Angel in Shining Armor
MARLENE WORRALL

Dedication
For Bill...just because.

Acknowledgements

I would like to extend my deepest gratitude to JoAnn Durgin and Teresa Lilly for their expertise and counsel. My heartfelt thanks also to Linda White, Lee Coryell, Debra Newell, Phd, Ann Bell, Cecil Murphey, Ramona Tucker, Helga Hamilton, Peter Paras, Alan Wong, Edward Rosario, NancyDeVreis, Sheila Weissberger, Caren Olson, Bettina Rogers, Lena Nelson Dooley, John de Simone and David Hawkins. Thanks also to my many friends, supporters and prayer warriors. You know who you are. And to my beloved sister, Verna Kallevig, for believing I could write before I began the journey. Most of all, I thank God Almighty for anointing me to pen this book and causing it to come to fruition. To Him be the praise, honor and glory.

Review

"Ms. Worrall creates a solidly-crafted real-life romantic adventure based on biblical principles. The characters are artfully woven and the story line draws you in. Marlene brings in a great deal of life adventure while illustrating how one can live a righteous life in whatever setting one finds oneself. I did not want to put the book down! Excellent read. Debra A. Newell, B.S., M.S., Phd. Author, Creative Director and Editor: A Strand of Pearls. April 14, 2014.

1

"I'll be leaving the Reservation real soon," Ayita High-Eagle told her mother.

"Good, 'cause this house is too crowdy for the three of us, and I ain't kickin' Wally out longs he brings in a paycheck. No matter how meager it is," her mother said as she stirred soup in a broad pot on the old stove dominating the cramped kitchen "One of these days I'm gonna move off the Reservation, too. 'Soons I find someone who's gonna support me better than Wally."

"I told you before, Mother, you don't have to put up with him. I can get you a job at Joey's. They're always looking for good servers."

"Ya, well I told *you,* I ain't interested in workin' for nobody. We git by on what Wally brings in."

"But you don't even *like* him!" Ayita lamented.

"I told you... I'm stickin' with him 'til I git someone better." Her mother continued stirring and alternately sampling the black bean soup, a steely resolve evident in her tone and manner. She sprinkled in more spices before pouring a generous dose of dark sherry into the soup and taking a long swig of wine from a tumbler.

The pungent aroma wafted through the air, tickling Ayita's taste buds. "May I sample it?"

"Help yerself."

Ayita tasted a large spoonful of the soup.

Her mother smiled, raising her eyebrows. "Well?"

"Delicious."

Ayita turned her face away from her mother so she wouldn't see the tears and overwhelming emotions surging inside her.

Today's the day

Her mother spooned the concoction into stoneware bowls and then placed them on the shabby wooden table. Fresh sourdough bread was cradled in a basket. Ayita broke off a crusty end and spread butter on it generously. She took a bite. Black bean soup was her favorite, but today she dawdled with it, preoccupied. She had no appetite.

She checked her watch: 2:30. *Time to leave.* It was her day off work, and she had a riding date with her best friend, Marjoi. She had other plans, too, but she had no intention of sharing them with her mother.

"Thanks for the soup, Mother. I have to go" She threw the remaining soup in the garbage and then washed her bowl, placing it on the drying rack. A few steps took her into her tiny bedroom. Once there, she slipped off her tracksuit and donned tattered, leather jeans, adding a weather-scarred, leather jacket to her woolen turtleneck. She tightened the strings on her cowboy hat, pushing back long, cascading, black hair.

Ayita glanced at the mirror above her dresser. Her suicide note was in plain view, scrawled on an envelope with some cash tucked inside it. When she failed to come home tonight, her mother would call the sheriff. The suicide note and cash would be easily discovered. Ayita was glad she'd had the insight and courage to pilfer money from the drunken men who hung around the shack with her mother while she often lay sprawled, half-naked, passed out on the sofa.

Ayita studied her face in the mirror.

Why had so many people fussed over her high cheekbones and almond-shaped, black eyes? Folks had raved about her beauty ever since she was young. But the reflection she saw mirrored the deep despair lodged within her.

Strangely, the shack on the Cherokee Reservation felt oddly cozy today. Standing at the door, she flashed it a last glance. *I'll never see it again.*

"Good-bye, Mother," she said, desperately trying to mask her troubled emotions as she peered into her mother's lovely face. She looked young enough to be her sister, and sometimes Ayita even called her by her given name, Juanita, because of it. She stared at her mother for a couple of minutes, choking back tears. *I'll never see you again. And I love you until my heart aches.*

"Bye, bye" Her mother's words were slurred. She didn't bother looking up from her coveted spot on the sofa, remaining glued to the blaring TV. The glass of wine rested in front of her on the coffee table.

Ayita stepped outside, surveying the tumbledown shack one final time, shivering involuntarily. It was a bitterly cold November day, and snow was forecast for the weekend. She climbed onto her bicycle, and began cycling the six miles to the Circle K ranch. Marjoi had been her best pal since their first meeting at school, when they had both been thirteen. Now, six years later, Ayita was an accomplished equestrian. She would always be grateful to Marjoi's folks, who had generously paid for riding lessons for both girls.

Marjoi was waiting for her in the barn, She was strapping the saddle on Black Diamond as Ayita walked in. They greeted each other with a customary hug before trading tidbits.

Brown Boy neighed his greeting, moving his large, lean body friskily about as Ayita approached him. She opened his stall and walked him over to a wall, laden with hooks and saddles. Pulling one down, she began strapping it on him.

Her secret weighed heavily on her mind, but she was determined not to burden her best friend with her decision. She didn't want to be talked out of it, for it was engraved in stone, as far as she was concerned. The trauma that had pushed her over the edge flashed back into her mind.

Wally had lasted over a month. One night, when her mother had stepped out, he had tried to rape her, crudely managing to rip off most of her clothes. A husky bear of a man, she was no match for him at 102 pounds.

Adrenaline racing, Ayita had smiled flirtatiously at him. "Let me get you a drink." She'd darted into the kitchen.

Wally had chased her, leering at her and trying to grope her, but she was too fast for him. Moving with the speed of lightning, she'd grabbed a colossal kitchen knife, its gleaming blade pointing at his chest. He lunged, trying to grab her arm and wrest it from her, but the knife carved into his arm. He screamed wildly as it plunged deeper into his upper arm, tearing a deep, long gash.

Wally went into shock. Ayita seized the opportunity to flee to the neighbors. They phoned the sheriff, but Wally somehow managed to roar off in his old rusted-out truck. Ayita knew better than to press charges. Her mother would never believe her. She would turn it around and say it was Ayita's fault -that she'd teased him.

Occasionally, one of her mother's boyfriends chipped in money for living expenses, but except for Wally's recent contributions, Ayita was the sole bread earner in their household. She loathed that responsibility. Still, she felt protective of her mother and didn't have the heart to leave her penniless. So, over the years, Ayita had pilfered cash from the pockets of visiting men too inebriated to be aware of her scam.

She could never refuse her mother, but she had come to realize that her love for her mother was not reciprocal. The only love her mother really had was the bottle. That...and her sex life. Juanita was never dry for a single day, although she *did* hit dry spells with men. It was during those times Ayita felt important. She would hand over some of her meager savings and, for a brief interval, they shared something akin to friendship. But she was quickly tossed aside the moment the inevitable new man showed up.

Marjoi frowned "Are you feeling all right? You look rather pale."

Ayita was jolted back to the present "No, I'm fine...just fine" She plucked down a saddle from its wall hook and strapped it on her beloved Brown Boy. Holding the reins, she walked him out of the barn. Shivers coursed up and down her spine as she reflected on the dark secret lodged in her breast. Mounting Brown Boy adroitly, she gathered her wits, trying to sound nonchalant. "Ready?" she asked Marjoi.

"Ready." Marjoi echoed.

Marjoi dug heels into the horse's belly. Ayita followed suit. They galloped off together, keeping each other in close range. Icy winds chilled them and bit at their faces as they galloped along the well-trodden paths that weaved throughout the mostly-cleared acreage on the ranch.

"It's such a beautiful, clear day." Marjoi cantered close to Ayita. "Doesn't it make you glad to be alive?"

Ayita wanted to scream her plan to her best friend, but she was determined not to share it. She would savor this last ride with her best friend. Later, when they returned to the barn, she would water her beloved Thoroughbred and take him out alone...for her final earthly ride. "I find winter depressing, in spite of the blue sky," Ayita's voice was flat.

"A brisk ride usually cheers you up," Marjoi reminded her.

Riding the winding, familiar trails that meandered throughout the acreage, Ayita felt strangely at peace.

At last they cantered back to the barn. It had been a long and arduous ride. Sweating profusely, the horses greedily gobbled water from the aluminum pails the pals had filled with water and placed in their stalls.

Ayita walked purposefully from one stall to the next, working her way through the barn, stopping briefly at each one. She was allowing herself the luxury of one last glimpse at the graceful Thoroughbreds she had grown to love. Bidding each one a silent farewell, she stroked some of them on their long, sleek necks and rubbed cheeks or foreheads of others. She would say good-bye to her beloved Brown Boy at the last minute.

Stopping in front of Brown Boy and Black Diamond's stalls, where Marjoi monitored the watering process, she lingered, watching the horses drink and cool down. A pang of apprehension churned in her gut. Trying to sound nonchalant, Ayita asked, "Do you mind if I take Brown Boy out again? I just feel like riding him solo."

"Of course," Marjoi was puzzled. "I don't know why you want more of this freezing weather, but suit yourself. I'm heading inside to warm up."

When Ayita was sure Brown Boy was rested and had had his fill of water, she unlocked the stall door. It was time to go. She tightened the strings on her cowboy hat, pulled on her ragged gloves, and led the thoroughbred out of the barn, holding the reins. He trusted her. She had loved him ever since the first time she had laid eyes on him. And they had bonded. A stab of guilt sliced through her. She shook it off.

They were outside of the barn. She mounted Brown Boy expertly and galloped off, easily in control. Barely a trace of nervousness remained. After all, she had contemplated suicide for a very long time. It was the only way to escape her intolerable situation. Her mind raced through the series of events that had led her to this final breaking point. *Was her life flashing before her as she neared the point of death?*

Ayita had to focus on her mission. Shivers of fear coursed through her in spite of her resolve to end her life. She had to snuff out the lonely, gaping voice screaming inside her, yearning for love, acceptance and a meaning to her sordid existence.

Galloping feverishly down the well-trodden trails, she dug her heels into the thoroughbred's belly, causing him to soar down the valley at a speed she had never before known. He raced faster and faster, his long, graceful legs moving with the speed and agility of a racehorse. Earlier, she had staked out the giant boulder looming in front of them.

She had only seconds to get it right.

Digging her spurs into his belly while simultaneously jerking back his reins would cause him to rear up and throw her. She held her breath waiting for it. She would hit her head on the boulder and die instantly. It was the perfect plan.

Brown Boy had a mind of his own. He became unsteady, his long, graceful legs barely managing to skirt around the massive rock while dodging the rocky terrain.

He slowed to an irregular gait and then suddenly sped up. He was acting erratically. Panic seized her as she realized he was spooked and crazed.

She was on a runaway horse!

Her plan had gone awry. Brown Boy reared up. Frantically, she struggled to hold onto him. She found herself praying he wouldn't throw her onto a small rock, for she might only be maimed if that happened. She became forced to guide him through the rocky terrain so he wouldn't stumble, perhaps breaking a leg. She didn't want *him* to get hurt. She cared about him, and she needed him. It was a long way back to the barn.

At last she decided, *I'll try again tomorrow.* Fierce winds stung her face and soared through her body, causing her to wish she had dressed with more layers. Brown Boy headed for the creek. The area was grassy and peaceful, with a smattering of Weeping Willows. A red-breasted Merganser chirped gaily from one of the tree's barren branches. A sandpiper flew overhead.

She dismounted, allowing her horse to roam and drink freely. The gentle hum of water trickled over the underwater foliage. She had to rethink her plan before she lost her nerve. Fresh determination settled over her. She would guide Brown Boy back to the massive rock and try again. Remounting, she cantered back toward the ominous boulder, passing clusters of Arbutus trees.

The sky was cobalt blue, accented by billowy, white clouds. In spite of the arctic wind, she found the weather stimulating. *Why does nature seem particularly appealing today?* She was losing some of her nerve in spite of her long-time plan to snuff out her own life. Niggling, fearful thoughts ricocheted through her brain. *Suppose I'm not killed instantly but instead break my neck. I could become a quadriplegic.*

She strained to think calmly. An expert equestrian, she planned to stage the perfect "accident." She would view the failed attempt as merely a rehearsal. Now she would perform the show and give a flawless performance!

Digging her heels into the horse's belly, she goaded him into galloping at breakneck speed. She felt elated in a dangerous way until she realized to her horror that her Thoroughbred was spooked and had become a runaway again. She had lost all control of him as he raced on in a wild frenzy, oblivious to her frenetic attempt at controlling him.

Through no logic she could identify, an instinct for survival kicked in. She struggled frantically to remain on top of him. Fear gripped her like a thousand icy fingers, choking her, clouding her judgment.

They raced frenetically through the grassy meadow. If he threw her now, she would probably break some limbs, possibly her neck. She doubted she would die instantly.

He sped wildly ahead. In the next instant, she lay on lush green grass in the meadow. Her whole body ached. A sharp pain shot through her right shoulder as she glanced toward Brown Boy. He stood frozen to the spot on which he had thrown her.

Dazed and in shock, she remained on the ground. Then, to her utter horror, glancing upward, she saw two sets of hooves poised to stomp her! In that split second, she stared, mesmerized, at a tall, blond man clad in shimmering silver. Astride the horse, he was forcing him backwards and away from her.

She scrambled to her feet, disoriented. Her body ached. She opened her mouth to thank the gallant stranger.

He had vanished!

Did an angel intervene to save my life?

Instantly, she reflected back on what her granny had told her. "You have a guardian angel. I have prayed for you every day since you were born."

Tears welled up in Ayita's eyes. She'd been so certain she wanted to die, but when she had seen the terrifying hooves poised to stomp her, she had cried out "Spare me, God." In that same instant, the thoroughbred was pulled back by its mysterious rider. He had backed the horse up and away from her, giving her a chance to get out of harm's way.

Ayita stood rooted to the spot. Stunned. Brown Boy mulled frantically before gradually settling down. She had been miraculously saved from a hideous finale. The prayers of her granny drifted into her consciousness. She remembered sitting on her granny's lap, while she read Psalm after Psalm to her, ending with her favorites-the twenty-third and ninety-first Psalms. She recited the twenty-third Psalm aloud in thanksgiving to God. *"Yea, though I walk through the valley of the shadow of death, I will fear no evil; for thou art with me, thy rod and thy staff they comfort me."* She shivered at how close she had come to death's door.

Ayita had been taught the prayers of protection from her earliest memories. The ninety-first psalm was a psalm of protection. Her grandmother had prayed the Lord's Prayer and the psalm of protection over her life every day until she went to Glory.

Her granny had told her that angels were a species entirely different from humans and that their mission was to guide, protect and help people on earth who requested this supernatural protection by asking God for it. She also said that in some cases-albeit a mystery-persons were chosen, seemingly at random, to be protected by angels. Someday God would reveal all these mysteries.

Her granny had been one of the few true believers on the Cherokee Indian Reservation. In times of crisis, many unbelievers had sought her out, requesting prayer. Known for her profound faith, she never turned anyone away. When she laid hands on the sick and prayed fervently, the person was invariably healed.

Tears brimmed in Ayita's eyes. God had loved her enough to spare her life. It was not her time to die. Did she have work to do on this earth, just as her granny had? Shakily, she remounted Brown Boy and trotted back to the barn, feeling as though she'd been reborn. She knew this miraculous event would shape her life forever.

After Ayita had watered her horse and led him tenderly into his stall, she whispered to him how sorry she was to have tried to use him to end her life. She stroked him and kissed him for a long time. Then, finally, she knew in her heart that he understood and forgave her.

She hurried from the barn to the Petersons' house. The door was unlocked, and she let herself in. Marjoi met her in the hallway and hugged her.

Ayita's face told the story. It was covered with dirt and deep scratches. A large goose egg jutted from her forehead. A long gash, matted with coagulated blood, zigzagged across her neck. Her leather riding gear was ripped, exposing her bruises. She knew she was a frightful sight.

"What happened?" Marjoi asked, eyes wide. "I thought you were acting strange. Right after you left, I sensed you were going to do something dreadful. I thought about riding out to find you, but I heard a scripture in my spirit: *"Be still, and know that I am God."* I began praying fervently for you instead."

Ayita began to sob. "I tried to take my own life. I wanted Brown Boy to throw me onto that giant boulder...where the path curves before the creek. I figured I would die instantly. But he wouldn't do it."

"Oh poor darling." Marjoi held Ayita close and let her cry her heart out. "I'm going to run you a hot bath in the Jacuzzi and bring you some tea. You'll feel a lot better after you relax in the tub and get cleaned up."

Marjoi led Ayita upstairs to the spacious, white marble bathroom. Turning on the water in the Jacuzzi tub, she added lavender and bath salts and turned up the dial on the piped-in music. "Brahms and Beethoven...it will help you relax." She placed fresh towels and a white terry robe on the green floral chair. "I'll be right next door in my room," she murmured, stepping toward the door but leaving it slightly ajar. "I want you to live with us. I'm going to talk to Mom about it as soon as she gets home from tutoring."

Grateful for this new turn of events, Ayita began to relax as the warm water and music soothed her. It was such a treat to bathe in the soaker tub-a stark contrast from the cramped, rusty shower at home. Dreamily, she glanced around at a variety of tropical plants lining the edges of the marble steps that led down to the sunken tub, as if she were seeing them for the first time. Suddenly, she felt everything was going to work out. She was reborn, and she was alive! *Dear God in heaven. I've never felt so intensely alive!*

After a long, leisurely soak in the tub, she felt refreshed and renewed. Wrapping the terry robe around her, she left a steamy bathroom behind and tapped lightly on the door to Marjoi's room.

"Come on in. Check out your new digs." Marjoi opened the door, grinning.

Ayita glanced around the spacious, familiar room and envisioned herself sharing it. A nice warm feeling enveloped her.

"I've made a pot of tea, and I want to hear the story right from the beginning," Marjoi said.

They headed down the curved staircase and into the kitchen. Marjoi served piping hot tea with fresh scones.

A pungent aroma wafted toward Ayita. "Something smells good. What is it?"

"Roast beef."

"Nice."

The yellow walls in the kitchen took on a sunnier hue, far more vivid than she remembered. Her senses seemed intensified. As she took a sip of tea, a torrent of emotions ripped through her again. "I tried to take my own life, Marjoi." Ayita broke down. Tears streaked her cheeks and she covered her face in shame and remorse.

Marjoi hugged her. "You'll be all right, my friend. You've been through a harrowing ordeal."

Ayita wiped her tears away with her fingers and relayed the details of the event. At last she said, "Do you believe in fate and angels?"

"I believe if it's not your time, God doesn't allow your life to end. And yes, I absolutely believe in the intervention of angels. It's all through the Bible."

"You've invited me to go to church with you many times, and I've accepted the invitation only a few times. Tomorrow, I'd like to go with you and your family to church."

Marjoi smiled. "I'd love that. I know my folks would, too. I'm serious about wanting you to move into our house for as long as you need to. We have plenty of room. I'm sure Mom will agree that it's the right thing to do."

"Thanks. Maybe when I get stronger emotionally, I'll be able to help my mother. But I can't live in the gutter with her anymore."

"I know, Ayita. Enough damage has been done to your psyche already."

"Yes, I shall start a new life," Ayita vowed. She took a leisurely sip of tea. "Do you think Satan was whispering in my ear, trying to coax me to take my own life?"

Marjoi nodded, solemnly. "Yes, I do. Evil spirits are real. It's just that they operate in a spiritual dimension that cannot be seen by the naked eye."

Ayita reflected on that statement. "That would explain why I felt this *compulsion* to hurry and get it over with."

"Satan is always in a rush. That's one way we can know that he's behind an evil scheme. God moves with an easy grace. When He's leading us, we are given a sense of peace in our spirits. It's awesome when you become tuned in to Him." Marjoi brewed a second pot of tea and then opened the fridge door and surveyed its contents. "How about a piece of chocolate cake?"

"I'd love a piece. Thank you."

Marjoi served the cake with the tea.

"I hope your mom agrees to let me stay here," Ayita said.

"I'll insist, if I have to," Marjoi grinned. "Mom has always told me we take on the characteristics of those around us. She has always believed that our surroundings color everything in our lives-all that drinking, swearing and ungodly living burrowed into your subconscious. I think that's what caused your black moods. I thought you'd been acting weird lately, but I had no idea you were contemplating suicide. I chalked it up to the winter blues. But when you rode off alone, I just got an awful feeling in my gut." Glancing at her watch, Marjoi jumped up from the table. "Time to put the potatoes on. Mom should be home in about half an hour." She picked out some potatoes from a rack in the pantry and started peeling them.

"May I help?"

In reply, Marjoi produced another peeler and handed it to Ayita. She filled a pot with water. The pals dropped the peeled spuds into it, as they chatted.

Dinner at the Petersons was congenial. Ayita thrived on their warmth and good spirits. She was like a sponge soaking up their love and support.

After dinner, Marjoi pulled her mom aside. She told her Mom a condensed version of the harrowing tale. Marjoi dashed back into the living room, where Ayita sat, fidgeting nervously on the sofa, pretending to watch the news with everyone else.

Marjoi gave Ayita a high five. "You're my new roommate!"

"Yes!" Ayita matched the gesture, springing off the sofa.

"How about giving me a hand with the dishes? That is, if you can come off your cloud long enough." Marjoi grinned at her best friend.

As soon as they were out of earshot of Marjoi's family, Ayita spoke from her deepest heart. "Thank-you, my dear friend." Gentle tears of relief and joy trickled down her cheeks. A new chapter in her life had begun. She would never look back. Someday, she hoped, she would be in a position to make a difference in her mother's life. She felt certain that sharing the Petersons' home would strengthen her emotionally. Through their love and her newfound faith in God, she believed she would go on to a bright future and have a chance to pursue her secret dream.

Later that evening, she placed a call to her mother to say she'd moved onto the Circle K ranch and would not be returning to the Reservation. There was a brief silence. "Thas fine." Her mother's speech was slurred.

2

A glimmering crimson sunrise heralded the dawn. Ayita peeked through the white plantation shutters. The swirling snowflakes driven by a howling wind made her feel safe and cozy in her new haven.

Marjoi bounded out of bed and slipped into a robe. Searching through her overstuffed closet, she found the white terry robe Ayita had worn yesterday.

"Keep this. I've got plenty more." Marjoi handed her the robe. "Bible class starts at 10:00, church at 11:00. Go ahead and take the first shower. There's a stack of fresh towels on the bathroom shelves."

"Thank-you," Ayita murmured sleepily. She found some slippers and padded down the hallway to their bathroom dreaming of a brighter future.

Marjoi was in her second year of a Bachelor of Arts program at Western Washington University nearby. Maybe, somehow, now that she was in this new environment, she, too, would be able to go back to school. Perhaps the counselors at the University would give her guidance in pursuing a music career.

After a long, hot shower, Ayita dried off and snuggled into the robe. Her aching body felt considerably better. Draping a Turkish towel around her masses of hair, she formed a turban.

When she reached the bedroom, Marjoi was seated at a Queen Anne desk reading her giant, red leather Bible. She set it down as Ayita entered the room. "How do you feel? Did you enjoy the shower?"

"Sure did. I'm ecstatic with the new turn of events."

"The snow is intensifying. There's almost ten inches on the ground. The news report said the roads are treacherous. I just turned the TV off," Marjoi said.

"Wow, that's a lot of snow." Ayita moved to the window to check it out for herself.

Marjoi joined her. "It's coming down in blankets."

Ayita watched, fascinated by the fat flurries swirling and dancing, driven by a fierce wind. It looked like it was rapidly turning into a blizzard, but she wasn't sure. She had never seen one before. This had to be a freak storm.

"The news report said we were fast approaching blizzard conditions," Marjoi said. "I seriously doubt if we'll be going to church today, but that decision will be Dad's. The SUV performs well in this kind of weather, but the roads aren't sanded yet. As you know, nobody around here prepares for massive snowfalls, because they so rarely occur. But just in case..." Marjoi walked over to the bed and pointed to a couple of outfits strewn across it. "I picked out a couple of combos from my closet. Maybe you'll like one of them. I hope they fit."

Ayita had always admired Marjoi's choice of clothing. She had great taste. It was going to be fun wearing her togs until they picked up her sparse wardrobe from the Reservation. She chose a royal blue turtleneck and mid-calf, tan skirt. Her cowboy boots would look great with it. She had carefully left them in the utility room by the back door, lining them up with other boots.

Ayita borrowed a coral lipstick and some mascara from Marjoi's makeup bag. She'd left her purse at the shack, believing she would never need it again. Marjoi nodded her approval of Ayita's outfit but added some chunky jewelry to give it cache.

"Thanks for being so generous with all your stuff." Ayita gave her hair its final fluffing as she glanced into the mirror.

"Don't mention it. You'd do the same for me."

"Yeah, I would."

They were both dressed early. "I'm heading downstairs to get us a couple mugs of coffee. I'll be right back."|

Ayita settled in on the window seat, staring at the snow, fascinated. It was a Winter Wonderland, out of a storybook. In less than twenty-four hours, life had become a joyful adventure instead of a sordid existence. She was mesmerized by the fluffy, white snowflakes descending from the heavens, backlit by rays of vivid sunshine, casting sparkly, silver diamonds on crisp snowbanks.

Christmas was barely a month away. She wondered half-heartedly if Wally would still be around. When Ayita imparted the news that she wouldn't return to the Reservation, her mother hadn't even mentioned the suicide note. Unshed tears threatened to spill out. Juanita had always been oblivious to the chaos in Ayita's life. She would be missed only when the monthly bills rolled in, and there was no one to pay them.

Thank-you, Lord, for watching over me and helping me escape my horrendous life. Somehow, Lord, I pray that some day...maybe with enough time and distance between us...I'll be able to help my mother.

As Ayita watched the snow, she reflected on past Christmas seasons. Nostalgia triggered fond memories of her granny, and others not so good. Only days after her granny's funeral, her folks had attended the wild seasonal bash held at the old dance hall on the Cherokee Indian Reservation. Ayita was only eight, but she had been left on her own until the wee hours of the morning.

It had been a lucky break-or maybe the answer to her granny's prayer, when she had changed schools at thirteen and met Marjoi. The next Christmas and every Christmas thereafter was spent with the Petersons. It was at one of the Christmas services that Ayita had heard the talented group from Prague perform. Chills shot through her, as a powerful feeling enveloped her. Someday she hoped to sing gospel music. Daydreaming had become a habit-a necessary respite from the harsh reality of her existence.

Marjoi's smile lit up the room. "Coffee is served!" She handed Ayita a mug of it and left. "Enjoy!"

Ayita sipped the delicious brew, the aroma titillating her senses. She peered out the window at the swirling snowflakes dancing in the harsh wind. *I've been given a second chance at life.* Fresh determination settled over her. *I will make something of myself. God will lead the way.*

Marjoi stood at the bedroom door. "Breakfast is ready. Come and get it."

Ayita fell in step with Marjoi as they descended the staircase together. The aroma of sizzling bacon and coffee brewing titillated her senses. "It's great to be alive!" Ayita said, turning to Marjoi.

"It is," Marjoi agreed with an amused smile.

Ayita joined the others around the sizeable oak table in the country kitchen. "Good-mornings" overlapped as Marjoi's folks and her brother, Rod, greeted them. Ayita barely heard Mr. Peterson blessing the food. She was so overjoyed to be here. Strangely, all her senses seemed sharpened since her brush with death. It was as though this was the first time she had ever had a good meal. She noted the burnt-sienna color of crisp toast, the vivid yellow eggs, crisp brown bacon, and even the sprigs of fresh, intensely green parsley garnishing the plates.

"The roads are slippery, and there's black ice in spots. I don't know if we can get to church today or not," Mr. Peterson said.

Was this a bad omen? The news report had warned folks to stay off the roads. Was an evil force still trying to drag her down? Somewhere she had read that when a soul drew nearer to God, Satan worked overtime trying to plant seeds of doubt, to counteract the powerful spiritual yearnings.

Was this what was happening to her? Was she a jinx to Marjoi's family? Had the years of emotional abuse left such a heavy scar that she was unable to mesh with a harmonious family?

Scriptures her granny had read to her as a child floated into her mind. *"Ask, and it shall be given you. Knock, and the door shall be opened..." Please dispatch sanding and plowing trucks to make the roads safe for driving to church. With all my heart, Lord, I want to worship and praise you for all that you have done for me."*

"Hey, let's get the weather update," Marjoi said, the moment they finished eating. The bosom pals topped up their coffee and taking their mugs, headed for the adjacent family room and settled onto the sofa. Marjoi clicked on the T.V.

"Generally icy conditions...patches of black ice in some areas make for hazardous driving conditions. The Meridian highway is littered with cars stuck in the ditches...ambulances and police are trying to keep up with accidents...watch for road closures. We advise everyone to stay off the roads except for emergencies. Most roads in the Bellingham vicinity are treacherous...crews are backed up..."

Rod peered out the family room bay window. "Sanders just drove up."

"Oh, good," Marjoi said. "Come on, Ayita. Let's watch the process." Soon, all three of them stood by the bank of windows and watched the sanders and swirling snowflakes. "Well, it certainly is a novelty to watch the dump truck pump out a steady stream of sand, spoiling the pristine, white snow."

Mr. and Mrs. Peterson moved into the family room to watch the news. Mrs. Peterson glanced at her husband. Her tone was dubious. "Well, what do you think, dear? Should we brave the storm and drive to church or just watch a service on T.V.?" Mrs. Peterson frowned, as she glanced over at her hubby.

"Well, the way I figure it, if we get stuck, we get stuck. As long as we're dressed warmly, we can ride it out. The SUV has never failed us before. Besides, we can always turn back if we think it's too treacherous to proceed."

"Well, to be frank, dear. I think it's foolhardy to drive in this weather, given all the warnings."

"Aw, bunk. Those newscasters always exaggerate to get folks riled up. Remember, there's always a special blessing attached, when we make a valiant effort like we'll be doing today," Mr. Peterson said. He had his arm around her, he pulled it away and clicked off the T.V. and stood up. "Let's get ready to go." he said, decisively.

Ayita glanced over at them, her heart filled with admiration. They were both far from handsome, but from their eyes shone a love that was powerful and deep. In fact, she'd often thought that their faces radiated such depth of love and joy. No wonder she'd been drawn to them and Marjoi from the moment she'd met them. *Lord, I'm so grateful to be part of this wonderful family. Thank-you.*

"Get your coats and gear on. We're going to give it a shot. Is everybody up to the adventure?" He said, challenging the group.

"Yes!" Marjoi and Ayita glanced at each other and

spoke in unison. Rod looked skeptical and remained silent.

The family converged in the utility room, where their winter coats and boots were stored. Mr. Peterson already had his black overcoat on and began pulling on a Russian-style, black cap from the coat rack and slipping it on. Soon, Ayita and her surrogate family were bundled up warmly, seatbelts cinched, ready for the adventure.

Ayita knew they would make it safely to church. She had often reflected on the placard her granny had given her before she departed this world for her home on High. It had the words *Jesus Never Fails* emblazoned in glittering, crushed silver paper, which illuminated brightly in the blackest of nights. It was one of her dearest treasures now.

It had stopped snowing and the sun cast a brilliant yellow glow on the crisp snow banks. Mr. Peterson drove slowly down the long drive to the main road. No other vehicles were in sight. In view of the grave warnings, Ayita was hardly surprised. At least their chances of skidding into another vehicle were minimal.

Vast white fields stretched endlessly on both sides of the road, broken only by snow-laden houses dotting the landscape and deep trenches bordering both sides of the narrow artery.

Then, suddenly, the SUV slid into a skid, veering to the right and heading straight for the ditch. *Black ice,* Ayita guessed, as she held her breath.

Dead silence. *Was everyone in the vehicle praying or holding their breath...or both?* Mr. Peterson resisted braking as he skillfully drove into the skid and managed to maneuver the SUV back onto the main grooves of the highway that previous cars had carved for them. Visibility was poor, but he stayed on the tracks until the massive church and its parking lot loomed into view.

"I think George was wise to cancel the 10:00 Bible class. There aren't many cars in the lot and the service starts in a few minutes. I guess most of the faithful heeded the warnings," Mr. Peterson said.

Blasts of frigid air snapped at Ayita's face as she stepped out of the SUV. She shivered, but at the same time, a warm feeling burst within her. Today was the day she would publicly give her heart to the Lord.

So many times before, Marjoi had asked her if she wanted to accept Jesus into her heart, but always before, Ayita had felt confused and had not wanted to make the commitment. But since her brush with death and the intervention of the angel, she wanted to make public the quiet decision she had made that life-changing day. Ayita wanted to invite Jesus to come and live in her heart. Marjoi had often explained He would, if she invited him to.

As the best pals entered the church foyer, childhood memories flooded back to Ayita with astonishing clarity. She'd been only seven when she had first accepted Jesus into her heart, while sitting on her granny's lap on their old rocking chair. *How had she strayed so far that she had forgotten the Creator until her brush with death?* She could not blame her mother for that. She had allowed herself to stray.

"One day, we will all have to answer to God for what we did with our lives," Granny had often warned her. It was a sobering thought. Sadness washed over her. How had her mother strayed so far from her beliefs? She'd known the Lord at one time-granny had told her so-but she had gone off the deep end. Booze and promiscuity dominated her life.

The group shed their overcoats in the church foyer, shaking the snow off their coats before hanging them up on the long coat rack.

Timeless hymns rang out as Ayita and Marjoi entered the sanctuary and chose seats near the front. The white baby grand was played by a courtly, elderly black gentleman in a white suit. Ayita recalled what Marjoi often told her. God lives within His praises. *Yes, that's true. Jesus is alive!* She could sense His presence as the small group of worshippers took their seats, singing joyfully. Usually the church was full but many folks had not ventured out in the bad weather.

The worship team was already on stage. Marjoi leaned toward Ayita and whispered. "There's usually six, but today only half showed up." The vocalists were smartly dressed in black and white. One glance at the group and Ayita burned with a desire to be part of their team. Their radiant faces beamed with the glow of the spirit of God. She felt an instant kinship. The music portion of the service ended much too quickly for her liking, and the minister, a tall, sandy-haired gentleman, stepped onto the platform, taking his place in front of the transparent podium. She listened intently as he delivered the sermon. At one point, he spoke about the Law of Reciprocity. *"Give, and it shall be given unto you,"* he said. *"Cast your bread upon the waters for thou shalt find it after many days."*

Her eyes misted. God had sent the Peterson family into her life to help her negotiate the choppy, black waters that were part of her growth. They would guide her into a new life. It would be a life that hopefully would allow her to make the most of her vocal gift. God would reward her faithfulness in using that talent for His Glory. In her heart, she had already recommitted her life to the Lord. Now she wanted to take the public stand.

When the altar call came, she was ready to step

forward. "Is there anyone here today who would like to receive Jesus as their personal Savior? Or anyone who would like to recommit their life to the Lord?" The minister asked them to slip up their hands, and then he extended the invitation to step forward to the altar, so he could pray for them.

A scraggly, young man stepped up to the altar from the front pew and Ayita went forward also. Marjoi accompanied her. The preacher asked them if they wanted to turn from their sin and accept Jesus as their personal Savior. They nodded and the minister recited John 3:16 *"For God so loved the world, that he gave his only begotten Son, that whosoever believeth in him should not perish but have everlasting life."* He assured them that God would be faithful to forgive their sins and cleanse them from all unrighteousness and restore the years that the locusts have eaten.

Ayita left her broken spirit at the altar. Her life was made new. *Restore the years that the locusts had eaten!* That was music to her ears! She was a brand new creature. Joy and peace swept over her. Finally she was on the same page as the Petersons. Not an outsider.

Gentle tears born of a grateful heart slid down Ayita's cheeks. God would make something beautiful of her life. Her best friend stood next to her with an arm around her in support of her decision to live for Christ. She was in a state of euphoria as Marjoi guided her back to their pew. She felt like leaping for joy.

"What did I ever do to deserve a God so awesome?" Ayita whispered to Marjoi the moment they resumed their seats.

"Nada. Salvation is a gift. You can't earn it. You can't buy it. It's a gift freely given to those who ask and believe,"

Marjoi whispered back.

"Amazing. Praise God!" She smiled broadly and lifted her hands toward heaven in praise, emulating other worshippers around her.

When the service ended, a few parishioners remained in their pews, silently praying. Ayita asked God to endow her with wisdom to deal with her mother and lead her back to the Lord. She had a burden for her, and prayed that she would be able to get her attention long enough to share her conversion story.

Ayita could hardly wait for the Bible class the following Sunday. Marjoi had been attending it for years- no wonder she had so much biblical knowledge.

Marjoi led Ayita into the lobby. "Come on. I'm going to introduce you to some new people."

The pals rose from their pew. Marjoi steered her into a section of the foyer where a bevy of young folks congregated. They were chatting and laughing animatedly. She broke into the group, promptly introducing Ayita.

Ayita gaped as she locked eyes with the most gorgeous man she had ever encountered. He was making his way over to their group. He looked Hispanic, but maybe he was Italian or French. His magnetic black eyes swept over her, resting at her eyes and holding them captive. Who *was* this man? Her knees felt like they could buckle. Her heart soared with a joy she had never before known. What was happening to her?

Marjoi's eyes twinkled mischievously as she introduced Valdez. "Ayita, I'd like you to meet Valdez Lopez. Valdez, this is my best friend, Ayita High-Eagle." She glanced around at the small cluster of people. "I think you've met everyone else."

Ayita couldn't help but notice two of the three young

women in the group smiling at Valdez as though their lives depended on attracting his attention. He ignored them. The strange, foreign thrills coursing through Ayita did not subside. He was absolutely the most handsome, exciting man she'd ever encountered.

"Pleased to meet you," he said, bowing slightly and kissing one of Ayita's hands. His grin was slightly crooked. His dark, swarthy skin contrasted starkly with the white turtleneck peeking out from an open, long black coat. Cashmere, maybe?

Her heart stopped beating.

"You gals are very brave to venture out in this weather." Valdez grinned, never taking his eyes off Ayita.

"So are you." Ayita barely recognized her own voice. It sounded thin and raspy. Valdez raised a hand in protest. "I can't take the credit. My aunt and uncle practically dragged me here. They've been attending this church for years. They keep telling me I'll meet someone special here one day. Today, for the first time, I believe them." Raven black eyes burned into hers, and she knew she should glance demurely away, but she could not bring herself to do that. Instead, she smiled at him, admiring his golden-brown tan. Or was that his natural skin tone?

She suddenly realized the other folks in their group had left. Only three persons remained: Valdez, Marjoi and herself.

"Do you like Mexican food?" Valdez asked Ayita, his eyes fixated on hers.

"Love it." Her smile emanated from somewhere deep inside.

"You?" He glanced over at Marjoi.

"I live for it," Marjoi retorted, wryly.

"How about joining me for lunch?" Valdez directed the

question to both of them.

"Hopefully, the roads are a little better by now." The bosom pals exchanged a knowing flicker of agreement. "I'll find Dad and tell him we'll be home later," Marjoi said, leaving the smitten couple to enjoy each other, as she went to hunt for them.

"Be sure to tell him I have a Hummer and I know how to drive in blizzards," Valdez called after her. "Spent a couple winters in Montana."

Excitement and a burning desire to know him better flared within Ayita. He was a stranger to her, yet somehow not a stranger at all. She had a niggling feeling she'd been waiting for him all her life. In the past, she'd had a couple of boyfriends, but they had not affected her in the way Valdez did. Never before had she known chemistry like this.

He reminded her of a prince. Impeccably attired, his black coat molded onto massive shoulders tapering to a slender waistline. Perhaps he was very rich. Maybe a tailor made his clothes. She wondered if his coat was cashmere or vicuna. Lord knows, she had read enough fashion magazines to know pricey fabric when she saw it. Waves of insecurity washed over her. The man was downright intimidating.

He seemed to sense her insecurity. "Have you been attending this church very long?" he asked, as if trying to make her relax and feel comfortable.

"I've only been here a few times so far, but I plan to attend regularly from now on. I accepted Jesus as my Savior today!" She beamed triumphantly, forgetting her social fears.

"That's great. Yeah, I saw you up there." He nodded politely but curiosity stole over his face.

She didn't tell him about her suicide attempt and the miraculous intervention of the angel. The timing wasn't right. After all, they had just met. "A dramatic turn of events occurred," she began, evasively. "It caused me to seek God. It's hard to explain. I think the Holy Spirit moved on me, and now I feel buoyant and happy. It's like being reborn."

"I confess I have never taken that step. In fact, as I said, I wouldn't be here today if it weren't for my aunt and uncle badgering me to come to church with them." Valdez flashed that crooked grin again.

She reached into her memory bank, struggling to remember what her granny had said. It came to her suddenly: "Before a person gives their heart to the Lord, there is a scrim over their eyes. The evil one blinds them. They need a committed Christian to encourage them to seek the truth for their life." Her grandmother's profound truths had embedded in her memory bank.

"That pretty much describes Aunt Millie and Uncle Paul," Valdez said with resignation.

Marjoi rejoined them. "we're on."

~~*~~

Lively Mexican music rang out as they entered the decorative eatery. The decor featured a wide array of bold colors, favoring pink, turquoise and magenta. Colorful Mexican hats and vases were interspersed throughout the restaurant.

Valdez insisted on ordering for the three of them. "Bring us fajitas with extra guacamole, black bean salads, quesadilla con ensalada and a side order of jalapenos with corn tortillas and sodas," he told the waiter.

In between bites of the spicy, pungent food, Marjoi brought Ayita up to speed concerning Valdez. "Valdez is a gifted artist. He and his dad came to America from Madrid, after his mom died. They moved here where his aunt and uncle live."

"Not so talented," Valdez replied modestly, dipping a crispy corn chip into the spicy guacamole.

I'd love to see your paintings," Ayita said.

"Perhaps you won't like my work, and then you might decide I'm not interesting to you, either." Valdez's eyes twinkled.

"Then it might be well worth you showing us your paintings, just so you can find out who your real friends are." She chuckled.

"You have a point." He was visibly amused.

"I may regret this-but why don't the two of you let me take you to my house, and I'll give you the grand tour. Dad paints out of the studio on the main floor. My studio is upstairs. We have a modest collection of the Masters' work. I'm sure you'll enjoy them. I study them to figure out how I can improve my work."

Ayita wasn't sure what he meant by the Masters, but she smiled at him.

He returned it, his eyes lingering on hers.

When they had finished their leisurely lunch, Valdez paid the bill and then drove the pals to his house in Fairhaven, nestled along the craggy West Coast near Bellingham. They skirted the unique downtown area on their way to his house.

"I enjoy the camaraderie of other artists. When I'm not focused, I drive through town and wander through the art galleries or bookstores-maybe grab a coffee or lunch at one of the quaint eateries," he said, as he cruised the Hummer past a row of ocean-front townhouses and homes overlooking the Pacific Ocean. "I've taken some classes at Western Washington University- nice to have it in such close proximity."

Valdez swung his vehicle into the circular drive, stopping in front of a turn-of-the-century mansion painted a robin's egg blue. He stepped out of the driver's seat and opened the door for Ayita first, then Marjoi.

Chivalry is not dead.

"We shoveled the sidewalk this morning, but you'd never know it." He opened the front door and helped his guests with their coats, hanging them on a brass coat rack in the entrance hall. "Mother was an avid art collector and antique dealer. May I give you the tour before we head upstairs to my studio?

Ayita nodded excitedly. She had never been in an ancient mansion before.

Valdez led them down a long hallway, through an archway and into a stately living room. The sweeping room had maroon, silk, embossed wallpaper adorned with wall sconces holding candles.

Having visited art auctions with Marjoi and her dad, Ayita had an idea that she was seeing Louis XV and XVl antiques and other rare pieces. She marveled at the soaring ceilings, which featured magnificent frescos. It was like walking into a museum. Even *she* was able to tell the paintings were priceless treasures. *Masters, he had said.*

He stole a lingering glance as he paused at the crystal-leaded French doors and opened them. He turned on the lights. Before them, loomed a stately, formal dining room. It was really quite magnificent. A glittering blaze of lights sparkled brilliantly from the ornate crystal chandelier overhead. The long, Jacobean table was surrounded by twelve chairs covered in a rich, burgundy tapestry. Even *she* knew it was a rare antique.

She stared at the furnishings and the room. He stared at her. Finally, she broke into an embarrassed smile. "Okay, ladies. Onward," he said, grinning, as the threesome left the glorious room.

He toured them through a spacious solarium occupying the south side of the mansion, facing the ocean. A breathtaking view of the azure blue sea flanked by craggy cliffs stood before them. Massive waves crashed against the shore. She loved the sound of the raging sea below. *It must be wonderful to live here...to wake up in the morning and see this.*

He continued the house tour, leading them up a polished, mahogany staircase. They passed a floor of closed doors with wide hallways-presumably bedrooms-until, finally, they arrived at the top floor of the mansion.

He ushered them into his quarters and massive studio. Ayita was dumbstruck as she glimpsed Valdez's work-in-progress. It was a giant canvas displaying a partially completed oil of a mature woman, clad in rich, dark maroon and cocoa-brown tones. The background for his subject was oppressive, shadowy chocolate hues mingled with gloomy, mottled grey tones. The woman's face was hauntingly real, the eyes extraordinary-both in their depth and in the ethereal quality that seemed to radiate from her soul.

It was as though the woman in the painting were alive-right here in the room with them. Captivated, Ayita studied it intensely, trying to absorb every detail. At first, she stood mesmerized, taking in every nuance of the face. Then, as Valdez motioned for her to join him, she walked to the back of the room so she could study it from a distance.

"Did you really paint this portrait?" Ayita asked Valdez.

"Yes. Why do you ask? Don't you like it?" A somber expression crept over his features.

"Like it? I love it! I've never seen anything like it before. It's as if she's *alive,* right here in this room. Who is she?"

"It's a portrait of my mother. She died recently."

"I'm sorry," she murmured. Her heart ached for him. "The painting is brilliant. Her...essence...lives on through the canvas."

"Yes, I shall treasure this painting forever. It will never be sold."

"Did you work from a photograph?"

"No. The memories of Mother are vivid. I chose to paint from those." Valdez turned his face from her.

Ayita knew instinctively that he was fighting tears. Stillness pervaded the room. *How recently had his mother died?* She would ask him another time, perhaps. She sensed he was making a supreme effort to pull himself together.

"We must finish the tour, ladies. There are three more rooms of paintings to view." He began walking toward the door.

Ayita was astonished by the magnitude of his talent. As they reached the last room, an odd sense of déjà vu descended upon her. Why? Had she dreamed of Valdez and this house? Perhaps even the art tour? They arrived at the Landscape and Still Flowers gallery.

"This room contains my Impressionistic work." Valdez gestured toward a couple of the paintings. "I was experimenting with light and shadows, as well as color blending. I'm always reaching up to a higher level. I never stop learning."

"I love your terra cottas and reds. They're my favorite colors." Ayita studied his work, noting the various hues of periwinkle and multi shades of turquoise. Although she knew very little about art, she did know what she liked. Viewing his work whetted her appetite for more. "I feel like I need to hang out here and just enjoy these paintings for a while."

Valdez nodded. "There are a couple of benches here, so you can do that. I sometimes spend hours here, analyzing a piece to figure out how I can improve it." He paused for a moment before continuing. "There's one more gallery-The Desert Room."

They followed him down a wide hallway brimming with portraits. Valdez opened the door to another room. It overflowed with paintings of the desert. He had used the true palette of the desert, encompassing a variety of pinks, lavenders and turquoises mingled with faded greens, giving the impression that it was bleached by intense sunshine. There were canvasses with backgrounds of sand and ochre hues, featuring varieties of cacti and desert vegetation.

"Did you ever live in the desert?" Ayita asked Valdez.

"Yes, before I moved here. Dad had already bought this house. I had always wanted to travel to Santa Fe and some of the quaint towns in Arizona. I wound up spending a year in Sedona. Now *that's* an artists' haven."

"If it's anything like your paintings, it must be magnificent," Marjoi said.

"Oh, it is, believe me." Valdez's eyes shone with the memory of it.

"I would love to visit there sometime," Ayita whispered spontaneously.

Valdez stopped talking. As his eyes swept over every part of her, she could sense his male appreciation. She felt small and delicate next to him. He was sizable and strapping. She sensed that he wanted to take her in his arms and smother her with his kisses. She wanted that, too. It was probably just as well Marjoi was with them.

"You will," he said. The whisper was laced with a promise.

Somehow, she knew in her heart that he had so much he wanted to say to her and share with her. She had never felt more treasured or appreciated in her entire life. It was a rare snippet in time, and she wished she could freeze-frame it on video and replay it repeatedly.

"When are you planning to have an art show?" Marjoi asked.

He pursed his lips. "I'm not sure I'm ready for one."

Marjoi frowned. "That's ridiculous. Your work is masterful. Surely you must know that."

"Maybe you just need a good gallery to represent you," Ayita said, tentatively.

"You're probably both right. But I despise promoting myself."

Marjoi rolled her eyes. "Get over it, Valdez. It has to be done. That's one good reason to get a reputable gallery behind you-they'll promote your work so you can keep painting."

"I guess you're right, Marjoi. I've been procrastinating."

"Is there another way you could sell your work?" Ayita took her focus off the mauve, craggy cliffs she had been studying.

"I've been thinking of opening a small chain of galleries and hiring a high-profile PR person. I could feature Dad's work and mine."

"Sound like an expensive proposition to me," Marjoi

chimed in.

"If our work is well received, it could turn out to be lucrative."

"Where would you open the galleries?" Ayita asked.

"I would probably start with Santa Fe, Sedona and Scottsdale-then move on to El Paseo in Palm Desert and Rodeo Drive in Beverly Hills."

Was he a multi-millionaire? Ayita knew nothing about market conditions in the art world, so she opted for silence. She had only just met him and hoped she would get a chance to know him before he started jetting around the country.

The rambunctious bark of a dog broke the spell.

"Dad is home. He takes the German Shepherd with him in his RV," Valdez said.

Moments later, a frisky, black Shepherd bounded up the staircase and into view. His tail wagged a friendly greeting. Ayita thought him handsome with his perfectly matched zigzag of white, enhancing each side of his long neck. He barked briefly, sniffing the visitors as he ambled around the room, and then focused on Valdez as he continued his tail-wagging ceremony.

"Hey, boy. Champ...meet my friends, Ayita and Marjoi." He leaned down and stroked the dog playfully.

"Hi, Son." The friendly voice drifted upward from somewhere on a lower floor."

"Hey, Dad," Valdez called out, and then added, "I'm showing some friends my work."

"Good."

Ayita glanced at her watch. Two hours had elapsed since their arrival at the house. The time had flown. Not only was Valdez remarkably handsome and impeccably mannered but a gifted, accomplished artist, as well.

41

She loved the way he looked at her, but she wondered what he saw in her. Niggling self-doubt surfaced but she strove to stifle it. Valdez was by far the most exciting person she had ever encountered. Nothing was going to spoil this potential relationship.

Marjoi was a psychology major, in her second year at college. She had tried to shed some light on Ayita's problem of low self-esteem. She had explained to her that the emotional abuse from her parents coupled with their lack of interest and encouragement in her life, had borne the problem. Her mother had fueled it since her father's departure by virtually ignoring her existence; except for odd occasions...usually when she needed a favor.

Recently, Ayita had begun to thank God for her dear, loyal friend, Marjoi. Was God so generous that He was giving her yet another terrific companion? Ayita had never really had an actual boyfriend-only a few scattered dates with goofy guys. It was almost too good to be true. What had she done to deserve this remarkable man?

"May I have the honor of serving you ladies tea?" Valdez struck a grand pose.

There was a playful side to him that reminded her of an actor in a play. He had a flair for making even the mundane into an exciting event. Ayita caught him studying her face again. Their eyes met. Dark, intense eyes burned into hers.

She held his gaze as though meeting a silent challenge. She forced herself to ignore the insecurity threatening to overwhelm her. A thrill coursed through her entire body. She could not help the blush she felt spreading across her face. There was no mistaking his raw, male appreciation of her.

"Tea sounds good," Marjoi said.

Ayita was grateful for Marjoi's presence of mind,

because she was a bit tongue-tied.

"Which painting did you like best?" Valdez set down a tray containing a silver teapot service and white china mugs.

Ayita watched him with pure enjoyment as his large hands grasped the delicate teapot's handle and his husky form leaned toward her as he poured the tea. "The portrait of your mother. It is magnificent." Ayita took a sip of the tea and then set the cup down carefully. She glanced around the living room, admiring the beauty of her surroundings. A roaring fire blazed from the antiquated, marble fireplace. *The mansion is a real treasure. He is so fortunate to live here.*

"Dad is shy sometimes. He probably made a fire and vanished into his den to read. I'll put on another pot of tea and serve him some, as well. "Sorry I can't offer you pastries to go with the tea," Valdez said.

Marjoi sighed. "I couldn't eat another morsel after that lunch.

"Neither could I," Ayita agreed. Questions about the antiques bubbled up in her mind, but she was too shy to inquire and afraid that she might appear ignorant.

Marjoi plunged right in. "Are the settees Queen Anne?"

"Yes, they are. We had most of these pieces shipped over from Spain. Mother was an avid collector. She grew up in London and later visited there frequently, picking up pieces from Sotheby's and Christie's. She found some great treasures in Madrid and often bought privately from country estates, as well. She had a good eye."

3

Their timing was perfect. The tumbledown shack was bathed in darkness. She could retrieve her meager wardrobe without being discovered.

Snow was falling again. Road crews had not sanded the driveway leading to the High-Eagle shack. Valdez didn't want to get stuck, so he parked his Hummer on the side of the main road, leaving his lights and blinkers on. The threesome bailed out and hiked the short distance to the shack.

Ayita had planned to knock before entering her former home, but she heard voices as they approached. Nasty, bellowing sounds. An ugly quarrel was in progress. A man's deep voice uttered drunken threats. She wasn't sure if it was Wally or some other guy. Then she heard her mother bellowing incoherently.

She froze. "Let's get out of here," she rasped, her voice shaking. Her lower lip quivered as it sometime did when she was upset. Her body trembled as she fought off tears.

Silently, the trio marched purposefully back to the Hummer.

"I'll give you directions to the ranch," Marjoi told Valdez as they settled back into the vehicle.

"Sounds good." Valdez carefully maneuvered the Hummer from the side of the road onto the main road grooves, which were strewn with sand. Then he glanced at Ayita. "Is your mother going to be all right?"

His concern touched her deeply. "I hope so. It's probably Wally. He's never been violent to her that I know of, but I can't handle being around them anymore," she said, shakily. "They're both so unpredictable."

"Let's not take any chances." Valdez fished out his cell

from an inside pocket on his jacket. "I'll call 911."

"Thanks." Sadness wrapped around her. At times like this she felt so helpless, and that feeling brought back dozens of similar memories-memories she wanted to blot out forever.

Once Valdez had the emergency operator on the line, he turned to her. "The address, please, Ayita." But by now she was sobbing uncontrollably, so Marjoi took over, giving him the information. Ayita could imagine the conversation with the sheriff. Juanita was infamous around the Cherokee Indian Reservation. The sheriff had been many times before.

She ceased crying. Valdez had taken care of it. The sheriff was on his way. If her mother was in any serious trouble, she would have protection now.

"I can sure see why you've moved out," Valdez said, gently. "It sounds like your mom might need professional help."

"Yeah...I guess she does. Sometimes I wish they would just lock her up and insist she check into a treatment center. But in the past, after she sobers up, she usually charms them into releasing her. She went to a clinic for a month once, but two days after she was released, she was hitting the bottle again."

Valdez wheeled the Hummer onto the long drive leading up to the Circle K Ranch. He parked the vehicle and turned to Marjoi. "Do me a favor?"

"You got it."

"Would you give me some time alone with Ayita? I'd like to talk to her, privately."

"Of course. I'll put the coffee on. Take your time." In minutes, Marjoi disappeared from Ayita's view, vanishing into a flurry of swirling snowflakes. A light dusting of snow blanketed the recently sanded roads and fluffed out the snow drifts. Fog rolled in, obscuring the ranch house from her view.

In spite of the fact that the Hummer's windows were closed, Ayita could hear the horses neighing restlessly from the nearby barn. She shuddered as she thought about what she had tried to do.

"Do you want to talk about it?" Valdez asked, tenderly.

"Maybe sometime...but not right now." She peered into her compact mirror, wiping off her smeared mascara with a tissue before applying fresh lipstick. Tucking the compact back into her borrowed purse, she glanced up at Valdez. "Why are you being so nice to me?"

A puzzled smile lit his face. "You must be joking. You are the sweetest, most gorgeous gal I've ever laid eyes on. Don't you *know* that?"

He gazed at her, tender admiration shining from his eyes. "Wrapping powerful arms around her, he pulled her close to him. Large, brawny hands stroked her long, silky tresses. He touched her face lovingly and drew her even closer until she could feel his heart beating.

Neither spoke. It was as if she had been born for him. It felt so right. How had he known how desperately she needed strong arms around her, protecting her and comforting her? She fit perfectly into his arms. She wanted to stay there forever.

Valdez wanted to hold Ayita forever. She was fragile and delicate, reminding him of a rare flower-a white orchid, maybe. She needed special attention, understanding and careful treatment. He was definitely up for it. He was so lucky to have found her.

~~*~~

"I guess I should go in," Ayita said, finally.

He released her but continued to study her. "When will I see you again?"

"I don't know. It's...all happened so fast."

"May I call you?"

She hesitated before answering. "I guess that would be all right."

When she gave him the number, he programmed it into his cell.

"What time do you get home from the restaurant tomorrow?"

"I work the dinner shift...so around 9:30." Ayita smiled, but she was shaking inside. *How did I attract this incredible man?*

"I'll call you then." He grinned back at her before stepping out of the Hummer and walking around to the passenger side to open the door for her. Taking her hand, he helped her out of the vehicle. He clasped her hand as they walked down the path leading to the front door of the ranch house.

A chill wind snapped at her face and whistled through her body. She double-wrapped her woolen scarf around her neck and formed a fortress against the Arctic air. Snowflakes swirled, collecting rapidly on their coats. The fog had become denser. She could barely decipher the outline of the house.

Upon reaching the veranda, he took her gloved hands in his and lifted one of them to his lips, kissing it tenderly. She thought her heart would stop. He opened the door for her and she slipped into the house on a cloud. So much had happened in the last two days.

Marjoi had told her that angels were an entirely different species from people, but she was beginning to wonder if that were true. She had so many questions about the unseen spiritual world. She'd also said angels sometimes appeared in times of great crises to guide someone or to save them from peril. In some instances, their presence could be felt even though the angel did not manifest itself in physical form. Ayita had a new thirst for biblical knowledge. Tomorrow, she would buy a Bible and read it every day. She would keep checking the thrift shops until she found one. Her granny had bequeathed her Bible to her, but she would leave it at the shack. Maybe one day, her mother would pick it up and read it.

Mr. Peterson and Marjoi met them in the front entrance hall. Marjoi introduced her dad to Valdez.

"Thanks for getting these gals home. It's pretty grim out there. You must have driven through some dense fog. The main roads are sanded, as you probably know, but in the last hour, the snow has intensified. I hope you'll be able to get home. Where do you live?"

"Fairhaven, overlooking the ocean."

"Real bad accident out that way. Three-car pileup. There are two tow trucks over there, according to the local news. They're saying it's the worst blizzard to ever hit the region. I wouldn't venture out in this weather, if I were you. Maybe you don't live far away, but you may not be able to get through. I think you should spend the night here, and see what the roads are like in the morning."

"I'll be fine, Mr. Peterson. Thanks for your concern. If I run into any problems, I'll use my cell to get help."

"Some of the trucks aren't operating; and the ones that are can't keep up with the requests for help," Mr. Peterson warned.

"I appreciate your concern, but I'll find my way home. I kind of thrive on challenges." Valdez grinned at Ayita and lifted his hand in a parting gesture.

Ayita stared at the door after he closed it. A warm glow saturated her entire being. She followed Mr. Peterson and Marjoi into the family room, riding on a cloud.

"The news should be on any minute," Marjoi said.

Ayita glanced out the living room window at the dense fog and dim blur of snow as dusk rolled in. There was no visibility. How would Valdez make it home? The newsflash announced what they already knew-Fairhaven and Bellingham were buried beneath dense fog and mountains of snow. To make matters worse, the blizzard was supposed to accelerate during the night.

Ayita was concerned for Valdez's safety. She sent up a silent prayer that God would send angels to protect him and guide him as he drove home...or bring him safely back to the ranch.

Marjoi changed the mood by announcing she was going to make mulled apple cider. Minutes later, she returned with a tray laden with tall glass mugs. The aroma had a spicy cinnamon scent.

"Delicious," Ayita said, after taking a swig of it. The cider warmed her but her mind remained on Valdez. In fact, she couldn't stop thinking about him. She wasn't sure if it was because she was worried for his safety-or because she was crazy about him.

Perhaps sensing everyone's mood and concern for Valdez, Mrs. Peterson decided she would serve dinner in the formal dining room tonight and make it an occasion. "Would you girls mind setting the table? Use the silverware and china. Maybe fix a salad. I'll make one of my favorite chicken dishes. I think we can count on Rod whipping up dessert." She glanced over at Ayita. "He's famous for his tasty, chocolate concoctions."

It wasn't long before Mrs. Peterson announced "Dinner is served."

Ayita's heart swelled with appreciation. "The table setting looks very elegant, Mrs. Peterson."

"I always think the food tastes better when it's served on fine china. " Mrs. Peterson said.

Ayita and her surrogate family enjoyed dinner, and then the girls did the clean-up. They had just plopped down on the sofa in the living room when the doorbell rang.

"Expecting anyone?" Ayita glanced around at various family members. Mr. Peterson shook his head. "In *this* weather? You must be joking."

The door chimes reverberated throughout the house again.

"Excuse me. I'll see whose crazy enough to be out on a night like this." Mr. Peterson rose from his chair and headed toward the front door.

Ayita's intuition told her it was Valdez. Simultaneously, both she and Marjoi popped up from the sofa and headed for the door, trailing Mr. Peterson.

Valdez stood shivering in the doorway-the image of a frozen snowman.

"Hey, Valdez, come in out of the cold!" Marjoi scolded, shutting the door behind him.

"The Hummer is in the ditch about a mile and a half down the road," he said, teeth chattering. "The roads are treacherous. I must have hit black ice, because the Hummer spun out of control."

Marjoi took his coat and hung it up on the rack in the hallway while Ayita collected his accessories and hung them on the rack.

Mr. Peterson wrapped a blanket around his shoulders. "Make yourself at home, Valdez."

Valdez plopped down on one of the living room sofas. "I called Bob's Towing. They told me it would be a five to six hour delay, but they couldn't guarantee they'd make it at all tonight. So I cancelled it. I figured I'd better take you up on your invitation, instead of freezing to death."

"I doubt they would find your vehicle in this dense fog anyway. I'm glad you found your way back here. That must have been a challenge." Mr. Peterson strode to the wet bar and fished out a bottle of brandy, pouring a generous amount into a snifter. He handed it to Valdez. "I keep brandy in the house for emergencies. Drink it while I stack more wood on the fire. Our fireplace throws off a lot of heat. You'll warm up in no time."

Thank you, Lord, Ayita said, silently. Her eyes never veered from Valdez. "God was watching over you. You walked away from the accident without a scratch, but you could have frozen to death, if you hadn't found your way back here."

She watched him as he drank the brandy. She knew it would revive him. After all, she was well schooled in the uses of alcohol.

Valdez winked at her, tickling her senses. Rising from his seat on the sofa, he crossed the room to join her on the loveseat. It hit her then, that she must have subconsciously chosen it, as though waiting for him to join her on it. Wordlessly, they sat together, enjoying the blazing fire. Marjoi's folks slipped out of the room, unobtrusively.

Marjoi rose from her armchair. "I'll put some dinner in the microwave." She strode toward the kitchen.

They were alone. Valdez regarded her with appreciation. "I sure got lucky."

"I'm the lucky one," Ayita thought. "I didn't expect to see you again so soon." She smiled at him, too shy to flirt

back, though she basked in his adoration. "How were you able to find your way here, through the dense fog?" Ayita frowned, thoughtfully.

"I really don't know." His brows knit in serious contemplation. "I can only tell you that I...somehow sensed what direction to walk in. Otherwise, I never would have found this house."

Marjoi returned to the living room. "It was probably your guardian angel that led you here."

"You might be right. I felt a presence on the entire journey here. I instinctively knew what direction to walk in. It really is a miracle I found your house," Valdez said.

"Praise the Lord!" Ayita exclaimed.

Valdez and Marjoi stared at her in amazement. She was usually so timid.

"I prayed the angels would surround you, guide you and protect you. It was a blessing the Hummer slid into the ditch before you got on the Meridian Highway. With the deep trenches on either side of that artery and the dense fog you might have been in *real* trouble."

Marjoi spoke in her usual, authoritative manner. "The Bible tells us to 'Ask, and it shall he given you; seek and ye shall find, knock, and it shall be opened unto you.' As children of the Kingdom, we should constantly be aware of the power we have. We can ask God to send our guardian angel to protect us and we can ask Him to lead and guide our lives."

Ayita silently marveled at Marjoi, who clearly had been an ace student in her mom's Bible classes.

A few minutes after Marjoi headed back to the kitchen, she called, "Dinner is on the table, Valdez. We'll keep you company."

The threesome settled in at the table and Marjoi prayed

the blessing. "Thank-you for this food, Lord. Bless it to Valdez's use." He was clearly starved. "The chicken is excellent," he said, in between bites. "I do the cooking at my house. I enjoy it."

Ayita jumped in, starting to relax in his presence. "Really? What do you like to cook?"

"Almost anything. I make a lot of classic Spanish dishes-paella, chioppino, black bean chili... I also create my own dishes."

"Are you sure you don't run a cooking school?" Marjoi teased.

"Actually, I did for a while, in Madrid." Ayita and Marjoi exchanged glances. "Is there no end to your talents?" Ayita asked.

He shrugged. "I didn't say I was good at it. Aside from it being a necessity, I like to keep busy. It's also creative."

After dinner, everyone returned to their former places in the living room.

It bothered Ayita that Valdez had driven back out into the blustery storm. She finally spoke up. "Why did you attempt to drive home in the blinding fog and blizzard? We barely made it here earlier."

"I told you I thrive on challenges." He grinned at Ayita.

"Don't you mean impossibilities?"

He chuckled. It was a derisive chuckle. "I've traveled all over the continent and driven through most of the States. Last winter, I got caught in a blinding snowstorm in Montana. I learned real fast how to survive the weather. Between white-outs, dense fog, black ice-the works-I guess you could say that this was just another adventure."

He was a Maverick. But weren't creative people often adventurous? Didn't they have to experience and understand life in order to be able to depict it?

"I see." Ayita nodded. She added, wistfully. "I'd sure like to travel someday."

"Me, too," Marjoi agreed. "I got a chance to see California last Easter. I traveled with my folks. Dad drove down the Coast to California. He took the scenic route. It was breathtaking, actually. The further south we travelled, the better I liked it. Balmy nights, palm trees and the most magnificent sunsets I've ever seen!"

Ayita listened to Marjoi with only half an ear, because Valdez had her mesmerized. His dark, brooding eyes held her captive. She trembled slightly. *What is happening to me? It's as though I'm under a spell. Do I affect him the same way?* She had never known anything like this before and she found it unsettling.

Could he read her mind? When Marjoi had "painted" a picture of the beauty she had enjoyed in California, Ayita had been drawn into her image-world. She envisioned herself traveling there with Valdez. She really hoped her thoughts weren't transparent, because sometimes it seemed as though he could peer into her very soul.

"I'm going to make a pot of herb tea," Marjoi announced, heading for the kitchen.

At last they were alone, and it was truly blissful.

"You're very beautiful," Valdez said, tenderly, tracing a finger over her features. "The flames from the fire cast an enchanting glow on your face...it gives you an ethereal quality. You almost resemble The Madonna-a face of mystery and magnetic beauty. I should like you to sit for me sometime. I would love to do a portrait of you."

Flustered and unsure how to respond, she finally murmured "Thank you...I consider that a compliment." Her thoughts jumped to next Sunday. "How about joining Marjoi and me for Bible study before church on Sunday?

Weather permitting, of course."

He hesitated for a long minute. "I don't think so. I've read the Bible and attended church several times. That's enough religion for me."

Ayita was frustrated. The bright lights of eternity had been switched on for her, and she longed to share that illumination with him. "Didn't you listen to the sermon last Sunday?" She was irked at his lack of perception.

"Yeah, so..." He shrugged.

"The preacher said we would grow spiritually if we meditated on even *one* Bible verse a day. Ideally, though, he suggested we read at least one chapter of the Bible daily, preferably before breakfast."

"Why before breakfast?"

She frowned. "Were you daydreaming all through the sermon?" His cavalier attitude was downright annoying.

"I guess my mind must have drifted off at some point."

"I guess it must have. The point was to put God first by starting your day with His Word."

Granny's words flooded back to her again, infiltrating her soul from her earliest memories.

"Faith cometh by hearing, and hearing by the word of God."

Ayita said to Valdez, "For you to have the Scriptures embedded deeply within you, you need to read the Word and listen to it being preached...and that's the end of my preaching." She smiled at him, nervously, hoping she hadn't said too much.

He glowered back, reminding her of a little boy just chastised by his mommy.

Marjoi returned with a tray holding a teapot and mugs. She set it down on the oval coffee table. "Tea is served."

"Good timing, Marjoi. I need a break from your Bible-thumping friend," Valdez muttered.

Marjoi arched a brow. "Pardon?"

"She reminds me of a reformed alcoholic - she's even trying to talk me into going to Bible class. That's really pushing it." He frowned.

"That's your loss," Marjoi shot back.

"All right. Now I have to contend with the two of you." Valdez rolled his eyes.

"I suppose if you feel you already know everything, there's no point in attending the class." Marjoi glowered at him.

"I didn't say that," Valdez retorted.

"Hey, guys, give it a rest. Why don't we take our tea and head for the family room and get the weather update?" Ayita suggested.

A weather news update grabbed their attention: The meteorologist, an attractive brunette, glanced at a map on the screen showing the air masses and projected weather. "The fog is expected to lift slightly by morning. If it does clear up, it will be short-lived. Another blizzard is moving in from Alaska." She pointed to the area on map. "The Arctic air will bring sub-zero temperatures. There's no end in sight for the cold snap. This winter we are experiencing a record snowfall here in the Bellingham/Seattle vicinity. If the storm escalates-and we predict it will-this could be the coldest, fiercest winter on record for the state of Washington."

Ayita could hardly believe her ears. Her mother and Wally could freeze to death. The house on the Reservation was poorly insulated, the heating system ineffective at best. On the other hand, her mother could be resourceful when she had to be. She had a few friends living on the Reservation and a couple of them had newer homes. She and Wally could probably keep warm in one of their homes, if they had to. They would survive.

Valdez stood, stretching his long, muscular physique. "I wonder if the fog has lifted yet. There must be pockets of visibility somewhere." He walked purposefully over to the large bay window facing the street. Heavy blue drapes covered the windows. He parted them, as well as the sheers beneath and peered outside. "Whoa, the fog is as thick as soup, and that snow is coming down fast."

"I guess you're stuck here for a while. If that blizzard worsens, the area will come to a standstill until the road crews can operate," Marjoi said.

Ayita couldn't remain irked with Valdez for very long. Her heart beat faster as she glimpsed his tall, male form. His back was to her as he surveyed the weather. He turned abruptly, as if sensing she was watching him. Midnight black eyes locked with hers, causing her to feel dizzy and somewhat euphoric.

She took a deep breath. She was playing with fire. He wasn't a Christian, even though he seemed to believe in angels and attend church occasionally. *But hadn't God sent him to her?* There was so much she needed to learn about the spiritual dimension.

It would never work. What did he see in her, anyway? He was an accomplished artist from an affluent family and held a Master of Arts Degree from the University of Madrid. She was an uneducated nobody. But she did possess an innate curiosity about most things and a compulsion to learn everything she could about music. She had wanted to sing and perform for as long as she could remember. Though she'd been unable to entertain the idea of studying music at a university because of her tumultuous home life, maybe she could do that now.

Marjoi was channel-surfing again. *Encounters with Angelic Beings* was on. "Anyone interested in watching this program?" she asked.

"I'm fascinated with the idea of angelic beings," Valdez replied. "I'd like to see the show."

"Me, too." Ayita smiled at him and felt her heart lurch. "I find it particularly fascinating since angels have been with us from the beginning of time. Numerous Scriptures refer to them throughout the Bible. And yet, only now, in recent years, has there been a huge revival of interest in the subject."

Marjoi nodded. "I think we're living in the last days. The Bible says, 'And it shall come to pass in the last days, saith God, I will pour out my Spirit upon all flesh...I will show wonders in the heavens above.'

"Maybe one of those wonders is the four blood moons. We've have three of them and the fourth one occurs in September of this year! They tie in with the scriptures from Joel. 'And I will show wonders in the heavens and in the earth, blood, and fire, and pillars of smoke. The sun shall be turned into darkness, and the room into blood, before the great and the terrible day of the Lord come.'

"You think that's enough evidence to suggest the world is going to end?" Valdez looked skeptical.

"No. But it could herald the rapture," Ayita said.

"Or it could mean that the rapture will occur sometime after the occurrence of the blood moons, I suppose." Marjoi said.

"Well... I tend to believe in angels...because of things that have happened in my life. Do you think they exist?" Valdez asked.

"I think us humans have always been fascinated by the supernatural. Maybe the manifestations of angels are another way God has chosen to wake people up. I'll let Ayita tell you about her encounter with one. Sometimes God sends them to guide us or protect us from evil...or warn us of impending danger. They're God's special messengers. And there's many different types of angel...I'm sorry...don't get me started, I have this innate tendency to lecture. Guess I inherited it from my folks. They're both teachers."

Ayita was a sponge, desiring to rapidly gain biblical knowledge. "I think we should watch the show. I'm sure we'll all learn something."

"Yeah. Maybe we should watch it." Valdez conceded.

4

Ayita awakened early, excited at the prospect of having Valdez as a houseguest, and intrigued by the impending blizzard.

The bedroom was cool. Pulling on her robe, she scampered to the window. Chunky snowflakes danced and swirled, driven by a fierce wind. She could hear it howling through the closed windows. The fog had lifted but in its place raged a fierce blizzard. She knew it was bitterly cold outside but she was curious to see how cold that felt. She had never experienced anything like this before.

She slid the window open a sliver. Frigid gusts stung her face, jolting her awake. Secretly, she was thrilled. There was no way Valdez would be able to hire a tow truck to come out in this weather. They would all be tied up with road emergencies. He would not be a priority customer for them-but he sure was a welcome guest at the Circle K!

She strained to glimpse the ground below, so that she could see how deep the snow was, but there was zero visibility. The wind howled, driving chunky snowflakes through heavy fog, creating a blurry maze. The sky was dark and ominous, as though warning the earthly inhabitants of impending disaster.

A wave of panic washed over her. Would there be enough food to last them for the duration of the storm? She had no idea of the extent of foodstuffs Mrs. Peterson had on hand, and there were two additional people in the house. Suppose the blizzard lasted for several weeks-even a month? What if the pipes froze and they were unable to access water?

She vaguely recalled an article she had read some time ago. A couple had died in a blizzard because they ran out of food and water. Their water pipes had frozen, so they were unable to access water, and since they had neither food nor water stored, they were out of luck. The power lines had been knocked out, so there was no way they could get help, either.

Panic seized her as her thoughts raced back in time to her childhood. She had gone to bed hungry. She was crying and calling for her mother, but her parents had already drunk themselves into oblivion and were passed out of their bed. Abandonment and hopelessness had welled up deep inside her. The old fears returned to haunt her now.

Somewhere she'd read you never got the chill of poverty out of your bones. Maybe you never got neglect and abuse out of your bones, either. Her mind whirled. Could she really make something of her life? The more she dreamed about what it could be, the more frustrated she became with the reality of working at the restaurant. *Lord, remove the panic and give me wisdom and peace.*

Like a gentle wave cresting on the ocean on a summer day, a quiet peace washed over her. She was, after all, a new creature-the minister had told her so-and God was her Father. She could talk to Him the way she had only dreamed of talking to her earthly father. She clung to the Scripture. "Old things are passed away: behold, all things are become new." Never again would she feel alone and abandoned, as she often had as a child. God promised never to leave her or forsake her. He would always lead the way, like a lantern in front of her, lighting her pathway and guiding her one step at a time.

Her eyes fell on the words of the *Footprints* plaque on the wall:

One night a man had a dream. He dreamed he was walking along the beach with the Lord. Across the sky flashed scenes from his life. For each scene, he noticed two sets of footprints in the sand-one belonged to him and the other to the Lord.

When the last scene of his life flashed before him, he looked back at the footprints in the sand. He noticed that many times along the path of his life, there was only one set of footprints. He also noticed that it happened at the very lowest and saddest times in his life.

This really bothered him, and he questioned the Lord about it. "Lord? You said that once I decided to follow you, you would walk with me all the way, but I have noticed that during the most troublesome times in my life, there is only one set of footprints. I don't understand why when I needed you most you would leave me?"

The Lord replied: "My precious, precious child. I love you and I would never leave you. During your times of trial and suffering, when you saw only one set of footprints, it was then that I carried you."

Author Unknown.

She read it a couple of times. She did not have the answer to her problems, but God did, and He would guide her to the right solutions.

Marjoi finally awakened. "Hey, you're up early," she said sleepily before heading down the hall and disappearing into the bedroom. Returning shortly, she stepped into her walk-in closet to select an outfit.

Ayita remained transfixed to the raging storm outside. Marjoi, clad in a navy wool sweater and matching slacks, her hair still wrapped in a towel from her shower, joined Ayita, who was comfortably nestled on the window bench.

"I can't believe this weather. I've never seen anything like it in my life!" Ayita exclaimed.

Marjoi located the remote control on her dresser and

started channel surfing until she found a newsflash.

"We interrupt this program to give you a weather update. There is no end in sight for the freak blizzard that has buried the West Coast area of Seattle and Bellingham. Fairhaven and the surrounding area has been hit particularly hard. Except for emergency vehicles, we are advising all drivers to stay off the roads. Hospitals are overflowing with accident victims and frostbite patients."

Ayita and Marjoi exchanged glances in stunned silence.

The report continued. "Massive power outages have been reported in those areas, particularly along the Coast. If you have battery-operated radios and flashlights, get them ready. If your pipes haven't burst, be sure to keep a small trickle running continually through the pipes and some extra water for backup..." Emergency preparations were exhaustive.

As they listened to the news bulletin, they remained fixated on the blizzard outside, faces pressed against the window.

"This storm has broken all existing records. It's the worst blizzard ever recorded in the state of Washington," the newscaster announced.

Ayita and Marjoi stared at each other, stunned.

"I hope Mother is all right," Ayita said.

"You better try reaching her now, in case the power goes out," Marjoi suggested.

"You're right." Ayita picked up the phone and punched in her mother's number. No answer. She let it ring about ten times before finally hanging up. "I hope she's at one of her neighbor's houses. We better lift her up in prayer."

They joined hands and prayed. Tears spilled down Ayita's cheeks as Marjoi finished the prayer. "You're such a wonderful friend to me." Ayita smiled at her. "I'm so lucky to have you on my side."

The intercom buzzed. "Shall I include the two of you for breakfast, or do you want to do your own thing?" Mrs. Petersons spoke in even tones infused with warmth, characteristic of her persona.

"We'll make our own," Marjoi said.

"Suit yourself. Valdez is joining us. He's at the breakfast bar having coffee."

At the sound of the name *Valdez,* wild thrills raced throughout Ayita's body. *I've never known a man that affected me like this.* Shaking it off, she decided to head for the shower.

Later, she pulled on Marjoi's red turtleneck and tan pants. The pants were a little loose in spite of being a stretchy fabric, but she was grateful just to have clothes to wear.

Mrs. Peterson cleared the table while her hubby and Valdez sipped coffee at the kitchen island.

Mr. Peterson glanced in their direction as they entered the kitchen. "Good morning, girls. You both look lovely."

"You say that all the time, Dad. We don't have any wrinkles yet."

Ayita muffled a snicker as Marjoi cracked eggs and poured in a little milk to make scrambled eggs.

"Join us for coffee. I'm sure it doesn't take two of you to whip up a little breakfast," Mr. Peterson grinned. "I was just telling Valdez that Betty and I feel like such fools. We usually do a big grocery shopping on Saturday, but because the roads were icy, we skipped it, thinking we would go later in the week. And now we've got a problem."

"Don't blame yourselves. I don't recall any warnings about this massive storm moving in. Do you?" Valdez asked.

"No, I don't. It's a big surprise."

"I don't think there *were* any warnings. Maybe somebody was sleeping on the job at the weather bureau. Or maybe they thought it just looked like more of the same," Ayita reasoned.

Valdez grinned at Ayita. "You have a point."

It was almost as if he were proud of her speaking up. She was sure he had already figured out how shy and insecure she was.

"Anyway, it caught us off guard, and probably a lot of other folks as well," Mr. Peterson concluded.

While Marjoi scrambled eggs for them, made toast and added a thin slice of tomato on each plate, Ayita set the table and poured freshly brewed coffee for them. She also poured a small glass of orange juice for each of them and topped up everyone's coffee.

Betty Peterson pulled up a stool at the kitchen island and joined Valdez for coffee. "You see, Valdez, my family is spoiled. I usually stop by the produce store several times a week to buy fresh veggies. Who knew something like this could happen? And I never store canned food. Henry and I are health fanatics, you know."

"Anyway, the fact is, somebody will need to walk to the supermarket...or one of the neighbors, so we can replenish our food supply. There's no end in sight for this weather." Henry's brows knit together in a frown as he puffed on his pipe.

Ayita got the distinct impression the Petersons felt foolish to be in this predicament. On the other hand, how were they to know a freak storm like this would move into the area? She had grown up here and had never experienced anything even close to this before. It seemed to her that the weather patterns were changing everywhere, and this was merely one more example of that.

Marjoi seemed to have read her thoughts. "Personally, I believe God uses freak storms and unexpected weather conditions to grab our attention. So many of us are lulled into believing that everything will remain the same as it is now, and we allow ourselves to become spiritually lethargic."

Rod grabbed a mug of coffee in the kitchen and then gave a little wave as he flitted by. The nervous twitch in his eyes was not lost on Ayita. "Let somebody else figure it out," appeared to be his motto.

Henry was drawing a map. "The supermarket and produce stores are both about ten miles away, and I'd be surprised if they're open. On the other hand, the Clayburghs live about seven miles away, and I know for a fact they keep copious amounts of foodstuffs on hand, because they entertain frequently and lavishly."

Betty picked up the phone and punched in her neighbor's number. She chatted briefly before placing the receiver back on the hook. She smiled. "We're in luck. If somebody can get there, Mrs. Clayburgh will be happy to give us a large supply of food. Apparently, she has a freezer full, as well as surplus canned goods and dried foods. We can have whatever we can carry back."

Valdez piped up instantly. "Hey, I'm on my way."

Marjoi disappeared from the kitchen, returning shortly with a woolen facemask, holes cut out for the eyes, masked-gunman style. Everyone chuckled except her. "You folks can laugh all you want, but the mask could save his face from freezing."

Suddenly everyone was silent. There was a ring of truth to her statement and everyone seemed to sense it.

Rod bounced in and out of the kitchen prancing around like a nervous cat.

"Maybe someone should go with Valdez," Marjoi said.

Rod quickly found the exit while Henry Peterson turned noticeably silent.

Ayita was disappointed to discover bravery was not a trait possessed by either father or son.

"I'll go with you," Ayita blurted.

"No, you won't," Valdez shot back. "For one thing, you don't have an ounce of fat on you; you'll freeze much faster than I would. Secondly, I can move faster alone, and I *do* have plenty of meat on my bones. Besides, I love a challenge, remember?"

Ayita knew she had no right to feel this way, but she brimmed with pride. *He's quite a man.*

"I'll pack you some lunch and fill a couple of water containers." Betty got up to start the preparations. "I'll go over the map I've drawn for you. I sure hope you can find their house in this dense fog. You'll need a miracle, young man," Henry said.

"I'll manage," Valdez said with an air of confidence.

Although Ayita was a brand-new Christian, she knew at that moment her faith was stronger than Henry Peterson's. She was amazed at how fearful he was. Though only in his mid-forties, he looked much older today, haggard and drawn. Betty Peterson definitely had greater faith than her husband. Yet Marjoi was a tower of faith. Was it because she saturated herself with the Scriptures?

Suddenly, Ayita sensed in her spirit that the whole family would be tested. She also knew, with sudden clarity, that this would be a rare opportunity to set an example for Valdez and witness to him in a unique, powerful way. She felt excited at the prospect that God might use her-perhaps even to inspire greater faith in Mr. Peterson!

"Are you scared?" Rod asked Valdez, pacing nervously around the kitchen.

"Of what?"

"Of freezing to death, or getting lost in the blizzard!"

"No," Valdez said dismissively, as though he found the question tiring.

"You're very brave!" Ayita blurted.

"Yes, you are." Betty handed Valdez an insulated transport bag. "This is the lunch bag we use when we go to the park. There are tuna sandwiches, two chocolate bars, and a small thermos of coffee. Oh, and a small flask of brandy and two bottles of water. We sure appreciate you doing this." She flashed him a warm smile.

Rod continued his anxious pacing. Finally, as Valdez was leaving, he spat out "What if you freeze to death? What if you don't make it back with the food?"

"I'll be back. Count on it." Valdez stared at him unruffled. "If my time on the planet is up, there's nothing I can do about it anyway-but the thought of this family doing without...possibly starving...*that* I have a problem with-because I can do something about it. I told you, I love challenges."

Henry Peterson and the family joined hands to pray for protection over Valdez, asking God for the ability to find the Clayburghs' house, get the food, and return safely. Then everyone discreetly vacated the back porch, except Ayita.

Valdez resembled an Eskimo, bundled up from head to toe. He held his woolen facemask and gloves in his right hand. He gazed at Ayita tenderly. Then, in one smooth move, he gathered her into powerful arms and pressed his lips on hers.

In that instant, every particle of her body, mind and

soul jolted, fully awakened. She felt as though she'd been in a deep sleep until this startling moment. *So this is what love feels like!* She could never live without him now. She finally admitted to herself that she was deeply, irrevocably in love with him.

Reluctantly and slowly they parted. "Good-bye for now, my darling," Ayita whispered, her heart still pounding.

"I'll be back before you know it. I would slay dragons for you," He grinned crookedly. "I'll call you as soon as I reach the Clayburghs, so you'll know I made it there." He donned the woolen mask and his gloves, and then strode outside into the driving snowstorm.

As she stared out the door after him, snowflakes propelled by howling winds swirled onto the glassed-in back porch. Some of the fat flakes sprung upon her, melting on impact. His form faded to a dim blur, lost to the fog and snow.

When she closed the door and walked slowly back into the house, it felt larger and eerily silent without Valdez's presence.

Rod was still pacing around the living room. "How will he be able to carry the food back through the blizzard, even if he *does* find the house?"

"He said he'd call as soon as he gets to the Clayburghs. He'll figure something out," Ayita reported. "So if they still have power, we'll hear from him. Do you think cell phones will work in this weather?"

"I doubt it," Rod said quickly.

"Why don't we try him right now," Marjoi suggested.

"I know the number. I'll try it." Ayita headed for the kitchen phone. She punched in Valdez's number and let it ring about ten times, but there was no answer.

5

Valdez trudged on in the frigid weather. The wind howled. Snow flurries pelted against him. The fog was so dense he could barely see a foot ahead of him. *It's impossible. I'll never make it.* He was lost, and there was no way he could find his way back. What a fool he'd been to think he could find a house he had never seen, while groping his way through the heavy snow and dense fog.

Taking the flashlight from his pocket, he checked the map. It was useless, because he had no idea where he was. He stuffed the flashlight and map back in his pockets. He had to speed up. He couldn't risk getting frostbite. Speed would be crucial. It would keep his blood circulated and shorten his travel time.

He walked faster, hoping he was going in the right direction. It was early morning, so maybe the sun would come out and burn off some of the fog, giving him better visibility. He had to remain cool. If he got upset, he couldn't focus on staying the course straight ahead. His sense of direction was usually uncannily accurate. He forced himself to remain calm. He believed he was walking south.

An eerie stillness surrounded him. Silver sparkles of glimmering sunlight struggled to break through the fog, but it seemed like a tease to him. He could not foresee how his trek would end. He suddenly regretted that he had not gone forward to the altar the day he had witnessed Ayita's formal conversion.

He wondered what his eternal destiny would be, if he were to perish in the blizzard. Normally he didn't give it much thought, but here, alone and freezing, a lone figure hidden in dense fog, plodding his way through deep snow, he began to have second thoughts about everything. The weary trudge, mile after mile, was a test of his stamina. It was silly, but he wanted to be a hero in Ayita's eyes.

His best calculation put him at about three miles until he reached the house. It had been relatively uneventful. Then, suddenly, without warning, the slight visibility dropped to zero. The snow flurries, which had ceased for a time, seemed to be in concert with the deepening fog. Chunky flakes swirled around him with increasing intensity, forming a white, mobile wall. Icy winds whipped mercilessly around him, chilling him to the marrow. He began to shiver.

He paused, pulling out his emergency flask of brandy, taking a healthy swig of it to warm up. He felt better, but now he noticed an itch from wearing the tight ski goggles. They helped his vision slightly, but he took them off and placed them in his travel kit to ease the pressure. The wool mask had been a brilliant idea. It lessened the impact of the biting wind slapping at his face.

Taking out the flashlight again, he reviewed the map and guiding notes. Henry had been thorough. Valdez guessed it came from teaching school for over twenty years. He checked his compass and felt sure he was heading south toward the Clayburgh ranch. He halted every once in a while to make sure the deep ditches continued on either side of the road, and he had not mistakenly headed off on a side road. There was apparently a large, abandoned farm in the area, and that was one of his markers.

Occasionally, he was able to see a couple feet ahead of him, but most of the time there was only a blur of white snowflakes mingled with dense fog, obscuring his vision to practically nil. Normally an upbeat and positive person, he started to have fearful thoughts. *What if I'm unable to locate the house? What if I'm walking in the wrong direction?* He wore a money belt, an old habit from travelling around Europe, but money couldn't help him now.

He was growing steadily more fatigued. He had to be nearing his destination. His legs felt like steel weights, his feet like blocks of concrete. There had been small breaks in the wind, but presently, he felt numb. If he didn't get there soon, he would collapse. He was sure his hands were frozen, and his whole body ached. *When will this nightmare end?*

Using the flashlight he'd brought with him, he beamed it around, hoping to spot the house at the side of the road, but it was futile in the fog-laden blizzard. How could he possibly hope to find a house, located down a long driveway, when he couldn't see more than a foot ahead of him? It had been a crazy idea for him to attempt this mission. The flashlight helped only marginally in his frantic search for the driveway. *God above, I must be only a mile or so from my destination.* In fact, his intuition told him he was close...very close to the Clayburgh ranch.

Like a scavenger at a deserted beach, scrounging for valuables, his instinct told him he was approaching the treasure.

The Clayburghs had promised they would leave a myriad of blazing lights on to help guide him onto their property. *Where are those blazing lights?* His soul cried out to God, to the same God he had been uncertain even existed. He had never pursued Him, yet somehow now he knew God was his only hope.

He could not do this alone. He wasn't invincible-he needed help. He couldn't stand it any longer. *God, please help me find the driveway to the Clayburgh's before I freeze to death. Reveal it to me, please. Make it crystal clear.*

Did he really believe God would answer his prayer? Yes, he did. He had to believe it. Weariness was overtaking him, causing his footsteps to become ponderous. He was hungry, thirsty, and bone tired. He pulled out the second water bottle and took a long drink, then took out the flask from the inner pocket in his parka and finished the last bit of brandy. He had eaten the tuna sandwiches and a chocolate bar hours ago. Now he munched on his last bar.

Suddenly, as if seeing a mirage, he spotted dim lights in the distance. As he walked toward the glow, the lights became more visible, gradually brighter until they shone brilliantly-a beacon of hope in the blinding storm.

As he moved closer to the source of light, he started to think it was a mirage. The lights seemed to flicker and fade and flicker back on again. Was he imagining that he had reached his destination? Were his eyes playing tricks? He walked closer and closer into the brilliant light, and then he saw it-a house emerging from the misty gray fog. It was bathed in bright lights. He had made it!

Now he could lights blazing everywhere, cutting through the dense fog. The Clayburghs would be waiting for him.

But, just as suddenly as he'd seen the vivid lights, they dimmed, along with the outline of the house. He realized with a sudden sinking sensation that they were only a figment of his imagination. A mirage. He was exhausted and hallucinating. It was a desert fantasy. Water springs for a dying man or, in his case, refuge for a freezing one.

He began to lose hope. He would die here, alone, in this freak blizzard. How long would it take them to find his body? No, that wasn't right. He must not dwell on morbid thoughts. Ayita and the Petersons needed him. He had to find the house and bring the food back to them.

Thank God, his dad would be all right. He had gotten through on the phone earlier, but he hadn't really been worried because they lived right next door to a corner grocery store, and his dad usually kept canned goods and bottled water for emergencies. It was unfortunate that that house he shared with his dad was located over fifty miles from the Circle K ranch.

An image of Ayita loomed before him. At first the image was fuzzy but then it came sharply into focus. She needed him-of that he was certain. And not just for the sustenance he could bring her, either.

He loved that woman. Fantastic as that was, he actually *loved* her. In fact, he could not imagine life without her now. Yes, he would make it. He had to. He had to know what she was really like. Had to learn all the tender secrets that marred her gentle persona. He wanted the chance to explore a relationship with her. He was going to find this house and get the supplies back to the Circle K. There had to be a way.

He had devised a method for locating the driveway he hoped was soon approaching. Every five feet or so, he stopped to see if he could find a driveway-but each time, all he encountered was the deep ditch. He could not give up. Sooner or later it would have to be there. It was slowing him down, but judging by his watch, lit by his flashlight, he should be pretty close to his destination. Surely, he would stumble upon it soon.

He grew more fatigued with every step. The frigid temperatures and dense gray fog that surrounded him, obscuring his ability to locate the house, was finally wearing him down. He strained hard to glean a bit more visibility but couldn't. Had he begun looking for the driveway soon enough? Had he passed it?

It was impossible to gauge how far he had come and how far he had left to go. All he could do was give it his best shot.

His mother had spoken of angels just before she died. He wished he knew more about them. Would they be watching over him? Would they guide him to the driveway? If only he knew how to tune into them.

He was exhausted, mostly from the sheer frustration of knowing he was lost and unable to see where he was going. Swirling snowflakes danced crazily about him, mingling with the misty fog. The hazy blur was his constant companion.

If he didn't find the driveway soon, he would surely freeze to death.

A raw, unsettling pain seared through him. His chronic back condition was flaring up, exacerbated because he was under pressure.

His body crumpled to the ground. The road beneath his aching frame was freezing cold. It was all a bizarre charade. If he didn't scramble back onto his feet quickly, he would be a goner. *Why had he offered to attempt this mission?* He knew the answer, but it did not alleviate his distress.

He didn't know where the strength came from, but somehow he found himself back on his feet. He had to keep moving.

Before he'd left the Circle K Ranch, he'd calculated about five hours to reach his destination, based on the fact that it normally took him about twenty or twenty-five minutes to walk a mile. He figured the blizzard and fog had slowed him down to about one mile an hour or less, which included his constant stops to check the side of the road searching for the driveway.

Gut instinct told him he was near the Clayburgh ranch. But where was it? Still, there was no sign of the driveway. Could he be miles off target? How would he know if he was? He stumbled again but managed to remain on his feet. He couldn't see any welcoming lights, and there was still no sign of a house or the ranch. The horses and cattle would be in the barn, so listening for their sounds was futile.

He reached into an inner pocket of his parka to get a drink of the bottled water and realized to his horror that his right hand was frozen! He used his left hand to reach the bottle and finished the water quickly. He had to find the house. No way could he head back. Emotionally, he felt depleted. He could not endure the elements much longer. *What was he going to do?*

There was only one thing left he *could* do-pray from the depths of his heart. *I give up, Lord. Without your help, I'll never make it. Please, God, help me!*

In that instant, he saw a huge, winged creature looming before him. Resplendent with white, feathery wings tinged with blush-pink, it had a serene, handsome face, and brightly shining eyes. The angel pointed to one side of the street.

Immediately Valdez was infused with strength and swiftly found himself at the side of the road the angel had directed him to. He turned to thank the Being, but it had vanished.

Now on the driveway he could see a faint light filtering through the dense fog. It emanated from the direction in which he was headed. Everything was going to be all right. He fairly spun down the drive, propelled by a second wind. The soft light loomed brighter. He was almost at the doorstep. Glimpsing the steps, he flew up them to the front porch and knocked forcefully on the door.

He tried the doorknob. Locked. Tense, he waited, his heart beating rapidly. Someone was unbolting the door *The face mask!* He ripped it off, hastily. He did not want to alarm the Clayburghs.

The door opened to reveal a delicate-looking Asian woman, standing next to a ruddy-faced man who gave the impression of being cranky. But when he spoke, his manner was gentle and kind. "You must be Valdez. We're the Clayburghs. Come in, come in! There's a blazing fire in the fireplace!"

"I get you something hot to drink." Mrs. Clayburgh smiled her welcome and ushered him into the house. "I'm Dottie...my husband, John."

Valdez followed the gracious, friendly couple into their spacious living room. A roaring fire blazed from the red brick fireplace. He drew closer to it, the welcoming warmth caressing him. Then he collapsed on the sofa, still clad in his parka.

Dotti brought him a snifter of warm brandy and followed it with green herbal tea. "Green tea with honey give you boost." His petite hostess smiled, revealing tiny wrinkles around her slanted eyes, cracking the alabaster skin. "I made lamb stew. Hope you like it." She spoke in choppy sentences, and as she spoke the curve in her lips sprang her Dresden doll face to life. He sensed she had a big heart and a gentle spirit.

"My hand...I think it's frozen," he muttered vaguely. He was delirious. Hot flames leapt from the wood fireplace, warming him while the hot drink burned its way down his throat and through his body, taking the edge off his chill. He was starting to feel better, but he still felt light-headed.

"Let me have a look," Dotti prompted.

He sensed expert eyes scrutinizing it. "Is it numb?"

"Yes."

"When you first realize...frozen?"

"About...a half hour ago...I think."

"Try to relax. I be right back." Dottie scurried away, returning quickly with a basin of hot water. She set it down on the coffee table. "I do not think frozen. If I'm right, hot water bring it back."

He soaked one hand and drank the steaming tea with the other. "I think I'm in good hands."

"I hope so. I was doctor in Shanghai before Revolution. One of the lucky ones. I got out in time. I bring you more tea and honey biscuits. You going to be fine." Dotti gave him an encouraging smile and disappeared into the kitchen.

John Clayburgh occupied a wingback chair opposite Valdez, who sprawled on the sofa. He rose. "Let me take your jacket, I'll hang it up for you so it can dry."

Valdez was only vaguely aware he still had it on. He glanced at the heavy parka. "Thanks."

His host helped Valdez slip it off, then threw it over an arm, and disappeared with it. He was back in minute. "Good thing you took a chance and came over here. There's no change in sight for the weather, and it's hard to know when the supermarkets and grocery stores will reopen. Tomorrow we'll have to figure out how you're going to get the supplies back to the Circle K."

Although Valdez did not share the visitation of the angel with his hosts, he knew that because of that majestic appearance everything would work out.

Dottie carried a tray with a pot of tea and biscuits into the room. She set the tray down on the antique console next to him. "You have feeling in hand yet?" she asked, inspecting it.

He tested it. "No."

"I think you will...soon."

He shared her optimism. It was in his nature. His father had always seen the positive side of every situation and, perhaps by osmosis, Valdez had a similar mindset. The grogginess of his ordeal gradually faded as he revived. The warmth of the house and his genial hosts elevated his spirits. He had made it here; he would make it back. He just did not know exactly how he would do that...yet.

His hostess hovered over him. "I prepare herbal bath for you. Maybe you like to soak hand while soak body. Good for you." The Dresden-like doll smiled.

He accepted her hospitality gratefully. "Thanks, I appreciate that."

"Follow me, I show you bathroom and bedroom you use."

He stood, feeling somewhat wobbly, and followed his hostess. She gestured toward a guest bathroom. "Robe is on door and plenty fresh towels. I run Bododos herbal bath for you. Revive you. This-your bedroom." She gestured toward it.

Minutes later, he immersed his aching body in the hot, foamy liquid, finally able to relax completely.

When he emerged from the warm water and toweled off, he realized he had been using his right hand as well as his left! His hand wasn't frozen, after all. He donned the robe and padded down the hallway to the living room. He couldn't wait to share the good news with his hosts.

Dottie smiled knowingly upon hearing his report. "I had hunch warm bath bring it around." Mysterious cocoa-colored eyes twinkled with delight. "I get fresh clothes;

then we have dinner. Lamb stew revive you. Then you rest. Ordeal has greater emotional impact than physical. You feel much better tomorrow."

"What time is it?" Valdez asked.

"Five o'clock."

The stew was perfect, and he knew he had made a wise choice by coming out here. It was stimulating to meet interesting people.

He parted the heavy drapes and peered outside. It was exactly as it had been when he had arrived a couple of hours ago. Maybe there would be a lull in the weather tomorrow. If not, he would start out early and carry the food to the Petersons. It would be heavy and burdensome, but somehow he would manage.

He glanced at the sole book occupying the night table in his room: *Oriental Wisdom through the Ages.* Interesting title. He flipped through the pages, stopping to read sections that seemed engaging. He skipped over others.

His concentration wavered as he thought about Ayita. *Why couldn't he stop thinking about her?* Finally, he doused the lights and snuggled under the warm comforter.

The next thing Valdez knew, it was morning. His first thought was of Ayita. Suddenly he realized he's forgotten to call the Petersons to let them know he'd arrived safely. He hoped that his hostess had phoned the Petersons to tell them he's made it. Folding back the comforter, he stepped out of the bed and slipped into the robe Dottie had given him.

Thoughts of Ayita dominated his mind again. So what if there was a vast difference in their backgrounds? He'd been educated in the finest schools in Europe, graduating cum laude with a Master of Arts from the University of Madrid. Later he had studied privately with world renowned artists in Venice and Paris. Summers were spent painting prolifically in Marbella, enjoying the family villa his mother had inherited. One day it would be his. He would take Ayita to Europe so she could enjoy the beauty and treasures he had grown up with. As a young student, he had spent hours at the Vatican, studying the magnificent frescoes gracing the grandiose ceilings and curved wall structures. Rome, The Eternal City, had always been his favorite. Ayita would love it.

Yes, there was a stark contrast between his beginnings in life and Ayita's. It made him appreciate her more than if she had been a spoiled rich girl, like the uppity dames he had gone to school with or hobnobbed with in Marbella.

His life had been one of privilege...Ayita's, one of poverty and misfortune. He wanted to protect her-to teach her and guide her. He could expose her to his world. It would be fun to see Europe through her eyes and make up for her rough beginnings.

He was sure Ayita was a clever girl, but very insecure. She needed a mentor. She could have a career as a recording artist. Why not? He would help her achieve it. He had only heard her sing once, and it was memorable. He got thrills and chills just thinking about it. She definitely had the potential to make it big in the music industry. He had been astonished by the rich quality her voice exuded, its depth and the unique sound erupting from somewhere deep inside of her.

He forced himself to push intrusive thoughts of her from his mind. He was on a mission, after all. After showering and shaving, he padded down the long hallway to the kitchen. The aroma of fresh coffee titillated his nostrils. The scent became stronger and mingled with the smell of bacon as he neared the kitchen. Dottie was humming as she hovered over a frying pan, coaxing bacon to crisp perfectly. "Good morning, Valdez. You sleep well?" She smiled, her eyes crinkling her Dresden doll face.

"I slept great. Thank-you."

"Coffee?"

"Love some. Thanks."

Dottie poured him a mug of the brew, handing it to him.

White frilly curtains graced the double kitchen windows. Outside was a thick blur of snowflakes mingling with dull fog. It had lifted slightly from the day before, but the snow had accelerated. He'd heard blizzards only lasted a day or two and then moved on to another location. This was definitely a freak storm. Unprecedented, as the news had stated.

The moment of truth was fast approaching. He had to return to the ranch with the supplies, but how could he do it? In the cold light of day, his faith wavered. Last night he had been elated to find the house-ecstatic to warm up and finally be indoors. But he was only halfway through his mission.

Daylight slowly filtered into the house, speckled with flecks of sun struggling to peek through the mist.

"The 8:00 a.m. news should be on soon. We'll see what the latest forecast is," John advised.

Dottie served them bacon and eggs with hash browns and rye toast. She dished up a small portion for herself and joined her hubby and Valdez at the kitchen island bar. It was obvious she thrived on taking care of houseguests and cooking for them.

"This nasty weather must have put a stop to your dinner parties," Valdez said.

"As a matter of fact, I had to cancel a dinner for ten I had planned for Friday. You're doing me a favor by taking the surplus food I bought."

"You're very gracious, Dottie. Thank-you."

After breakfast, Valdez opened the front door to get a feel for the temperature. Fierce winds howled, blowing fat flakes inside. He shivered and slammed the door shut. It was still bitterly cold. He hurried back into the family room, shaking off the residual trauma of the previous day.

A newsflash came from the T.V.: "Good-morning, this is CFCW News. The freak blizzard *Raging Tiger* continues to break all existing weather records. It is wreaking havoc in the Bellingham/Seattle vicinity, with more Arctic air moving swiftly along the West Coast. No end is in sight, with up to two feet of snow in some areas. Roads remain treacherous, most of them are still unplowed. Tow trucks, snowplows, and dump trucks are unable to operate because of the dense fog. The I-5 and Meridian Highways remain closed until further notice."

"Schools, churches, shopping centers, and supermarkets also remain closed. Emergency road crews are overtaxed, working on frozen pipes, downed power lines, car-accident victims, and other problems. If you're watching this broadcast on T.V., you are among the fortunate with power. Most folks are tuning in to broadcasts by battery-operated radio. There is an unprecedented number of accidents, and cars remain stuck in ditches. The number of stranded motorists has increased alarmingly."

"Snow warnings are in effect. Stay indoors. Repeat. Stay indoors. Emergency delivery services for groceries are being organized. The military has been dispatched to dispense foodstuffs and other essentials. Water pipes have burst in some areas. Bulldozers will begin plowing as soon as visibility permits."

"Do not-repeat, do not attempt to walk long distances

in this weather, and do not drive your vehicles. Black ice warnings are in effect. That problem, coupled with the fog, make it virtually impossible to travel. Conditions may worsen before we see a break in the weather. Brace for it."

John clicked off the news. "There's not a thing we can do. We've just got to ride it out. Thank God we still have power, and thank God for my wife, who thrives on entertaining. Otherwise we'd never have this overabundance of food."

Valdez made a conscious decision to remain positive. He *had* to make it. "Thanks for the great breakfast."

John rose from the table first. "I better put more wood on the fire."

Valdez followed his host into the living room and settled into a wingback chair to meditate. In minutes the blazing fire crackled.

Valdez reflected on the angel visitation. That event caused him to *know* that everything would work our favorably. He really had no reason to be apprehensive. *I made it here. I'll make it back.*

He had no idea how long he had been sitting on the sofa when he heard a knock on the door. *Visitors...in this weather?*

Dottie was still puttering in the kitchen. She must have heard the knock also, because she poked her head around the corner. "See who is at the door, would you, Valdez."

Valdez opened the door. A lean, young man reached out his hand. "Name's Trig."

"Valdez. Come in. Let me get the lady of the house." A few long strides took him to the kitchen. He frowned at Dottie. "It's a young man. Looks Scandinavian. Says his name is Trig."

Dottie's expression changed from an initial startled

85

look, back to her Dresden-doll smile. "Oh, Trig. We sometimes give him meals. I really don't know where he lives or if he has a home, so I call him *The Drifter.* He's a gentle soul." She walked into the living room. "Good morning, Trig. Coffee?"

"No coffee, ma'am. Thank-you." Trig glanced over at Valdez. "Get your supplies, and we'll be on our way."

Valdez was dumbfounded. *How did he know what I needed?*

"It's packed and ready in the fridge," Dottie said, as a knowing expression crossed her face.

Valdez moved toward her and pressed some bills into her hand.

"Absolutely not, Valdez. It is an honor to help. This surplus food would have gone to waste, anyway."

"I sure appreciate your hospitality. When you're in the Fairhaven area, please come and be my houseguest. Dad and I share a comfortable, old mansion there."

"Sounds like fun." Dottie hugged him. "You'll be fine. Bye for now."

The mysterious traveler tucked the hamper into a compartment in the back of his snowmobile while Valdez shook John's hand. Then Valdez and his newfound friend climbed aboard and headed out into the swirling snow.

6

Ayita and the Petersons were relieved and joyful at the sight of Valdez and his companion in the snowmobile. Valdez jumped off, soon carrying the hamper into the kitchen. "Trig did not say where he was from or where he lived," Valdez told Betty.

Henry Peterson was as pale as if he had seen a ghost.

Betty turned to thank him, but The Drifter had already gone. The other family members crowded around as she unpacked the groceries. "What a generous supply of food. And she refused to accept any money for all this?"

"I tried to pay her, but she wouldn't hear of it," Valdez explained.

"Was Trig a kind, young man wanting to help...or was he an angel?" Ayita asked Valdez as she helped Betty unpack the food and put it away.

"It certainly is mysterious. Most young men have ravenous appetites, especially when it's bitterly cold like this. I thought it very odd that he refused breakfast," Betty said.

"Is that what the phrase we heard on T.V. the other night means? '*Some of us have entertained angels unawares*?'" Valdez directed the question to Marjoi.

Marjoi smiled. "You're becoming an impressive Bible student, Valdez." She turned toward Betty. "Mom, I'll finish putting everything away and then make some breakfast. Why don't you relax?"

Betty smiled. "Suits me just fine."

Valdez shed his jacket and made a beeline for Ayita, looking remarkably handsome in the borrowed gray cashmere sweater and worn, ill-fitting jog pants. His black, twinkling eyes fixed on hers. "I need to get out of these wet clothes. I'll slip into the slacks and sweater I was wearing when I took up residence here." He headed for the guest bedroom.

Ayita bubbled with joy. She and Marjoi had prayed almost the entire time Valdez was gone. Last night Marjoi had reminded Ayita of the time the disciples of Jesus had been in a storm-tossed boat in the middle of the sea. As Jesus walked on the water toward them, Peter asked if he could walk on the water to meet the Lord.

"Come," the Lord said.

But as Peter walked toward Jesus, fear overtook him as he focused on the raging storm. Taking his eyes off Jesus, he began to sink. Jesus stretched out his hand to Peter and said, "Why are ye fearful, O ye of little faith?" When they returned to the boat, the wind ceased.

As the parable permeated Ayita's mind, she made two decisions: *I'll never take my eyes off Jesus. And I'll pray for an increase of faith.*

~~*~~

By late afternoon, four days later the snow began to subside. Ayita gazed out the living room window, watching the snowflakes lazily float to the ground.

Two days later, the fog vanished as quickly as it had appeared.

The military had already started moving in. Road crews began the daunting task of clearing the roads to allow trucks containing food into the area. Bulldozers cleared the main arteries. Cars, trucks, and RVs littered the ditches. TV showed folks pushing vehicles, helping eject them out of ruts or ditches. It was a chaotic scene.

It started to warm up. The temperature rose to just above zero. Businesses and shopping malls reopened, along with schools. Joey's Sports Bar reopened for the weekend, so Ayita was back to work.

Valdez finally managed to hire a tow truck. "The Hummer is out of the ditch," he announced, talking on his cell phone to Ayita. "Maybe I'll stop by Joey's and order a steak for dinner tonight."

"You better make a reservation. It's crazy here," she reported. "I've never seen lunch this busy. The place is jammed, and there's a long line-up outside. I guess folks went stir-crazy, stuck indoors during the blizzard."

"Could you make me a reservation for 7:30 this evening? If I can't take you out, at least I can see you and drive you home. You're off at 9:30, right?"

"Yes. See you then. Bye."

Valdez kissed Ayita good-night on the doorstep at the Circle K. She felt like she belonged to him. As she stealthily entered her shared bedroom, she realized Marjoi was asleep.

She undressed noiselessly and slipped into bed, exhausted but thinking about Valdez. He was such a hunk. She adored everything about him. Well, except that he had not made a decision to live for Christ. He seemed to be moving in that direction, though.

Lord, help me understand what's going on. Why have I fallen so hard for Valdez, given that he's not a true believer? Help me to have the courage to end it.

Sleep eluded her. She wanted him. She longed to be near him. He had just left, and she felt an unexplainable hollowness. Was she obsessed with him? Or was this what love was about? She had never experienced feelings like this before.

Finally, her eyes closed.....

~~*~~

The alarm clock buzzed loudly. It was 8:00 Sunday morning. Her favorite day of the week.

Marjoi appeared from their shared bathroom. "Good morning. Shower's all yours."

"Thanks," Ayita said sleepily.

Mr. Peterson insisted on driving the girls to church in his SUV when they were ready. "Your Honda doesn't have snow tires, Marjoi. You could get stuck."

A short while later Marjoi and Ayita walked down the main aisle of the church. Ayita's heart lurched. Valdez sat alone, the third row from the front. They slipped onto the seat next to him.

"Hey, gorgeous, I figured neither snow nor sleet would keep you away from church. I thought I'd find you here," he said, grinning at her.

The worship team was already on stage, belting out music through their microphones. Their voices blended harmoniously, and they moved with the grace and poise of seasoned professionals. Ayita was riveted as she watched their every move, studied every nuance. One day soon she would be on stage, singing. God had placed that overwhelming desire in her heart.

The service ended with an altar call. Valdez remained in his seat.

Marjoi excused herself. "I'm going to find Karl, the music director."

I'm going to the CD library. I want to take some CD's home," Ayita told Valdez.

"Mind if I tag along?" He caught up with her and

walked with her to the library.

While Ayita studied the CD's in the library, Valdez studied her.

Marjoi appeared with Karl at her side. "Hey, Ayita, I want you to meet Karl Davis, our music director."

"Pleased to meet you," Karl said.

"Nice to meet you," Ayita's hands were laden with CD's, so she didn't offer to shake his hand. Then, suddenly, she realized Valdez had stepped out of sight.

"Any chance Ayita could audition for you?" Marjoi asked.

"I don't see why not. Choir rehearsal is Thursday at 7:00 p.m. Why don't you get there at 6:30 and I'll hear you sing then? Bring a vocal selection with you, and we'll see how it goes."

Ayita's heart beat faster. *A vocal selection?* She didn't have a vocal selection. Panic welled up inside her, and she felt like bolting.

Marjoi must have sensed her panic attack, for she draped an arm over Ayita's shoulder, smiling confidently, as though she had enough courage for both of them. "Ayita just gave her heart to the Lord last Sunday, so I'm guessing she probably only knows secular music," Marjoi explained.

"Oh, well, in that case..." He fished in his suit jacket and pulled out a card, handing it to Ayita. "Give me a call at my office tomorrow morning, if you would. I'll line you up with one of the church pianists. Helen loves working with new singers. Take a hymnal from the sanctuary and look through it. See if there's something there you want to work on. If you find a song you're familiar with, rehearse it, and then Helen will record it for you, so you can work on it at home. I mainly just want to hear your voice and vocal range as well as your rhythm at your first audition, anyway."

"Thanks very much," Ayita placed the card in the side flap of her purse.

"We welcome new talent in our church. See you later," Karl said, walking away.

"Come on, girlfriend, let's go find Valdez," Marjoi said.

They entered the foyer and found Valdez chatting with two male parishioners. When he spotted the girls, he headed their way. "Do I get to do the honors for lunch?" he asked, glancing from Ayita to Marjoi.

Ayita had not slept much lately, with the long hours at the restaurant. She mustered up the courage to turn him down. *Maybe I would stop thinking about him if I spent less time with him.* Besides, she wanted to keep him on his toes. "I'm sorry, I'm just too tired. But thanks, I'll take a rain check."

"Sure. May I call you later in the week?"

"I'll have my new schedule on Monday, so I'll let you know what days I'm off." Her resolve had already gone out the window.

"Sounds good to me," Valdez said.

Ayita phoned the church first thing Monday morning, and the secretary gave her Helen Sorenson's phone number. She said Helen would be expecting her call.

Marjoi had been given permission to drive the Honda, since the roads were better. She drove Ayita to Helen's house, promising to pick her up in two hours.

Helen lived in a rambling old house, located on the crest of a hillside in Fairhaven. She was boney and energetic-a "no-nonsense taskmaster." The minute Ayita arrived, she hung up her coat and scarf and directed her to the piano, which was the focal point of her living room.

"Have you found some hymns you want to try?" she asked Ayita.

"I have, Mrs. Soresenson. *His Eye is on the Sparrow* and *Amazing Grace.* I remember them from when I used to attend church with my granny. I found them on YouTube and brushed up on them."

Helen took her seat at the grand piano. "We are going to begin with some vocal exercises. When I'm sure you are doing them correctly, we will record them so that you can build up your voice. We will start by opening that little space in the back of your throat, known as the larynx this will help facilitate a resonant and vibrant sound..."

Forty minutes later, Ayita had earned the right to sing. She sang the two songs, doing all three verses of each. Then her teacher broke them down, instructing her as they went.

By the time Ayita left, she felt exhilarated and excited. Helen had taped the songs, instructing Ayita to work on the vocal exercises and music for a minimum of an hour a day, preferably two, until her audition on Thursday. "We'll meet at the church at 5:00 sharp on Thursday for a final rehearsal before your audition," Helen said.

"How much do I owe you?" Ayita asked, when the lesson and rehearsal was concluded.

"Nothing, dear. I do it as unto the Lord. I've been given my gift to share it with others. My hope is that you will do the same. You *do* have much vocal talent, my dear."

"Thank-you for all your help, Mrs. Sorenson. I sure appreciate it," Ayita said.

~~*~~

On Thursday night, Ayita shone like a brilliant star.

Karl booked her to do a solo and promised to personally take her under his wing and coach her. She would sing one month from the upcoming Sunday. There would be plenty of time to select and prepare the music.

"Incidentally, who did you study with?" Karl asked.

"Study?"

"Study. Train. No one sings like that without having studied music for years."

"I've never taken a lesson before I worked with Mrs. Sorenson earlier in the week."

Karl regarded her skeptically. "You're unusually gifted, then. You have perfect pitch and rhythm, and a rich voice that could surely move all but the dead...and even them I'm not so sure about." Karl grinned. "If I can use you sooner, I'll let you know." He stacked the hymnal on a bookshelf next to the piano.

Ayita had brought her own sheet music so she wouldn't have to drag hymn books around with her. Besides, it made her appear more professional.

Marjoi waited outside in her Honda. "Hey, Ayita. How was the audition?"

"Awesome. Absolutely awesome!"

She floated through her shift that night, joyously happy. When she tallied up her tips she saw that it was shaping up to be a good week all around.

Sunday and Monday were her days off. She could hardly wait to work on her music and begin to build a gospel repertoire. Ayita bought an inexpensive CD player and a mini tape recorder and rehearsed diligently, day after day, perfecting her music. Every chance she had, she listened carefully to the gospel greats, learning from them. They were her inspiration.

She had not pursued her ambition to become a vocalist

while she lived on the Cherokee Indian Reservation but felt in her spirit that the move to the ranch had opened the way for her future to unfold in that direction. When she had played the lead in *Bye, Bye Birdie,* and her mother hadn't even bothered to attend the musical, Ayita had been devastated and depressed. It was the turning point in her life. She felt worthless and hopeless. There was no point in going on.

But now she wanted to make Valdez and Marjoi proud of her. They were both encouraging her to nurture her talent. Every night Ayita prayed fervently that God would grant her the opportunity to use her talent for His honor and glory. Yes, she wanted to excel in the gospel music industry. She fell asleep dreaming of music and a certain Spaniard.

Valdez phoned Saturday. "May I take you to dinner Sunday night?"

"Valdez, I'm sorry I've got to focus on the music. Maybe next week."

"Tired of me, already?" Valdez asked.

"No, just confused. I...like you a lot. Maybe too much. But there is no future for us. My life is about serving the Creator. Yours is about having a good time. Our goals are different. Surely you can see that, too."

"So, you're not even going to give me a chance?"

"My focus is on the music. I really want to develop as a singer. I want to make something of myself."

"Well then, call me when you come up for air. Sooner or later you need to come out with me. We'll have fun, I promise you."

So Ayita worked at the restaurant and studied music in her spare time. But she couldn't get her mind off Valdez. However, since there was no future for the two of them, she ignored his calls.

A week later, Ayita was reading her lyrics, while going over some music in her mind. Marjoi was on her bed, reading a book. Her cell rang. Though she had not returned other calls from Valdez, something made her pick up this one. "Hi," she said.

"Where have you been?" He sounded a touch irritated. "I haven't been able to reach you. I've been calling several times a day for the last three days. Why haven't you returned my calls?"

"I've been busy. And, Valdez, we've got to end it between us, anyway." The old feelings of insecurity and feeling that she wasn't good enough for him had been welling up inside her lately.

"I don't get it, Ayita. I thought we got along great. What's goin' on?"

"We do get along, I..." How could she explain the low self-esteem lodged inside her? Residual effects from the tumult she'd endured with her mother? She did not deserve a man like Valdez. She could never match up to him. After all she was only a server. The vocal thing, as much as she desired it, was only a dream...so far. What really bothered her, though, was the fact that he had not taken a stand for Christ. "I guess I just need time to get used to the idea of us dating. I don't know what you see in me, anyway." She felt better after that admission.

~~*~~

Valdez could scarcely believe his ears. Didn't the beautiful Ayita understand the effect she had on him? Didn't she realize he had risked his life just to impress her? *Doesn't she know I'm in love with her?*

He was speechless for a few minutes. Somehow he had to win her over. "Let me take you to dinner, and I'll explain it to you," he finally said. There was so much he wanted to share with her, so much he needed to tell her, about how he felt about her and how much he believed in her.

~~*~~

Ayita was still overtired from working late nights. The hours and hard work were taking a toll. A new wave of insecurity washed over her. Marjoi had labeled Ayita's mood swings as *post-traumatic stress.* She had to turn Valdez down-she wasn't good enough for him. Surely, he understood that, or he would, in time.

"I...I have to rest and work on the music on my night off," she mumbled. "I've been working a lot of overtime."

"Good food and great company will revive you. It's just what you need," Valdez cajoled.

"I don't think so. I think I need sleep."

"I'll pick you up after work Saturday. Just give me the time, and I'll be there. We can have a late supper, and then I'll drive you home."

Ayita was amazed at his persistence. Some part of her admired him immensely for it. Still, the harder he pushed, the further she backed away. They were worlds apart. Couldn't he see that? The relationship couldn't go anywhere. Didn't he get that? True, in the privacy of her own thoughts, she dreamed of them sharing a life together. But it was just that, a dream, and nothing more.

Fatigue mingled with frustration suddenly overtook her. "Leave me alone, can't you!" she barked.

The silence was deadly. After a couple of long minutes, Valdez broke the ice. "Am I losing it, or what? I thought we had terrific rapport. Have I imagined it?"

"Can't you see we don't belong together?" She threw the words back at him, but as she did, a part of her died. *Can't you see we do belong together? Don't you know I'm in love with you?"*

"I can't imagine what kind of game you're playing," Valdez murmured.

"I'm not playing games! I have no wish to pursue this relationship!" There, she'd said it, and she felt much better...sort of. Tears streamed down her face from a deep well of sadness, a sense of utter futility. She had to end the relationship now, before they got in any deeper.

It was the only way. If she pulled out now, she could deal with the pain. If she got involved any deeper, she couldn't handle it when it ended. She had to protect her tender psyche, battered since early childhood. "I'm hanging up now. I'll see you at church on Sunday."

"Something's really bothering you, and I want to find out what it is," he pressed.

Ayita didn't answer.

Valdez spoke gently. "Perhaps we can talk about it on Sunday."

Choking back sobs, Ayita whispered, "Good-night."

~~*~~

The call from Karl came much sooner than she expected. "Can you fill in for one of the singers in the group? Janice has a sore throat. Are you available to sing this Sunday? Rehearsal is at 8:00 a.m. Sunday. You'll be singing in the group at the 9:00 a.m. and 11:00 a.m. services."

Karl could not possibly know how much this call

meant to her. When she finally found her voice, she said, "I would love to."

"All right, it's settled then. I'll e-mail the music to you. Let me just make sure I have your e-mail."

"That's it," Ayita said, when he read it off to her, her head in the clouds. She turned to Marjoi, who was at her desk studying. "I...never told him I don't read music. Maybe I should have."

"It doesn't matter, Ayita. You can pick that up later. Meanwhile, you can probably find all the songs on YouTube, I'm surprised he didn't mention it."

"Oh perfect. You can rehearse in the games room. As you know, there's a computer there, so you're good to go."

"I sure hope I can memorize them in time...although he did say the words would on Power Point on the overhead screen."

"From what I've seen, you pick up music fast," Marjoi said. "It's your God-given gift."

Ayita walked over to Marjoi and gave her a hug. "Thank-you for believing in me, Marjoi. You're such a good friend. My whole life has changed for the better because of your generosity. I sure hope I can pay it back someday."

Marjoi pointed upwards. "It's the man upstairs. Give Him the praise and glory."

Ayita didn't get into bed until well after midnight. It took her until then to memorize the lyrics cold, and she refused to sleep until she knew the music backwards and forwards. This was her break and she was not about to blow it.

~~*~~

On Sunday, the other singers in the group were already onstage rehearsing when she arrived, even though she was ten minutes early. Had the rehearsal been rescheduled for an earlier time? If so, why hadn't she been notified? Her cell read 8:19. She watched and listened from the front row while the performers finished their song.

Karl introduced her and waved her onto the stage. "Let's take it from the top." He grinned at Ayita. "You're right on time, Ayita. Dora and Connie were early. The call time for the men was 8:30-just so you know."

She was grateful he had answered her unspoken question. It was her first church vocal rehearsal, and she was glad to discover she was not the only singer who was keen. Clearly, it was a privilege to be chosen as a group vocalist in a church of this magnitude. The singers and musicians took the music seriously and Karl was clearly a devoted and excellent musical director.

Ayita reached for the microphone from one of six stands set up on the stage. Dora and Connie stood in front of their respective microphones. Ayita found her place next to Connie. The other women singers did not seem overjoyed at her presence. She'd probably broken into a tight little clique. Normally, a somewhat shy person, she felt invincible and empowered when she stepped on stage. Her usual feelings of insecurity and inadequacy took wings. She had found her niche.

She turned toward Karl. "May I please listen to the last two bars of the first song again? It sounds slightly different from the YouTube version I worked with," Ayita said. She realized as she spoke, that she was speaking with uncharacteristic boldness.

"You don't read music?" Dora raised her eyebrows.

"No, I don't." *Not yet,* a little voice inside Ayita said.

"That's a terrific idea, Ayita. You have a good ear. There are two different versions of endings for that song, I forget to mention it."

Helen rolled out the ending on the piano. Ayita listened carefully, glad she had had the courage to bring the point up.

"From the top," Karl called out after the warm-up.

Ayita hit every note with uncannily perfect pitch. Helen had told her that ability was an innate gift. Her hard work paid off. Her taskmaster had trained her well. She sang all five songs flawlessly and she knew it. As she glanced over at her colleagues, she saw respect written in their eyes. Even *she* knew her voice was pure and melodious, her pitch perfect, and her innate sense of timing accurate. Karl smiled proudly. He knew talent when he saw it. Soon, the men joined the women as the rehearsal continued.

The sextet sang three songs at the beginning of the church service, preparing the spiritual mood before the minister stepped up to the podium. Valdez sat in the center of the front pew. She glanced quickly in his direction and then swiftly shifted her concentration back to the music.

The sextet performed the songs laudably, and Ayita found she possessed only a modicum of stage fright, which evaporated the moment she began singing. She felt, as she always had whenever she performed, that she truly belonged on the stage. That she'd been born for it. This time, though, there was an added dimension. She was performing for the Lord, singing gospel music for his glory and honor; not musical comedy songs in musicals she has performed in high school and local theatre. Innately, she understood that there was a new, deeper, exhilarating dimension to the quality of her voice reflecting her new life

~~*~~

The sermon was based on the first commandment. "I am the LORD thy God...Thou shalt have no other gods before me." The message seemed to muscle its way into Valdez's mind. Had painting become a god to him? It was true he put his work first in his life. Surely God understood that art was his passion.

"'I the LORD your God am a jealous God,' " the minister said.

Wouldn't God know I need to be dedicated, even obsessed, in order to excel in a field as competitive and demanding as the fickle world of art? Surely He knows I don't have a lot of extra time to devote to Him.

Valdez's dad was a name in the art world, but Valdez himself had not yet made his mark. He had been offered representation and a One-Man Show at a world-class gallery that vied for his work. His dad had invited collectors from around the globe, certain his show would be a smash success. Still, Valdez did not feel ready to make the big splash. Like his dad, he was a perfectionist.

As the service ended, his spirit was troubled. Something deep within cried out for a closer relationship with God. *Later, I'll pursue God later, when I have more time.* His priority right now was to get his relationship with Ayita back on solid footing. He had no idea what had gotten into her lately. Didn't she realize what a good catch he was? He was tempted to tell her about the family fortune, but first he had to know if she wanted him for himself. He would tell her about the money and the houses he'd inherit on his father's passing sometime in the future.

Valdez waded past the hordes complimenting Ayita on her marvelous singing. She was a star basking amidst throngs of admirers. He finally made it through the bevy of people. "May I see you privately, Ayita?"

She nodded, and they walked outside. "Why don't we get in the Hummer and talk there?"

She nodded again, subdued.

"I'll drive you home." Valdez took one of her delicate hands in his brawny one once they were sitting in the Hummer. "Ayita, Ayita, what am I going to do with you?" he ask rhetorically. When he saw her body quiver, he asked. "Why won't you allow me to take you to dinner? Have I hurt you in some way? Tell me what you want me to do to make things right. I want to be your friend most of all."

Ayita peered down at her hands. "You haven't hurt me..."

"Is this a one-way street? Am I the only one who feels this powerful attraction?"

She didn't answer for a minute. At last she said, "I've spelled it out for you, Valdez. To use the Bible term, we are *unequally yoked.*"

Valdez cupped her face in his hands and raised it, then tiled her toward him. "Surely we can at least be friends, can't we?" He was irked with her, but a part of him was frightened. Maybe Ayita didn't feel as strongly toward him as he felt for her. Maybe she wasn't in love with him. Maybe she was serious about dumping him.

Finally, he sighed, crushed. "I'll walk you back to the church. Hold on, I'll get your door." He climbed out of the Hummer, strode around it to the passenger door, and opened it for her. Taking her hand, he murmured as he helped her down from the vehicle. "I love you, you silly little fool."

Ayita peered at him strangely but didn't say anything.

Valdez walked her back to the church and then hurried

back toward his vehicle.

Ayita walked straight over to her best friend, who was chatting with some parishioners in the church foyer. "May I have a ride home with you, Marjoi?"

"Of course. I thought you were going with Valdez...?" Marjoi lifted a brow.

When Ayita said nothing, Marjoi grabbed her hand and tugged her out the church door and toward her Honda. Once they were nearly there, Marjoi stopped and peered at Ayita. "What's going on with you and Valdez? I thought you two were getting along great."

"It's over between us. I want it to end."

"Why?" Marjoi was puzzled.

"Doesn't *anyone* understand? I'm not good enough for him. Surely *you* can see that." Ayita stared at Marjoi.

"Not *good enough* for him? Whatever gave you that idea?"

"Can we just drive back to the Circle K?"

"Of course we can."

They drove in silence. Finally, Marjoi tried again. "This is about your past, isn't it?"

"That, and other issues."

"I'm going to give you a book to read when we get home."

Ayita did not respond.

Marjoi persevered. "It's called *See You at the Top,* by a renowned motivational author, Zig Ziglar. The book has been widely used with remarkable results for people in sales as well as other fields."

"So...what's the theme of it?" Ayita asked.

"It talks about how we have an opinion of ourselves based usually in error, and frequently formed by the opinions of only two unqualified-in many instances-persons. Namely one's parents. We tend to live out that opinion whether it's good or bad, until we decide to change our image."

Ayita frowned. "How do we do that?"

"I thought you'd never ask." Marjoi smiled and then plunged in. "You need to sit down with pen and paper and construct an image of who you believe you can be-in your dreams, in your heart of hearts. When you're finished, you should memorize it, believe it, speak it aloud and picture yourself transformed into the new image."

"That's powerful stuff," Ayita said.

"Yes it is. I mean, think about it. Why isn't your new image you've decided on as accurate as an image constructed haphazardly by an unqualified person?"

That hit home. "I can't wait to read that book. That theory certainly makes sense to me. Meanwhile, at least until I have time to digest this new information, I still don't want to speak to Valdez...I mean, if he calls."

"Suit yourself."

~~*~~

Valdez didn't call. The following Sunday he was not in church. In fact, he dropped completely out of sight.

Monday she hounded Christian music stores searching for new music and buying CD's of famous gospel singers. She found the book *See You at the Top* at her local library. Rushing home, she began reading it on the bus. By midnight, she had finished it.

On Tuesday at Joey's, Ayita fought hard to concentrate as Valdez kept infiltrating her mind. Normally, she enjoyed brightening up the patrons' days with her infectious smile and cheery comments, but, today she hoped someone would smile at her and encourage her in some way. And customers did smile at her. Her shift went well, and she pocked some generous tips.

Once home, she delved back into the book, carefully rereading it to embed the concept into her psyche. The book illuminated her problem: she was her own worst enemy. She reread it and carefully made notes, meditating on what she'd learned.

Two weeks later, enlightened, she dropped the book off at the library. She knew God was guiding her, and this self-image aspect of her life had been the missing link. It was like a pink neon light flashing. She understood what she had to do: reprogram herself from a negative, low self-image to a positive image. With God' help, she could do it.

Karl Davis called the next day, inviting her to sing a solo on Sunday. Rehearsal was Thursday night as usual. She was glad she had started to build a repertoire. She selected a song, worked with the back-up tape, and came to rehearsal well-prepared as always.

~~*~~

Ayita awakened on Sunday before her alarm went off. She jumped in the shower and warmed up her voice as the water warmed her body. She used the vocal exercises she had learned from Sondra, the musical director from *Bye, Bye Birdie*, along with ones Helen had given her.

Happily, she snuggled into her favorite red wool dress. It had long sleeves and fit her like a glove. The big decision now was whether to wear her long tresses back with a ponytail or let her hair fall naturally. She opted for letting it cascade freely down her back. Her face was a bit too boney without the framing of her masses of hair enhancing it. She slipped into her black pumps and padded downstairs to rehearse in the games room. Marjoi hadn't stirred.

It was very early, and everyone in the house was still asleep. She kicked off her shoes so she would be comfortable. The acoustics in the games room were ideal for music. By the time everyone rose, her rehearsal would be finished.

Sometime later, there was a tap on the door. Ayita opened it.

Betty smiled. "Good morning, dear. My, you're certainly industrious."

"I was just rehearsing the song I'm going to sing in this morning's services."

"Good for you," Mrs. Peterson encouraged. "I'm rustling up some coffee and breakfast. Come on down when you're ready."

~~*~~

The roads were finally back to normal when Ayita and Marjoi drove to church. Ayita went over the song twice with Helen in the rehearsal studio there. Then she slipped into the back of Mrs. Peterson's Bible class and slid into the seat next to Marjoi. Her best friend smiled her welcome and handed her a notebook.

When the class was over, Marjoi and Ayita sat in the front pew so Ayita would be close to the stage when her moment came. Butterflies darted through her stomach, but it was a heady kind of anticipation, not stage fright.

Her solo followed the sextet's first song at the start of the church service. She stepped out on stage, the adrenalin rush buoying her up. She commanded the stage with her presence, but it was the joy of salvation and the power of

God that lifted her as she sang a song of praise and thanksgiving to the Almighty with clarity and majesty.

Ayita knew it wasn't customary for the congregation to clap after a church solo, but today a resounding, spontaneous applause echoed through the church. She was tempted, just for an instant, to bow theatrically as she had done after the standing ovation she had received while starring in *Bye Bye Birdie*- but she knew it wasn't protocol in church. She was here to worship God, not to take glory for herself. So she simply placed the microphone back in the holder on the stage and walked serenely down the stage steps to her seat in the front pew.

After the service, as she chatted with friends in the foyer, a tall, distinguished, gray-haired gentleman approached her. "Hi, I'm Melvin Donner. I have a recording studio in Nashville-Praise Studios. Your singing is remarkable, and I was wondering if you would be interested in flying to Nashville, all expenses paid, to audition for my partners and meet them. If they like you as much as I do, we might be interested in signing you to our label."

Ayita was so excited she could barely breathe. Never in her wildest dreams did she think someone would make an offer to her of this magnitude. Had Karl set this up? Had he believed she was ready for the big-time? "I'm very interested," she said, glad she had begun programming her new image.

"In all the years I've known Karl, he's never phoned me, insisting I hop a plane to hear a new singer at his church. I was curious, so I decided to take him up on it. He knows I like to play talent scout every now and then. Of course, with the wealth of talent we have in Nashville, I don't usually travel to find singers. They find me." He grinned at her. "But there are always exceptions. My recording company will require a demo reel in advance, of course."

"A demo reel? What is that? I've never heard of it," Ayita blurted.

This young woman wasn't a phoney. Melvin could see it. She really was that green. Instead of being put off by it, he found it charming and refreshing. "A demo reel is a professional video or audio of songs from past performances...maybe snippets from songs that show you at your best," he explained. To put her at ease, he added, "You're everything Karl promised and more."

"I'm afraid I don't have one."

Her naked honesty touched him. He was used to the tough, seasoned pros pounding on his door daily, laden with show reels and promo packages. She was delightfully refreshing and just what their studio needed-a sparkling new talent-an unknown. They could start fresh with her and build her image. His PR people would love her and so would his associates.

"Have you seen Karl?" Ayita asked. "He's usually milling around, socializing after the service."

"He probably ducked out. He said it would be more fun that way. After all, how many singers do you know who have been approached by a talent scout?" Melvin asked.

She smiled nervously as him.

He was struck by how the smile lit her tilted eyes with sparks of something close to pure joy. "If everything works out the way I think it will, you'll have a great story of how you were discovered. Our press agents will love it."

She floated on air as she sat in the Honda, Marjoi speeding them home. Her most fervent prayer had been answered.

~*~

The next week she had the night shift, so she used her days to prepare her demo reel. Karl had generously offered to help her with it. Karl and Helen were thrilled for her and agreed to do everything to help her make a great reel. When it was ready, she would courier it by FedEx to Nashville.

She was on a cloud. This was the best thing that had ever happened to her. Well, the second best thing; the first was her conversion. God has given her the desire of her heart. She had committed her gift to Him, and she was being rewarded for it.

Ayita had no knowledge of the Nashville music scene, and now she wished she had not been so final with Valdez. She sensed he had a sharp business mind. Should she phone him? Clearly, he was making a statement by not calling her. It had been three weeks since she had last heard from him. He probably had a new girlfriend by this time. Who could blame him? A gorgeous hunk like him certainly wouldn't be without female company for very long.

Karl admitted orchestrating the meeting with Melvin Donner. "You have what it takes, Ayita, so you might as well get on with it."

Flashes of insecurity plagued her as she tried to concentrate on getting the music together for her demo reel, while continuing to work a full schedule at the restaurant. She had embraced the concept of creating a new image. She forced the negative, insecure thoughts to the back of her mind whenever they niggled at her. If Karl and Melvin believed she could make it, who was she to disagree?

After two weeks of intensive rehearsal, she made the demo reel at a local studio Karl found through the internet. He personally insisted on paying for the demo reel.

Ayita was thrilled and scared the day she sent the demo by FedEx to Nashville.

~~*~~

Three days later, Ayita received a call from Melvin's assistant, Suzie. Her airfare and hotel accommodations had been arranged. She was to fly there on Monday-only four days from today.

She quit Joey's, giving only four days' notice.

"Hey, I forgive you, Kid," her boss said good-naturedly, "Just remember me when you get to be a big star."

Karl drove her to the airport. She hugged him goodbye through tears of gratitude. "How can I ever thank you?" Ayita said, a trickle of tears sliding down her cheeks. "Make the most of the opportunity God has given you, and you will have thanked me." Karl gave her a fatherly hug. "It was a privilege working with you, Ayita. You have a brilliant future ahead of you."

7

The American Airlines flight touched down effortlessly at Nashville International Airport. As Ayita walked down the off-ramp, she spotted a rotund man holding a large sign with AYITA HIGH-EAGLE emblazoned in bold black letters.

She smiled. *That was easy.* "I'm Ayita High-Eagle."

"Welcome to Nashville, Ayita. I'm Melvin Donner's driver. Name's Sam Schiff. Mr. Donner extends his apologies. He couldn't break away from recording. I'll be driving you to your hotel. Melvin will call you the minute he's free. This way to the luggage carousel."

They stood together watching the luggage on the belt. After some time, Ayita pointed. "There it is, that leopard one."

Sam grabbed the suitcase and headed for the exit doors. "Here we are," he announced as they approached a sleek white Mercedes limo. He helped her into the back seat.

"Wow, this is amazing," Ayita said, overwhelmed.

Sam drove her to the Gaylord Opryland Hotel and parked the limo at the roundabout in front of it. Ayita was so excited she could hardly contain herself. Sam stayed with her while she checked in. The bellhop led the way to her room.

"My boss instructed me to give you the V.I.P. treatment and make sure you got settled in. Anything you need, call me." Sam handed her his card, then exited.

The bellhop opened the drapes and set her suitcase on a holder. "Is the temperature fine for you?"

"Thank-you, it's all good."

Ayita extended some folded dollar bills his way, but he

raised a hand in protest. "Thank-you, Ma'am, but I've already been taken care of." He smiled and closed the door quietly behind him.

She walked around the luxurious peach and teal room, barely able to believe her good fortune. A crystal vase containing a generous spray of fresh flowers was perched on the console. Fishing out the card, she read: *To Nashville's new singing sensation! Welcome to Nashville, Ayita High-Eagle. Warmest regards, Melvin Donner*

"Does it get any better than this?" She addressed the wall.

The hotel room phone rang. She grabbed it on the first ring.

"Hi, this is Suzie, Melvin Donner's assistant. Welcome to Nashville, Ayita. Are you getting settled in okay?"

Ayita was charmed by the Southern accent. "It's all wonderful."

"Take down my phone number. Call me if there's *anything* you need, or anything I can do for you. By the way, Mr. Donner would like to take you to dinner tonight. I've made reservations at the French Chateau, one of the finest restaurants in all of Nashville. He'll send his driver to pick you up at 7:00 sharp. I hope these arrangements are suitable. If not, please let me know and we can change them."

Ayita was awestruck. It took a moment to digest the barrage of blessings. "It's all perfect...and thank you for the beautiful flowers. You probably chose them. Birds of Paradise are my absolute favorite. How did you know?"

"A little birdie told me."

Ayita laughed.

She dressed leisurely, slipping into her little black jersey dress and adorning it with chunky, gold jewelry.

Marjoi had helped her pick out both items for the trip. She had carefully put jumbo heated rollers in her hair and was pleased with the large, loose curls that bounced on her shoulders. She fussed with her makeup nervously before slipping into her new black pumps. Then she carefully placed her makeup bag and company into her clutch purse, slipping in her card key and settled back to relax and wait for her date.

Sam buzzed her from the hotel lobby.

"I'll be right down, Sam."

Sam walked over to her as soon as she got off the elevator. He whistled. "You look great. You belong right here in Nashville. I can tell."

Thank-you Lord, I needed that word of encouragement. Feelings of inferiority and insecurity niggled at her. She ignored them. "How is *your* day going?" Ayita asked.

"It's been a lazy day, but I'm working tonight, as you know." He walked her outside to the limo. Melvin stepped out of it and grinned at her, then opened the back door. "Good evening, gorgeous." A bottle that appeared to be champagne was cooling in an ice bucket on the pull-out bar in the back of the limo.

"I appreciate everything you're doing for me," Ayita said. Then, in a serious tone she added, "I don't drink though. You see, my mother..."

"Hey, little lady, I'm way ahead of you. This is sparkling apple cider. Take a closer clock."

Relief washed over her, replacing the beads of sweat that had started to form on her face. The last thing she wanted to do was offend Melvin.

The French food exceeded her expectations. It was an enormous difference from the food at Joey's. Melvin briefed her on what to expect on Tuesday. They had watched her demo reel and loved it, but she would meet with his partners and audition live for them as well. If they were on the same page as he was, she would be signing a contract very soon.

"I'm sold on your talent, but my partners have other artists they're touting, and I need to convince them that you should be their number one priority. I'm the majority partner in the recording studio, but I have worked with my partners for over ten years. I value their input and abilities, and I want to continue having a good working relationship with them."

Melvin walked her to her room and bade her goon night after a fabulous evening. She wanted to pinch herself. It was still early, just after 9:00.

"Get lots of rest, Ayita. Your voice needs to be at its optimum for your live audition tomorrow. No late movies tonight," he teased.

Ayita was smart girl. No way would she blow this opportunity of a lifetime. She'd have to win Melvin's partners over tomorrow to snag the recording contract, and she determined to do just that.

Strolling around the suite, she reveled in the luxury and beauty. After finding some classical music on T.V. she settled into the tub for a leisurely soak. She would have a very early night and just go over the audition songs in her mind while she relaxed.

By the time she doused the lights, it was just after 9:30. Her wake-up call was set for 7:30. Helen had told her, "Rest the voice thoroughly and take good care of it." Melvin had subtly confirmed that.

~*~

The next morning Ayita awakened before the front desk called her and strolled over to the French doors. Opening them, she glanced at the lush vegetation below. Resplendent gardens weaved colorfully throughout the central courtyard. She was Cinderella at the ball. She turned on the mini-coffee maker. Minutes later, she poured a cup of coffee and set it on the desk. Picking up her Bible from the desk, she turned the pages to Psalm 138, David's praise for answered prayer. The Psalms were her favorite book in the Bible. It has been her granny's favorite, also.

Lord, thank you for the gift of singing and this awesome opportunity. She reflected on the various biographies she'd recently read. Without exception, every bio relayed a journey of a long, arduous climb to ultimate success. Certainly, some artists received breaks sooner than others-but everyone paid their dues one way or another. She resolved to work diligently and learn everything she could as fast as she could. Her journey had just begun. It would be exciting watching her future unfold.

The phone rang. Ayita picked it up.

"Melvin here. I'm about ten minutes early. Leave your music satchel in your room. We'll get it later."

"Sure. I'll be right down." It was exciting to have an 8:00 breakfast date. She was glad she'd been ready early.

Melvin was trolling around the lobby when she got off the elevator. He looked handsome in a pale yellow cashmere sweater and cream-colored slacks. Tall, with silver hair framing his deep tan, he was a perfect father image. "Good morning, gorgeous. Are you hungry?"

"Actually, I am. Are you?"

"I will be when I see their menu. Everything is good and so fresh here."

A pert hostess greeted them with a charming Southern accent. "Good mornin'. Two?" she drawled, handing them menus. "We also have a buffet. It's $19.95." She showed them to a table by the windows. The eatery bustled with activity.

Ayita couldn't help but overhear shop talk at the tables on both sides. "Does everybody in Nashville dress in Western gear?" she asked Melvin.

"Pretty much. You'll probably be wearing it before the week is out."

The waitress hovered over them. "May I take your orders?"

"Ayita, what would you like, dear?"

"I don't know. What are you having?"

"I think I'll have the number three. Crisp bacon, scrambled eggs, hash browns, and well-done rye toast please."

"I'm not really a copycat, but that sounds great. I'll have the same but make the rye toast dry, please," Ayita told the waitress.

Melvin waited until they were halfway through their delicious breakfast before he updated her. "Ayita, I'm sorry, but your audition has been rescheduled for Friday. My partners are finishing work on an album with another artist. They're running behind schedule. The vocalist had some throat issues."

Ayita's heart sank.

"But I'm going to show you around Nashville and get you oriented"

She hid her disappointment. "That sounds like fun Melvin. Thank-you."

Breakfast over, Melvin escorted Ayita to the limo, settling in the back seat with her. "I've told Sam to start with the landmarks. The Parthenon is our first stop. It's a reproduction of the Greek Parthenon, located in Centennial Park. There's a forty-two foot statue of Athena that's pretty amazing and casting fashioned from the famed Elgin marbles. I'm sure you'll agree the art galleries have impressive collections."

"It's very kind of you to take the time to show me around Nashville, Melvin. I wasn't expecting that."

"If I have my way, you'll be too busy real soon to see any of the sights. And, after all, since you're going to be living here, you should at least know where the landmarks are located," Melvin told her.

"Yes, I'm sure you're right." She was soaring on a cloud at the possibilities as Melvin helped her into the limo.

"Take us to the Grand Ole Opry Museum, would you, Sam? Ayita needs to check out the venue she will soon be performing in."

Ayita smiled nervously. *Would that really happen?*

They viewed some landmarks, and then Melvin said they would soon see his personal favorites: "We're approaching the Grand Ole Opry Museum. It's actually the Minnie Pearl and Ray Acuff Museum. The exhibits here honor Patsy Cline, Jim Reeves, Marty Robbins...to name a few."

He toured her past exhibits of current artists, including Reba McIntyre and Garth Brooks. "There's a lot of memorabilia here. It's probably overwhelming for you, but it will give you a sense of what Nashville is all about. For the first year you live here, you'll be a tourist. There's that much to see and do. I'm merely showing you a few highlights to whet your appetite."

"It's a far cry from my little hometown of Bellingham, in Washington."

"Yes it is. You're going to love it here once you get into the swing of things. Next stop: The General Jackson Showboat, Sam," Melvin told his driver.

Sam cruised up right near the famous boat and double-parked the limo. Melvin stepped out and helped Ayita onto the boat. "This paddle wheeler cost twelve million dollars. It cruises down the Cumberland River every day."

They lunched at a casual little fish place with Sam joining them. Then Sam drove her back to the Opryland Hotel.

"We'll pick you up at 6:45 for dinner. Will that work for you?" Melvin asked.

"Perfect," she murmured. "What a great tour. I feel so privileged to have seen it with you, Melvin."

The day of her audition, Ayita arose at 7:00, made coffee, and looked over the music she would sing. She vocalized for the better part of an hour, warming up and listening to tapes she had recorded earlier of her audition material.

It was zero hour. Sam picked her up at 10:00. Her audition was at 11:00. She met him outside the hotel. Sam opened the door for her and she slipped onto the soft leather seats. It was easy to adjust to luxury.

Ayita wore her audition dress. It was red silk, short, fitted with long sleeves and flowed easily over her body. She was in good voice and ready to rock. The live musicians were warming up as she entered the studio. The executives were seated on the periphery of the studio, she was barely aware of them.

Ayita stepped up to the microphone. She was relaxed, rested and extremely well-rehearsed. She felt comfortable; she was born for this. She sang five songs consecutively and felt good about all of them.

Melvin rewarded her with a big hug after the audition. "You did great, Ayita. Matter of fact, you were brilliant." He gave her a thumbs-up. "I watched the other producers' faces. They were mesmerized. Astonished. You beat out all the competition. And, frankly, I'm not surprised."

"I give God the glory. He has gifted me and opened doors for me. Praise His mighty Name!"

She signed the contract with great excitement. She couldn't wait to have a leisurely chat on the phone with Marjoi.

Her cell rang on the ride back to the hotel. "Hi, this is Suzie. Congratulations, Ayita, you're in! Now that we know you're staying in town, Melvin has asked me to help you find an apartment. It may take some time, of course. Meanwhile, enjoy the hotel... it's tax deductible, anyway."

Ayita laughed. "I'm beginning to get used to the fast pace in this town."

Suzie chuckled. "It's about to get faster. We'll see if we can find you a spot downtown. Somewhere near Music Row and Praise Recording Studios."

Ayita was on the fast track, no doubt about it. She could hardly believe it. She was really here, living her dream!

"Now. Let's work on your schedule. Got your appointment book handy?"

"Sure do." Melvin had given her one at their first meeting. She used it constantly.

"Okay. Here's your schedule: January 7 we start back to work. There's lots of staff holidays. You can use that time for preparations. I've scheduled in rehearsals for your new material..."

"My new material?"

"Oh, hasn't anyone told you? One of our writers

penned some new songs for you. You need to meet with Lou. He'll be your accompanist. You'll rehearse every day for as long as it takes until the producers are satisfied with the song."

Ayita could barely catch her breath. One part of her wanted to leap for joy and yell, "Hurray!" at the top of her lungs; another part was a scared little girl, getting in over her head. She was grateful to Marjoi for working with her on her fear and feelings of inadequacy. Every time a fearful or negative thought entered her mind, she forced herself to cancel it out with positive, faith-filled thoughts. She spoke the affirmations aloud. *It's all going to be just fine,* she told herself and believed it.

Suzie prattled on, asking Ayita to jot down dates of an upcoming cocktail party, as well as a dinner party. They would provide a suitable escort for her. She wrote in music events and concerts.

"The press is on it. You can anticipate seeing your name in various columns in the coming weeks. Oh, tomorrow at 10:00 you have a meeting scheduled with a prospective manager. Melvin thinks Tizzy will be good for you, but if you don't like him, let me know and we'll set you up with someone else. There's no shortage of managers in this town. Make a note of my holiday schedule. Call Tizzy for anything I would normally handle. He's been around this industry for a long time. He'll be able to answer any questions you may have."

~~*~~

She liked Tizzy, sort of, but for some reason did not totally trust him. She shook it off. Melvin had recommended him, after all. She had to give him a chance.

Tizzy insisted she program her appointments and rehearsal times into her cell phone, as if she could forget! "I want you to get into good habits. Rehearsals are from 10:00 to 5:00 with an hour's break for lunch. I would like to hear you sing the new music as soon as possible. Any chance we can drive over to the studio now and just take a chance that a piano is available?"

"Sure. But who is going to accompany me?"

"I will. I'll stop by and pick you up, if you like."

Tizzy showed up within a half hour and buzzed her from downstairs. "I'm in the lobby."

"Great, I'll be right down." She picked up the black satchel containing her music and headed down the elevator.

In minutes, they drove to the studio, parking in front of it and walking in together. Ayita was surprised to discover Tizzy was an accomplished pianist. He seemed familiar with every song she had brought with her. Folks took their music seriously in Nashville.

"I didn't know you played the piano, Tizzy."

"There's a lot of things you don't know about me, Kid. You're doin' a great job...especially since you just got this music. With the right breaks, Ayita, you'll make it right to the top. By the way, my birth name is Thaddeus. But everybody called me Tizzy."

After Ayita sang the new songs a couple of times, Tizzy smiled, clearly excited about handling her. "I...was just curious how fast you would pick up new music. Now I know. You can put the music away. I'll take you to some of Nashville's best music stores. We can do a little browsing-maybe pick up some CD's and sheet music for new songs. I'll give you a hand selecting some new material for your upcoming album. The producers have the final say on what you sing, but you're the one who needs to love the song and identify with the lyrics."

Ayita felt like she was in Disneyland as she glanced around the music store. She was amazed at the volume of music available. She recognized a famous country singer leafing through some CD's and soon spotted another hiding under an enormous white Stetson. There were maybe a couple dozen other customers in the store. Almost everyone in the store looked like someone important.

Ayita found three songs she loved. Tizzy found two more he wanted her to try. He picked up the bill and drove her back to the hotel in his black BMW.

She spent considerable time working on the material they had selected. It was the only way for her to see if she could truly make the song her own. In the end, she scrapped two and kept three. It was all a learning experience.

Melvin took her to dinner at Ruth's Steak House. The filet mignons were perfect. She took home a doggy bag, determined to eat smaller portions because she'd already put on a couple of pounds with all the dinners out. She wanted to remain petite. Since she was a size four, a couple of extra pounds really showed on her.

"I'll be out of town for two weeks over Christmas," Melvin said. "I visit my kids every year in Aspen. We hang out together and do a little skiing."

Finally, her curiosity got the best of her. "What happened to your wife?"

A long silence ensued, causing her to wish with all her heart that she had resisted the temptation to pry into his personal life.

"She died last year, during the Christmas season," he said softly.

"I'm so...so sorry." Ayita fumbled for the right words.

"What happened?"

"Brain aneurism. It was sudden. Here today, gone tomorrow. It's a real wake-up call, let me tell you."

Why hadn't she allowed him the courtesy of telling her in his own time? She was young and had a lot to learn, and she intended to learn it as fast as she could.

Most evenings, she dined with either Tizzy or Melvin. They took her to a variety of good restaurants. Tizzy favored Italian and Southern cooking, while Melvin took her to the famed La Paz restaurant for Mexican food and to the Nashville Palace for prime rib and live country music, featuring *Grand Ole Opry* stars. If she had a sliver of doubt about whether or not she wanted a music career, it had vanished during her first week of constant exposure to music greats and her total immersion in the Nashville music scene.

While Melvin was away for the holidays, Tizzy assured her he'd be at her beck and call. He squired her around town and took her shopping for new clothes. "Melvin told me to buy you a suitable wardrobe and retain the bills for income tax purposes. You're going to need the write-offs, anyway."

Who was she to argue? It was heady stuff shopping at Nashville's trendy boutiques. She picked out some great clothes.

"Now I'll take you to Robert's Western World. It's in the historic section of Nashville. They have the most extensive, interesting collection of cowboy boots. You'll need a couple pairs of boots just to be part of the scene here. If you exceed the budget, I'll let you know. Meanwhile, have fun. You have a lot of events coming up, and you need a good wardrobe to choose from."

Tizzy wore a candy-striped shirt with navy golfing

sweater and looked spiffier than usual. He dropped her off at the hotel with all her designer bags. "I'll pick you up at 7:00 to go to the Belle Meade Plantation. They've replicated the way it might have looked in 1895 during a gala Christmas Ball."

When they arrived at the mansion, she drew in her breath at the remarkable sight, decorated in pink, gold and white with towering plants featuring mistletoe and narcissus. Tizzy had lined up an exciting evening for her. Next on the list was the Nashville Ballet's *Nutcracker*.

"It's quite an elaborate production isn't it?" he commented when the production was over.

"Yes, and the staging is brilliant," Ayita noted.

Finally, they attended *Dickens of a Christmas*, featuring carolers in Victorian costumes, a horse-drawn carriage, strolling minstrels, street vendors, and theatre productions. Her head spun from all the events as Tizzy guided her past throngs of tourists, leading the way to her car. Ayita was glad to get back to the hotel. The whirlwind tourist immersion was wearing thin.

By the time the Christmas and New Year's celebrations were over, she was anxious to get into the studio and record her debut single. She had fallen into a few weepy moments over Christmas, when she had nostalgically thought of her mother and Marjoi, not to mention an overwhelming sadness regarding the distance between herself and Valdez. Why couldn't she simply expunge him from her mind?

The producers hovered during her final two days of rehearsal, making minor suggestions about her performance. They listened intently during the final run-through.

Tizzy imparted the good news. "The producers are thrilled with your work."

Melvin returned to Nashville on January 5 and so did his assistant, Suzie. It was business as usual again.

After the final rehearsal, Melvin took Ayita aside and told her to take the day off before she came into the studio to record. "Rest your voice and relax for the day. Try to put the music completely out of your mind until you walk into the studio on Friday. I promise you, it will be brilliant."

Ayita snapped up every morsel of advice, following it to the letter.

~~*~~

Her big moment finally arrived, the day she would record her first single. If it was well received, she would likely be put under contract. Tizzy confided that the contract had already been drawn up, since she was the front-runner as the studio's new protégée, but the producers still wanted to see how it turned out. "If everything goes according to plan, they'll hand you a contract and ask you to sign it."

Ayita clamped the headphones on her head and sent up a silent prayer. The music began. The red light signaled zero hour. She stood on her mark, nodded to the musicians, and began singing. It was an awesome experience. She had a sense of transcending her earthly state of being, as if she were an eagle soaring in the sky, far from everyday existence. As she sang, wave upon wave of pure vocal tones drifted and soared not only within her immediate physical space but spiraling into the infinite. Her voice was floating on the breath.

She was cognizant of nothing except the music. She neither saw nor heard the subtle direction her producers gave her, yet she infused it into the work. It had all been carefully rehearsed, and this moment of performance was hers to cherish. She would glorify God now and forever and share her gift with the world. She finished the song to a standing ovation. The sound technicians, musicians, and producers all clapped exuberantly. *It must have gone well.* Gradually, she emerged from her focused state and smiled, thanking everyone involved.

Melvin Donner was the first to hug her. "Congratulations, Ayita."

The associate producer, Sandy Trollier, was next. He smiled and shook her hand heartily. "Nice work," he said.

Finally, Tizzy rewarded her with a bear hug. When they pulled apart, she saw that he wore a jubilant grin. "You were great, Kid!"

"You know, Ayita, I never really believed in overnight sensations, but you've caused me to change my mind," Sandy said. "Well, the contract is ready. It's a one-year contract, renewable and changeable with money and terms by both parties a year from today. Tizzy has already approved it. We think it's fair, and I trust you will, also. Everything is spelled out clearly. Read it through and ask any of us to clarify anything you don't understand. Suzie will witness your signature, and we will start the ball rolling. Our work has just begun."

She read it over carefully in the studio office. There were some things she did not quite understand, but she trusted Melvin and was thrilled to be under contract for the major label. She signed it, and Suzie witnessed her signature.

Melvin held her at arm's length and stared at her as though amazed by her very existence. "Lunch is on me. We're going to have one terrific celebration! I've been around this business long enough to know when I have a hit on my hands. We've struck gold with this one."

Melvin took everyone to Mario's for Northern Italian cooking. "I have to tell you, Ayita, that I'm spoiled rotten. This is my favorite Italian restaurant in Nashville. You're going to love it."

She did. The food was amazing.

After the celebration, Melvin dropped her off at her hotel. "You really came through for us. You have a great future in this industry."

"How can I ever thank *you* for the opportunity?"

"Just stay in Nashville and use that talent. The rest will take care of itself."

8

She awakened the next day, sensing she had slept through the morning. Glancing at the clock on her night table, she realized it was almost noon. Sunlight peeked through the shutters in her suite, beckoning her to enjoy the day. She jumped up, spooned gourmet coffee into the filter, and stepped into the shower while it was brewing. She sat at the kitchen table with her magnifying mirror, applying makeup in between sips of coffee. Then she pulled on her stretch jeans with the multi-colored stones embedded on the seat and legs, a new sweater, butter-colored leather jacket, and tan cowboy boots.

She checked her image in the full length mirror. "Hey, I'm part of the Nashville scene. I even look the part!" she told the mirror, feeling spunky.

Grabbing her new tan leather purse, she headed for the elevator. Pressing the button, she soon stepped inside it, humming a tune. A young mother with a baby smiled at her.

The sun warmed the hotel lobby. The mild winter was a nice change from the bitter winters in Washington. A few patrons milled around, some reading newspapers and magazines. She picked up a local newspaper from the hotel newsstand and settled into a comfortable chair to read it. But she couldn't concentrate. She had become weary of pushing away intrusive thoughts of Valdez. He hadn't called, and she held little hope of a blossoming relationship with him, still she allowed herself the luxury of thinking about him.

Glancing through the music section of the paper, she spotted several photos of herself, along with a promotional article touting her soon-to-be-released single. The campaign to raise her profile was underway.

She picked up her messages from the front reception desk, flipping through them as she headed back to the elevator. "Marjoi...Tizzy...and Valdez!" What uncanny timing! She started at the phone number. The prefix was a local Nashville number. He was in town! He must have known she had just finished her recording session. Marjoi must have advised him of her schedule. That had to be it. He had been respectful enough of the pressures she was under to wait until the recording session was over.

The elevator stopped on the eighth floor. She stepped out of it in a daze, walking down the hallway to her room. She could hardly contain her excitement.

A crystal vase filled with Birds of Paradise flowers stood on the white marble hall table, a card perched next to it. Excited, she picked it up. It was from her producers. *Congratulations on your first single! Great work! Welcome aboard.* All three producers at Praise Recording Studios had signed it.

As she walked into her room, she spotted another far more lavish bouquet of flowers. *Two dozen red roses!* Tearing open the card, she saw it was from Valdez. *For Ayita: My gorgeous and gifted friend. Love Valdez.* At the bottom of the card, he had written his hotel phone number and his cell with a brief message: *Please call me.*

She phoned him immediately, anxious to hear his voice and make a date to see him. Her resolve to end the relationship had flown out the window.

"Crown-Plaza Nashville, good afternoon."

"Valdez Lopez, please."

"Thank-you, I'll put you through," the operator said.

Moments later, Valdez was on the line. "Thought you could lose me, did you?"

"I tried," she shot back with a stab at humor, her heart fluttering.

"Not hard enough," he slammed back.

"What are you doing in Nashville?"

"I came to see you."

She was unable to halt the wild surge of excitement soaring through her right down to her toes. Her hands trembled as she cradled the telephone.

"May I have the honor of taking you for dinner tonight?"

"Thanks for the invitation, Valdez. But my manager and one of the producers left a message for me. I'll need to talk to them first before I can make a commitment."

"So get back to me. I'll be in my room-at least for the next hour or so."

Ayita wanted to be with Valdez more than anything in the world, but she'd already figured out that success came with a hefty price. Business had to come first, at least for now. Once she became a household name, she would be able to call her own shots. Powerful men had catapulted her rapid rise in the gospel recording world. They had guided her and believed in her, and they came first. She phoned Melvin thanking him for the flowers and asking him to convey that message to the producers. "And thanks again for the lovely lunch yesterday."

"My pleasure. It's only the first of many celebrations where you're concerned, my dear." As if reading her mind, he added, "I need you to stand by for the rest of the day. Tizzy is out of town catching a new act, and he managed to book you as a fill-in for one of the stars at Nashville's Breakfast Theatre. You'll need to get with Jeannie Stuart for wardrobe coordination. She'll meet you at Boot Country to select an outfit to compliment hers and tie in with the rest of the cast."

"What time?" Ayita asked.

"She's rehearsing for another show today, and I don't know what time they'll break. She wondered if you could stand by until you hear from her."

"Of course."

"I need to get with you later in the week to go over some things. With all the meetings I have scheduled during the day, it might have to be dinner, if that's all right," Melvin said.

"Sure. Whatever works for you, Melvin."

She was grateful to Melvin for taking her under his wing and wanted to show appreciation any way she could. Besides, she really enjoyed his company. Sometime she secretly thought of him as the father she never had. Aside from being her mentor, he was protective toward her, and she liked his maturity and wisdom.

She wasn't looking forward to breaking the news to Valdez, and she wanted so much just to be with him. Maybe he would bring over Chinese food or pizza and hang out with her until she received her calls for wardrobe and a possible dinner meeting. Would he understand?

He did. To his credit, he took it all in his stride. "You're busy tonight. Why don't we get together tomorrow?

"I have rehearsal all day tomorrow. Then I have to go over the musical director's notes and be available in case they want to go over anything,"

"I'll be there within an hour."

Thrills danced through her body. He was on his way. Although she had not spoken to him in over a month, not a single day had gone by without thinking about him. He had gotten under her skin, and the only way she knew of to rid herself of the obsession was to see him again. Then she could put him out of her mind and get him out of her system once and for all.

Valdez looked gorgeous. He had obviously gone shopping since arriving in town. He sported alligator cowboy boots with jeans and blue Western shirt. He carried a buttery tan leather jack with fringes. *Guess he plans to hang around for the evening.* As she let him into her hotel room, a wave of shyness washed over her. It had been some time since she had seen him.

He swept her into his arms with such force it almost took her breath away. *He feels incredibly wonderful!*

"I love you," he whispered huskily into her ear. "It's so great to see you. I've missed you so much, Ayita."

"I've missed you, too," Ayita whispered. She felt helpless to control the intense emotion she felt toward him. Her resolve to end it had vanished.

After a long embrace, Valdez held her a foot or so away from him, just drinking her in. "You're beautiful...so very beautiful."

His lips came down on hers in a passionate kiss. She felt euphoric joy, almost as though she transcended her earthly form.

Lord you've given us love, our greatest earthly gift. Surely You brought Valdez into my life so we can enjoy this gift together.

At that instant she heard the phone ring. Pulling herself away from his embrace, she picked it up. It was Tizzy. Even though he was calling from Chicago, he was in one of his chatty moods and started telling her all the plans he had for her career. She had never lost that gut feeling he was somehow off-base, but she hadn't been able to put her finger on it, and the longer she worked with him, the harder it was to unload him.

"I just called to check on you and make sure you got the wardrobe call with Jeannie," Tizzy said.

"I did, thanks, and I have to leave right away. She's waiting for me."

"I'll be back tomorrow. See you then, Hot Shot." Tizzy signed off.

She plunked down on the sofa next to Valdez, in spite of knowing it was an indulgence and she needed to leave in minutes. "I've missed you."

"I tried to forget about you, but I couldn't," Valdez said, stroking her hair. "Then Dad got sick and I've been taking care of him. I didn't hear from you, so I assumed you didn't want to see me. Then Marjoi told me you were recording a single at Praise studios, right after the New Year. I decided to pay you a surprise visit, because I didn't want to risk you turning me down if I called from Washington."

"You talk way too much," Ayita gave him a peck on the neck.

Valdez pulled her closer to him, and she melted all over again. It felt so right to be with him. She never wanted to let him out of her sight.

The sharp ring of the phone jolted her back to the real world. She wrenched herself away from the strength and protection of his powerful arms to answer the phone.

"Sorry I didn't get to call you earlier," Suzie said, "but I've been in meetings most of the day. Do you have your appointment book handy?"

"I do." It was open at today's date, on the desk in front of her.

"Ten o'clock tomorrow, you have a meeting with your new press agent. Outline your career story. You know, the first time you sang for the public, the musicals you played the leads in, church solos...that sort of thing. You'll like Johnny Clark; he's one of the best in the business. You may have seen the preliminary blurb he put in the local paper. It broke today. Make a note of everything that might be relevant. He'll come up with a great article. Bring three or four sharp outfits to the photo shoot. He's planning to shoot a few roles."

"What papers will it be in?"

"Music industry papers across the States. He's booked you on a couple of talk shows and radio shows. He will call you today to make sure you don't have any time conflicts. Oh, and you're back on *Grand Ole Opry.* There'll be other personal appearances around town, as well."

It was hard work, a lot of discipline, and a whole lot of fun. She was headed for the big-time in a hurry.

"Oh, and I made an appointment for your hair with Diana. She does hair and make-up for photo shoots and T.V. She'll come over to your hotel about 8:30 tomorrow. By the way, you might want to squeeze in breakfast while your hair is drying. Get used to a tight schedule. Diana will make you look like a star-guaranteed."

Ayita had begun to feel the pressure. Melvin had been serious when he had said she would not have much spare time once the single was released.

She returned to Valdez's waiting arms, expecting him to be irked by the interruption. Instead, he shrugged it off. She appreciated his easygoing style.

"Hey, Babe, you're one busy lady. I'll head back to the hotel, watch a little TV, and catch a nap. Phone me when you're ready to be picked up, and I'll take you for a nice dinner."

It was becoming obvious to her that Valdez had his

own strong sense of identity. He wasn't intimidated by her meteoric rise in the music world. That was sure a bonus.

She had recently discovered she had a real streak of independence. It came with the territory. She didn't like others driving her and picking her up. She much preferred to drive herself in her own car. However, Tizzy and Melvin had suggested she get her bearings in the city and focus on preparing for her upcoming album. Once that was done, Suzie would help her set up driving lessons, so she could get her license. The studio would lease a car for her. She could hardly wait.

Meanwhile, when time permitted, she hopped on the Trolley and traveled to the studio and rehearsal rooms that way. She discovered the city of Nashville was designed around the music industry. It was ideally set up so the musicians, lyricists, music publishers, and all the music people could function efficiently.

Jeannie looked great in a yellow dress with Western styling and matching alligator boots. She had set aside a similar costume for Ayita to try on. "Hi, I'm Jeannie. Great to meet you. I hear you're pretty hot."

Ayita blushed, even though she knew what Jeannie meant. It was industry lingo for "Hot new talent." She remembered what Tizzy had told her. *"Every business has a language. You'll catch on to it pretty fast. Just do more listening than talking for the first little while. In no time you'll be part of the music scene here."*

Ayita tried on the dress, and Jeannie approved it for her show.

"In the second act we'll be wearing turquoise suede with matching boots. Try that outfit on next, please." Jeannie handed her the garment and boots.

Ayita checked herself out in the full-length mirror:

Dynamite! It would be great on stage. Jeannie nodded her approval of both costumes. The size four dresses fit perfectly and needed no alternations, except for a tiny nip-in at the waistline. The size six boots were a good fit also.

"I'm glad we don't have to worry about a lot of alterations. They just have to take in the waistline on the garments," Jeannie said, comparing figures. "Where do you work out?"

"I-I don't. Not yet, that is. Where is the best place to work out?"

"Private trainer, Jody Scott. Best one in town. I'll give you his number."

It was the last thing on her mind, but she was determined to fit in and do what it took. She programmed the number into her cell. Who knows, she might even do that sometime.

Valdez picked her up and took her to Mario's, an elegant Italian restaurant nestled in the heart of the city. They had veal dishes and dined by candlelight to violin music. She was in heaven-almost.

The serious discussion about Valdez's spiritual state needed to be addressed as soon as possible, but the timing never seemed to be right. Sadness trickled into her mind. They were unequally yoked, and that was definitely a problem. Unless Valdez committed his life to Christ, they had no future. *So why did God allow me to meet him? And why am I so crazy about him? I better get over it.*

Dessert was a chocolate concoction, and both ordered espresso. Valdez surprised her by ordering de-alcoholized champagne. The waiter served it in crystal flutes.

"I would like to propose a toast." Valdez felt in his pocket, pulled out a tiny, black velvet box and opened it on the table. Then he slipped the dazzling pear-shaped solitaire on her ring finger. "Will you marry me, my darling?"

Staring at the ring, dumbfounded, she finally found her voice. "It's stunning, Valdez...but I can't marry you."

"Why not? I love you and I think...you love me. I can support you in grand style. I'll take care of you forever, my darling girl."

In many respects, Ayita felt as though she had not been truly alive before she had met Valdez. Only since he had turned up did she feel that spark, that passion, that *joie de vivre* .In fact, the passion and love she felt for him was downright scary. Where would it end?

"I would like to propose a toast," Valdez said. "To the most beautiful and charming lady I have ever met and, I hope to my future wife."

They clinked glasses as Ayita tried to recover from the shock of his proposal and the magnificent diamond ring. The sparking "champagne" was refreshing and gave Ayita a few moments to gather her wits.

"It's only fair to tell you, Ayita..that I tried to forget you. After you rejected me, I worked very hard at trying to get you out of my mind...but nothing worked. Finally, I had to face the fact that I'm deeply in love with you. Frankly, darling, I can't live without you."

She felt like she was watching a love scene from *Romeo and Juliet.* "Where would we live?" she asked, dazed.

As soon as the words had left her mouth, she knew it was a fatuous remark, give his lack of commitment to Christ. If only she *could* marry him! If only she could have a career and a happy marriage. Still, she'd already been blessed beyond her wildest expectations. Becoming a recording artist in Nashville with the likelihood of a long, exciting career was a dream she had harbored since childhood.

"We would live in Fairhaven, of course," Valdez said, easily.

Slowly, it dawned on her. He probably figured that once she had finished the PR campaign and the album, she could move back to Fairhaven, marry him and have his babies. It was not what she wanted. Not now. Not yet. Maybe not ever.

She chose her words carefully. She could not deny that she wanted him more than she had ever dreamed she could possibly want any man. "I'm in love with you, too," she said carefully, placing the ring back into its velvet case and handing it back to him. "We need to talk."

"So talk. I'm listening." But his mood reflected that of a sulking, spoiled, rich kid, unable to have his way. It made her more determined to hold her ground.

"To begin with," she said, sadly, "I'm a believer-you're not." She waited for the words to sink in. "Also, I want a career as a gospel singer. I believe God has opened doors for me and called me to do this. And now that I've discovered the joy of living in Nashville, I can never go back to living in Washington."

Valdez's featured took on a serious demeanor. "Dad is still very sick and he needs me. I have not wanted to burden you with this, particularly when you were preparing to do the CD, but he has worsened considerably."

"I'm so sorry to hear that. I thought his cancer was in remission."

"It was. It came back again. The operation was not successful. They have given him three months to live. He's only fifty-six-much too young to die," Valdez said brokenheartedly.

He seemed to age before he eyes. She had a sudden

urge to hold him very close...soothe his aching heart, caress his face with her lips, smooth his unruly hair with a gentle touch, and promise him everything would be all right. But she knew it wasn't going to be. "I had no idea. Of course you must stay with him, comfort him and do everything you can for him. You shouldn't even be here now. What if..."

"Now you understand why I have to go back tomorrow. So think about what I've said." He apparently chose to ignore that she was here in Nashville to build a career and that she'd made it abundantly clear she wanted Nashville to be her permanent home. "I'll tell you now, although I was not planning to: I'm going to inherit a great deal of money when Dad passes on."

Upset that he'd even ask her to give up a promising career, she was barely listening. He was selfish. Of course. Why hadn't she seen that side of him before? He wanted everything his way.

"...so, as the only child, I will inherit the entire estate. There's the villa in Marbella and the houses in Madrid and Fairhaven, as well as my father's substantial portfolios. I'll be worth...over ten million."

His words broke into her thoughts. *Ten million!* They could produce their own records, buy a studio, hire their own people...maybe buy an estate in Nashville; *if* she married him and he agreed to move here.

Grand images flashed into her mind: She was bejeweled and wearing a stunning designer gown. They were guests at a grand gala in Monte Carlo. Another image replaced that one: She was galloping joyfully across lush acreage on their ranch. In another flash, they were globetrotting, visiting cities she had only dreamed about seeing. The possibilities were endless. It was all within her reach. In fact, he was handing it to her on a silver platter. She forced herself to come back down to reality. She needed time to assimilate this new information.

"I can't give you an answer right now. Give me time to think about it." It was the best, most noncommittal response she could come up with, but deep in her heart, she knew she would have to turn him down. She remembered Jesus' promise in Mark 10:30 to give back a hundredfold anything we give up for him.

"Don't think about it for too long. I want to marry you, Ayita. I can give you a fabulous life. All you have to do is say yes."

She felt heady. She had to calm down and think about this. "I'd like to go home, if I may," she said, softly.

"As you wish, my darling." He was tender and attentive. He requested the bill, and when it arrived, he plunked his Gold American Express card on the tray.

What would it be like to live a lavish lifestyle? But wouldn't she have that on her own by staying the course? Almost everyone in Nashville was betting on her.

The hostess helped them into their jackets. Ayita was amused by the young woman's smile beamed toward Valdez. He *is* gorgeous. No doubt about that.

The carhop brought the black Sports model Mercedes convertible around to the front, and Valdez drove her home. She did not invite him in. They stood at her front door gazing into each other's eyes. Then he whispered huskily into her ear, "My beautiful princess." His lips found hers, his passion sweeping her along, soaring her to dazzling heights.

Slowly, he pulled out of the embrace. "Good night, sweet princess." His breathing was still ragged. He took both of her hands in one of his and planted kisses on each of them. Her toes tingled. *Darn him, anyway.* He was determined to get to her one way or another.

She locked the door behind him. She was alone. Tonight she felt lonely. Thoughts swirled around in her mind. The proposal and dazzling engagement ring had come as a complete surprise.

Scriptures flashed into her mind. *"Delight thyself also in the Lord; and he shall give thee the desires of thine heart."* And *"Seek ye first the kingdom of God, and his righteousness; and all these things shall be added unto you."*

God had promised her everything she would ever need or want. She already knew what her answer would be. She had a mission in life-a destiny. God had chosen her to sing His praises, and it was her privilege to do that. Her future was in heaven. She would enjoy eternal wealth and beauty in that crystal city above. Everything on earth was temporal. No one had ever accomplished the feat of taking wealth to the world beyond. Wealth was fleeting. Tempting, yes, but fleeting.

She also knew she was in love with Valdez. She should not have seen him. It was far tougher to end their relationship now. Just seeing him this one time had spun her head.

She finally fell asleep, exhausted, after batting ideas back and forth, and arguing with herself for or against marrying Valdez. No matter how great a guy he was, he had not committed his life to Christ. That was the bottom line. She needed to take courage in hand and walk out of his life. It would be the hardest thing she'd ever have to do, but she would be in line with Scripture. God would be pleased, and that was all that mattered.

9

The sharp jangle of the phone startled Ayita out of a deep sleep. It was Valdez. "I've decided to stay on a couple of days. How about letting me take you for lunch today?"

Ayita was nowhere near awake. "Maybe. I'll have to check my schedule."

"Give me the address of your rehearsal studio, and I'll meet you there whenever you break for lunch. Call me on my cell."

"I don't know what time we'll break, but I'll call you when I find out." She was groggy, a zombie before she had the infusion of caffeine. She spooned in the gourmet coffee and poured some orange juice from her mini fridge. She drank some coffee. *Now* she awake. After breakfast, she hopped into the shower and then slipped into designer jeans and a bright, funky top.

Diana arrived at 8:30 sharp, laden with plastic kits brimming with hair products and makeup items. She was cute and pert and wore short platinum hair with a red streak running through it. She wore a pink, silky track suit and high corked pink sandals which added several inches to her short frame. She was somewhat overweight but bright and bubbly and obviously thrilled to be in the "biz."

Ayita was somewhat skeptical of Diana, but Suzie had told her she was one of the best in the industry. Who was she to argue?

Diana set her products on the dresser, batting false lashes. She hummed as she assembled her paraphernalia. "You're gonna look sensational when I get finished with you!" she cooed. "I'd love a cup of coffee. Do you have a pot going?"

Ayita poured Diana a mug of the brew. She was

already plunging into her task. Heating up jumbo rollers, she curled Ayita's hair. Next, she started the meticulous process of making Ayita up for photography. When Ayita finally consulted the mirror, she was delighted at the glamorous image before her.

"It's actually more difficult to work on someone who is naturally beautiful like you are, than someone who is plain. Well, what do you think?" Diana asked.

Ayita studied herself in the mirror. "I'm thrilled with the way I look. Thank-you, so much!"

"The camera is going to love you," Diana said.

"I'm counting on it." Ayita meant it.

Diana packed up her makeup and hair products and clacked over to the door. "The studio gets the bill, but I guess you know that. I'm going out for coffee and meet you at the shoot. I'll be there the whole time for touch-ups, powder, hair, etc...well, Suzie said you're new, that's why I'm telling you all this."

Tizzy picked Ayita up at 9:30 and drove her to the studio. The photographer was already there, and so was her new press agent. Tizzy made all the necessary introductions and mercifully had another engagement, so he left her on her own. She was getting tired of him hovering all the time.

Diana showed up in good spirits with all her supplies and hovered on the sidelines, checking hair and doing minor touch-ups. The photo session went smoothly and Ayita enjoyed every minute of it

Rehearsal was set for 2:00 P.M. She was unable to focus on the lyrics because she kept visualizing herself as Valdez's wife, in spite of her resolve to end it with him. Though she had returned the ring, he still claimed her heart. Perhaps Valdez wanted to stick around to try to talk her into taking the ring back and wearing it.

She agreed to meet Valdez for lunch. After all, he would be leaving soon. He picked her up and drove them to Music row, parked and walked a block and went into a cafe she knew music folks frequented. He ordered corned beef sandwiches on eye with extra pickles, lots of mustard and two diet cokes. Valdez pulled the pear-shaped diamond ring out of the inside pocket of his jacket. He placed it on her finger and lovingly slid it down. She felt helpless to stop him. Sparkling lustrously, the diamond's resplendence captivated her. Was it five carats? She had no wish to be gauche and ask him, so she said nothing.

Was she losing it? She'd just resolved last night to end the relationship. She couldn't marry him. So why had she allowed him to place the ring back on her finger again? As if in a daze, she pushed the ring snugly onto her finger and admired it. She opened her mouth, hoping some words of protest would spill out, but she'd been struck mute.

Valdez put his hand up as if stopping traffic. Then he raised an index finger to her lips and teased her, "Ssshh. Just wear it, my darling. You think too much." He changed the subject masterfully. "How are rehearsals going?"

"Terrific." She smiled at him, grateful for the change of topic.

"What sort of new material are you working on for the live show?"

He was doing a fabulous job of diverting her attention. She rattled off the titles of six songs.

"May I give you a piece of friendly advice?"

"Sure."

"You're the talent; you should be calling the shots."

"What do you mean?"

"For example, yesterday you allowed your manager to bend your ear at an inconvenient time for you. The same scenario occurred with the press people. Instead of allowing them to lead you around by the nose, you should be leading them."

She frowned. "I thought you wanted me to give up my career and be a happy housewife?"

"Maybe I *would* like that, but as long as you're in this business, you should be calling the shots. You're the talent. Without you, they have nothing."

"Are you going to tell me what songs I should sing, also?"

"No, but that should be primarily your decision not theirs. From what I've gathered, your manager and producers have a large hand in selecting your songs. You're fresh, new talent in Nashville, maybe you should check out songs written by unknown writers... as opposed to doing the stuff everybody else had been doing for a while. "

"Since when did you become an expert in the music business?"

"I can usually size up a situation pretty fast."

She lifted a brow. "So I see."

"It's hardly a secret there is an enormous amount of talent in Nashville. You have your own unique sound- maybe you need a unique writer to work with. There might be some great songs out there that would suit you better than the music your manager has selected for you."

Impressed by Valdez's interest and input, Ayita wondered if he'd be a better manager for her than Tizzy. "I think you're right. I could start by going to Writers' Night. It's a showcase for unpublished songs, performed primarily by new artists."

"Now, there's a great idea." Valdez took a bite of his sandwich. "Incidentally, who has Tizzy worked with in the past? Can you name one singer he guided to stardom?"

Ayita was silent. Her niggling feeling about Tizzy resurfaced. She felt embarrassed for not asking Tizzy those sorts of questions. She'd been so thrilled just to be in Nashville, to have a manager and be living her dream, that she hadn't given serious thought to qualifying him. But she'd never said she was an astute business woman. She was singer; that was her gift.

"We didn't discuss any of his other clients. We talked primarily about the direction he wanted to guide me in within the gospel field. He made song recommendations and artist suggestions...vocalists he wanted me to listen to."

"Why?"

"What do you mean, why? I guess he wants me to listen to the top recording artists and learn from them."

"They put you under contract because they love *your* unique sound, and of course, your persona. They think *you* are one of the best talents out there. They also love the way you deliver a song-your personal style. The last thing you want to do is copy any other artist. If they start messing with your individuality, you'll lose your natural edge."

"Tizzy suggested I take sight-reading classes and perhaps work toward a degree in music. He said the sky was the limit for a talent like mine."

"Okay, so he says a lot of the right things. Anyway, more to the point, I gather you have already signed a contract with him."

"Yes, I have."

"Too bad. I think you could have done better."

"You're probably right, but it's too late now." She sighed.

"Maybe not. Did you read the contract or take it to an attorney before you signed it?"

"No. Tizzy was in a big rush to get the contract signed.

He pressured me into it, to be honest."

"Well, maybe you can get out of it, particularly if you signed it under duress. We should check with an attorney. Something bothers me about him, but I can't quite put my finger on it."

"I know exactly what you mean, because I feel the same way."

Valdez glanced at his watch. "Your hour is up. I had better get you back to rehearsal. I'll pick you up at 5:00. If you're not ready, I'll wait in the lobby."

"We could go until 6:00 maybe later."

"I'll take my chances. I'll be there at 5:00. If I have to wait, I'll wait."

She knew she had no backbone. She was as weak as mush and had just proved it. She flashed him a big smile. He really was a sweetheart. He had spent the entire hour discussing *her* career

Suddenly, she realized she still had the solitaire on her ring finger. It glittered brilliantly. She had been so involved in their discussion that she'd forgotten she had it on. It was outrageous, given she had no intention of marry him-but she felt proud to be wearing it. Someone really wanted her. All her good intentions of telling him to get lost had fallen by the wayside. Impulsively, she slipped the ring into her cosmetic bag in her purse right before entering the studio. She wasn't in the mood to field questions about the diamond, especially since she had to muster up the courage to break off with Valdez, anyway.

Ayita found it exhilarating, rehearsing with celebrities for the *Breakfast Theatre Show,* but she wasn't concentrating as much as she normally did. Thoughts of Valdez intruded. She could hardly wait to see him again.

Rehearsal ended a few minutes after 5:00. True to his

word, Valdez was waiting in front of the studio, sitting in his car.

Ayita couldn't stop smiling when she spotted him. "Hey, handsome."

He got out of his car and opened the door for her. "How did it go?"

"Great...thanks."

He drove her back to her apartment. As soon as they were inside, he said "May I see the contract?"

She fished it out of the desk in the small living room. He sat at the desk, immersing himself in the contract. She watched him flip the pages. Occasionally his brow furrowed; other times his eyes narrowed. It felt so comfortable, watching him read the contract as she sat on the sofa next to him, brimming with admiration. She had placed the ring back on her finger and now allowed herself the luxury of admiring the brilliant stone. Would she dare keep it?

It wasn't long before he had finished speed-reading the contact. "Looks like you have an iron-clad contract for five years with this character. I seriously doubt if a good attorney could get you out of this, except for the fact that any self-respecting manager should have recommended you have an attorney look over the contract before signing it, to begin with."

She adored him. He was protecting her, and it warmed her heart.

"His cut is 25 percent. Isn't that rather steep?" Valdez asked.

"Yes, it can be as low as 15, or so I've heard. I asked him about it, and he said the fee was theoretically negotiable, but he has never worked for less than 25 percent. He told me he was the best in the business. He said he would look after my taxes and all my personal business. He pointed out that his fee was tax-deductible anyway, and I would have very high earnings, if the producers' projections proved accurate. I would need lots of write-offs."

"There is some truth in that statement about the write-offs, but you might feel the dint until you actually see the big money. He's clever, all right. I'm just not sure I trust him."

Valdez gave her a mini-lecture on the theory of real income and taxes and net income. She was more confused when he had finished than when he had started. She hated business, and it was obvious he loved it. Maybe she needed him more than she realized. She was happy to let someone else run her business affairs, but she wished with all her heart that person was Valdez, not Tizzy.

"I didn't realize how good you are at all this," Ayita said, with admiration.

"No, of course you didn't. You've been too busy judging my worth based on my level of Christian commitment." He searched her eyes

"That's unfair, Valdez. I just want us going down the same road if we intend to build a marriage. But at the moment, I don't see how we could."

"I told you...I don't mind going to church occasionally. But no one has yet been able to prove the existence of God. Until they do, why should I believe?"

She was deeply saddened at his remarks. He was almost a flat-out atheist. She would have to walk away from him, after all. "That doesn't make sense. You told me an angel guided you to the Clayburgh home when you were desperately searching for it in the snowstorm, and then an angel or a mysterious man drove you back to the Petersons with the supplies. How many God-incidents do you need to believe in His existence?"

"Look, I *do* believe in angels, but I have trouble accepting the concept of the Triune God."

"And I thought you were clever," she said, exasperated. "Either you believe the Bible is the inspired Word of God or you don't. So you believe the part about the existence of angels, yet other parts of the Bible you don't believe. Does that make you a half a believer?"

He grinned. "I believe in angels, because I have encountered their presence. I'm just not sure about God."

"Don't you see? You accept Jesus by *faith.* According to Scripture, man has a scrim over his eyes and cannot see the truth *until* he accepts Jesus by faith, and *then* his eyes are opened and he understands the truth of the Bible."

Maybe someday I'll believe. Right now, I have other things on my mind."

This was her cue to return the ring to him, once and for all. "This is exactly why I broke off with you before." How could she justify continuing this relationship, if he was not a believer? She knew the answer: she couldn't. She would have to muster up her courage and end it. Slowly, she eased the sparkling diamond off her finger. The relationship wasn't meant to be. She had to be strong and make the break. She fought back a mountain of tears as she slipped the jewel from her finger and handed it back to Valdez.

Comfort and peace descended upon her like a soft breeze on a summer day. God was faithful, and He would help her move beyond this. Maybe her destiny was to be friends with Valdez. Could she turn the romance into a friendship? It sure would be nice to have him around as a friend to protect her, as well as guide her through the jungle of the Nashville music scene.

She realized now how naive she'd been when she thought everyone in the gospel music industry would be moral. She was fast learning other harsh realities. There were committed, awesome Christians, but also lukewarm believers and even people parading as Christians in order to fit in. Could she handle the pressures of making it big on her own? Could she trust Tizzy to guide her into making all the right decisions? She wished now that she had followed her gut instinct and not signed with him. Why hadn't her producers suggested she hire an attorney to look over her contract?

Then she remembered a comment Melvin Donner had made, an apology of sorts. He'd assumed she would have an attorney study her management contract and was surprised when he learned she hadn't. He had been busy and had forgotten to suggest it. "Hey, I'm used to veteran singers who have been kicking around for years. By the time they get a break, they know everything about the music industry." She would see an attorney as soon as possible.

Valdez did not react verbally to her giving him back the ring. He simply retreated in silence. She was learning that this was his way of dealing with situations that bothered him. It was definitely a "guy thing." Shoving the ring into his slacks pocket, he stood. His brooding eyes now bore a wounded look. The last thing she'd wanted to do was hurt him, but she had done that.

"I have to leave. I have an early flight tomorrow," he said.

She knew then that he would make himself scarce. This was the end-marriage or nothing. She walked with him to the door and retrieved his jacket from the hall closet, helping him slip into it. Her heart caught in her throat.

He leaned down and gave her a peck on the cheek. "Good-bye, my beautiful one," he murmured in her ear, then left.

She stood rooted to the spot. She opened her mouth to say good-bye, but no words came out. Somewhere deep in her heart, she did not want to bid him farewell. Her suite felt eerily silent without the presence of the robust Valdez. If it was a portent of what was to come, it would be a very lonely life.

After trying unsuccessfully to concentrate on the lyrics for tomorrow's rehearsal, she finally gave up. Instead, she ran water for a bath and then cranked up the music on the radio. She would take a break. After the bath, she climbed into bed to study the lyrics just before she turned out the lights. She had discovered that that was the best time to let memorization sink in.

Ayita phoned Melvin at home and asked him to give her the name of an entertainment attorney. He seemed surprised at first, but gave her two names, assuring her they were both excellent. "Go with whomever gives you the first appointment. They're two of the best in the industry."

She entered the appointment into her cell phone and duplicated it on a hard copy in her appointment book. A glance over her week revealed she'd have to start scheduling grocery shopping and errands. She would soon need an assistant.

The next day she had a breakfast date with Tizzy. She arrived early, as was her habit. She thought she spotted him, but it was hard to tell, because a newspaper obscured the face, along with the brilliant rays of winter sunshine. Tizzy was obsessed with the news and was constantly reading all sorts of newspapers. She craned her head to the side to check the identity of the reader. Sure enough, there was the bronzed face and dark, curly mop of hair. His tortoise-framed glasses were perched on his beaked nose. His face was bent down, immersed in the *Los Angeles Times*.

Although he appeared to be concentrating on his newspaper, sometimes she thought it was his "cover," because he was always glancing around, apprehensively. She wasn't sure whether it was to avoid someone or perhaps because he thought he might be missing a celebrity.

She plunked down in the booth facing him. "Good morning, Tizzy."

He smiled at her as he folded the newspaper and set it down to one side of the table. "Good morning, gorgeous. Did you sleep well?" Tizzy's eyes traveled over her, appraising her. Was it a professional assessment of his "property?" Was he strictly checking out her public image?

A stout, red-haired server waddled over to their table. She topped off Tizzy's coffee and yawned. "Coffee?" The question was directed to Ayita. The coffee pot was poised mid-air, above Ayita's empty mug. She hoped the server wouldn't spill it on her.

"Yes, please," Ayita said quickly.

The server filled her mug and handed Ayita a menu, before sauntering off.

"I heard the photo shoot went great," Tizzy began.

"It did. How was your trip?" Ayita asked.

"I signed a new artist. Donny Douglas."

"Girl or guy?"

"Girl. She's pretty hot stuff right now."

The redhead stood by again, waiting to take their orders.

"Scrambled eggs, hash browns and dry toast, please," Ayita said.

"That's an ala-carte. Four ninety-nine," the waitress droned, speaking in a monotone.

"Fine," Tizzy said. "And I'll have the number three, with an extra pad of butter on the side"

"That'll be $5.99 plus 50 cents for the extra butter."

"Fine. Top up the coffee please." Tizzy waved a hand over both cups.

"The photo shoot was five hundred dollars. I signed for it. Who pays for that?" Ayita asked.

"You do. The studio pays the hair, make-up and photo people, as well as the publicity people; then they issue you an expense accounting at the end of each month. Expenses are automatically deducted off your salary, the same as my commission."

"That's fine. But what didn't you explain all this to me before?"

"You snagged a recording contract. I assumed you were a seasoned pro, like everybody else in this town."

"You assumed wrong." She had been thrust into the middle of a business she knew absolutely nothing about, and she was fast getting the feeling that if she didn't figure everything out real quick, she would be the loser."

There was a loud page, booming above the noise and bustle of the busy restaurant. It was for her. Suddenly, she realized she'd forgotten her cell phone. Who was tracking her down during her breakfast meeting? She picked up the phone at the front desk of the eatery.

Valdez's warm, sexy voice caught her by surprise. "Hey, beautiful, my flight was cancelled due to a bomb threat. All the flights are delayed until they get the threat under control. Any chance of taking you for dinner tonight?"

Her knees turned to mush. She heard herself say, "I'd

love to" It was the polar opposite of what she meant to say. He was a master at catching her off guard. She would see him tonight, since she'd already agreed to, and that would be the end of it.

"I'll pick you up after rehearsal. I'll get there at 5:00 and wait outside. Don't worry, I'll be there waiting, no matter how late you rehearse. I'll pick up some CD's to listen to."

"Well, you're popular. Who would be calling you at this hour at Denny's?" Tizzy asked, the moment she returned to their table.

"Personal," Ayita said, proud she had the guts to stand up for her privacy.

"Interested in doing a concert tour in the Orient?"

"It depends on what it pays. What cities are you thinking?"

"I'm just throwing out feelers right now. If you're interested, I'll see what I can do. As far as the money is concerned, I'll get you as much as I can negotiate. The more tours you do, the quicker we can build your name internationally and sell your singles and albums."

Lately, she had begun to feel the pressure of being a highly paid performer. She was a commodity, a cash cow, and every day she felt a little more like one.

"As soon as we finish your promo package, I'm going to start pushing for a North American tour. By next year, I want you to be playing concerts in the hottest venues in the UK, the continent, Asia and maybe South America."

She was tempted to remark that she would probably be doing tours, though not with him as her manager. But that would be contingent on her attorney finding a loophole in the contract. She remained silent and polite. She always believed in being gracious, Mrs. Peterson taught her that.

Ayita was finishing her third and last week of rehearsal for the *Breakfast Theatre Show* and was very excited to be appearing in it. It would be good for her to be on stage working in front of an audience every day. Further, it would be a boost to her name value for her upcoming appearances promoting her single.

It was well after 6:00 when Ayita finished rehearsal. After a "good night y'all," she headed outside into the balmy evening, with a spring in her step. She was on top of the world, blessed, beyond her wildest dreams. Having problems to deal with was just part of the growing process.

Spotting Valdez waiting in his car jolted her back to reality. He was a temporary person in her life, and no matter how much she procrastinated, it was inevitable their relationship would end.

Valdez stepped out of his rented Mercedes Sports Coupe and greeted her with a big grin. "Fate has allowed us one more day to be together, my darling." He took one of her hands in his and kissed it, before she could discourage him.

She would enjoy his company tonight. He would leave town soon, and then she would will herself to forget him. Ayita had made an appointment with her attorney for 6:30 and they would just make it.

It was handy having all the music business people in the vicinity. They located the office quickly. At room 302 they spotted a bold sign: Lars Thalberg, Entertainment Attorney. She felt empowered just being here.

A mature secretary glanced up from her computer and greeted them with a warm smile. "Come in. You must be Ayita and Valdez. Mr. Thalberg is expecting you." She buzzed the intercom and announced their arrival. Minutes later, she ushered them into the attorney's office.

Mr. Thalberg was an impressive, surprisingly young attorney. He stood about six feet, five inches. As if his height was not enough intimidation, he spoke with power and confidence. His wit and quick intelligence impressed her. She was in the right place. His office was spacious and included a large desk and a comfortable seating arrangement, consisting of a pair of leather sofas and club chairs. The walls were lined with masses of shelves, brimming with law books.

"So, young lady, let's have a look at your contract." He proceeded to speed read it, half-moon glasses perched over his nose. "Right off, I can tell you it's not a standard contract. The wording appears to have been altered to favor your manager, but that's not necessarily a bad thing. We'll see what we have here, shortly."

When he flipped to the third page, a concerned look crossed his face. "I'd like you to leave a copy of this with me. I need to go through this contract with a fine-tooth comb. I can already tell you I don't like it." He buzzed his assistant. "Mary, would you please come into my office. I need a copy of a contract."

Mary arrived quickly, taking the contract her boss extended to her.

"Make Ayita another appointment, would you. She'll advise you of her schedule."

"You work in the music industry, Mr. Thalberg. What kind of a reputation does Tizzy have?" Valdez asked.

The attorney hesitated a moment, appearing to mull the question over, or more precisely, perhaps deciding how he would respond to the question.

Valdez decided to help him out. "Is he bad news?"

"He can be. You have to watch him carefully. He can be sneaky. He hasn't really done anything blatantly crooked, to my knowledge, but I have reason to believe he has had unscrupulous dealings with some of his artists in the past. On the other hand, he's helped some singers up the ladder, although he hasn't had a winner in a long time. Maybe he's lost his touch. He's not known around town as one of the best managers. I'm baffled as to why Melvin recommended him to you-unless he owes him a favor. Anyway, we'll have another meeting after I've had a chance to go through the contract thoroughly. If we are able to get you out of this contract, I'll give you the names of a couple of good managers."

As Valdez drove her to a French restaurant, he said, "At least we know it wasn't all in our imagination. The guy doesn't have a good reputation. If Melvin recommended him, then how can we trust Melvin?"

Ayita only wanted to sing. She hated having to deal with the business side of things. She wanted someone else to look after it for her. If only Valdez was on the same page as she was, they would be an unbeatable team.

They enjoyed a hearty dinner as The Pinnacle restaurant revolved, featuring breathtaking views of the city. Ayita's head spun in synch with the revolving restaurant. Everything was happening so fast. Would she be able to keep up? She shook off the niggling doubts and glanced across the table at Valdez. He had finished eating, his knife and fork resting on one side of his plate. He just sat there, grinning and gazing into her eyes. He was an ideal date and an ideal man, but until they were able to resolve their major difference, they had nothing. This was a fact she would just have to face, like it or not.

Ayita declined Valdez's invitation to join him in his room for a late movie. She had to rest her voice for tomorrow's rehearsal. Besides, it was dangerous for her to be alone with him. She didn't trust herself.

Valdez's cell chirped. He read the text message quickly and silently. Tears sprang to his eyes. "I'm afraid it's bad news. I had planned to be back in Fairhaven tonight, as you know. Dad was just taken into emergency. My aunt and uncle...the couple you met at the church...drove him to the hospital. The live-in male nurse apparently called them."

She wanted to hold him close and comfort him. They were in a public place, she couldn't. "Oh Valdez, I'm so sorry. I'll pray for him"

He paid the check and drove them back to his hotel. "Maybe...by some miracle...the flights will be operative again and I can get home," Valdez said, as he helped her out the car.

He strode into the lobby with Ayita at his side. *He needed her. She would stay with him for an hour or so, until he adjusted to the situation.*

As they entered the lobby, his cell rang. He read the text message: *All flights operative. You are on top priority to fly out on emergency medical.* He shared the text with Ayita, then grabbed her and kissed her.

Don't go, Valdez. I need you so much, Ayita thought. She smiled weakly as tears filled her eyes. "You see Valdez... God is watching and He cares."

"I'm going to grab my suitcase, throw everything in, drop you off and head to the airport. Maybe I can get a connector and get in tonight, or close enough so I can drive to the hospital."

She watched him quickly pack his suitcase. Overwhelming love mingled with compassion for his plight stole over her. His father was dying. He had lost his mother only a few months ago. She wanted to hold him and never let him go. He was an only child and so was she. No wonder he needed her so much. He had no siblings to share his sorrow with.

When they reached Ayita's hotel, he walked her to the door of her studio. Then he wrapped his arms around her, pulling her close. She couldn't stop him, and she didn't want to. She didn't want him to go. She turned her face away because she didn't want him to see her tears. She was in love with him-deeply in love-and because of it, she shared his sorrow.

"Thank-you for a lovely dinner," she whispered. "And thank you for looking after me. You don't know how much I appreciate it."

He held her slightly away from him. "I'm going to miss you, beautiful. I'll call you as soon as I know what's going on." He saw her into her suite and turned sadly, walking down the corridor.

It was only after he had gone and she was alone in her suite that she became aware of her upper lip trembling, as tears trickled down her cheeks. She had fallen hard for him. Still, she determined to cut him out of her life. Somehow, the floodgate of emotion set off a chain of reactions inside her. It triggered a well of sadness mixed with the trauma she had known as a child and teenager. It had returned to haunt her, causing a rush of insecurity and deep sorrow.

10

Vivid sunlight streamed through the cracks in the louvered shutters on her bedroom windows. Ayita bounded out of bed and opened the slats. A crimson morning sun greeted her. God was in his heavens and somehow everything would work out for the best.

She brewed a pot of coffee before stepping into the shower stall. Grabbing a fluffy, white towel, she formed a turban on her head. She wouldn't take the time to shampoo her long tresses today. The towel would help keep her hair dry as she showered.

Afterwards, she slipped into some jewel-encrusted designer jeans and a sporty white shirt, downed a large mug of black coffee, gathered her music and rode the elevator downstairs to the eatery for a light breakfast.

The hostess seated her at a table by the long bank of windows. Ayita checked her schedule on her cell and double-checked it with her appointment book, while she waited for the server to take her order. While she nibbled at breakfast, she habitually glanced over the music she would be rehearsing that day. She did the serious work at night just before she fell asleep.

She had a dinner date with Melvin tonight. He wanted to discuss some of the marketing strategies with her. She was looking forward to the meeting-it was stimulating riding on the learning curve and Melvin was an ideal mentor.

Ayita was early for rehearsal as usual. She heard classical music played beautifully on a piano as she neared the rehearsal room. Chopin? Beethoven?

Melvin had been giving her a crash course in music,

exposing her to a variety of composers and testing her on them later. It was great fun receiving a classical music education in an unorthodox manner. She slipped soundlessly into the room. None of the cast members had arrived yet, so the accompanist was obviously doing his own thing.

She slipped onto a seat quietly, determined not to disturb him. When he finished playing the concerto, she approached him. "That was brilliant. Why aren't you a concert pianist, Lou?"

He laughed. "I had aspirations to be one-honest. I just don't have what it takes. I don't have the discipline or overwhelming passion...and commitment required to succeed."

"I'm sorry." Ayita said.

"I guess I would have to admit I sold out. That's how life is sometimes. You're much too young to know about that."

His plight struck home. God had opened doors for her and that was why she had to make every hour of every day count for something. Maybe someday she would be able to inspire others to use their gifts as well.

Singing classic country for the Breakfast Show was a challenge and departure for her, and she took it in her stride. Rehearsal went great and she could hardly wait to perform at the famed Nashville Palace.

During the first coffee break, while Jeanne, along with the back-up singers and musicians stepped out for coffee, Ayita chose to remain and speak with the director, who was presently going over some nuances with the accompanist.

Ayita picked Lou's brain for a few minutes, and then he surprised her with a compliment. "You're one of the most gifted singers I've ever had the pleasure of working with. You have a great future in this industry."

Ayita blushed and smiled up at him.

He returned the smile. "Considering you're untrained vocally and musically, you're somewhat of a phenomena. If you continue to get the right breaks, you're going to soar to the apex of this industry. I'm available to help you in any way I can. I've been disappointed over the years, occasionally putting untold hours into a singer's career. Then, once they hit the big-time, they don't even bother to say "thank-you." I find that disheartening. I think you're destined for stardom and in you, I see the humility of a great artist."

"So, I've found a loophole and I can get you out of the contract," Mr. Thalberg said. "You can?" Ayita said, thrilled. "I believe so." He went over some points in the contract explaining details as he went. Ayita was only half-listening. *If only Valdez were here.* But, she knew she had to grow up. As Tizzy had said, "You're in Show Biz kid, with an emphasis on the Biz."

Mr. Thalberg was way ahead of her. "You'll probably want to run this by Valdez. I have the important points to consider written up. Take this explanation letter and review it with your friend. If you decide you want me to pursue breaking the contract, I believe I will be successful. Just let me know what you want to do."

Ayita took a taxi home and freshened up just in time to be ready for her dinner date with Melvin at Mario's. Melvin ordered Saltimbocca Alla Romana, and she ordered Osso Bucco Alla Milanese, while Tizzy had Scaloppini Alla Bolognese. A serious gourmet, Melvin only dined at the finest restaurants. Mario's had apparently won every major restaurant award in the industry. The accolades were artfully displayed in the foyer for all the guests to see.

"Mario's has won the Mobil Four Star Award for the last five years in a row, so the food should be up to your standard," Melvin said, eyes twinkling.

Ayita determined not to say a word about hiring an attorney to advise her in breaking her contract with Tizzy. She would sign with a new manager and play it down. After all, Melvin wanted the best for her. Maybe Tizzy had bullied Melvin into recommending him. Maybe he really did owe Tizzy a favor.

Sam dropped her off at the hotel as usual, and she sank into bed early, lyrics in hand. She thrived on the all-consuming aspect of the business. She adored the rehearsals, the performances and recording. Her career was moving full speed ahead and she treasured every minute of it. Still, conflicting thoughts and emotions and unsolved problems with Valdez constantly intruded into her mind.

Melvin had ordered another photo shoot to take place on location at the Opryland Hotel tomorrow. The photographer would photograph her with an established male artist named Ronnie Clark. Her mentors were working diligently to catapult Ayita to the top.

Ayita was quickly getting used to wardrobe fittings, working closely with the costumers to incorporate her unique style into her costumes. Tizzy and her producers didn't want Ayita to be seen in public in an outfit she had previously worn. Image was everything and they guarded hers diligently. She was being groomed for stardom and everything had to be just right.

~~*~~

Working with Ronnie, the photographer, was a hoot. He clowned around a lot, relaxing her. When it was over, they laughed together at his jokes and she felt certain the photos would be excellent.

Soon, she was spirited back to the studio for rehearsal. She joined the other cast members for the final run-through for the newly revamped *Breakfast Theatre Show.* Tizzy had finally managed to get her an audition for the *Grand Ole Opry* for next week. So, after an intense rehearsal, she walked the short distance to the another rehearsal studio to meet Lou, so she could polish a couple of her best songs she would use as audition pieces for the *Grand Ole Opry. Talent is 99% hard work, that old adage is true,* Ayita thought.

She thrived on the hectic schedule during the week, but always looked forward to Sundays. The day of rest. The day set aside for worship and praise of the Creator, and the day she recharged her batteries. She always attended church and spent the rest of the day relaxing, occasionally watching a Hallmark movie or listening to classical music. But often, she spent most of the day meditating on God's Word. He had been so good to her and she would always be grateful and never forget Him. In the five months she'd been in Nashville, she had church-hopped looking for a church home. She still hadn't settled on one. This Sunday she planned to try yet another.

~~*~~

The moment she entered Trinity Baptist, she felt she'd found her new church home. The closer she drew to God, the more He spoke to her. Lately, she had begun to receive a quiet peace in her spirit, telling her when to move, where to go, how to operate. She was no longer the master of her own ship. God was calling the shots. He always had, but now she listed for that still, small voice.

Ayita had gained considerable confidence since moving to Nashville. She decided to approach the music director and offer to sing in one of his services. Why not?

George Smith was an eloquent and seasoned minister. But the best part was that he was on fire for God. An elderly man, he nevertheless knew who she was and was pleased that she had visited his church.

"We would love to have you sing here," George said when she approached him after the service. Let me know when you can work it into your schedule."

A couple weeks later, Ayita sang "How can I say thanks" by Andrew Crouch. The song erupted from a wellspring of gratitude to God. It came from the depths of her soul. The congregation received it joyfully, applauding her with a standing ovation. She was taken aback by the enthusiastic applause. She knew that most congregations did not applaud their soloists, and she really wished they hadn't done so for her. She wanted all the praise and honor and glory to go to God. Still, she was humbled and touched by their spontaneous response.

Once the service was over, Ayita joined throngs of folks milling around in a recreation room, decorated gaily in a Southwest theme. A long table was set up with large cylinders of gourmet coffee, tea, and lemonade, and an assortment of cookies available, as well. She poured herself some lemonade and glanced around the room, hoping to connect with some new people.

The small round tables that filled the room made it very easy to mingle and meet new people. Several people looked her way and smiled. She sensed they were ambiguous about approaching her, because of her celebrity status. But one woman, a mature blonde, walked over to

Ayita.

"Hi, I'm Anne Talbot." She smiled warmly. "First time here?"

"Yes," Ayita said.

Anne was striking and elegantly attired in a red silk suit, accented by black accessories. "I loved your solo," she said, in her rich, husky voice. "We're in the same business."

"Are you a recording artist, also?" Ayita asked.

"Twenty years, honey. Mind if I join you?"

"I would like that."

Anne sat down. "I just got back from Buenos Aires. I'm a widow. It's been three years now, but I still have a lot of loose ends in business to tie up, and some of my closest friends live there. I usually go back once a year."

"Do you like living in Nashville?" Ayita asked.

"Very much. I've decided to settle here. I bought an estate a couple of years ago. Why don't you come over to the house for lunch? Dalia usually has something tasty prepared by the time I return from church. I often surprise her by bringing guests. I promise you won't be disappointed."

"Thanks, I'd like that." Ayita was delighted to be making a new friend. But she felt kind of silly that she didn't have a driver's license or own a car yet. "Could I hitch a ride with you? I came here by taxi. I get around mostly by limo or taxi."

"Of course, my dear. I'd love the company."

Annie's Hybrid was bright red and perfectly matching her suit.

Santa Rosita Estates was a magnificent gated community of acreage properties, clearly designed for Equestrians, Ayita noted.

Anne pressed her remote control as the imposing iron gates parted. She drove through and parked in the roundabout in front of a stately, white colonial home. They dined on lobster bisque and scallops. Ayita felt as though they had been friends for ages. They had as easy rapport, made easier by their shared passions for music and horses.

"I married an older man when I was only twenty-six. He was almost thirty years my senior, but I must tell you, Ayita... it was love at first sight. He was a businessman. The love of my life...recently died of a massive heart attack...right in front of me. I thought I would never get over it. But God has been gracious. Slowly, I'm recovering from the shock and horror of it all."

"I'm so sorry," Ayita said, deeply touched by the story.

"The Lord has been good to me. I was born in Nashville and a lot of my family is here. After my husband died, I no longer wanted to live in Buenos Aires. I loved living there when we were together, but everything changed the day he died. It's been an enormous adjustment."

Ayita looked away when she realized Anne was fighting tears. She couldn't imagine how devastating it must have been to see her beloved husband die so suddenly.

Anne poured them both more apple cider. "Let's go out on the back veranda and get some fresh air."

Ayita followed her hostess outside, and they sat on wicker chairs, enjoying their ice-cold cider. A soft breeze rustled the leaves on the grass below them. Spring was just around the corner, but it was still a touch cool outside.

"It's a beautiful afternoon. Would you like to go for a swim? I have bathing suits in assorted sizes with the tags still on. I keep them in the guest house."

"That's a great idea. I don't get much time for swimming and lounging and that pool sure looks inviting."

Ayita glanced over at an Olympic-sized lap pool and adjacent hot tub. The area was shrouded in privacy. Masses of white Oleanders grew wildly over the high walls, surrounding the estate. She felt privileged to be here.

"Let's digest our lunch first." Anne suggested.

"Yeah, we don't want to drown," Ayita said.

Anne laughed heartily.

"What a fabulous place you have," Ayita added.

Anne nodded. "Thanks. It proves dreams really can come true. I've wanted a colonial mansion ever since I was a little girl and Daddy drove me by one. Anyway, the estate was in serious disrepair when my realtor first showed it to me. I got a great buy on it because it was so dilapidated. I restored the home. The project kept me busy for the better part of a year, and it was precisely what I needed emotionally."

"You must absolutely love it here," Ayita said, glancing around.

"I really do. It was very lonely at first, though. I don't think I would have made it without my dog, Shep."

At the sound of his name, the handsome Shepherd bounded toward them.

"He's been great company. I also placed an ad in the local paper and found Dalia. I had advertised for a live-in couple, but when I met her, I knew she was the one God had set aside for me. She dances around the house, singing all the time. Just what I needed after my mourning period. She's a real comedian- very witty. I keep telling her to get an act together and entertain people, but she insists she's doing it right here and she's happy with that."

"Are you working on an album at the moment?" Ayita asked Anne.

"Actually, I am. We can go back into the house later

and I'll play some of my other recordings for you if you like. Or I can just give you a couple CD's to take home. I'm much more excited about the new album I'm working on right now. Why don't you drop by and watch rehearsals next week if you have time? I'd love your opinion on the songs I've selected. I think they suit me and my voice, but I value input from other professionals."

"Tell me when and where. I'll be there if I can get away. I'm on a tight schedule right now, but maybe during lunch if that could work."

Anne pressed her hand. "I'll let you know, and I understand." She got up. "It's starting to cool off outside, so let's go inside. Maybe I can scare up some dessert. Will you have some?"

"I'm not on a diet."

Anne opened another bottle of chilled cider and brought it into the living room. "Are you dating anyone? I hope you don't mind me asking." She set the glasses on the coffee table.

Ayita hesitated a couple minutes. "I was. But I'm breaking off with him."

"I'm sorry to hear that, but I'm glad you're free, because I know a great guy I'd like to introduce you to. Just a minute...I'll show you some photos of him. We're good friends, but there's no romance there and there never will be. I think you might enjoy meeting him." Anne disappeared, returned shortly with a packet of photos. "See what I mean?" Handsome, isn't he?"

Ayita had to admit he was. "But what's he like?"

"He's a really great guy, that's why I want you to meet him. I have a hunch you two might click."

Ayita studied the gray-blue eyes and silver flecked hair in the photo. "He looks old enough to be my father."

"He probably is, but don't let that stand in your way. Forty-six is not exactly ancient. It's just that you're so young." Anne sighed. "I don't think age should be a factor. Once a person becomes an adult, I don't think it matters if the woman is older or younger than the man by dozens of years, and vice versa. I think compatibility, chemistry and... ultimately love, are the primary factors in a good relationship. The rest can be worked out. Anyway, Dad always told me it was better to be an old man's darling than a young man's slave. Personally, I enjoy the comforts of life. I admit I'm spoiled rotten. My husband left me very well fixed. I'll never have to worry about money as long as I live." Anne assessed Ayita, interested to see her response. Ayita seemed deep in thought. "I'll tell you what. I'll throw a dinner party in your honor next Saturday night. Are you free?"

"I'll make sure I am. I'm flattered. That's very generous of you."

"I think it's getting too cool to enjoy a swim. Let's take a rain check on it. Maybe I'll have an indoor swimming pool installed. No...it's too complicated of a renovation."

~~*~~

The days flew by and soon it was Saturday, the night of the dinner party at Anne's. Ayita had mixed emotions about meeting a new man. Strangely, she felt like she was cheating on Valdez, despite her resolve to end it with him.

She took the studio limo so the driver could wait for her and take her home after the party. It gave her a boost of confidence knowing her driver would be waiting outside. She arrived early for the 7:00 dinner.

Anne greeted her and escorted her into a bedroom.

"You can leave your purse and wrap here, if you like."

Ayita followed Anne into the living room. They passed the formal dining room, where a decorative table was set for eight. A cluster of guests arrived. Dalia showed them in.

As Ayita chatted with the other guests, she became aware of the fact that they were all in the music industry in one aspect or another. She was grateful to have something in common with them. Finally, Anne winked at her. She had linked her arm with a tall, distinguished man and brought him toward her. She was certain it was Jerry, because she'd seen photos of him.

Jerry was urbane. She loved the flecks of gray in his hair, and his elegant deportment. She had an instant rapport with him. He was everything her dad wasn't, and nothing like Valdez, either.

By the time dessert was served, Ayita had managed to extract a mini-life story from him. He had been a successful film producer in Buenos Aires. That was where he and Anne had met. He had always wanted to be in the music industry, so he had moved to Nashville. He and Anne resumed their friendship. She had promised to show him around and help him in any way she could and she had gladly done that.

"I have a passion for both country and gospel music," Jerry said. "Dad ran a big studio in B.A., and I took the line of least resistance by going to work for him...but my heart wasn't in it. I longed to get into the music industry. Finally, after Dad passed on, I moved to Nashville to try my luck as a music producer."

"And," he hesitated, "I got a divorce around that time. Amelia, my wife wanted it. She said she was fed up with my "churchy" ways. She wanted to do her own thing. I really didn't have much choice in the matter. We had three children, so the courts made me pay her over a million. No big deal. I wanted my family to be well taken care of."

"I arrived here with about a million, but it doesn't go very far. The first thing I did was buy a lot and contract a house. I plunged into the music scene, immersing myself and finally began signing artists and producing singles and albums."

Jerry programmed Ayita's number into his cell phone and called her the following day, inviting her to lunch. It would be easy to meet up; since they both worked on Music Row, only blocks from either other.

Ayita felt good about meeting Jerry. He filled a void she had not realized even existed. Quickly, they became good friends. Although she still thought of Valdez frequently, and continued praying for him, he faded out when she began a whirlwind courtship with Jerry. His timing had been uncanny.

Jerry wined and dined her. They frequented the best restaurants, and he bought pricey tickets for hot events. Money seemed incidental. He spoiled her, picking her up after rehearsal in a black limousine and whisking her off to a concert, a private party or a chic eatery. Jerry had brought a cook with him from Argentina. She spoiled them with her fabulous South American and Spanish cooking. Her paella and cioppino were among Ayita's favorites.

Jerry became another mentor to Ayita. Like Valdez, he exposed her to the world of the arts. They frequented antique auctions, art gallery openings, fund-raisers, theatre and opera galas, and a few celebrity galas. He educated her on the finer things in life. She was an ace student.

At last it was opening morning of Nashville's new *Breakfast Theatre Show.* Ayita was on cloud nine. Her dressing room was brimming with flowers from Tizzy,

Melvin and his partners, as well as Jerry and the PR group.

Valdez sent a lavish spray of red and peach roses. She was touched he had not forgotten the date she opened and had not given up on her, in spite of her rejection when he'd proposed. It warmed her heart that he went right on caring about her.

Jerry was in Nashville. Valdez was in Washington. As long as Valdez stayed there, she might have a chance of forgetting about him. She was becoming increasingly fond of Jerry, at times even believing she could fall in love with him. Still, if she were to be completely honest, Valdez had stolen her heart a long time ago.

Still, it was futile. She was not about to chuck her career and move back to the small town of Fairhaven, even for him. And if his father did die, and Valdez moved to Nashville, being engaged to an unbeliever was the antithesis of what she was trying to accomplish as a gospel singer. She pushed him out of her mind.

~~*~~

Ayita's single was released the first week of April. It climbed to number one on the charts, surpassing expectations by her producers. Invitations poured in, inviting her to appear on *The Nashville Network Show, Music City Tonight with Lorianne Crook and Charlie Chase,* and with a little push from Tizzy, another appearance on *The Grand Ole Opry.* She was well on her way and finally began shopping for her own apartment. Hotel living was wearing thin.

Apartments in uptown Nashville were expensive and in short supply. Ayita dreamed of the day when she would have her own house like Anne and Jerry. Suzie finally helped her get her driver's license and Melvin leased a new Toyota Camry for her to drive. She felt a new sense of independence.

Jerry continued to do nice, thought things for her. He bought a stunning pink dress she had admired in a shop window and helped her track down apartments that were in good buildings but not too pricey. He was a father figure as well as a friend.

Jerry sometimes worked late, and on those nights, he usually asked his driver to fetch Ayita. He had often told her that he loved it when he came home and found her there. Tonight was Friday and Ayita was weary. *Yippee, it's the weekend, I get to relax.* The driver picked Ayita up at her hotel and drove her to Jerry's home

Maria greeted her in Spanish. "*Buenos noches, senorita.* I'm making a special chicken dish tonight. Have a taste and see what you think." She hovered over a large pot on the kitchen stove.

Ayita entered the familiar bright and airy kitchen. She loved the Mexican terra-cotta tiled floor and the sizable, tropical plants scattered throughout and overflowing onto the patio. Beyond it was a circular pool and spa, with swaying palm trees gracing the yard. Jerry's place had become a second home, and Maria like a second mother to her.

Ayita sampled the chicken cacciatore, which was bathed in a tomato and pepper sauce, then opened one of the French doors leading to the patio. A soft breeze caressed her face. She glanced at the thermometer: *75 degrees. Perfect.* The tourist bureau had been right in touting Nashville as having one of the most desirable climates in the world.

Maria brought her a glass of iced tea and the local

newspaper before joining her on the patio. "Anything interesting?"

"Not so far."

But as Ayita opened the entertainment section, she spotted a huge photo of herself. Farther down the page was a group photo of herself and the other entertainers in the *Breakfast Theatre Show.* She read the article in amazement. It featured *her!* Tizzy and the PR group had done their work well. A stab of guilt sliced through her as she thought about her plan to break the contract with him. The article wouldn't win her any friends at the *Breakfast Theatre Show.* She knew the other singers had been around Nashville a long time, but the press had grabbed onto Ayita as a fast rising star. She was, after all, almost twenty years younger than her co-stars. Tizzy had told her that Nashville thrived on hot, new talent. It was her moment in the sun.

At that instant, Jerry came up quietly from behind and startled her. "I saw the paper. Congratulations!" he said, beaming. After giving her a peck on the cheek, he joined her at the patio table.

Maria poured him a glass of iced tea, topped up Ayita's tea and set the pitcher of tea on the table. "What time would you like dinner?" she asked Jerry.

"Ayita, what time would you like dinner?" Jerry asked.

Ayita grinned. "I'm starving. The sooner, the better."

Maria set the patio table and served the dinner promptly. She had prepared a salad with lots of avocados and tomatoes to go with the chicken.

"Maria, please join us," Jerry entreated. "Don't you dare eat by yourself. We have no secrets from you."

"Thanks, I will." She smiled and created a place setting for herself.

Maria was solid and chunky. Her dancing brown eyes

reflected warmth and intelligence. She was jolly and found a thousand reasons to laugh. Ayita could readily understand why Jerry had become fond of her, treating her more like a sister than an employee.

"We'll have coffee and desert at the dining room table, please, Maria. It's starting to cool off, and it looks like it might rain," Jerry said.

Maria served a rich chocolate pie for dessert, along with demitasse cups of steaming espresso.

They lingered at the table after Maria left to tackle the dishes. Ayita gazed at Jerry's art collection gracing the walls. Ever since she'd spent the better portion of the day at Valdez's house scrutinizing his work, a fascination for art had been triggered.

"Who is the Impressionist?" Ayita asked.

"That's Peggy Hopper, one of my favorite Hawaiian artists. Those are originals, not limited editions. Maria is a collector; those are hers. She worked for a family in Maui ages ago. They lost their fortune and were unable to pay her wages. Instead, they gave her an extensive art collection over time, which, as it happens, is far more valuable than her accumulated salary would have been. In fact, Maria is wealthy because of it."

"She really is a special lady. How long did she work for them without pay?"

"I don't know, exactly. The couple had been married over seventy years and they died within weeks of each other."

"It sounds like Maria has led an interesting life."

"It got better for her after they passed on. They left her their entire estate!"

"Are you serious?"

"Absolutely."

Ayita frowned, puzzled. "Then why does she work?"

"She loves it. It's her life. It's all she knows."

"Was she ever married?"

"I don't know for sure, but I don't think so. She's very private. She was working for some affluent people in Buenos Aires when her daughter was murdered. After that happened, she wanted to leave the country. She worked for my mother for a short time. I begged Mom to let her come to America with me. She finally relented. So you see, we share a little history. Well, do you want to watch a movie or listen to some fine music?" Jerry asked.

"You keep promising to show me the movie you produced. Can we see it now?" Ayita asked.

He grinned. "Sure, why not?"

They moved into the elegant dining room. Once again Ayita admired the luxurious decor, from gleaming, white marble floors, French gold-gilded ornate mirrors and white custom-built sofas.

A smattering of Palm Fronds lent grace and charm to the room. *Someday I'm going to have a beautiful home.* Jerry swore by his decorator. Maybe she would hire him to decorate her new apartment when she found it.

The white plantation shutters were open. She peered outside at the lavishly landscaped gardens interspersed with tall Grecian sculptures and water fountains with cherubs. She loved relaxing at his place.

The "Made-for-TV film was a simple but touching tale of a young female polo player who had a tragic fall, crippling her, but through her profound faith in the miraculous and her indomitable spirit, she is healed and able to ride and resume playing Polo.

"What did you think of the film?" Jerry asked, when it was over.

"Amazing story! I loved it."

"It was based on a true story. That young gal apparently used to pray around the clock. One day she was healed and actually played Polo again. Isn't that something?"

"You'd never know that you heart wasn't in making films," Ayita said.

"I had a lot of help. Mother co-produced it and was executive producer. A couple of other producers were involved also."

She was touched by his honesty. It was decent of him to share credit with his mother and others. She felt strangely proud of him when the titles rolled. She wondered, fleetingly, what it would be like to be his wife. They had never made love; she was still a virgin and she planned to remain that way until her wedding night. That certainly didn't mean she was unaware of his sexuality, as well as her own. He was a good man and as time went on, she appreciated him increasingly. He never spoke of a future for them, but she was sure it would come in time.

However, something about him made her feel that he was withholding secrets from her...perhaps information that could enlighten her about him.

She sighed. "I'll need to go home soon."

"Let me guess. You have an early rehearsal."

She nodded in agreement. They had driven a short distance when Jerry asked her for another date. "I know it's short notice, but my tennis club is having a barbecue tomorrow night. I wondered if you'd care to join me?

"I'd love to," she said without hesitation "I'd like to learn tennis."

"It would be my privilege to teach you. Better yet, I'll pay for tennis lessons, and you can work with the pro at the club. Then we can rally together. You'll progress faster that way."

It was one of those charmed evenings, when Ayita felt kissed by the stars. Jerry gave her a peck on the cheek at her door. She stepped into her suite, glowing from a great day and a terrific evening.

Tizzy phoned her at 9:00 a.m. sharp. He had an offer for her to appear on *Grand Ole Opry* again. The publicity had worked. She had created a buzz around town.

Ayita leaped at the chance to appear on the show again. Tizzy managed to negotiate a substantial raise from her last appearance. They needed her to guest on the Saturday show, only three days away. She would be filling in for Shania Twain, who had taken ill. Her mirror told her she resembled Shania, but she never copied anyone. She was unique and she liked it that way.

She rehearsed intensely, as always, and finally, the big night arrived where she'd be performing at the *Grand Ole Opry* in front of a live audience. The limousine driver drove her to the theatre. The stage manager showed her to her dressing room and minutes later, the makeup artist arrived. The make-up artist had lots of tricks up her sleeve, because the show would be filmed as well. "Technically, two different types of make-up need to be merged to encompass both mediums. But I have my ways of getting around it," Tally, the seasoned brunette make-up artist, said, as she set to work on Ayita's face. The hairdresser performed miracles with her hair, and finally, the dresser helped her into her custom-made costume. She was grateful Tizzy had stayed away this time. He had gotten the message that she liked solitude before she performed.

Porter Wagoner was hosting the show. He introduced her as a talented newcomer. She beamed as she walked onto the stage, confident, but with a touch of nerves. She was certain her royal-blue lame' gown was a knockout. Ayita was rested, in good voice and ready to rock.

As Porter introduced her, the audience applauded enthusiastically.

"Well, little lady, what are you going to sing today?"

She drew a blank. She couldn't believe it. She hadn't realized how nervous she was. Vacantly, she gazed at his glittery, gold-and-white costume and forced herself to remain calm as she sent up a silent prayer.

Porter, to his credit, smiled encouragingly at her while chatting about her new single. Her confidence gradually returned. Then, mercifully, the title flashed into her mind. " 'We Shall Behold Him,' " she said, smiling weakly at him.

"Ah, the Dottie Rambo song made famous by Sandi Patty. Great choice."

Fortunately, the ragged edge of nervousness flew from her like a flock of geese flying south in the winter, the moment she began singing. The long months of grueling rehearsals had paid off. Her voice soared to a new plateau, hitting the high notes with ease and sustaining them as she sang in praise to the Lord. Ayita and the music became as one. Never had she been more attuned to the Creator than at this moment.

After the show, she relaxed in her dressing room, sipping Perrier water. Someone had put four bunches of flowers in vases in her dressing room. The stage manager, no doubt. She read the cards. To her utter amazement, the first card she picked up was from Valdez. How had he known she was performing here today? The others were from Tizzy, Jerry and Melvin-predictably. A stab of guilt sliced through her. She hadn't even called him to find out how his Dad was. The flowers were an ice-breaker. They could be friends, maybe.

Whatever reservations she had about Tizzy, she respected the fact that he was usually where he was supposed to be. She heard a knock on the door and figured it would be him. It was. He was grinning from ear to ear. He had been in the audience.

"I'm proud of you, Kid. You're really something!"

Pangs of shame swept over her as she thought about how she was trying to unload him. In fact, she had an appointment to stop in at the law firm for an update. Tizzy was thrilled for her, that much was apparent. Maybe he wasn't such a bad person, after all.

"Star material, Kid." Tizzy grinned. "How about letting me take you for dinner?"

He had her on a pedestal, and she felt somewhat uncomfortable because of it. She missed Jerry tonight, but he had told her that one of the artists he'd signed was opening a new show at Chaffin's Barn tonight, and he was obligated to go there and take the artist for dinner after the show and socialize with some of the cast. She wondered, fleetingly, why he hadn't sent his driver for her to join them. Why hadn't she been invited to join them after the show? She reminded herself that they weren't married. Jerry didn't owe her anything. Get over it.

"Actually, I'd like to head home and unwind. Maybe we could order some pizza."

"Sounds good. Am I invited?"

"Of course."

"Are you sure I can't talk you into dining at the Wildhorse Saloon?" Tizzy pleaded. "A lot of entertainers will be there-you never know who you might meet."

Ayita considered it for a nanosecond. No, she was spent emotionally by all the pressure she'd been under lately. She needed to kick back in her apartment. Ayita was an intensely private person. It was Tizzy's business to mix and mingle with celebrities, but it wasn't her thing. She much preferred the quiet relaxation found with close friends after a performance.

It would have been fun to share the success with her new friend, Anne, but since she was performing in a concert with other artists at the Starwood Amphitheatre, they had agreed not to connect socially after their respective performances. Both valued their privacy and shared the need to relax after a show in the comfort of their own homes-perhaps with a close friend or two.

The intense pressure of performing had various effects on people. Ayita knew she was a bit odd, because other artists her age often partied into the wee hours after a gig. Most of the time, lately, Ayita wanted to be alone to thank the Lord, instead of celebrating with friends, because she was so grateful for all that he had given her.

The chauffeur whisked Ayita to her apartment. Tizzy drove his own car and met her there.

The pizza tasted great. As she took the first bite, Ayita realized she was starved. Tizzy bade her good night shortly after they finished the piping-hot pizza.

Ayita put on a CD with one of her favorite opera stars-Renee Fleming. While taking off her make-up, she reflected on past events. Ever since the angel had intervened in her life, events had fallen naturally into place. Meeting Jerry had been the icing on the cake. Hanging out with him helped ease her mixed emotions where Valdez was concerned. Some days, she wondered what it would be like being married to Jerry. She wanted kids though, and she knew Jerry didn't. His two sons were grown, and he'd had enough of raising kids. He wanted to be carefree now and just enjoy life. His ex-wife had been very difficult and demanding and had brought up willful children. He had often told her how much he appreciated the fact that she made no demands on him.

Ayita desired a real home with a hubby and kids- maybe partly because she'd never really had one. Though Valdez was her first choice, she had humbly told the Lord that she would honor Him no matter what the cost-and she would only marry a believer. She would stand firm on the Word of God, no matter what went down. *"Lean not unto thine own understanding, in all thy ways acknowledge him and he shall direct your paths."*

She recalled a story from a guest on a Christian Talk Show who revealed a marriage of an unequally yoked couple, and the horrendous sorrows that had ensued from attempting to build a life with a husband who did not share the same beliefs. She decided she was better off focusing her energy on her relationship with Jerry, even if he wasn't her first choice in potential hubby. There were some inherent problems, but there would be issues and challenges in any relationship.

Ayita caught herself again. *We're only good friends. Jerry has never talked about us having a future together, and I'm nowhere near ready to take the plunge, anyway.*

Exhausted, she crawled into bed. The moment her head hit the pillow she fell sound asleep.

11

Ayita's single was flying off the shelves. It had quickly risen to the top and was holding there. The PR campaign had worked and her local appearances on *Grand Ole Opry* and *The Breakfast Show* had given her continued visibility and popularity. She was in fact, the fastest rising, new recording artist in Nashville, according to research Tizzy had done. He continued to receive requests for personal appearances as well as TV talk shows and radio shows.

She reimbursed her producers for her living expenses and settled her account with her accompanist. She paid Tizzy back for the wardrobe, settled her expenses and still had enough cash left to purchase a white baby grand and start a savings account.

The more successful she became, the larger her vision for her future became. Lately, she'd dreamed even more of owning an estate like her good friend, Anne. She wanted a swimming pool and tennis court as well as a gym, maid's quarters, rehearsal room and a few acres so she could ride horses. Southern plantation homes like Anne's were popular in Nashville. Ayita was grateful for her modest suite, but she knew God had greater blessings in store for her. She also knew she needed to be faithful to Him, in order to tap into His blessings. She diligently tithed from every dollar she earned.

She was unclear about the amount of money she would make from her two singles and needed Tizzy to explain to her how much money she could reasonably expect to earn in the next few years. She could not possibly consider buying a home without knowing that. She was starting to form a vivid picture of her goals. She even had a bulletin board tacked to the wall in her dressing room displaying a picture of her dream home-a colonial mansion on acreage.

The three primary men in her life were all positive thinkers, and they all encouraged her to think big, reminding her that everything begins with a dream, long before it becomes a reality. Jerry helped her locate a spiffy, two-bedroom penthouse in a good, slighter older low-rise. Her suite was on the eighth floor of the well-maintained building.

She loved the roof garden. The former tenant had left masses of mammoth clay pots filled with palm varieties. She could hardly wait to dine on the roof garden, while savoring the sweeping vista of Nashville. The apartment manager lived on-site and although her appearance was sloppy and she seemed worn out, Ayita had a hunch Lilly was a conscientious manager.

"The rent is two thousand, five hundred. I need first and last. The deposit goes into an interest-bearing account and you get it back when you leave, provided there's no damage. You're lucky you saw the sign on the lawn. It hits the papers tomorrow and prospective tenants will be ringing my phone off the hook."

"I'll take it," Ayita said, "And since it's vacant, I'd like to move in right away-tomorrow, if possible."

"Normally it takes a few days to run a credit check and check you out, but I know who you are-saw you on *Grand Ole Opry* the other night. You're quite the singer. We'd be thrilled to have you in the building."

"Thank-you. What do you need from me?" Ayita asked.

"Come on down to my office and I'll have you fill out the application form. Then we'll take care of the money so I can give you the keys."

The threesome rode the elevator down to the manger's

corner, ground suite. Her grubby, off-white poodle barked and jumped onto her lap while she tried to finish the paperwork. Ayita and Jerry ignored the negatives. She really needed her own little net that she could settle into. Her new baby grand would look marvelous in the penthouse

~~*~~

The following morning, Ayita stood among her suitcases and boxes at the hotel. Jerry had arranged to have his chauffeur pick up a few of her basic clothing and personal effects from the hotel and deliver them to the penthouse, so she'd have some items available there for her comfort. The rest would be delivered once the penthouse had been painted. Jerry and Ayita spent the rest of the day selecting a mattress and frame, as well as the rest of the basics to set up housekeeping. All the items, as well as her piano delivery from Nashville Pianos and Organs, were scheduled for delivery right after the paint in the apartment would be dry.

It was nice to be a local celebrity. Everyone assumed she was very busy and gave her stellar service. She handed out a lot of free singles for goodwill, since everyone had recognized her and treated her like the celebrity she was fast becoming. Ayita ordered the apartment painted in pale yellow because she planned to furnish the entire penthouse in white, using lots of mirrors and palm varieties, with the white baby grand as the focal point.

Next on her agenda, she and Jerry would hound estate sales to find good paintings and accent pieces to transform the penthouse into the picture of elegance. She set herself a goal: in one month, she would have the penthouse decorated. If she and Jerry worked at it every spare minute, it would happen. She had a little time off before she started rehearsing for her first USA tour, which was scheduled to begin in April of next year. *Yeah, she would have a home to come back to when it was over!*

Jerry knew how to get things done. At 6:00 in the morning, the day after Ayita took possession of the penthouse, the painters were on the job.

"Good-morning, Ma'am. I am Santos; this is my assistant, Carlos. Maybe I paint a sample on the wall to see if you like the color?"

"No, thanks, Santos. My decorator selected the colors. I'll go with her judgement." Clutching a large Starbucks coffee, Ayita glanced at the open can of paint, barely awake. "Go ahead and get started. The furniture will be here on Friday. Two days will do it?"

"We work a twelve-hour day, Ma'am. It will be finished and dry before then," Santos said.

"I'll stop by at lunch time and see how it's going," Ayita said, as she strode to the elevator. She'd met them and given them access to the suite. Now she would turn the situation over to the building manager, who had promised to keep an eye on them. She could tell that Lily was very protective of the building and its security. That was a bonus."

Ayita drove back to her hotel suite. Once there, she scrambled two eggs and ate a piece of rye toast with marmalade. She packed the few remaining items, adding them to the suitcases and boxes sitting by the front door. She would miss some of the musicians she'd met at the hotel, but she was thrilled to be finally moving into her own place. Gathering up the rest of her music in a few shopping bags, she put them in her car with the sundry items. She would drop them off at her new apartment during her lunch hour when she checked on the painters.

As she drove to the rehearsal studios, she thought about Valdez. Would he like her new apartment? Would he ever see it? Would she ever see him again? She hated to admit it, but she missed him terribly.

She wondered vaguely if touring would be lonely. Tizzy had told her that road tours were the fastest way to build an audience for her music. He'd set up a four-month bus tour, covering most of the states, except for New York City. He was saving that city for the last, and she would fly there. He was already working on a European tour. Ayita was on cloud nine!

Ayita's new home had come together quickly with the help of Jerry's decorator. A month to the day she'd moved in, she celebrated the milestone with Jerry in the new penthouse. It was even better than she had envisioned.

On Saturdays, when Ayita wasn't expected to rehearse, she worked with private coaches. She hired Olita to teach her piano and the famed Madame Carlotta to drill her on reading music. Madame had an operatic background and was a great disciplinarian. Ayita enjoyed just being around her. She knew that if she hung around with enough great people, she would rise to meet their level. Her natural ear and bent toward music made it easy for her to learn. But Ayita knew it was her total commitment and God's favor, as well as her gift, that caused her to soar faster and higher than she'd ever dreamed possible.

She immersed herself in all aspects of music. Her life consisted of Bible reading, prayer, church and her music. She saw Jerry once or twice a week-mostly for dinner.

Through hard work and determination, she learned to accompany herself on the piano when she sang. Reading music was speeding up the learning process and giving her more confidence. Her life was full and rich

Yet there were two thorns in her side. Her mother and Valdez. She wished with all her heart she could do something about both of them, but she knew only God could draw them to Him. She reminded herself she had to pray earnestly and then leave the results with Him.

Occasionally, Ayita played tennis with Jerry or took a lesson at his club. Her passion for music and learning began to fill her life to such an extent that she did not want to see Jerry as often as she had in the past.

Valdez suddenly started sending a dozen red roses to the studio daily. He always signed the card" *Love, Valdez.* It warmed her heart that he cared enough to pursue her. It felt as though he were personally greeting her every morning.

Ayita's calendar was now full of events. There were several First Night Invitations: one to the opening of a dinner theatre show, as well as private parties and investment seminars, to name a few. She would soon need a social secretary.

Sales of her two singles were brisk, and subsequently the demand for personal appearances increased substantially. Her manager had received invitations asking her to perform at charity events and to be part of a celebrity concert. Everything was happening so fast her head spun at times.

~~*~~

It was March fourth, the day Ayita turned twenty. As she awakened in her new apartment, the cell phone rang. She picked it up and heard the husky voice of Valdez singing "Happy Birthday" to her.

Overwhelmed, Ayita finally found her voice. "How did you remember my birthday?"

"I remember everything about you, my darling. When will I see you?"

"I don't know," she hedged. *Oh, if only he shared her spiritual beliefs.*

"Have a wonderful day, beautiful."

Minutes later, three dozen red roses arrived. As she opened the envelope, she found a gift card for $5,000. for Christine's a local jeweler. *The diamond cross we looked at together! He remembered!* The thoughtful, generous gesture touched her deeply.

After rehearsal, jerry's limo driver picked her up and whisked her to his place for a celebration dinner.

"Hey gorgeous," Jerry said, giving her a hug when she arrived.

Ayita was radiant. He surprised her with a five-course dinner, serving it to her in the dining room. Maria joined them for dessert. She'd whipped up a delectable chocolate cheesecake. Jerry warbled a pathetic version of "Happy Birthday," with Maria joining in.

After dinner, Jerry handed her a beautifully wrapped gift. She opened it to discover a bronze sculpture of a young woman playing a grand piano. It was exquisite, and she would cherish it always. She thanked him profusely for the thoughtful gift. "Mind if I play some of the music I've been working on?"

"Be my guest. That's why the piano is here. I wish I could play it."

Ayita played on Jerry's gleaming black baby grand, accompanying herself as she sang for the better part of an hour.

As she rose from the bench, Jerry put his arms around

her and drew her close to him. He whispered in her ear. "I'm crazy about you, Ayita." He stroked her ear and nibbled on her neck teasingly. "I think I'm falling in love with you, Ayita."

Then he kissed her fervently.

"I'm very fond of you," Ayita said, gently pulling back from him. She felt appreciated but conflicted, because even though she had some feeling for Jerry, in no way did it compare with the burning passion she harbored for Valdez. She ached for *his* arms around her and missed him terribly.

Then, in an instant later, she gave herself a reality check. She could count on Jerry. He was solid, mature, affluent and most importantly, he was a believer. Surely, Valdez would fade from her memory in due course. But when would it happen? Next month would be the eighth month she had dated Jerry. It was time to get engaged or move on. Even though she wasn't quite ready to take the plunge with him, she wanted to know if that was an option. Her mother had been married at sixteen, and Ayita was now twenty. Her music career was on the fast track, but she saw no reason to let her personal life lag behind. She made a decision: She would confront Jerry tonight, so she could line up her options.

"Why don't we get married?" She just threw the idea out there.

A shocked expression clouded Jerry's sculpted face. Dead silence followed. Finally, after several minutes had lapsed, he walked over to his favorite leather chair and plunked himself down, but still said nothing.

"I guess I'm thinking I don't want to waste time. I really need to know if there's a future in this relationship, before I get more deeply involved."

"Look...Ayita...I don't want to get into this right now.

It's your birthday-let's just enjoy it. I don't want to taint it with my personal problems."

"What personal problems?" Ayita snapped back. She quickly regretted pressing him. Common sense dictated that she back off, because he was obviously uncomfortable with the issue. But now the fiery, tenacious side of her rose to the forefront. She wanted to find out the underlying cause of his hesitation. She decided to pressure him until she got some answers. Surely she deserved that, after spending almost eight months with him.

"I'll drive you home," Jerry said.

She knew he was very upset, but she had no idea why. Why couldn't he share whatever was bothering him?

Three days went by without a word from Jerry. What was going on? Finally, she phoned him and invited him over for dinner. He accepted the invitation. He turned up at her penthouse with a large bouquet of flowers and a couple of tins of Russian caviar. He was excited about grooming his new find.

"I think you'll be impressed with my new artist. She calls herself Dona Babe. She's a striking redhead. I really think I've got a winning ticket with her. I'll leave you one of her CD's. Let me know what you think."

Jerry was in a chatty moot, complimenting her on the vast strides she had made in her tennis games, confirming dates with her for charity events they would attend together.

Ayita served Jerry his favorite dinner- roast beef, Yorkshire pudding, mashed potatoes and candied yams. She was working up her courage to confront him. She needed to find out what was going on, and she was determined to bring up the subject of marriage again.

"Coffee?" Ayita asked.

"Yes, thank-you."

Ayita set the coffee down on the table. "I left the drapes open, so we can enjoy the night lights of Nashville. Isn't the view up here fabulous?"

"It's a great spot, Ayita. You'll enjoy living here."

Ayita put on a CD of Beethoven and moved next to Jerry on her new white sofa. He smelled fresh with a scent of masculine cologne.

He stroked her hair sensuously. "You're something really special, Ayita. I'm so lucky to have you in my life." He held her close to him.

She refused to allow him to deter her. "So you love me, but I'm not good enough to marry you, is that it? Is it because of my mother, or my lack of formal education? She waited for a response, and not getting one, she continued. "Well, which is it?"

Jerry pulled away from the embrace and strode toward the sliding glass doors and the spectacular view. His back was to her. She waited.

"All right, Ayita, you deserve the truth. But I'm warning you, you won't like it." He turned toward her.

Her heart seemed to stop beating for a moment. "What is it? What's wrong?"

"As you know, my mother lives in Buenos Aires. She is Catholic, as is the rest of my family. That is, everyone except me. This may come as a surprise to you, but I feel the time has come for me to tell you more about myself. Besides, you won't let me off the hook, so I don't have much choice in the matter, do I? The money I have isn't all from my own efforts. My father made a ton of money. He hoarded away mountains of cash in a Swiss numbered bank account. Most of the money he earned came from producing some important films." Jerry shuffled his feet, his eyes darting around the room.

It was obvious he was not comfortable sharing this private information. Nevertheless, he continued. "When Dad died, Mom became executor of his estate. She had always been more astute at handling money than either my adopted brother or me. Mother was the catalyst, driving Dad forward. He became a successful producer through no small efforts on her part. It was her money, and frankly, her business acumen, as well. There is nothing that woman cannot do. She is really quite brilliant...an amazing woman."

"When I first immigrated to the States, it was with the stipulation that I employ a minimum of six people. I set up a recording studio and hired six people to help me run it. But because I was a novice record producer, I made a lot of costly mistakes and racked up some debt. For starters, a manager here in Nashville coaxed me to sign a couple of rising artists. Unfortunately, they both bombed. They were a husband-and-wife team, great singers with a lot of promise. What I didn't know, until it was too late, was that they were Coke heads. They didn't show up half the time. To put it bluntly, I lost a bundle."

Ayita sat stunned, listening intently as he continued.

"This all happened about four years ago. I was so heavily in debt at that time that I declared bankruptcy. I planned to return to Buenos Aires to run the film studio Mom owned. Well, my dear mother stepped into the picture and insisted she loan me three million. She wanted me to live my dream. She said the studio was churning out good pictures, and she was happy with the people she'd hired to help her produce the films."

"She really *does* sound like an amazing woman," Ayita murmured.

"You better believe it. She still gets up at the crack of

dawn and runs everything. She's the mastermind behind the studio our family owns. Because of the money and Mom's belief in me, I made a comeback and started to run a pretty solid business, producing albums and singles with hand-picked talent. I've managed to turn things around."

"Yeah-so what's the catch?"

"There are strings attached to the money."

"What exactly do you mean?"

"Mother asked me to promise not to remarry in the States-and not to remain here permanently."

"Have your fun, but come back to Mama?" She scowled at him.

Jerry blushed. "It's not quite like that. Mother's health has been failing in the last few years, and she longs to spend more time with me. Frankly, I want that, too. I don't know how long I have her for, and I love her deeply."

"When are you going back?"

"Mother asked me to return within ten years...three years from now. She wanted us to enjoy her money together. You know...take cruises and travel around the world. She's young at heart...in fact she's only seventeen years older than I am. In Argentina, girls marry young and have their babies while they're young. Mom wanted a large family but was unable to have more children. My parents adopted a boy, but Mom and my half-brother, Donald, never got along."

Ayita was crushed and upset. She just let him ramble on. For a moment, she felt like hurtling pots and pans at his head and kicking him out, but she thought better of it and remained silent, waiting to hear the rest of his story.

"You see, Ayita, I love Mother with all my heart. She had always been more like a sister than a mother to me. I cannot betray her, nor can I let her down. The only reason she was not heart-broken when I left is because I promised I would return. She wanted me to realize my dream in America and then return to my roots."

"If you have felt my distance lately, and I think you have, it's because it is soon time for me to honor my promise. Recently, I have learned that Mother has cancer. She is gravely ill. I must return...alone...to Buenos Aires. I must fulfill my obligation as her oldest son and honor her and live up to the deal I struck with her. Otherwise, how can I expect God to bless me?"

Tears glistened in Ayita's eyes, and then she started to sob uncontrollably. Her biggest security blanket had just been ripped away, leaving her trembling, cold and alone.

Jerry pulled Ayita closer, wiping away her tears with his kisses. "My darling, I'm so very sorry. Please try to understand. These complications in my life do not change the way I feel about you. I love you, my dearest Ayita, and I always will."

She was inconsolable. "You mean... that we can *never* get married?" she asked, hiccupping in between sobs.

"I don't see how we could...certainly not in the near future. I must visit Mother and spend time with her before it's too late." Jerry took both her hands in his, and then he kissed her tenderly, soon pulling apart. "Maybe we will find a way to work something out, when I return," he said

Sobbing, in a broken voice, Ayita said, "Forgive me, Jerry...but if she dies, then we're free to marry, is that the deal?"

To her utter amazement, he shook his head. "No, I'm afraid not. I was married once and Mother wants me to adhere to the rules of the Catholic Church which forbids divorce. I must remain married to my wife or be reconciled to her. I am divorced, as you know, but in order to honor

Mother and the church, I am not at liberty to take a new wife."

She was angry and hurt. "Why didn't you tell me all this sooner? Besides, Jesus forgives all sin except blasphemy, so adhering to the rules of the Catholic Church doesn't necessarily honor God. And as long as we're on this subject, I must tell you that no one has the right to forgive sins except God. The fact that priests have the unmitigated gall to stand there and play God and forgive people their sins is outrageous! Only Jesus Christ, who paid the penalty on the cross, by dying a savage death, can forgive sins...no man or priest can do this."

He searched her face, his eyes gentle and filled with understanding and love. She was sitting on his lap, her arms around his neck. He dabbed at her tears with soft kisses. "Can you ever forgive me? I've been in love with you since I first laid eyes on you. I was selfish. I was afraid I'd lose you if I told you the truth. I knew it would come out sooner or later... but I wanted to spent time with you for as long as I possibly could."

"But surely you want more out of this relationship than just friendship."

She had stopped crying and was trying hard to be rational. She remembered the times recently when it had been awkward for her to hold him at bay, when he had pleaded with her to let him make love to her. Yes, he wanted her as much or more than she wanted him.

"Take me with you to Buenos Aires."

He sighed. "I'd love to, darling...but you know I can't."

"So, I'm history. Abandoned. Just like that! She snapped her fingers for emphasis. "It's my childhood, all over again."

Ayita jumped up from the sofa and strode over to the windows to gaze at the city's twinkling, majestic array of evening lights. After a minute, she looked back toward Jerry. He hadn't moved from his spot on the sofa. She was astonished to see tears trickling down his cheeks. The dilemma was affecting him the same way it affected her. He really *did* care. *SO he does truly love me, but to what avail?*

She waited until his tears stopped and then mustered up all her courage. "Please leave, Jerry. I need to be alone."

With a mournful face and no further words he heeded her wishes.

Ayita hurried into her bedroom, throwing herself across her bed and letting out a guttural wail. "How could you do this to me?" she cried.

After she had exhausted herself from crying, she slept fitfully.

The next day, she felt awful. Her life seemed surreal. Everything had been so perfect, so wonderful. Her career was thriving, and Jerry had been her best friend, bringing new joy and possibilities into her life. But possibilities of a future with him didn't exist. Bitter tears threatened to fall, but she wouldn't let them. If God closed one door, He would open another. In some ways, it was blessing, at least she knew where she stood. Maybe this is what the scripture *"The Lord giveth and the Lord taketh away, praise be the name of the Lord,"* meant.

That night as she prayed and read her Bible, she felt the Lord nudging her. *Deep in her heart, she didn't really want him! It was Valdez, and Valdez alone, that had stolen her heart. It hit her then, that Jerry had been merely an emotional crutch. Someone she thought she could count on.*

She dried her tears and since she didn't feel tired, she

headed for the piano. She always received solace from playing it. Of course, she hadn't mastered it yet, that would take years, but she played some songs by ear and it gave her great joy and solace.

She couldn't concentrate, and kept striking wrong notes. She began mindlessly playing around on the piano. A song began to emerge. She was creating a tune! Excitement soared within her. She had never given any thought to the possibility of *writing music.* She began to play...slowly, deliberately, tapping into her inspiration. Soon, she was astonished as a song began unfolding, a song breathed from the Lord himself.

Soon she had composed her first song, complete with lyrics. Quickly, she depressed the record button on her CD player. She wanted to play it through again immediately in case she forgot some part of it. She played around with some minor changes of the lyrics, leaving the melody intact. Time stood still. The music and she became one.

Ayita played it straight through a second time, recording it as well, and then played it back. She could hardly believe her accomplishment. She thanked God for this new and amazing gift. He had surprised her by inspiring her to create original music at a time when everything seemed black. God's love was so much greater than all the world had to offer.

A title popped into her mind and she went with it. *Agape Love.* She sat on the piano bench in awe. She had just written her first ever gospel song. She knew what she had to do. She would love Jerry with agape love. If that was the way it had to be, then so be it. If God in His wisdom had allowed her to form a relationship with Jerry, then it was up to her to figure out what that relationship should be.

Perhaps he really *was* too old for her. Was she

subconsciously seeking a father image? Would she outgrow the connectedness she felt with Jerry as she became more secure and moved further up the ladder of success? It didn't take a rocket scientist to figure out that a natural gap in her life without a solid father image would tend to make her gravitate toward older men.

She played the song again, listening to it with her trained ear. She made a few minor changes with the lyrics and then sang with the recorder a couple more times, thrilled anew by this new gift that had been unearthed. She did it one last time, this time moving into full performance mode. As she performed, she imagined herself in front of a vast audience. In fact, she would add the song to her repertoire for her upcoming tour. It was an exciting breakthrough, and for a moment, she could hardly wait to share her new discovery with one of her friends. But whom? Anne? Jerry? Valdez?

The more she mulled it over, the more she realized she wanted to keep it a secret for now. It was a treasured and amazing gift that she wanted to cherish before sharing with anyone. She sat down at the piano with the thought of creating another song, but after a few false starts, scrapped the idea. She spent the next couple of hours rehearsing various songs and reviewing last week's piano lesson, in preparation for her teacher who would be arriving at 11:00 a.m.

The ring of the phone startled her out of her deep concentration. She picked it up from its resting place on the baby grand. "Good morning," Ayita said cheerily.

"You sound chipper this morning," Jerry said. "Are you on some unknown drug?"

"Meditation on the Word and inspiration from above."

"Good for you."

"I wrote a song about us. The words...and melody just erupted somehow."

"You did?" Jerry sounded pleased and flattered.

"God gave me a beautiful song-a composition. You see, I wrote about us. I think our future is as friends- Agape love. I felt God was showing me that.

A pause ensued before he spoke. "I don't know. Perhaps in time. I can only tell you that what I feel for you is far more powerful than friendship. It's a deeper love than I've felt for anyone in my life. And...I'm sure you have romantic feelings for me, don't you?"

For the flicker of an instant she wanted to say "Except for your mother?" But she wouldn't. She sensed the words came from somewhere deep inside him, and his sharing of that private part of himself touched her profoundly. Yet her frustration with him rapidly returned. "Yet you are perfectly willing to throw away what we have? You are unwilling to fight for us?"

What existed in theory was often different in reality. Wasn't *he* supposed to be more mature than *she* was? Shouldn't *he* have a hand in figuring out where the relationship could go also? Tears clouded her eyes again. It was difficult to turn off the deep feelings she had for him, as though it were a tap, but she knew she had to.

"I'm on my way over," Jerry said. "Let me take you to an early lunch."

"Sure." The words popped out of her mouth before she knew it.

The moment Ayita opened the door, waves of joy flooded over her like a warm ocean-caressing her, lapping up against sunny shores.

~~*~~

Jerry gathered Ayita into his arms and held her tight. No words were needed. He wanted her...God only knew how much. But could he break the pact he had made with his mother? Should he? And dare he defy the rules of his mother's beloved Catholic church?

True, he was a Protestant now-a Baptist-but in his heart he believed what had been ingrained in him as young boy. Were the rules he grew up with more powerful that the forgiveness of God Almighty? Was he not entitled to a second chance at happiness?

Wasn't that what the cross was all about? "There is therefore now no condemnation to them who are in Christ Jesus." Didn't that mean that God would forgive the sin of divorce, just as He would forgive the sin of stealing or lying or breaking any of the other commandments? Why was this commandment isolated? He certainly had not thrown away the wife of his youth. She had insisted on the divorce.

Jerry held Ayita close to him for a few precious minutes. He had been over this scenario a thousand times in his mind. "Get dressed, gorgeous. I'm taking you somewhere nice. The jeans won't be appropriate."

Jerry looked at her full in the face this time, and what he saw broke his heart. She reminded him of a little kitten-vulnerable and trusting. She was delicately sweet, and her face held a faint blush some women get when they gaze upon their beloved.

"I'll just be a minute," Ayita vanished into her bedroom.

Jerry was not a musician, but the piano was the focal point of her living room. He walked over to it now, as though it knew something he didn't. He sat on the bench and plunked a few keys, wishing he had the talent to play.

Sunshine played throughout the penthouse. Fresh evidence of God's love and majesty. Would it be possible to make her his bride? He wanted that with all his heart.

Ayita returned minutes later, beautifully turned out in an exquisite dress.

Jerry gazed at her with approval She was beautiful even without a trace of makeup. Her olive complexion was flawless. Her tilted black eyes shone like shimmering lamé, perfectly contrasting with the white frock she wore. A sparkling diamond cross adorned her neck. She was breathtaking. Her jubilant personality filled the room as she walked toward him and the gleaming, white baby grand.

"Off," she teased, pushing him off the bench playfully. Sitting on the bench, she poised her fingers on the keyboard. She concentrated for a few moments before beginning. Then the fingers began, slowly at first, then more intensely, as the music dictated.

The world stopped.

She performed admirably, considering she had only recently taken up the piano. The rich, beautiful voice glided over the music. The words were easy and natural, inspired by God. Jerry was mesmerized. When she had finished her performance, she stood, giving him a full, theatrical bow to reward his enthusiastic clapping.

"You're really something," he said, taking her in his arms. "If only you weren't already under contract, you could record for my label. Well, maybe someday." He sighed. "You have a galactic career in front of you. You've sure made rapid strides since hitting this town."

"You're making me blush."

"You look very pretty when you blush."

"Tut,tut,tut...agape love," she teased.

How could she be so light-hearted with him? Again he admired her strength. Jerry believed in destiny. *God, if You want us to spend our lives together, You'll find a way to do it.*

He took Ayita to the best restaurant in Nashville that he could think of: Mario's Brasserie. They ordered eggs Benedict, Caesar salads with coffee and virgin Caesars. They joked during lunch, dispelling the heaviness of last night's conversation. When the server recommended the strawberry cheesecake for dessert and assured them it was delicious, they agreed to split one.

Ayita took a couple of bites. "Now that's delicious." In between bites, she asked, "When do you leave for B.A.?"

"I should go as soon as I can arrange my ticket. I'll see a travel agent right after I drop you back at your apartment."

"I see." The sadness he saw in her eyes was nearly his undoing. "I'll miss you very much," she said in a tiny voice he barely recognized.

"Me, too."

~~*~~

Jerry drove Ayita back to her penthouse in silence, yet she sensed a new level of commitment between them. Was it a deepening of their friendship? Her future was in God's providential hands. She would learn to accept that her future with Jerry was to be friendship.

Agape love.

As soon as Jerry left, her cell chirped. "Hi, this Jeanne. I need you to come out to Boot Country as soon as you can."

"I'm leaving right now."

12

Jerry phoned frequently from Buenos Aires proclaiming his love for her. She concentrated on the music in the daytime, meeting with her manager to discuss her upcoming album, tour and promo campaign.

Valdez phoned early one morning. "I'm in Nashville. Any chance you're free for dinner tonight?"

Ayita was barely awake. His call was total surprise. "I would like to see you, Valdez...but..."

"Please say yes, Ayita. I need to talk to you. So much has happened. Dad died.

She needed a cup of coffee badly, but his words got through. "Oh, Valdez, I'm so sorry. Yes, of course I'll see you."

"You better give me your new address. You've moved from the hotel, right?"

"Yes, it's 2020 Monterey Lane, Penthouse three. Six o'clock tonight?"

Ayita had trouble concentrating on her music at rehearsal. The day seemed to drag by. Finally, she left the studio around 3:00 and drove home early. She ran a bath, turned on some opera music and soaked in the tub. She slipped into a robe and relaxed, puttering around the kitchen. Maybe she could at least be friends with Valdez. He was nice man, after all.

At 5:00 she had finished her hair and make-up. She was ready except for choosing what she would wear. She pored over some choices, finally selecting a trendy dress she had bought on the shopping spree with Tizzy. She chose tan alligator pumps with a matching bag for accessories.

At 5:45 her bugger rang. Valdez was early. She buzzed him in, then waited at the penthouse door for him to step off the elevator. Her heart beat faster. She could not still the excitement welling up inside her. He stepped off the elevator. *He looks so handsome I can hardly stand it.* He grinned when their eyes locked, but she saw his sadness, too.

She couldn't stop herself. She ran toward him and threw her arms around him. "I've missed you, Valdez. Oh, I've missed you so much."

He turned his face away from her, and she knew he was fighting tears.

She took his hand. "Come in. Let me show you around." She toured him through the penthouse. Then she led him to the sliding glass doors and the roof deck. It was a balmy evening, the start of an early spring. They stood together silently, peering at the lights below. His hand felt warm and strong. She sensed he wasn't ready to talk yet.

"It's a great spot, Ayita. Shall we go?" Valdez asked.

"Yes, let's do that."

Valdez closed and locked the slider, and they walked to the door.

Once at the restaurant the valet parked Valdez's rented Mercedes.

"Good evening. Do you have a reservation?"

"Lopez for two, please."

"Right his way, sir." The maître d' showed them to a table and handed them menus. "Nice to have you with us this evening. Enjoy your dinner."

A waiter appeared at their table. "Good evening. May I bring you something to drink?"

"Two Perrier waters, please," Valdez said.

Ayita smiled her approval.

"What are you going to have, Ayita? I'm thinking of ordering the Duck L'Orange."

"Make that two," Ayita said without studying the menu.

"Should we start with a salad?"

"Sounds good."

The waiter set down the salads and baguette.

"The funeral was yesterday. Oh, Ayita, I didn't know it would be so hard to see him go. We've been so close since Mom died. He was such an awesome mentor. I never would have come as far as I have with my art without his input. He was a gifted artist. A fine man. A good father." He fought tears welling up in his eyes.

"I'm so sorry, Valdez. What are your plans, now?"

"I don't know. I'm his sole heir. I'll inherit a great deal of money-in the neighborhood of ten million."

Ayita's mind spun. She couldn't even imagine that kind of money.

"I'm putting the house on the market as soon as the estate is settled. Too many memories. I don't want to be there alone. I dropped Champ off with my aunt and uncle. I'm going to start a new life." He gazed at her, as if evaluating her response. "Maybe I'll move to Nashville."

When she didn't reply, he added, "I guess I could move to Europe. I'll be inheriting a house in Madrid, I could live there."

Do you prefer living abroad to America?"

He shrugged. "I don't know. I'm not thinking very clearly right now. I suppose I could move to London or Paris. There's a good market for my work there. I don't know what I want to do. I can't decide right now."

Valdez no longer had the arrogant edge-in its place was a mellow and heart-broken man.

Ayita had spent more time with her friend Anne since Jerry had gone to Buenos Aires. Valdez was a refreshing change from female company. Her emotions were confused. As she sat across from Valdez, she felt a deep stirring in her soul and in her heart. She was excited just being in his company. She cared for Jerry, but what she had always felt for Valdez topped the charts.

However, the bottom line had not changed. Until Valdez committed his life to the Lord, he was not a candidate for a husband.

"I gather your career has really taken off." Valdez's eyes shone with his pride in her.

"I've been very blessed, yes."

"Are you still seeing the older guy-Jerry?"

"We're just friends," she answered swiftly. "You know, agape love."

"I must tell you, Ayita," he murmured. "I've met someone."

Her heart stopped. "What do you mean?"

"I couldn't wait around for you any longer." Valdez stated matter-of-factly. "You made it clear there's no future for us, so I've had to move on. I may never really get over you, but...I'm getting married."

Her heart stopped. She couldn't breathe. Somehow, she had been operating in a vacuum. She had believed that if she just snapped her fingers, he would come running. Instead, he had given her a harsh reality check. "What about the flowers? And the birthday gift? What was that all about?"

"I wanted to do it. I guess I hoped it would bring you to your senses, and when it didn't, I...just had to move on."

She fought tears.

"Jan is an art student..."

The sound of his voice faded, as if he was speaking from a tunnel a hundred miles away. She tried to force herself to stay in the moment.

"...I met her during an art show and reception in Seattle. I'll be meeting her in two days in L.A., and then we'll fly to Madrid. I wanted to tell you in person. Maybe we can still be friends."

Ayita's head was spinning. *Friends?* She fought the impulse to start bawling. "Would you have the waiter bring me another piece of the chocolate cheesecake, please, Valdez."

Her emotional choice was not lost on Valdez. He looked at her strangely and sadly. "Are you all right?"

"Yes, of course." Her response was merely a reflex. She was in terrible shock. "Would you like me to play some music for you? I-I've started composing music. Maybe you'd like to hear some of it?" Uncharacteristically, she prattled on nervously.

Valdez was suddenly quiet. He seemed to be in deep thought. Soon he whisked them back to her apartment. They stepped off the elevator at PH1, and he inserted the key in the door for her. She stood there, staring at the freshly painted white doors with gold edging. At least she had her own little nest. That gave her a lift.

Valdez found a seat on the white sofa. She made coffee for them.

"You have a real nice place here." Valdez glanced around the penthouse.

"Thanks. I feel like my life is just beginning. God has much greater things in store for me...for all of us."

Valdez peered at her. She sensed his confusion. Was he jumping into the marriage on the rebound? Was it an irrational decision made during the trauma of his father's death? She wanted to tell him to slow down, but it was none of her business.

"Ready for a mini-concert?" Ayita asked. She felt anxious. She had to throw herself into the music. It would soothe her, and sometimes she discovered secrets in the midst of the music as her spirit merged with it. She played him the first piece of music she had composed. "Agape Love." It was ironic that she seemed destined to share agape love with the two most important men in her life. A bitter laugh threatened to erupt within her, but she held it in check.

She wanted to belong to a special man, wanted to make a lasting home with one. Perhaps even consider having a child or two. Was that merely a dream that would never become a reality? Was she destined to be a big country and gospel star, devoid of personal fulfillment?

She was bewildered. She realized with sudden clarity, that she would need to seek God's face for wisdom and answers.

Valdez complimented her on her music and left shortly after she finished playing her new composition. "I have an early flight to L.A., so I'll say good-bye now." He gave her a peck on the cheek and headed for the door. Then, suddenly, he turned and just stared at her.

She sensed he was exercising extreme restraint. In that moment she knew, with every ounce of her femininity, that he wanted to kiss her. Instead, he pivoted and swiftly walked out of the penthouse.

A minute later, she heard the buzz of her doorbell. Peering through the peephole, she saw it was Valdez. She opened the door, knowing what he was about to do. In fact, she didn't want to stop him. Couldn't, even if she wanted to.

He took her in his arms and held her so tight she thought she would break. Then he kissed her deeply, passionately.

In that instant her heart told her they were destined to be together forever. She felt in her spirit that somehow his pending marriage would not happen or something would go amiss with his plans.

When Valdez finally pulled away from her, his breathing still ragged, he apologized. "I'm sorry...and I'm not sorry. I had to do that. Yes, I still love you...so deeply I can barely stand it, but I can't wait around forever. I have to get on with my life."

"I understand," Ayita said, and to her great sadness, she did.

Nothing in her life had been harder than watching him walk away from her.

13

After Valdez was gone, Ayita was at loose ends. She decided to invite Marjoi to be her houseguest. They had talked about it several times, but Ayita's schedule had been so full, it never seemed like the right time. Now she really needed to talk to her best friend. She hoped Marjoi would be able to make the trip soon.

Five days later Marjoi arrived. It was Thursday morning, and she had to return to classes at Western Washington University on Monday. But they would have a few precious days together.

Marjoi strode through the apartment, peering around. "Your penthouse is great. I'm impressed."

Ayita made soft-boiled eggs for breakfast that first morning and served them with rye toast and fresh orange juice, as well as coffee. They chatted a mile a minute, overlapping each other, both thrilled to have the reunion.

Finally, Marjoi plunked down one of the matching white sofas and Ayita settled onto the one facing opposite her. How dramatically their relationship had changed. In the past, Marjoi had always played the older, wiser sister; now Ayita took on that role. She had become worldly wise, while Marjoi retained the small-town flavor. It struck Ayita just how much she had grown in the short time since leaving Bellingham.

Marjoi was full of compliments for Ayita's achievements. It had always been the other way around. Marjoi's scholastic achievements and spiritual maturity no longer intimidated Ayita as they once had. Seeing her old friend suddenly made her realize that she had moved with the speed of lightening, making the most of her opportunity.

Finally, after they'd caught up on a lot of life happenings, Ayita looked over at Marjoi. "Okay, now that I'm over the initial shock of Valdez telling me he's getting married, what do you really think, Marjoi? Do you think he'll do it?"

"No, actually, I don't. I still believe with all my heart that somehow things will work out for the two of you."

"And then there's Jerry. My buddy-my back-up guy. The guy I thought would always be there for me. "I'm so disillusioned. I thought he was such a great guy, until I learned how weak he was. He's really just a mama's boy." She sighed. "And then, when Valdez told me he was getting married, I guess I went into shock. I couldn't handle it. After he left, I cried hysterically. Thanks for calming me down. We must have been on the phone for an hour. I felt so much better after you prayed."

After Ayita had a good cry in Marjoi's arms, Marjoi started cracking jokes to ease the tension. Before long, both were laughing uproariously.

"How is Mother? Have you heard anything?" Ayita asked after a short lull in the conversation.

Marjoi pursued her lips. "Are you sure you want to hear it?"

"Yes. I sent her several notes telling her about my life here and the music, but I've never heard back. I called her several times and left my phone number on her answering service. She hasn't returned my calls."

Marjoi took a long sip of the iced tea. "Nothing has changed. She's still bar-hopping and picking up men. She was involved in a brawl at Sam's recently. It was in the local papers. They held her overnight in jail."

"I'm surprised Sam's hasn't closed down. It's the worst of the worst."

"I hate to have to tell you this stuff." Marjoi wrinkled her nose in distaste.

"I pray every day for Mother and then leave it in God's hands. Only He can help her. I sure can't."

"I know it breaks your heart to think of how your mom lives. Just keep holding on to your belief that God is working in her life even though we can't see it," Marjoi encouraged her.

Ayita exhaled heavily. "If I held onto my sorrow over the way she lives, I wouldn't be able to perform or write."

"She's on the prayer chain at our church," Marjoi told her. "A lot of folks are concerned about her."

Finally, they had talked themselves out. Both girls crawled into bed and slept soundly.

Friday morning Ayita made omelets for breakfast and served them at the kitchen table. Marjoi reverted to the role she'd assumed ever since the beginning of their relationship-that of advisor. She spoke without restraint, as only old friends dared. "I really think you should break off the relationship with Jerry. Chill out for a while. You've got a lot on your plate. Focus on using your God-given talent, and the rest will naturally fall into place."

Ayita frowned thoughtfully. "Maybe you're right. I thought I was sort of falling in love with Jerry until Valdez walked back into my life. Then I realized I'd been kidding myself all along."

"I think you fell for Valdez the moment you laid eyes on him. I bet he's still crazy about you. I don't know what the story is with his new girlfriend, but I'll bet anything it won't last," Marjoi said. "And as for Jerry, I think he's a surrogate father for you. I mean, he sounds great and everything, but I really don't think he's husband material for you, anyway."

"Why would you say that?"

"Well, for one thing, he's been there, done that. You've told me he had a marriage that went sour. Plus, he's got two kids." Marjoi shot her a serious glance. "Can I be really honest with you?"

"Of course." After all, they had rarely had secrets from each other.

"I think you hit the nail on the head. He's a mama's boy. Some guys never grow up, and some mothers like it that way."

"I guess I know that, too. If I'm honest with myself, I've become very fond of him, and sometimes I think I'm falling for him. Other times, I know I'm not. But I've never been able to shake the powerful feelings I have for Valdez." Ayita let out a self-deprecating laugh. "My knees almost buckle when he touches me or kisses me."

"Ayita, a lot has happened to you with the speed of lightening. I think you need to chill out for a while. It sounds to me like you can't trust your emotions. Twenty is hardly ancient, you know. You've got lots of time."

"I know, but I would like to get on with my life."

"Maybe you're just lonely. It's a huge shock to the system to be alone in a big city. I don't know how you do it. I don't think I could. I wonder if you're investing Jerry with more good qualities that he actually possesses, simply because you don't want to be alone."

"Could be," Ayita pondered. Marjoi had a way of bringing her back to earth. "Let's slip into some track suits and go for a walk around town. I need to get out of the apartment before I go stir crazy."

"Great idea. What time do you rehearse today?"

"Actually, I won't be rehearsing until Monday. I talked Tizzy into arranging for me to take a few days off.

Everybody knows I work too hard, anyway. It wasn't a problem."

Ayita slipped into a tangerine tracksuit and Marjoi put on a turquoise one. They walked around Music Row and visited the quaint little shops in Nashville, browsing around. "It's fun showing you around town, Marjoi. What kind of food do you want for lunch?"

"I'm leaving everything up to you. This is your city- you decide."

"All that power. Careful, it might go to my head."

"I love the architecture in Nashville. It's so different from Bellingham and Seattle," Marjoi commented, as they passed a cluster of brick townhouses framed by lavish gardens and wrought iron gates.

"I'm blessed to live here. I love this city."

"And the temperature is perfect. It's so mild. Bellingham was raining and cold when I flew out of Bellingham airport." A minute later Marjoi added, "You know what I'm thinking?"

Ayita chuckled. "No, but I bet you're going to tell me."

"Here's the spin I'll put on it. Your childhood and teen years were devastating. Your Mom didn't care about anything you were doing. She gave you no support. Jerry is the parent you lacked. He's a solid, stable, supportive person in your life. That's it. That's all it is."

"Agape love. He's just a friend. Maybe you're right."

"I'll be interested to see how much you miss him. How long is he gone for?"

"About three months. It's halfway around the world, you know."

The pals finally arrived at an area of boutiques and cafes after hiking past numerous townhouses and chic condo projects.

"Ready to power shop?" Ayita said, anxious to cater to Marjoi's passion for fashion.

Marjoi smiled. "I just happen to have my plastic with me."

"You're not paying for anything."

"Is that so?"

They ducked in and out of several boutiques, their arms laden with designer bags. At last they stepped into Monroe's, a funky boutique. The decor was fifties and included some excellent reproductions of Marilyn Monroe. Ayita wondered how they were able to use her name for the store.

"Welcome to Monroe's," a breathy blonde whispered.

The store was long and narrow and overflowed with sexy, slinky togs, both casual and dressy. Marjoi started leafing rapidly through reams of garments, waiting for some of them to jump off the rack. Ayita was used to shopping with her. She just let Marjoi do her thing while she tried on a couple of tops.

"Mom spent a fair bit of time and money to arrange for limited use of her name for our boutiques. It was all negotiated with the executor of her estate. We have to give a percentage of our earnings every year to the estate," the Monroe fan lamented.

That explained it. Ayita thought it was sad that people were still obsessed with her. She didn't want to be anyone's idol, no matter how big she got in the music industry. "I wish life could be simple," Ayita told Marjoi.

"No, you don't. It wouldn't be nearly as much fun if everything was simple," Marjoi said, still leafing patiently through every rack in the store.

They laughed. It had been too long since Ayita had fully relaxed. She had worked like a dog since coming to

Nashville. "Tomorrow we hit the landmarks. I knew shopping would be your highest priority."

Four days flew by. Ayita gave her best friend a big hug at the airport Sunday night. It had been hectic and a wonderful respite for both of them. Ayita felt recharged. She had needed Marjoi and she had been there for her. Ayita made a promise to herself: she would always be there for Marjoi, no matter how busy or famous she became.

Ayita rehearsed with her band in the morning and lunched with Tizzy. They met at a deli for corned-beef sandwiches and coffee. They discussed her upcoming tour among other things. He stayed in close touch, talking to her almost every day.

"Hey, hot stuff," Tizzy lifted his eyes from a newspaper he'd been immersed in when she entered the eatery.

She was becoming increasingly more confident and spunky the longer she hung around Nashville. Lately, she'd noticed that she worked harder than anyone she knew. "How much money were you able to negotiate for me?" Ayita asked Tizzy, seconds after she had settled into their usual booth.

"Plenty." Tizzy grinned triumphantly.

"Excuse me. I think I'm entitled to know *exactly* what I'll be earning on this tour. In fact, if you made this deal two days ago as you said, I fail to see why you are only just now filling me in on the details. You have an explanation, I'm sure." She smiled tentatively, knowing she had come on strong and was on the defensive. This was not the first time he had done this.

"Give me a chance, Kid," he shot back, an acidy edge to his voice.

She recoiled inwardly at his casual use of the word

Kid. It was starting to get on her nerves. *Disrespectful. That's what it was.* But that was hardly the main issue here, so she made no comment on his use of slang. "I'm waiting."

"I was out of town, Doll. I don't like wasting money on long-distance calls. Business managers have to be frugal. Capiche?"

She capiched all right. He was hedging. She glared at him, eyeball to eyeball. She had never yelled at him before, but she came close to it now. "How much did you get, Tizzy?" Something just didn't feel right. But the number would be on the contract, so how could he cheat her?

In lieu of a verbal response, Tizzy produced the contract from an inside pocket of his jacket. He unfolded it and spread it out on the table, pointing to the numbers.

"You know those numbers don't mean anything to me. I don't know how much I have to pay the band when we perform, plus I have wardrobe and rehearsal costs. How much would hotel, meals and bus rental come to for three months? She was frustrated because they had had similar conversations before, but Tizzy had never illuminated her on the details. Was he deliberately withholding information? She needed him to spell it out so she could understand where all the costs were and what she would net. "What *should* I be earning? You're my manager. You tell *me.*"

She finally had his attention. He became serious and respectful.

"This is a gross figure. You pay for everything," he stated bluntly.

"I know, and the expenses are all deductible. Is this my copy of the contract?"

"Yes."

She snatched the copy from him, staring at the numbers, which meant nothing to her. Then it struck her. She hadn't signed anything yet. She had not agreed to the deal. He had not even had the courtesy to phone her and tell her the numbers. There wasn't even a verbal contract in place. "Wait a minute. I haven't signed anything yet. I don't have to agree to anything in this contract."

Tizzy cut in swiftly. "Oh yes, you do. I've given them my word that this contact will be acceptable to you, and I represent you."

"Did you really? You underestimate me, Tizzy. I may be a novice in the music business, but I am not a fool." Her smooth, husky voice barely concealed her steely resolve to understand his tactics.

Suddenly, she had his number. She knew how and why he was sleazy. Simply put, he took advantage of the lack of knowledge with industry newcomers. Did he have a second contract? Maybe a secret deal with higher numbers with the venue owners, that he wasn't showing her? She decided not to pussy-foot around him any longer. "I'm not signing anything until my attorney reads this contract over thoroughly, and I understand everything that's on here. Oh, and don't be surprised if you get a call from him. His name is Lars Thalberg."

Tizzy looked stunned.

Lars Thalburg squeezed Ayita in for a lunch meeting in his office. The firm had a small board room and his assistant served them lunch. He had sandwiched her in between two other meetings. She knew this was important. If she didn't get a handle on her business, she might be out of business overnight. She had heard plenty about the flash-in-the pan artists and those who had poor management, as well as artists who wound up broke in spite of earning millions. She wanted to excel in the music industry, and she knew it was time to take charge.

She sat opposite her attorney as they nibbled on lunch, while he perused the contract. "This is less than half of what an artist of your caliber would normally receive," Lars reported. "You have two singles, and an album about to be released. Your first single hit the top of the charts. You're one of the hottest artists in Nashville right now. Nothing is forever. You've got to save your money. Unfortunately, the public is fickle, we don't know how long you have to be a hot property, we've got to make the most of it, and save everything you can."

"I wish you were my manager. I appreciate your advice. Thank you, Mr.Thalberg." Lars pulled out a magnifying glass from the top drawer in his desk and held it over the signatures. "We may have him," he said ruefully.

"What do you mean?" Lars pointed to the line that read *Artist's salary.* "These numbers have been altered. This is not a true copy of the original contract. In the first place, you should have the original of the contact, not a copy. Who has the original?" He glanced over at her. "Tizzy, right?"

She nodded. "I think so."

Lars centered the magnifying glass closer to the paper. "Yup, these numbers have been altered. The monies are sent to Tizzy, and then he pays you, right?"

"Right."

"Only a small handful of artists do it that way anymore. The majority gets paid direct and then they pay their manager. Looks like he's creaming money off the top, to the tune of about 50 percent. Then you pay him 25 percent commission. So he's actually getting 75 percent of the money you earn, and you're getting 25 percent, if you see what I mean."

"I do now." She sighed. "On gut instinct alone, I knew he was not being straight with me. But I didn't even think to check it out until Valdez prompted me to hire an attorney. Okay, so now what?"

"He goes to jail if I can prove it. What he's doing is called *graft,* and it's very serious."

She frowned. "I can't believe he underestimated me like this."

"He's famous for helping "kids," as he likes to call them, get their start. When they're eager and green and trust him, he takes advantage of them. If they make it big, he readily lets them out of their contract. They go on to a classier manager, and he goes on to the next victim."

"But if he already has an artist signed, wouldn't he try to keep that artist?"

"No. Because in most instances he knows he can't. Ayita, you're very young. You're new in this business. If Tizzy has a redeeming feature, it's that he knows what he is. And he doesn't try to reach beyond it. He lets the artist out of the contract. They move on and he moves on. It's a sickness in a way. Certainly a great insecurity on his part. He's sleazy and he knows it. He lives up to his reputation."

"Wow, this is really a lesson for me, Mr.Thalburg. I sure appreciate it. I'm surprised he hasn't had dozens of lawsuits."

"Maybe he has. Though I'm not aware of them. Most artists are hugely involved with their careers. They don't have the time or money to start lawsuits. It takes a certain kind of person to pursue nailing a career crook like Tizzy. Many artists change managers every few years anyway. They outgrow their managers...or something happens. Various sorts of conflicts arise."

"How long do you think Tizzy has been getting away with this?" She was stunned by the revelation.

"Who knows? A long time, I suspect. He's clever about it usually, but he picked the wrong gal this time. I think he has this scam down to an art. I'm not surprised some of the other artists, especially if they were novices, didn't catch it. You're not the average newcomer. You're exceptionally bright and perceptive. Most singers aren't flown in with all expenses paid and signed to a prestigious label, like you were. Most merely turn up here and grab any gigs they can get and slowly work their way up the ladder. They become so busy clawing and scratching their way to the top, while trying to hold down a day job, that it doesn't occur to them to check up on their manager. Most are thrilled just to have one."

"When a manager like Tizzy takes an interest in them, they caught up with the concept that they're finally going to make it. When they see his pricey home and the way he lives-the whole image he creates for himself-they think they're really on their way. It doesn't occur to them to question him. Even if they did, he always has an answer. He's glib, as you know." Lars leaned back in his chair and shook his head.

"Hey, you've barely touched your chicken salad."

Lars grinned and took a few bites before continuing his dissertation. "The graft he does is well thought out and skillfully executed," Lars said, thoughtfully. "If he thinks he has a sharp cookie on his hands, he probably plays it straight. He really goofed this time and totally underestimated you. I wonder how he that?"

She sighed. "Probably because I told him I was a high-school dropout. He didn't think I would pose much of a threat to his scam."

"You're kidding me. You didn't finish high school? I figured you had a couple years of college, maybe a B.A. How old are you, anyway?"

"Twenty." Ayita smiled at his kind words.

"Well, you're astute. You think things through and don't accept everything at face value. You just seem somewhat educated."

"Thanks for that encouragement. Someday I hope to attend university. Right now, though, I need to cease the opportunity I've been given."

"Smart girl." He shot her an admiring glance. "Anyway, looks like Tizzy got careless. If he had observed you a little more closely, he might have realized how sharp you are, despite your lack of formal education."

"I didn't tell him I read voraciously. It never came up."

"What do you read?" Lars finally was biting into more of his lunch.

"Anything I can get my hands on. I love the classics, mystery and suspense novels, romance, history, biographies...you name it."

"My, my, I daresay you're a lot more educated than Tizzy. He's in for a big surprise."

The intercom buzzed." Five minutes until your next meeting," his assistant said. The state-of-the-art intercom system allowed the attorney to be heard in his assistant's office, without picking up the phone. "Offer Mr. Roberts a cup of coffee. I'll be about five minutes wrapping this up."

They both finished their lunch in silence then Mr. Thalburg rose and shook Ayita's hand. Ayita took his cue, rising to her feet. "I'll have my assistant mail you the bill," Lars said.

"I can write you a check now, if you prefer." Ayita was anxious to keep him in her corner. She could only guess at the Pandora's Box he'd opened.

"That won't be necessary. This thing has only just begun." He shook her hand and smiled warmly. "Call me tomorrow."

"I will Thank-you so much."

"Sure. A little piece of advice. Don't let on anything has changed. Give Tizzy the idea that you're happy to have the tour, busy rehearsing and haven't given another thought to the contract."

"I can do that."

"You could invite him to rehearsal with your band and ask for his input. He knows everyone in town. He does have a lot of savvy in the music business, and he's not *all* bad. It's just a shame he may prove to be a crook. Don't bring up the contract. Pick his brain as much as you can. Get him to flesh out the details of the tour. Remember, the more he talks, the more he gives away. He might stick his foot in his mouth."

He shook her hand for the second time, and she noticed again how large his hands were and how powerful his presence was, almost filling the room. A gold-linked bracelet slipped below the starched French cuffs on his black, pin-striped shirt. He wasn't really her type, but Marjoi was right. There *were* a lot of attractive men in Nashville.

~~*~~

It wasn't long before the jarring ring of the phone reverberated throughout Ayita's penthouse. She picked up the receiver, admiring her antique gold, reproduction telephone.

"Can you meet me at my office tomorrow morning?

I've just had a cancellation for 9:30." The highly charged, confident voice of her attorney always made her feel good, as well as confident that a resolution to the situation would soon be forthcoming.

"Yes." Pursuing the lawsuit with Tizzy was a priority. She would call the band leader and tell them she would be an hour late. They wouldn't complain, she was paying them.

~~*~~

The next morning Ayita was ushered into the attorney's office. It made her feel empowered just being there. God had given her brains and talent. It was up to her to use them.

Lars didn't mince words. He believed he had sufficient evidence to convict her manager of graft and to arrest him that very day. Lars had already called in a handwriting expert in forgeries, who had confirmed the forgery, and he would have an assistant dig up old contracts with similar forgeries to strengthen their case in court. Meanwhile, he told Ayita not to sign anything. She was to refer everything and everyone to him. As her entertainment attorney, he would advise her and analyze offers, as well as any subsequent contracts.

"I've already taken the liberty of hiring a private detective to help with the investigation. We need to move on this fast. If there are any leaks to the press, we'll deal with them as they come up," Lars promised. "After today you can start looking around for new representation, but don't sign anything and try to be discreet. Alternatively, as an entertainment attorney, I can handle your contracts, if you're comfortable handling the rest of your business. Be prepared for a scandal, but remember, any publicity is good. It gets your name out there."

She thanked Lars and drove to the rehearsal studio. When she arrived, rehearsals were well underway, with the dancers going through the numbers with her two back-up singers. She'd told her choreographer to rehearse without her. She wanted to see how the show looked, anyway. She settled into a studio chair and waited until they finished the song they were rehearsing. Then, without a word, she stepped onto the stage, picked up her microphone, and began singing the next tune. She had fast become a consummate professional.

They broke for lunch shortly after 1:00.

She called Lars, and he advised her that Tizzy was reportedly "out of town," so he hadn't been able to proceed with the arrest. "I guess he has a guilty conscience," Ayita said.

"He might have a house in the Bahamas or some other tax-free haven. A lot of crooks and high-rollers vanish to some exotic locale once their scam is exposed," Lars explained.

"He's never mentioned one, but come to think of it, he *has* gone out of town on several occasions since I've known him. He never leaves a phone number. A couple of times I tried his cell but could never get through. He says he's traveling around, and it's easier for him to call me. I never thought anything about it."

"It's not much to go on-he could be anywhere in the world-but don't worry, we'll find him and nail him," Lars said, in a determined tone.

She had a full calendar of costume fittings, wardrobe and fabric choices, vocal exercises, and singing lessons. Recently, she had added private dance lessons to her already over-crowded schedule. Jerry was due in on Sunday, and she looked forward to seeing him. It had been a long time, and she'd missed him. Her evenings had been spent reading and playing the piano. It would be nice to have a dinner companion again. But now she knew the break had been a blessing in disguise. It had given her time to get a fresh perspective on their relationship.

Finally, Sunday afternoon rolled around, and she anticipated Jerry's call. He'd told her he'd call his chauffeur to pick him up at the airport, so she wouldn't have to worry about the inevitable delays of travelling.

Ayita's cell rang, and the call display flashed Jerry's home number. *He's home!* "Hi, Ayita, I just got home. I'd love to see you, and Maria has cold antipasto and some special dishes prepared."

"Sounds good."

"May I send my driver to pick you up?"

"Yes, please. I don't feel like driving."

She slipped into one of the new outfits she'd bought during her shopping spree with Marjoi-a silky, leopard body suit. She pulled on tan lizard backless shoes. She freshened up her make-up and stuffed a few things into the matching leopard purse. She had just misted herself with Joy perfume when she heard the buzzer. The driver had arrived.

Jerry was waiting at the front door when she arrived at his house. He bounded down the stairs and over to the limo, opening the back door. He offered his hand to help her out of the vehicle. "Ayita, how nice to see you." He hugged her and then took a step back, checking her out. "That cat suit is great! I've never seen you wear anything that...flamboyant."

"Marjoi's influence...she's a fashion diva. She came to

town for a long weekend. We went shopping together. I'm glad you like it."

Jerry clasped her hand and walked with her inside the house.

"Hey, Ayita, nice to see you," Maria said, hugging her. "It was awfully quiet around here without the two of you."

Jerry presented her with a duty-free bag of gifts. She tied one of the designer scarves around her neck, then walked over to the hallway mirror to check out the look. She noticed a separate bag and glanced into it. "Perfume. Good heavens, what did you do? Buy out the store?" She opened several bottles of expensive perfume, checking out the scent of each one and recognizing the name brands. "Maria, I want you to take half of these," Ayita said, sweeping a hand over the perfume bottles.

"That's very generous of you, Ayita. Let's figure it out after dinner. Everything is ready," Maria announced, leading the way to the dining room.

It was a feast fit for royalty. Maria vanished, allowing them privacy.

"Lobster Thermador! My favorite dish. And cold eggplant...love it!" Ayita then lifted up a prayer of thanksgiving for all the blessings they had been given. Jerry was silent and reverent as she prayed.

About halfway through dinner, Jerry surprised her with some news. "Mother has decided to come to Nashville to live, and she wants to meet you."

Ayita was overjoyed. "That's great news, Jerry," but even as she said it, she remembered Marjoi's assessment of their relationship.

"Wait, there's more," Jerry said. "If she doesn't approve of you, she wants me to honor the promise I made and move back to B.A. as soon as possible."

Ayita's heart sank, in spite of her misgivings about the relationship. No matter what happened, at the least, he was a treasured friend. "She's probably just humoring you by coming for a visit."

"No, you're wrong about that. Mother is a very curious woman. She has been threatening to come to Nashville ever since I moved here, and since her cancer is in remission right now, she wants to travel while she can. She feels she may not have another chance."

"I see."

"Wouldn't it be wonderful if we could get married and have God's blessing? While I was in Buenos Aires, I realized how much I love you and decided that, no matter what it takes, God willing, I shall make you my wife. But if Mother doesn't approve of you, for whatever reason, it will be very difficult for me to marry you. If she doesn't forgive the loan, I will be a slave to paying it off-and I'm not in a position to provide you with the lifestyle you deserve."

"I see." Boy, did she ever. He was financially dependent on his mother. Did he mean he would have to sell the house and get a modest condo or rent an apartment? Did that mean he would have to give up his live-in cook/housekeeper and his driver? But what did that matter? She was supposed to love him for who he was-not for his image and his money. Besides, everyone in the music industry was predicting a brilliant future for her. But did she really want the added burden of providing an affluent lifestyle for both of them? She was still praying to reunite with her Mother and she wanted to provide for her financially.

Jerry's image was fast diminishing in her eyes. She had lost respect for him after learning he had been primarily living on a mega-loan from his rich mother. Suddenly, it seemed nothing in this town was as it appeared. First Tizzy, now Jerry. Disillusionment swept over her like a gathering storm.

She pulled herself together. "Why do I think you're using your mother's objections as a smoke screen? I have a hunch *you're* the one who isn't anxious to remarry. But don't worry about it. I told you before that we can be friends. Agape love, remember?" Ayita smiled shakily at Jerry. She wanted him, and she didn't want him. Thoughts of Valdez kept returning.

"I *do* want to marry you," he said slowly, punctuating each word. "And I want Mother's blessing on the union. The last thing I need is to upset her. Her health is fragile, and given her age, she could die at any time."

Ayita could see his point. *There's been enough weighty conversation for one night.* She switched the subject. "What's for dessert?"

"Strawberry cheesecake. I peaked."

At that moment, Maria brought out freshly made cappuccino, serving it with the cheesecake while Jerry put on Beethoven and Brahms CD's. Ayita knew that, wherever their relationship led, knowing Jerry had been a respite and a blessing. He had helped her adjust to living in Nashville.

She also realized she had become very spoiled since moving here-accustomed to servants, hairdressers, drivers and dining in the finest restaurants. Strangely, it felt so right, as though she had been born for this. She had grown up in poverty, living in squalor with the dredges of society. Now she was soaring on top of the world.

When insecurity struck, she reminded herself she was a "King's Kid" and recalled one of her favorite Scriptures. *"I wish above all things that thou mayest prosper and be in health, even as thy soul prospereth."* God wanted the best for her! She didn't have to feel unworthy of her prosperity- or Jerry's. What did it matter if his money was an early inheritance of sorts?

As they finished their dessert, Jerry said, "We need to pray and believe God for a solution to our problems. I want God's best, and I know you do, too."

"That reminds me of a song Tammy Faye Baker recorded," she quipped. "The lyrics say 'We don't deserve it and yet we're blessed.'"

Jerry grinned appreciatively. They sat in front of a blazing fireplace, catching up the happenings in their time away from each other. Even though she had used Jerry's decorator, her place didn't hold a candle to his. She knew he'd dropped a small fortune decorating it, and his home reflected that.

"One day I'm going to win a Grammy award. Then I'm going to launch my own gospel show along the lines of the *The Barbara Mandrell Show,*" Ayita said.

He smiled. "I always told you the sky is the limit where you're concerned, Ayita. Would you forgive me if I let Bob drive you home? I have jet lag and would hate to fall asleep at the wheel."

"I'm way ahead of you. I told him to wait and asked Maria to feed him. He's in the kitchen reading the paper. I figured you'd have jet lag after your long trip."

After telling the driver they were ready, Jerry walked with Ayita to the limo and opened the door for her. He took her in his arms and kissed her tenderly. Then his kiss became more demanding.

She wrenched herself away from him. "Enough, Tiger," she teased, knowing she herself was dressed like a jungle animal. "Go get some sleep. Thanks for the gifts and dinner."

She shooshed him away and settled into the limo for the drive home.

14

It was July fifteenth, Juanita's birthday. Ayita wanted so much to phone her, but the last time she'd tried, she'd discovered it had been disconnected. She had sent a follow-up note with some cash inside but had received no reply.

Marjoi checked on Juanita routinely. She'd informed Ayita that nothing had changed.

Ayita sipped a Coke and absently watched television, her thoughts focused on her mother. She firmly believed that if she was thinking strongly of someone, that person was usually thinking of her. She wasn't sure if it was just because it was Juanita's birthday, or if they really did share a kind of mental telepathy.

The buzzer rang on her intercom. She was puzzled because she wasn't expecting anyone. Jerry didn't usually pay surprise visits, nor did Tizzy or Melvin. But curiosity got the best of her, and she pressed the button down.

"Hello."

"It's me...Juanita."

Her mother had often asked Ayita to call her "Juanita" instead of Mom or Mother. Ayita was never quite sure if it was because she wanted guys to think they were friends instead of mother and daughter, or if she was simply refusing to call herself a mother because of feelings of inferiority or rebellion. Ayita had gone along with it over the years, never questioning it

"Mother, is it really you?"

"Let me in. My feet are killin' me."

"It *is* you. Press PH1. I'm in the penthouse." Ayita buzzed her in.

She hugged her mother the moment she stepped off the elevator. "Happy birthday, Mother. I'm glad you're here.

I've been worried about you." When she finally released her mother from the hug, she asked, "How did you find me?"

"I got your letters and cash with your address. Marjoi told me you'd welcome me."

A side glance at her told the story. Her mother had come to stay. Juanita handed Ayita her torn garment bag while she held onto the scratched black vinyl bag and her shoulder bag. She plopped her CD player onto the kitchen table.

"I would have gladly sent you more money, but Marjoi said she thought you moved out of the house. She had no idea where you'd moved."

"I moved in with a man. It didn't work out, so I moved back onto the Reservation. I didn't bother reconnectin' my phone."

"I could have helped you, financially," Ayita began.

"It's not too late, baby. I'm still broke," she said wryly.

Her mother's timing had been uncanny. Sunday afternoon was the one day Ayita usually relaxed and loafed around the apartment, and always spent time in the Good Book. *Maybe Marjoi tipped her off.*

Juanita walked around the apartment, smiling. "My baby lives in style." She made her way to the sweeping outdoor deck, which had a wrought-iron table and chairs. Ayita had added a few, potted Calla Lilies to the other plants.

"Make yourself at home. I'll make some iced tea and rustle up some sandwiches," Ayita offered.

They sat outside and lunched together.

"Talk to me. What's going on?" She finally asked.

"I saw ya on *Grand Ole Opry* a couple times. You sang like a bird. I was mighty proud of ya. They give the name of yer CD on TV and I went right out and got it. Bin listenin' to it ever since. Played it over and over every day fer weeks. Then I jest got up one day and made up my mind I was goin' to Nashville to find ya."

"I'm so glad you did, Mother," Ayita said...and meant it. "How did you manage to get the plane fare?"

"Borrowed it from Henry."

"Henry?"

"Last guy I dumped...the one I was livin' with. I phoned Marjoi, and she picked me up and took me to the airport."

Ayita couldn't miss the nervous helplessness in her mother's eyes as she glanced around the sweeping deck. "Oh, by the way, Mother, stay as long you want."

Juanita did not look convinced that she was welcome, so Ayita elaborated. "You're welcome to say as my permanent house-guest, Mother. I'm glad you're here." She hugged her mother to emphasize her sincerity. After all, this was her golden opportunity to share the Lord with her mother, and she wasn't going to blow it. She was a great believer in actions speaking louder than words. She sensed in her spirit that her mother was more open to hearing about salvation than she ever had been.

"Come on, I'll show you to your room. Let's get you settled in." Ayita led the way to the guest bedroom, picking up her mother's meager belongings from the hallway and taking them with her. She felt momentarily sad as she glimpsed the pathetically small cache of worldly goods Juanita had brought with her. She was determined to help her mother turn her life around. "I'm glad you've traveled light. I'm going to knock off early at rehearsal tomorrow and take you shopping for a new wardrobe."

"Are ya serious?"

"I sure am."

Ayita fished around and found a robe and a nightgown. She did everything she could to make her mother feel like a welcome guest. She did have some misgivings, though. She would have to spell out a few things, including some rules and guidelines. But right now, she wanted her mother to feel good about being here. She knew it must have taken a great deal of courage to show up, after everything that had happened between them.

Ayita popped in one of the CD's she had made. "Mother, why don't you take a nice herbal bath and just relax?"

"Sounds perfect," her mother said.

Ayita began running her bath, determined to spoil her. After all, the men she'd met in Nashville had all spoiled her. It was her turn to spoil someone. "Mother, I'm very impressed that you know all the lyrics and melodies of every song on the CD!"

"I should. I listen to your CD's night and day."

It was then Ayita noticed her mother's words were slurred. Had she smuggled in a bottle of wine? Was she hiding it somewhere in the bathroom and taking secret sips? Ayita decided she would not broach the subject until tomorrow...if then. Her mother was no doubt tired and probably relieved she didn't have to turn around and head straight back home.

"I'm goin' right to bed after the bath. I *am* a little drowsy. I had a couple of glasses of wine on the plane." It was a start in the right direction. Her mother had admitted to drinking today, though she didn't really know the extent of it.

Ayita granted her mother privacy and headed back to the living room and the music. She played the piano and sang, worshipping God. When she looked in on her mother, she was fast asleep, snuggled under the comforter.

"Dear, dear Mother," Ayita murmured as she kissed her gently, first on one cheek and then on the other, before turning out the soft light on the night table.

Her eyes fell on the partially open vinyl bag, out of which peeked a large bottle of red wine. She picked it up and noted that it appeared to be a cheap brand. She had seen it on display in grocery stores. She remembered being sent to the store to buy it for her mother when she was only fifteen. She'd used Juanita's I.D., since they looked strikingly similar. Only fourteen years apart, some folks thought they were sisters.

Disappointment flickered, but she was not surprised. Settling down on a sofa, she opened her Bible, reading a chapter from the Psalms and meditating on it. Then she began praying. The Lord brought a scripture to mind. *"If ye have faith as a grain of mustard seed, ye shall say unto this mountain, Remove hence to yonder place, and it shall remove; and nothing shall be impossible unto you."* She drew all her strength from the Word daily and it helped her cope with the problems and challenges in her life.

She went back into the bedroom and watched her mother sleep. Juanita was snoring. Ayita stood over her, softly speaking life and healing into her spirit. "God is healing your addiction, Mother. I don't know when and I don't know how, but He is." Ayita knew that God moved in mysterious ways like the wind. *You don't know where it comes from or where it goes, but it exists.* She kissed her mother gently on the forehead, and then closed the door quietly behind her.

Ayita was very conscious of the enormous difference in the dynamics of their relationship. Now that her mother was in Nashville, her mindset was different. Her mother was in *her* apartment, and the dynamics of their relationship were very different than when she had lived on the Reservation with her mother and her "man-of-the-moment."

Ayita had a sense of control. In spite of the bottle of wine her mother had smuggled into the apartment, she knew her mother was on her best behavior and had come to the end of her rope.

~~*~~

Ayita finally woke her mother at 8:00 a.m. She had a big day planned for them. "Coffee and breakfast is ready," Ayita called out, opening the door to the guest bedroom.

"I can smell the aroma of coffee. I'll be right there," Juanita said, groggily, getting out of bed and pulling on the robe.

Jerry's driver whisked them from one exclusive boutique to the next. They stopped briefly at Ayita's favorite shopping mall in Nashville. She loved helping her mother select new outfits with matching shoes and purses. They hit a lingerie store. "I think I'm shopped out Ayita, you've been very generous. You sure you're not gonna run out money?"

"My credit card has a high limit, Mother. I'm keeping an eye on what we're spending. We haven't exceeded the numbers I had in mind." Finally, they were shopped out and ready for lunch.

She discovered she loved indulging her mother. They went to a little French Bistro and insisted Jerry's driver, Hortense, join them at the outdoor eatery. Juanita ordered a glass of wine but didn't order a second one. This was her day. Ayita had no intention of spoiling it. *One day soon, God would take away her compulsive desire to imbibe.* She smiled inwardly as Juanita flirted with Hortense. In a way, her outrageous, indiscriminate interest in all men, any race, any type, any age, was amusing, as long as it stopped there, and was actually part of her Mother's unique charm.

Next stop was the hairdresser. They both had their hair washed and blown dry. Juanita also had hers trimmed and styled. They didn't hit the makeup department because Juanita was stunning without a speck of makeup and usually didn't bother with it. She wore her usual coral lipstick, and it was all she needed. They both had long, thick, black lashes. Ayita wore mascara, but her mother didn't bother. Ayita wore fake lashes when she performed, even though they were a hassle to apply, because she knew the bright lights on stage would wash her out if she didn't.

Manicures and pedicures were next, following by a half hour massage. "Time to go home, Hortense," Ayita told the driver, who was patiently waiting in the limo outside, as he worked on crossword puzzles.

Ayita enjoyed giving her mother the star treatment for a day, and her mother clearly relished every moment of the outing. Jerry had insisted his chauffeur drive them around, so they wouldn't have to bother with parking. Shopping with a limo standing by was surely one of life's premier experiences. The culmination of an exciting indulgent day ended perfectly when the driver insisted on carrying the collection of decorator bags up the elevator to the penthouse. Ayita rewarded Hortense with a generous tip. It was worth it when she saw the joy in her Mother's face as she reveled in the luxury of this last touch of extravagance for an indulgent day. It was the *crème de la crème*-like the icing on the cake. Since dating Jerry her vocabulary had increased and so had her use of French and Spanish phrases. It was a perfect ending of a perfect day.

Ayita kicked off her shoes and her mother did the same. Music and tea were next on the agenda. Both relaxed with the blackberry herbal tea and then her mother disappeared into her bedroom, laden with designer bags. Minutes later, Ayita popped her head into the bedroom and caught her mother singing along with her CD while she admired one of the new dresses she'd already slipped on. It was a Southwest creation in soft turquoise suede. The sandals and handbag were a perfect match.

Juanita walked around the apartment proudly modeling it. "I don't deserve all this. How are ya ever goin' to pay fer it all?"

"It's not about what we deserve. We, as sinners, don't deserve the free gift of salvation, either. Jesus died for our sins long before we appreciated it. I look at it this way, Mother. My vocal gift is on loan to me, and I intend to use it to the max to glorify God. It's the same thing as my finances. God is my source, and I know He wants me to share what He has given me."

Juanita gestured toward all the bags. "But can you afford all this?"

"Yes, Mother, I can. I think you have no concept of how much money I'm earning and how fast I'm earning it. Let me put it this way. I hope to buy a house within the next year or two."

"I had no idea you were capable of doin' all this." Juanita seemed awestruck.

"You probably have a lot of dormant talents, too. I put *all* my trust in the Lord. Once I understood how the principles work, I knew prosperity would be mine forever."

Juanita frowned. "I'm not sure what you mean."

If you tithe from the *first* fruit of your earnings, God promises to bless you financially one-hundred fold. I trust *God* with my money, not the stock market."

"Ya sure have come a long way since ya found God."

"Without Him, I can do nothing. I am a mere vessel to sing His praises."

"I wish I had what you have, but I think I'm beyond it...a hopeless case." She emitted a harsh, grating laugh.

"No, you're not! You can accept Jesus as your personal Savior, just as you are. That's the beauty of it. The Bible says, 'And ye shall seek me, and find me, when ye shall search for me with all your heart.' " Ayita's soul stirred, and she felt compelled to sing one of the songs on her album *Believe and Receive.* She had loved the song from the moment she'd heard it played by the composer, Elliot Barnes.

The rich timbre of her voice and the Holy Spirit's anointing upon her stirred her mother to tears. Ayita leaned toward her mother, who sat in a white Louis XV replica chair, tears streaming down her cheeks. When the CD ended, Ayita took tissues from on top of the piano and wiped her mother's tears away.

"Would you like to invite Jesus to come and live in your heart?" Ayita asked her mother.

Juanita nodded. "I hate my life. I hate it!" She spat out the words in a broken, sobbing voice. "I'm tired of the sin. Sick of drinkin' and the hangovers. I want to follow God."

"Do you want to say the sinner's prayer? I'll help you," Ayita prompted. So Ayita spoke the sinner's prayer and her mother repeated it after her. "Dear Jesus, I believe you died on the cross to save me from my sins. Forgive all my sins and come and live in my heart." Juanita said the words with sorrow for all her sins in the past and great sincerity at wanting her life to change.

Ayita threw her arms around her mother. "I love you, Mother."

"Ya mean ya forgive me for all the crap I put ya through?"

"Yes, Mother. I'm so happy you're here and that you've found the Lord."

"Thanks, Baby. Yer the best daughter a mother could ever have." A heart-wrenching smile flickered across her mother's lips.

"At the risk of sounding preachy, may I share a Scripture?" Ayita asked.

"You sure can, honey." Her mother beamed.

Ayita took one of her mother's hands in hers. *He removes our sins as far as the east is from the east.* "Jesus does not remember our sins once we're forgiven. So you can live life with a clean slate. Isn't that great news?"

"It is, Baby. It really is. Wanna hear something weird?"

"Sure."

"Well...ever since you became a Christian, I felt kinda jealous. I wanted what you had. I jest wasn't sure how to go about it. To tell the truth, I was hangin' onto my...ways. But God in His wisdom closed the doors on what I didn't have the courage to walk away from."

"What happened?"

"I didn't drop the men like I always told ya I did. They dropped me usually. I told ya it was the opposite, jest to save face. I would meet a guy...we'd be together...but when he found out the extent of my drinkin', he was gone in a heartbeat."

Her mother stood and walked toward the rooftop deck, stopping at the long bank of sliding glass doors. "They was all louses, only interested in sex and my looks. But when they saw how out of control I was, and how much I spent on booze and gamblin', they hit the road, leavin' me in greater pain every time it happened."

Juanita paced around the apartment as she unburdened herself. "I felt like no one loved me or wanted me, and that's why I gave myself so freely, because for a brief time I felt loved. I always believed the current boyfriend was gonna be different. I'd tell myself *"This is the one that will last."*

"What finally got you off the treadmill?"

"The last man I was with. Henry. I fell hard for him. He was different from all the rest of 'em. A cut above. A shrewd businessman...he had money. He was kind...and special. A widower." Juanita paused, her back to Ayita. "So I moved in with him. He had a nice, big house." She choked on her words.

Ayita sensed that a dam of tears threatened to break loose. She also knew that her good listening skills had been the key to her survival and the reason she was wise beyond her years. Ayita had understood the seamy side of life at a tender, young age, and that knowledge had served her well in the jungle of Nashville's music industry. She was overjoyed that today her mother had not only accepted Jesus as her Savior but had finally chosen to confide in her, sharing the large portion of her life that she had tried to keep hidden from Ayita all these years.

"Anyway, one day his favorite daughter came to visit. It was early afternoon, and I was plastered. She had dropped by, unexpectedly on a Sunday, hopin' to find her father home. He was an avid tennis player and had gone to his club for a game with a buddy. He'd invited me to come and watch, but I didn't feel like going. I told him I would stay home, relax and cook up somethin' real nice for dinner."

Her shoulders slumped. "Instead, I hit the bottle. His daughter treated me like dirt, like garbage under her feet. She made a pot of coffee, drank a couple of cups without offering me one and then left without even sayin' goodbye." A long silence followed this latest confession. "The next day, Henry told me to pack my bags and leave. He couldn't look me in the eyes when he said it, but I knew he was heartbroken."

Though Juanita's back was still turned, her tone changed as though she were strangely drained of all emotion and talking now about someone else's life. Swiveling toward Ayita, she walked toward her and the pair of matching white sofas. Plunking herself down opposite Ayita, she stated, "That was the turning point in my life. I really loved him, and I thought he loved me. I think he *did* love me, but he was weak and loved his daughter very much also. And she said I was all wrong for him, that I would drag him down into the gutter with me. She gave him an ultimatum: 'Get rid of Juanita, or you'll never see me again. If you hook up with her, I'm gone from your life.'"

"That's a sad story," Ayita replied. "But there's good news. When God closes one door, he opens two new ones. I'm going to do everything in my power to see that you are happy here. You stay as long as you want...forever, if you like."

"Oh, Honey, that is so generous. But you'll git married one of these days...soon..a beautiful girl like you..."

"I don't know when that will happen, Mother; but when it does, I see no reason why you couldn't live with us wherever we live."

Tears trickled down Juanita's eyes. "Oh, Honey, yer

my miracle daughter."

"And you're my miracle mother."

Her mother's laughter pealed out and jogged Ayita's memory. She realized that the sound of her laughter was the way it had been when she'd been a very young child, long before her mother had begun her tragic, downward spiral. Ayita was grateful to God for the blessing of the new leaf her mother had turned. She also realized it would be up to her to mentor her mother, now that she had become a new creature in Christ. After all, Marjoi, her parents and her grandma had mentored Ayita. It was her turn to give back.

"I wish I hadn't wasted so much of my life," her mother said.

Ayita was amazed how quickly her mother assessed the truth of her situation. Then she remembered how the Bible says a scrim is removed from a person's eyes when they accept the Lord, and they are then able to see God's ways clearly. "The Bible says, 'I will restore unto you the years that the locust hath eaten.'"

"Maybe I could become your assistant, Ayita." Juanita said.

"What did you have in mind?"

"There's no reason I couldn't shop and cook and do all the cleanin'. You know I love to cook."

"You can cook for me anytime you want, Mother, and I'll appreciate it, but I won't allow you to do the cleaning. I have maid who comes in once a week to change the linens and vacuum and keep the place looking good. But yes, I would be very grateful if you would do the shopping and cooking. And, frankly, if I didn't have to worry about shopping for groceries and cooking, I'd have an extra chunk of time to put toward my career."

"It's a deal, then. Where's the nearest supermarket?"

"The nearest one is a couple miles from here, but there's a fresh vegetable and fruit market only two blocks away. I usually drive to the supermarket once a week or every two weeks to stock up on staples and meat; then I pick up fresh veggies and fruit every few days, if I'm going to be eating in."

In that instant, Ayita's attention fell on two of her plants. They were wilting. She had forgotten to water them. Locating the spray bottle under the kitchen sink, she walked around the apartment, misting all her plants. "I'll help you find some hobbies to keep you busy, Mother," she called out.

"No need. You haven't done so badly, so I think I'll just copy you. Maybe I'll get involved in the church, like you been doin.' All my fun was always temporary. If I didn't have you, baby, God only knows where I would be now."

"Never mind. God knows your life from beginning to end. He knew that you and I would be here together at exactly this time. Awesome, isn't it?"

"It really is."

Ayita knew her mother had many stories to share, and she wanted to hear them. But it was well after the dinner hour, and Ayita was getting hungry. "Maybe I'll order pizza," Ayita suggested.

Her mother nodded and continued talking.

It was after 8:00 when the buzzer rang, and she buzzed Nick's delivery boy into the building. After he handed her the steaming pizza, she thanked him and tipped him generously.

Ayita happily served the pizza on her new pale yellow and white dinnerware. After making a jug of iced tea, she filled two tall glasses with crushed ice. She ignored the fact that she knew her mother preferred red wine with pizza. She determined not to dwell on her mother's weakness. She would need to lean on God's wisdom to handle that one; it was far too big for her. But she was fairly sure her mother hadn't taken a drink so far today. She had heard of God supernaturally lifting some alcoholics desire to imbibe. Other folks had deliberately replaced habits of the cocktail hour with habits of doing a sport or taking a class, and moved on from their compulsion. Ayita resolved to take one day at a time and believe God had it under control.

They enjoyed the pizza, finishing every last morsel.

Right afterwards, Juanita vanished into her bedroom. Ayita wondered how much wine remained in the large bottle her mother had brought. She was sure whatever remained would swiftly disappear. But she hesitated to confront her mother. She would let it go for now. Instead, Ayita crawled into her bed and turned out the lights.

~~*~~

The next morning, as she opened the sliders on her roof deck to usher in the fresh air, she spotted a couple of sandpipers, flitting overhead. They swooped onto her roof deck. She had recently watched a documentary about birds and recognized them by their markings. There was a red knot sandpiper and red-necked phalarope. She observed the latter closely, recognizing the black, brown and gray upperparts and brown face and sides. The medium-sized sandpipers flitted off as quickly as they had swooped down onto her deck.

Ayita padded into the kitchen and ground whole beans into fresh coffee. She made a pot, waiting for it to brew. She enjoyed the feel of the silk Japanese robe as she sat down at her beloved baby grand. Slowly, and with great concentration, she began to play the songs she had composed. The words she penned flashed into mind as she sang with a joyful and grateful heart. She had just started playing her second composition when her mother emerged from the kitchen, touting a yellow mug of coffee. Juanita sauntered toward the sofa, plunking herself down on it. In spite of her face being somewhat ravaged by years of hard living and too much booze, she was a striking beauty in her turquoise Japanese robe, one of many purchases from their shopping spree.

She had never been able to identify with her mother's cravings for alcohol, but she did know that an unseen spiritual battle raged over her. Merely telling her not to drink would be like applying a tiny Band-Aid to a broken leg.

Instead, she would shower her mother with mountains of love and gently instruct her in the ways of the Lord. Ayita had to re-educate her mother, helping her replace bad habits with positive, inspirational thoughts from the Good Book. The music was a perfect place to start. The songs she had written were praises to God, and He lived within His praises. As her mother closed her eyes, the music seemed to permeate her entire being. Ayita could sense the new joy there.

At that moment the phone rang. Ayita was tempted to let the answering service pick it up, but when she saw Jerry's name flash on the screen, she decided to answer.

"Hi, gorgeous. When can I see you?" Jerry sounded unusually chipper.

"You can come over for a cup of coffee in an hour if you like. I have someone I want you to meet. She's my house-guest. You'll love her, I promise."

"If you say so. I'll see you soon."

"Just a quick coffee, though. I have rehearsal at 10:00."

"Sure. Your place is on the way to my studio, anyway."

Ayita showered, dressed and whipped up egg-white omelets for herself and her mother.

When Jerry arrived, he carried a bouquet of yellow roses.

"For me?"

"Enjoy." He handed them to her.

She cut the stems on the diagonal, adding floral preservation into the warm water, and arranged them artfully in a crystal vase. Then she placed it on top of her white baby grand, so she could enjoy them while she played.

Her mother was engrossed in the local newspaper while she ate the omelet.

Ayita took Jerry by the hand and brought him into the kitchen.

"Delighted to meet you," Jerry said, his eyes sweeping over her mother. His appreciation of her mother's beauty was hardly lost on Ayita. Her mother had always had a powerful effect on men, and Jerry was no exception. She had to admit her mother looked particularly youthful and vibrant today, sporting her chic new hairdo and outfit. Panic surged as Ayita suddenly saw her mother through a man's eyes. She was stunning-sexy and svelt in a white jumpsuit accented by a wide, jewel-encrusted gold belt, showing off her lithe body.

Ayita glanced at Jerry. Juanita and Jerry appeared to be sizing each other up. Jerry was the first to speak, and he put his foot right smack in his mouth.

"You're absolutely gorgeous! I had no idea..." He quickly returned to his senses. "I...see where Ayita gets her looks from," he finished, lamely.

Ayita shot Jerry an irritated glance and he winced. Clearly he regretted gushing over her mother. *How dare he fall all over mother like a love-struck fool?*

Her mother had been a femme fatale for as long as Ayita could remember. Had she caught Ayita's wounded look? Her mother may have been a boozer but that didn't mean she was insensitive.

"My daughter is not only gorgeous but an accomplished singer as well."

That comment was music to Ayita's ears. She had waited all her life to hear something nice from her mother.

"Indeed she is," Jerry agreed.

Still, Ayita was crushed. She hadn't realized how vulnerable she was, and how traces of her past could still come back to haunt her when she least expected it.

Had she over-reacted with jealousy? Or had Jerry become smitten with her mother? *Love at first sight?* Dozens of other men had fallen in love with her mother, in spite of the fact that none had stuck around for the long haul.

Ayita breezed out of the room and strode to the open patio doors. The sun streamed into the penthouse as she struggled to maintain her composure. Walking over to the baby grand, she plunked her music folder from on top of the piano and flicked through some songs. She was waiting for Jerry to come over to her and apologize - or to at least explain his reaction. He didn't.

She forced herself to focus on the music. Sooner or later, either Juanita or Jerry would return to their senses. She had to leave for rehearsal soon, and Jerry always went to his studio in the morning.

Finally, when she was fully immersed in the music, she

heard joyful laughter. Glancing toward the sound, she saw red! Jerry and her mother sat on the sofa, chatting as merrily as two lovebirds. They were discussing politics, of all the lame things! She wasn't even aware her mother had an interest in such things. Maybe some of the men she knew had taught her something, after all. Perhaps the special man she had lived with most recently.

In that second, Ayita's annoyance morphed into a seething rage. "Get out!" She screamed the words, shrilly. "Get out of my house and don't ever come back! How dare you come in here and flirt with my mother! You...you rotten sod!"

She had no idea where the British expression had sprung from. Likely some of the classic British mysteries she sometimes read.

Jerry looked stunned and got angry. "Lighten up. We're talking. We're not...flirting," he said, defensively.

Ayita knew her mother. She could hardly miss the sparkle in her eyes or the way Jerry leaned toward her, captivated by her beauty and charm.

Her mother didn't seem hung over. Ayita suspected she'd snuck a few glasses of wine at various intervals during each day, but it was early morning and her mother was clear-eyed and sober. She had a tendency to chatter like a hillbilly when she was inebriated. Sometimes Ayita thought her mother hid behind the uneducated speech pattern, forcing people to accept her with all her defects-or reject her. Most of the men she met liked her just fine as long as they were sleeping with her. Ayita couldn't help wondering how Jerry would have reacted if he had met her mother on one of the many days she was stoned.

Ayita had had enough. "If you don't leave right now, Jerry," she yelled, "I'm going to call the police." She glared from Jerry to her mother sending them both a clear message.

"Okay, okay, I'm leaving." Jerry put his hands up in protest.

Ayita rushed to the door and held it open for him. "Don't you *ever* come back here again," she barked, slamming the door behind him so hard it almost rattled off its hinges. She swiveled to glare at her mother from across the room. She was not proud of the way she was acting, but their outrageous behavior had pushed her over the edge.

"What was that all about, Ayita?" I've never seen you act that way."

"Are you going to sit there and tell me that the two of you weren't flirting outrageously?" Ayita asked.

"No. Actually, I'm not. I'm way ahead of you on this one."

"I beg your pardon?" Ayita scowled in disbelief.

"Well, once I realized Jerry was flirting with me, I fed the fire to see how high it would blaze."

At first Ayita was speechless with shock. Soon, she found her voice. "Are you saying you deliberately goaded him into flirting with you, even more than he already was?"

Her mother lifted her chin. "Yes."

"Why?"

"Because I wanted to find out where his loyalties lay, and if he really loved you. I have to confess Marjoi tipped my hand. She told me she wasn't sold on Jerry. She said she didn't trust him, somehow. So, when I saw the opportunity to test him, I did exactly that. I brought out his true character. He's not for you, honey."

Ayita was stunned. "You...you actually did this...to smoke him out?"

"Darn right." Juanita's eyes narrowed. "Think about it.

Forget *him* for a moment. Let's face it; I'm at your mercy. If you don't like something I do, you could throw me out on my ear."

Ayita rolled her eyes. "Mother-I wouldn't."

"But you *could."* Her mother appealed to her reasoning powers and Ayita chose to believe her. "I'd never have flirted with Jerry to deliberately upset you, except for the reason I told you about. The last thing I'm lookin' for right now is another man. I've finally turned a new leaf and this is our special time to become reacquainted."

Her mother had finally struck a chord. "Oh, Mother, that's what I want, too. He really is a louse, isn't he?" Ayita sighed.

"I'm afraid so, dear."

"But I really thought I was in love with him and vice versa."

"I know you did, dear. Come on," Juanita said abruptly. "Let me help you find a sharp outfit for today's rehearsal. There's a wonderful man out there somewhere, jest waitin' for you. Come here, darlin'," Her mother curved her arms around her daughter and held her close. Ayita glanced up to see tears glistening in her mother's eyes. She really loved her, after all.

A few minutes later, Ayita drove to the rehearsal studio, barely making it for 10:00 a.m. God was in his heavens and everything would work out according to His perfect plan.

15

They settled into a comfortable routine with Juanita doing the shopping and cooking while Ayita pursued her music career.

Jerry hadn't called, and she was surprised to find she didn't miss him that much. Her mother had masterminded a reality check and helped Ayita get things into perspective. She focused on rehearsing songs she'd written and composed for her next album; in addition to rehearsing for the big production that was scheduled to go on tour.

She had received yet another request for a guest appearance on *Grand Ole Opry*. This would be her third time on the show in six months. She was becoming part of a small coterie of favored performers. This morning, a local reporter was coming to the penthouse to interview her.

She chose a blue Donna Karan suit she had picked up at a big sale at Saks. It was a small size. The saleslady had cooed, "Honey, nobody can squeeze into it. My usual customers loved it, but they couldn't wriggle into it. Otherwise, it would be long gone." The luxurious silken fabric caressed her skin. She felt great in it.

Her mother whistled as Ayita modeled the elegant suit around the penthouse while waiting for the reporter to arrive. "I'm going grocery shopping," her mother announced, heading for the door.

Ayita was grateful for the privacy. She had warned her mother that a reporter was interviewing her. "It is no one's business about your past, Mother," she'd told Juanita. "That's just between us."

Allan Greenwald was a touch early for his appointment. Bright and inquisitive, he seemed impressed with himself as well as his job. She wasn't impressed. For all Tizzy's bad points, he had clued her in on reporters and interviewers, warning her to be very leery of them. "Think carefully before you answer any of their skillfully crafted questions, unless you're willing to accept butchered quotes and comments taken out of context. They often have a hidden agenda," he'd warned her. Too bad Tizzy had turned out to be a criminal. He'd been arrested and was now serving jail time.

The aggressive young reporter started digging away at her personal life. She stopped him in his tracks but sensed he knew something, because he continued to dig relentlessly, clearly to ferret out skeletons from her past. He even stooped to planting words in her mouth, but Ayita refused to take the bait.

Innately shrewd, Ayita sidestepped his intrusive questions. She knew her knowledge could only come from one source, and she relied on it. The right words usually sprung to her lips as the need arose.

She could sense the reporter was frustrated when he finally said good-bye. She smiled because she knew she had won the unspoken challenge of wits. She didn't like this side of the business, but it was part of the game, and she was learning to be masterful at it. But her woman's intuition told her that the reporter was not through with her. She was willing to bet he was going to look for another opportunity to exploit her and uncover her past.

Juanita came back to the penthouse around noon. A taxi driver was with her, helping her carry the groceries. She let herself into the apartment, and began putting things away in the kitchen.

Ayita heard her come in. She stood on the front deck waiting for Alan to drive off. There was a white Porsche visible from her vantage point. It was parked at the curb, slightly up the street from the entrance of her building. She figured it was Alan inside the car. Whoever it was, he wasn't driving off.

Ayita buzzed the doorman downstairs. "Is the reporter who just left my apartment still parked at the curb?" she asked.

"I don't think so, Miss High Eagle, I saw him leave."

"I'll be back in a minute, Mother," Ayita said, grabbing her purse and heading down the elevator. She handed the doorman a fifty-dollar bill. "Tell me, Bart, how long has that Porsche been parked at the curb?"

He hesitated, glancing at the crisp bill. "Ma'am, he's been parked there ever since your mother left the building earlier this morning. I guess he's that reporter I let up to your suite a while ago. I was sure I saw him drive off, but now I see he's back."

Ayita was livid. "Did that reporter ask you a lot of questions, Bart?"

He shrugged. "I was evasive. You always told me not to give out any information about you. It's part of my job description, anyway."

"What kind of questions?"

"He seemed to know your mother was staying here. He asked if I had ever seen her drunk."

"What did you say?" Panic welled up inside her.

"I told him it was none of his business, and to stop loitering or I would call the police."

"What did *he* say?"

"He said he was just leaving."

"But he didn't leave." She narrowed her eyes.

"He left, but I just now realized he must have come back when I was on break. I don't know how long he's been parked there, because his car is hidden by the corner of the building and the shrubbery."

"All right. I should have been more explicit in warning you, Bart. The press is scrounging to get some garbage on me to put in the rag papers. If you spot him loitering around here again, warn him. If he doesn't leave immediately, call the police and report him...and advise me immediately."

"I'll do that Ms. High Eagle. I bought his story the first time. He said he was early for his next appointment and was just killing time."

"What a line."

~~*~~

The following morning, Ayita followed a hunch and took the elevator down to the lobby. Sure enough, a different young man loitered in the lobby, chatting up Roberto, the doorman on duty at the time. The men were laughing, munching on croissants and drinking coffee, neither of which the doormen were allowed to do while on duty.

Ayita formed a plan. "Well, see you later," she called to Roberto, slipping out the front door. She went around the side of the building and using her key, she slipped unseen in the back door of the lobby. Crouching behind the enormous, leafy plant, she listened to their conversation.

"So I can give you a hundred if you can get me some information on Ayita's mother. I've got it from a good source that she's a big boozer. I bet Ayita is, too."

"Why do you need this information?" Roberto asked.

"I work for a tabloid, and it's the only way I can get a promotion. I've got to come up with some juicy insider stuff."

"A hundred bucks?"

"Yup. Got it right here." He flashed the hundred-dollar bill at Roberto.

"Let me see what I can do. Well...there is something. I did hear a rumor that her mother is a heavy boozer and party girl."

"Evidence," the reporter insisted. "I gotta have evidence. Photos would be good."

At that instant, Ayita stepped out from behind the California fan palm. Its leafy branches had hidden her perfectly. "Young man," she announced loudly, "my private life is just that-private. If I see you snooping around here looking for dirt, I'll make sure you're removed. As for you, Roberto-doorman have been fired for far less. Consider this your final warning."

Ayita didn't like being tough, but where her mother was concerned-particularly now that she was making an effort to change-Ayita was determined to do everything possible to protect her. The last thing she needed was bad press or a scandal.

After reporting Roberto to the office, Ayita let herself into the penthouse. Her mother was sipping tea, but her posture revealed she was disturbed about something. "Mother, what is going on?"

"I hate to tell you this, but I think I was spied on today."

"So what? You were grocery shopping."

"Ayita, I...stopped at the liquor store. Jest as I was leavin' and payin' for a...big bottle of wine, I had a sense I was bein' watched."

Ayita exploded. "How dare they spy on you!" There's no law against you buying a large bottle of wine. How do they know it's not for a party? It's nobody's business but ours and the Lord's that you have an addiction. I'll take care of this, Mother," she said with steely resolve.

~~*~~

The next day, Ayita accompanied her mother to the liquor store. Sure enough, she spotted a sleazy creep slinking around a display. They walked out of the store empty-handed, the young man on their heels.

"Are you having fun yet?" Ayita snapped, pivoting on her heels and glaring at him.

The spy's face turned red as he blubbered. "What are you talking about?"

"Look, I already know what you want. So why don't you give it a rest? You're trying to get a photo of my mother and me buying wine or looking inebriated. Then you're planning to trump up a phony story and plaster it all over the rag trades in the hopes of getting a promotion. Did I miss anything?"

The rangy young man stuttered and started walking off. He pivoted back toward Ayita. "I don't know what you're talking about, lady."

"Sure you do. Scram."

This was another incident where Ayita didn't know where she got her courage from. When it came to messing with her livelihood or her mother, Ayita was a tiger. Her mentors had warned her to watch out for the predators. They'd said that if the press ever twigged to her mother's sordid past, it might be splashed across every trade paper in the industry and could seriously tarnish Ayita's image.

~~*~~

Juanita determined not to go near the liquor store all

week, even though she craved a drink. Finally, she became desperate. She walked by the liquor store a couple of times to make sure the sleazy reporter was nowhere in sight. *I can be in and out of the store in minutes, and no one will be the wiser,* she told herself.

Juanita didn't see the spy until it was too late. The light of a camera bulb flashed in her face. She was already blasted from the wine she had drunk earlier that day, which had been culled from her secret supply, bought from previous shopping forays.

That night at home, Juanita cooked a lamb roast with roasted vegetables and set the table carefully, placing fresh flowers as a centerpiece. She was ridden with guilt but couldn't bring herself to say anything to Ayita.

~~*~~

A few days later, Ayita stopped in at a grocery store to pick up a newspaper. A tabloid cover grabbed her attention. To her utter horror, she glimpsed Juanita's face plastered all over the paper. "Singing sensation Ayita High-Eagle covers up sordid past," blared the headlines. Horrified, she opened the tabloid to the next page. There was a photo of Ayita and her mother, laden with shopping bags. The article said the mother and daughter look-alikes had been on a nonstop party boozing and shopping. The lies were incredible.

Heartbroken, Ayita snapped up all the copies in the store, and then ran, sobbing to her car. She phoned her attorney on her car phone, leaving a message with Mary, his assistant.

Opening the door to the penthouse, still reeling from the horrific article, she froze. Juanita languished on the living room sofa, smashed.

"I've bin drinkin' all day. I'm so...o...sorry, Ayita. I jest had to drink. I made ya nice dinner, though."

Ayita had wondered how to broach the subject of A.A. with her mother. Now her hand was forced. She did not possess the strength to lay down the law to her mother, but God did, and she felt the leading of the Holy Spirit. "Mother, either you give up drinking and call A.A. right now, or I'll have to arrange for you to go into rehab tomorrow. It's your choice. I refuse to allow you to mess up your life and mine. Not to mention that you're destroying your health."

Ayita paused for effect before she delivered the punch line. "This is the end of the line for me." Ayita's voice was steel.

As smashed as her mother was, Ayita could see the shock value of her statement reflected in her mother's eyes. She looked scared, almost terrified, as if she'd just had a moment of utter clarity. Ayita knew her mother had never glimpsed this tough side of her...the mettle inside her that drove her to survive, succeed and excel.

Juanita struggled valiantly to focus. "I'll call A.A. Have you got the number?" Her words were slurred, but underneath Ayita sensed her crippling fear.

"I'll get it for you." Ayita strode to her small den and punched the name onto the screen of her laptop and printed out the details. "They meet at a church near here. The next meeting is at 8:00 a.m. I'll get them on the phone, but I want you to speak to them, Mother."

"What should I say?"

"Tell them you're an alcoholic and need help. Give them your name and cell number. Tell them you want to attend their next meeting."

Juanita took the phone. "I'm an alcoholic and I need

help," she said, slurring her words. "I'll be at the meeting tomorrow morning."

"The party's over. You're either going to stick with their program, or I'll throw you out on the street," Ayita said, with fierce determination.

"You wouldn't do that, Ayita." Juanita's words were slurred, but there was terror in her eyes.

"Watch me," Ayita said with stern resolve.

Wordlessly, she helped her mother into bed. Juanita glanced up at her. Neither spoke.

~~*~~

The alarm jarred Ayita out of a peaceful sleep. Why had she set the alarm for 6:30? Then she remembered her promise to drive her mother to the meeting. She jumped out of bed, got dressed swiftly, and then made coffee and breakfast before calling her mother.

"I will accompany you to the meetings for a lifetime, if that's what it takes," she told her mother as she insisted Juanita get out of bed.

The tabloid spies would notlikely be on the job at this hour of the morning, but if they were, rehab would not make as exciting news as relapses or benders.

The mother and daughter team arrived fifteen minutes early at A.A. A bevy of folks milled around, sipping coffee from Styrofoam cups. Several folks were already seated around a long table.

Ayita sported large sunglasses. Her long tresses were clipped into a knot at the back, held by a large clip. She wore a baggy, old gray sweat shirt and ill-fitting gray pants that went with it. It wasn't much of a camouflage but maybe it would suffice. God had given her the clarity to grab them at a thrift shop right after she'd scooped up the remaining tabloids. That was when the plan of action had been born.

As some of the members spoke, Ayita reflected on the first and only time she had ever tasted alcohol. It was vodka, and she had been sixteen. She had become sick as a dog. Between that experience and the horrors of living with an alcoholic mother, she had promised God and herself that she would never touch another drop as long as she lived, and she never had.

Ayita listened to the sad, laborious tales of recovering alcoholics and silently thanked God that she had never had a drinking problem. She also thanked Him that her mother was finally making an effort to end her boozing. That first day, at the end of the session, the group joined hands and admitted their helplessness over the demon of alcohol.

The miracle happened right away. Her mother vowed to stop drinking. Still, Ayita promised to accompany her mother every day to the meeting, to give her emotional support.

Once they were home, Ayita reread the article in the rag trades with a sickening feeling. She studied the large color photo of her mother, standing by the counter in the liquor store as she handed the clerk some bills for a large bottle of red wine. Ironically, Juanita looked attractive, sporting her new hairstyle. The glittery-gold embossed sweater she wore tucked into white jeans was flattering. The photographer had actually gotten a great shot of her.

Desperate for ideas and input, Ayita phoned Jerry, only to discover that he had already moved on and seemed to have little interest in her dilemma. *Thank-you for illuminating me, Lord.*

"You're in the limelight. What do you expect?" he

threw back at her. "Any press is good press, don't forget."

Ayita decided to take the bull by the horns. If show business and publicity was a chess game, she would master it. She phoned the sleazy reporter and made a lunch date with him for the following day.

16

Ayita entered Antonio's at 1:00. She found Alan Greenwald at the bar hobnobbing with artists and their managers. It occurred to Ayita that he probably had a sadly lacking personal life. Maybe he lived vicariously through interviewing celebrities and trashing them. Alan looked like a movie-star in a polo shirt with a navy blazer and cream-colored slacks. He was draped over the bar, a bottle of Perrier and a glass in front of him. He was laughing animatedly. He stood next to a young female singer Ayita vaguely recognized from celebrity events.

The server found them a private table near the front of the restaurant. Masses of magenta bougainvillea plants grew outside the open-shuttered windows. Brilliant sunlight streamed through the windows. It was a glorious day.

The energy and bustle of affluent folk dining at a chic eatery was stimulating. She was starved. And she had carefully rehearsed what she wanted to tell Alan. "I want to thank you for getting my name in the rag papers."

Alan practically choked on his Perrier. "I beg your pardon?" he croaked.

She repeated verbatim what she had said. For one split second, Ayita could see him buying it. Then, quickly, he reverted to his normal stance-that of the hard, seasoned reporter. His reaction was laced with skepticism. "I don't know what you mean," he sputtered, blushing slightly.

"Oh, but you do..." She flashed him her most charming smile.

"You must have me confused with another reporter. I write *Rising Stars, Falling Stars.*"

"Confused? Me? I don't think so." She ignored his sputtering protests. "There is a smattering of truth in your articles, but most of it is blatant lies. I'll be suing, of course." Traces of steel showed through her velvet voice. If she had to play the classic iron-lady housed in a pussycat voice and gentle mannerisms, so be it.

His face hardened into concrete. He no longer appeared handsome. In fact, he looked downright devilish. "You won't be successful. I've been around for over twenty years in this business, and no one has ever successfully sued me."

"Don't get cocky. There's always a first time, and trust me, I'll be it."

The server brought their salmon patties and salads. Ayita moved her purse closer to Allan. Inside the flap she'd concealed a mini-recorder.

"Doesn't the editor have the final say on the copy? Doesn't he or she verify all the details and information before the article goes to press?"

"Of course," he said, swiftly.

"Then you have nothing to worry about. It's all about the rag paper's editors, not the individual reporter. Just for the record, Allan, Mother has given up drinking. And I never touch alcohol."

"If I hadn't broken the story, someone else would have, sooner or later," Alan said, defensively.

"Maybe-maybe not. Is *your* Mother still alive?"

"Very much so. She's a vital and wonderful lady."

"Would *you* feel protective if someone assassinated *her* character?"

His gaze hardened. "I'd probably kill anyone who dared hurt my mother."

"So you understand how fiercely protective I am of *my* mother."

"Yeah, I guess I do." He shrugged.

"Is it really necessary to dig up dirt on people? Perhaps you would last a lot longer and have a more blessed career if you cancelled ugly stories defaming people. You could write about my mother's sobriety...after a lifetime of boozing. Now that would make a good story."

She tilted her head toward him. "Do you know how much courage it takes to give up drinking when you've done it most of your life? Yes, she was a wild woman, but that's all in the past. She's turned a new leaf. Mother is about to morph into a fabulous new woman. You'll see. She talked about doing philanthropic work the other day. I could see her doing that sort of thing."

Alan rolled his eyes. "I'll get the check," he said, when the bill arrived and was placed between them on a tray.

"No, Alan, this is on me. I invited you, and I insist on paying."

"Please let me pay."

"If you insist." Somewhere inside this man lurked a conscience, after all.

~~*~~

Ayita had called the rehearsal for 3:00, which would give her plenty of time to jot down some notes for the meeting with her attorney. Mary had squeezed her in for 2:15 today.

Ayita arrived early and studied her notes. At exactly 2:15 Mary motioned to her. "Mr. Thalberg will see you now. You know where his office is."

Lars Thalberg made brief notations based on what she told him and soon glanced at his watch. "I'm sorry, Ayita, I have another meeting. I can give you about ten minutes. I know you want to move quickly on this, so could we do a dinner meeting tonight? Do you like steak?"

"Very much."

"Chuck's Steak House on Music Row-seven p.m. I've been preparing for a big trial. But tonight I'm all yours," Lars said. Ayita gave him a thumb nails sketch in case he wanted to do any research and left within ten minutes.

After rehearsal, Ayita changed into a dinner dress, warning her mother, "You better behave yourself. I'm going to sue that sleazy reporter, so you need to stay off the sauce."

The steaks were cooked to perfection. They both ordered baked potatoes with sour cream, chives and bacon bits. "So, Lars, which is the best way to go? Do we sue the reporter personally, or do we sue the rag paper? Or both?"

"Well, this is definitely character assassination. You have a lot at stake here. Problem is, if you fight them, they'll fight back. It could get uglier and expensive, not to mention time-consuming. The reporter is going to say he's within his rights, because what he said was true, and the photo was partial proof."

"Partial proof?" Ayita asked, confused.

"Theoretically, she could have been buying the wine for someone else, or for a party. He did not actually see her consume it, correct?"

"Correct," Ayita said.

"My advice is to let the bad press fade. By next week, they'll have another cover story, and the public will already have forgotten yours. I do not advise you to rush into a court battle. Court cases are expensive and time-consuming. Your time is valuable. Focus on helping your mom kick the habit and get back to work. And don't forget, the press will be keen to cover the court case, and the new reporter may dig up even more stuff than the last one."

"So you're saying I might be opening a can of worms? Is that it?"

"Precisely. Unless you can prove loss of earnings relating specifically to the bad press about your mother, you could lose the case. Keep in mind it was your mother's character that was defamed, not yours."

"But..." She entwined her fingers in frustration.

"I know. It reflects badly on you, and the press might start digging into your former life on the Reservation. But I say take a walk. If they manage to sidetrack you on your career path, then they have won a small victory, haven't they?" He took a bite of steak and then a long sip of the Pellegrino water.

"I think we should instigate an article with a photo of your mom sipping Perrier and attending A.A. meetings," he added. "Get some great photos of the two of you, attending sporting events or something like that. There is a lot of truth to the adage, 'There's no such thing as bad press.' I'm betting your CD sales will soar because of this. You may find this incident boosts your career. If we can get some sort of public apology, stressing that your mom is diligently attending A.A. and has stopped imbibing, you'll save yourself a lot of time, aggravation and money. Alan has never seen your mom drunk, has he?"

"No."

"All right. You have nothing to worry about. The paparazzi are notorious for planting unflattering photos of celebrities and their families. If Alan doesn't retract his statements in the rag papers and the local press, we can nail him quite easily. He won't be able to provide proof that she consumed the wine she purchased, and is a habitual drunk. Even if he digs up all kinds of dirt from her past, it won't mean a thing. We'll make sure a lot of photos of your mom at A.A. show up in the press in the next few weeks.

"That certainly puts it all into perspective, doesn't it?" Ayita sighed.

"In theory, the wine your mother bought could have been for a party or social purposes."

She nodded. "Good point."

Lars leaned forward, resting his forearms on the table. "My goal will be to put a positive spin on this whole scenario. I was thinking we could check your Mom into the Betty Ford Clinic in Rancho Mirage, California, and make sure a publicist follows her. We'll play her problem up as a point of interest. If you believe that part of her motivation to stay sober is because she loves you and doesn't want anything to put a crimp in your career, people will identify with her and warm up to her."

She saw his point. "The Betty Ford Clinic is a great idea. I'll check it out."

"The public is interested in every aspect of a celebrity's life. It's really up to the artist to direct and educate their interests. Help them get involved in her sobriety. Make them want to root for her and believe that she can triumph over her addiction. Once we get sympathy on our side, you'll find the public will want her to overcome her weakness and move on to a better life. The general public tends to identify with the underdog."

Ayita left the dinner meeting feeling on top of the world. But the moment she walked into her apartment, she sensed something was amiss. For one thing, it was eerily silent. Normally when she returned home from rehearsal, either there was music playing or the sound of one of the T.V. sets. The apartment was in darkness, devoid of even a night light.

"Mother?"

Silence.

Ayita had a sudden foreboding. Sure enough, her mother was snoring loudly. passed out on her bed. On the nightstand, stood a magnum of open red wine, revealing only a tiny portion remaining. Ayita shook her head. *Mother, how could you?* It was her former life on the Cherokee Indian Reservation all over again.

She sighed deeply, whispering to her mother. "I'll let you sleep it off. But tomorrow we will deal with this."

~~*~~

It was almost noon the next day when Juanita, dressed in a yellow silk robe, her hair disheveled, ambled into the kitchen. Ayita had cancelled rehearsal. She had been waiting for hours for her mother to wake up.

She served her mother coffee, inserted a slice of bread into the toaster, and depressed the level. "Mother, we need to talk," she said, taking a seat at the kitchen table.

Her mother was stooped over her mug of coffee, her shoulders sagging. Her face was blotched, her eyes bloodshot. The remorse and shame she felt was palpable. It seemed to weigh her down like a heavy cloak.

"What happened, Mother?" Ayita asked.

"My desire to drink jest overwhelmed me, and I bought some wine."

"But you were supposed to call your sponsor or someone from the group. They would have talked you out of taking a drink."

"I didn't have their numbers handy because...I thought I had this thing licked."

Ayita was afraid to ask, but she did. "That reporter...he didn't stop by last night, did he?"

"Yeah, he showed up here."

Ayita was flabbergasted. She took a deep breath, trying to regain composure. "Were you loaded when he got here?"

"The buzzer rang, and I answered it. Yeah, I was loaded. I'm not gonna lie to you after all you've done fer me."

"Oh Mother, I've been trying so hard to protect both of us..."

Juanita put her hands over her face and began sobbing like a child. "I wish I could stop, baby, I jest can't. I better go back to the gutter where I belong, instead of destroying yer life."

"You can quit; you already have. This was only a relapse. We'll get beyond this. I swear we will. No pity parties. We're moving onward and upward."

"I wish I could believe that," Juanita lamented, disheartened.

But Ayita was a survivor, and *she* would make sure her mother would survive too, with God's help.

"I feel guilty and terrible about it, and I wish with all my heart I didn't have this weakness, but it's bigger than both of us, baby. I fought the impulse to take a drink all day...well, up 'til 3:00. Then I couldn't stand it any longer. I walked past the liquor store twice, tryin' to resist goin' in, but finally on the third time, I caved in. Juanita sighed. *"Just this once,"* I told myself. I'll drink this bottle of red and then I'll give it up forever."

"Let me pray with you, Mother. I don't have any answers but God does. And I believe the recovery group has some answers. After all, they share your compulsion. You must connect with them in a meaningful way, listen to their stories. They have sagas of sobriety and survival. You can do it," Ayita said firmly. "No, you *will* do it. Come on, let's look at the schedule and see if we can find a meeting."

The schedule was tacked to the fridge. Ayita glanced down the list of meetings and found a 12:00 meeting at the church up the street. "We have to leave right away. Get dressed. We're going. I chopped up some fruit. I'll put it in the fridge for you. You can have it as soon as we get back from the meeting."

Juanita shuffled into her room, emerging ten minutes later in a black silk V-neck sweater and a pair of tan slacks. Remarkably, she looked good.

~~*~~

Alan was pleased with himself. He tape-recorded Juanita's inebriated voice when she'd answered the buzzer. Armed with that, he had weaved a story around Ayita and Juanita, careful to pepper it with as much truth as he could muster up. He planned to drop it off to all the rag papers, in the hope someone would pay him for the story and print it. He felt a bit sheepish doing it, but he had to make a living, after all.

He was doing her a favor anyway, because the sooner she realized it was a jungle out there, the sooner she could learn to cope with it. Besides, he really disliked her goody-two shoes attitude. It grated on him.

~~*~~

Lars Thalberg phoned Ayita late the following morning. He had contacted the rag paper that had run the story on Ayita and her mom. "I told them she does not touch alcohol anymore. She was buying it for a party." But Lars said he got the big brush-off at the newspaper. He added that it wasn't the first inquiry about the headquarters of the sleazy rag paper.

Ayita saw red. "Where is their head office, and who runs the paper?"

Lars flicked through his rolodex. He located a name and number and gave it to Ayita.

She wasted no time. She flew to Orlando the next morning and marched right into the paper's head office, minutes after it had opened. It was 9:00 a.m.

"May I speak to the president?" Ayita asked the receptionist.

"He's not here. But Ms. Munarez pretty much runs everything. Do you want to see her?"

"I do." The receptionist announced her name and buzzed Ms. Munarez. "She'll see you right away. She's between meetings. Coffee, Ma'am?"

"No, thank-you."

"I'll show you the way."

Ayita followed her down a long hallway until they came to a door marked *Ms. Munarez, General Manager.*

The tall, striking black woman ushered her into a posh office, overlooking manicured lawns and a smattering of date palms. She sported an Afro and wore a bright orange blouse and white pants, cinched by a wide tan leather belt. "I just love your music," she said, "Can't get enough of it. I'm delighted to meet you. I saw you on *Grand Ole Opry* a couple of times. Your singing is absolutely amazing."

"Thank-you."

"What can I do for you?" Ms. Munarez asked as soon as they were seated.

"I'm here to correct a false story that was published involving Mother and myself."

"I think I know the story you're referring to. Allan

wrote it, am I correct?"

"That's right, Ms. Munarez."

Ms. Munarez flicked through the most current issue of the rag paper before passing it over to Ayita. "Is this the article?"

"Yes."

Ms. Munarez held a notebook and a pen was poised at the ready.

"My mother has stopped drinking. She is in the A.A. program, but she had a relapse. The spin put on the article makes it seem like we're a couple of drunks on a non-stop party. That couldn't be further from the truth. Don't you check content before you publish it?"

"We try, but we don't have the manpower to verify every story. That's supposed to be the reporter's job."

"He has some bold-faced lies in his article."

Ms. Munarez frowned. "Can you be more specific?"

"He said Mother was continuously spotted buying vast amounts of alcohol and that he had seen us both inebriated on several occasions," Ayita said. "Let me set the record straight. I don't drink. I never have. Mother has stopped drinking. She had a brief relapse, but she's back in A.A."

"Okay, so he lied. What are you going to do about it?"

Ayita took a deep breath. "Sure, of course. I just wanted to make sure I was suing the right person. Did anyone here punch up the story, or was it printed exactly as he presented it?"

"Let me buzz the editorial department. We're going to find out right now."

After a brief chat with a staff editor, Ms. Munarez turned to Ayita. "The story was published as presented, with only a couple of words edited, which did not alter the story content."

"Thank-you for your help, Ms. Munarez."

So, Alan was her man. She would sue him on the personal covenant and then find out what her remedy was for the rag paper for publishing blatant lies.

Ayita flew back to Nashville the same day, arriving home late that night. Her mother was sleeping soundly. She kissed her lightly on the forehead before heading to the den to snatch some sleep. She flicked on her reading light and picked up her Bible to read a psalm.

There was a note on her night table. It was folded in two. She opened it.

Dearest Ayita,

You cannot possibly know how much happiness you have brought me by sharing your home with me. If I live to be a hundred, it will not be enough time for me to compensate for the happiness you have brought into my life.

I never shared this with you, but now the time is right to do it. I have been contemplating suicide off and on this past year. In the last few months, I had become increasingly attracted to the idea. But when I heard you sing on the Grand Ole Opry, I knew once and for all that it was not the solution to my suffering and frustration.

I realized that only God could help me. I understand now, in retrospect, that God was speaking to me through your music. I realize, also, that there was an unseen spiritual battle raging over my soul. Satan almost won!

If I had slashed my wrists and died as I'd been planning, I would be in hell right now. When you sang "Amazing Grace," I knew God was calling me to Him. I knew then that I had to find you and see you again. As soon as I laid eyes on you, I knew everything was going to be all right. I have a confession to make. I have already asked God to forgive my sin. I have been a secret drinker ever since I moved into your apartment. But this day, God has removed my desire to drink. Praise His Name! I don't know how, but I know in my spirit that this is the end of it. Thank-you, my precious, precious daughter, for helping me through this valley of tears, and entering the joy of living for Christ.

Tears spilled down Ayita's cheeks. Tears of joy mingled with love and compassion. What if she had not allowed her mother to move in with her? What if she had been too ashamed of her to have her around? What if she had accused her mother of being negligent or a shameless hussy? Or a hopeless alcoholic?

"For with God nothing shall be impossible" reverberated through the very depths of her soul. As Ayita dried her tears, she couldn't stop smiling.

God had turned her mother's scars into stars, just as he had done for Ayita. Her tears were now diamonds for Him. Diamonds that would sparkle and shine throughout all eternity. She fell to her knees in jubilant prayer. Moments later, crashing on her bed, she dropped off to sleep.

~~*~~

The fingers of dawn crept slowly across the horizon and it burst into a glorious, crimson sunrise. It was confirmation of the beauty and rejuvenation of her mother's soul.

Ayita spooned coffee into the filter basket, reveling in the early morning rays. She was fortunate to have an apartment that faced southeasterly. After pouring a cup of the freshly brewed mocha java, she sat at the kitchen table.

Every day was a new beginning.

"Good-morning, Ayita," her mother said appearing in the kitchen. She yawned as she poured herself a cup of coffee. "Mind if I join you?"

"Good morning, Mother. Since when did you become an early riser?"

"I used to be an early riser when you were very young. You probably don't remember that."

"How old was I?"

"Two, maybe three. You had a habit of waking me at the crack of dawn."

"No kidding."

"I didn't drink last night, and somehow because of it, I woke up early...and with a clear head. It feels great."

Ayita rose from her chair and gave her mother a big hug. "I'm so proud of you. I love you so much. I read your note, and I can only praise the Lord for His perfect timing. This proves God is never late. I'm so happy," she said, finally releasing her and sitting back on her chair.

"Valdez called while you were gone," her mother said.

Her heartbeat accelerated. "Where was he? What did he say?"

"He was still in Fairhaven. He made it a point of telling me that he had recently broken the engagement with his fiancée. He wants you to call him at home."

"Let him call me."

"I'm sure he will."

It was over between them, wasn't it? So why did she feel this sudden surge of excitement and anticipation at the possibility of seeing him again?

"I'm starved. I'll rustle up some breakfast for us," Ayita said.

Juanita smiled. "Sounds good."

She could never know how much her sobriety means to me, Ayita pondered. *Or how receiving her love and attention now means everything to me.* Ayita had been neglected most of her life. Now her mother was doting on her. Oh, joy unspeakable! Ayita had prayed for this love for as long as she could remember. No longer did she have to share her affection with the current man.

At that moment her mother took the eggs out of Ayita's hand. "I feel like making breakfast for us, honey. You don't mind, do you?"

"No, of course not. Maybe I'll plunk out a tune on the piano."

"Do that. I'll cook to music."

Ayita sat on the bench in front of her piano and began to play. Her creative juices flowed as she created a new one. The healthy, new relationship she was forging with her mother fueled her talent...sparked it. The song expressed what she was feeling even before she could identify it. She could almost glimpse into the infinite and understand that if she had not known such deep valleys and intense sorrows, the joy she was experiencing now would not be as profound.

The world was full of hurting people, and she and her mother had been part of that syndrome. Now her songs, both the lyrics and the music she wrote, would surely inspire other sufferers to believe in bright, new tomorrows. God had lifted them out of the mire, and maybe she could be the catalyst inspiring others to move out of their pits.

Her mother served breakfast on the deck. They chatted, making social plans and confiding secrets. They were becoming close friends.

"Do you mind if I go shopping today?" her mother asked. "I need to pick up a few things-a couple of casual sweaters and some hair products."

"Take my credit card. That's what money is for, so we can enjoy it and have a good life. And guess what? It's only the beginning. My producers called me a couple of days ago. They want to meet with me about doing a new album featuring the music I wrote. They want my own compositions to be the focal point of the tour, also."

"Great." Juanita frowned. "You're sure about loaning me the credit card?"

"I'm absolutely sure. I trust you totally."

She fetched the card from her purse and handed it to her mother. But Juanita's shopping expedition was incidental. It was the call from Valdez that had started her mind and heart racing.

17

Airlines flight 697 touched down effortlessly at Nashville International Airport. Ayita watched it as it landed. Dusk was settling in. She checked her watch-three minutes early. It was 4:49. She waited near the off-ramp. She could hardly wait to see Valdez.

When he strode down the arrivals ramp, their eyes met. They rushed toward each other. She hugged him and knew he didn't want to let her go.

Finally, he released her and gazed at her. "I love you, Ayita." Emotion brimmed in his eyes.

She accompanied him to the luggage carousel. He pulled his suitcase off the carousel and rolled it outside. She led the way to her car and drove him to the Hilton. He checked in, handing his suitcase to the concierge, then hopped back in the car. Juanita would have dinner ready by the time they reached Ayita's penthouse.

The swordfish was perfectly cooked, and so was the asparagus and salad. Juanita also served one of her many desert creations-a concoction consisting of cherries, Jell-O and Philadelphia cream cheese. Right after dessert, Juanita vanished into her room.

Valdez surprised Ayita by scooping her up in his powerful arms and carrying her out onto the terrace. She laughed gaily, relishing every moment of it, but as a lady, she felt she had to pretend to protest. "Put me down. What do you think you're doing?"

"I'm practicing carrying you."

Ayita blushed. She knew what he meant, of course. But was he teasing or serious?

"You're so gorgeous. And I'm so grateful you didn't marry Jerry."

"I'm glad you're still single, too."

"Ayita, I have a confession to make." He set her down then, and they both gravitated to the loveseat. "I was trying desperately to get your attention when I told you I was getting married. I wanted to make you jealous. I wanted you to fight for me. You're the one I've always wanted. If we can agree on theology, maybe we can build a life together," he pleaded.

She put up a hand. "I don't want to talk about it tonight. I just want to enjoy you, with no complications."

"I can offer you a great life. With Dad's passing, I'm a wealthy man. My attorney tells me it will be about another month to settle the estate, but it's much larger than I realized, and I'm the sole heir."

"I don't care about the money."

"But I want to share it with you and build a wonderful life together."

She didn't know what to say, because as far as she knew, his theology hadn't changed.

"Dad had three portfolios, a Swiss bank account, and of course, the house in Fairhaven. Then there's his vast art collection, as well as his own work. Oh, and the villas in Madrid and Marbella."

"This is a sorrowful time for you, Valdez. Please...let's not talk about your wealth." She found it gauche. Was he so insecure with her that he had to brag about all the money and property he's inherited? Money was clearly his god.

He was trying to buy her again, and that didn't sit well with her. After all, she earned her own money. If he were totally broke, she would still find him wildly attractive. The responsibility that came with having that kind of wealth was scary. So much had happened to her so fast. It was overwhelming to learn about his newfound wealth and that he wanted to share it with her. Sometimes she felt like she was in a race car on a speedway with no end in sight.

Still, she had always loved him. She knew that now, without a doubt, as she gazed upon him. She had tried to make it work with Jerry, had tried doggedly to thrust Valdez from her mind and heart, but she had failed. Valdez was the love of her life, and he always would be. He was the man she was born to love.

"I will need to make a trip to Europe...line up some art exhibits there, perhaps mingle Dad's work with mine. The price for his work will skyrocket as soon as the public realizes he's dead." He shook his head. "Dad never wanted to sell his work. He only parted with a few pieces to close friends. Maybe that's part of the reason collectors were always clamoring for his work."

"I love his paintings. He was very gifted," Ayita said.

"He just kept on painting. He sold a couple pieces to friends and that was about it. He didn't need the money. Of course, he knew his paintings would be more valuable after his death. Perhaps he planned it that way from a business perspective."

"What did he live on?"

"Stock dividends, and the interest from investments, mostly. He did sell the odd painting to collectors. He wanted to leave me a nice inheritance, because he had more than he could ever spend. After Mother died, he became a recluse. That's why I insisted on moving in with him. He had no interest in eating out or spending money. Dad was always a saver."

"It sounds like he was an astute businessman."

"Very much so. He taught me how to manage money and invest it. There has been a great deal of money in our family for generations, and the wealth just keeps growing."

"You're very fortunate."

He gazed tenderly into her eyes. "I'm hoping you'll help me spend it."

"I don't know, Valdez. But I'd love to see the villas sometimes. What do they look like? Do you have pictures of them?"

"Somewhere in the Fairhaven house, probably. They're both ancient. The villa in Madrid is an old mansion, well over a hundred years old. My granddad bought it very cheaply. It's in considerable disrepair. It has masses of ivy growing over one side of it. There's an Olympic-sized pool in the backyard and masses of garden statues and fountains and such. The house sits on two acres. It's very private because the estate is walled, and the entrance has a tall iron gate. It's been rented to friends of Dad's for years."

"Do they still live there?"

"Yes, they do. But I've often thought I'd like to move in. I might pay them a visit and give them notice to vacate," Valdez said.

"You would live on that large estate by yourself?"

"Maybe with you." He waggled his brows and grinned.

She felt herself blushing.

And then Valdez leaned down and pulled her close to him, wrapping his arms around her in a tender embrace. His lips came down on hers in a long, slow, sensual kiss, and she knew in her heart that someday she would belong to him completely. God would work out the details. She was certain of it.

The events shaping his life would mold him into the man God wanted him to be. He was notably more mellow and humbler than he had been the last time she'd seen him. She felt more deeply connected to him, perhaps because of his sorrow. If it was true that tragedy united people, then that was happening with the two of them. He had poured his time and life into his work, but now he was mourning and reflective, vulnerable and hurting. She knew he needed her more than he ever had, and she wanted to be there for him with all her heart.

Because she'd known heartache as a child, she had become a woman wise beyond her years. Her crude beginning, and the sufferings and challenges she'd survived had filled her with compassion.

He strode to the deck and opened the sliding glass doors. She followed him. "I just never thought he would go so soon...so suddenly. Death is always unexpected, isn't it?" His shoulders heaved and he sobbed, brokenly.

Her heart ached for him. "Always...it's always too soon. I felt that way when my granny died." Her stomach lurched. She reflected for a brief moment on the day she had stared death-her own-in the face, and cheated it.

"I'm going to make a pot of tea," Ayita said. She was feeling teary herself, and she wanted to be a tower of strength for him.

He kept his back turned. Suddenly, he spoke with passion. "You'll be pleased to know that my dad became a Christian on his deathbed. The hospital chaplain led him to the Lord only days before he went to meet his Maker."

"I'm thrilled to hear that," Ayita said, but she was done witnessing to Valdez. The Holy Spirit would have to convict him of his sins and his need for Jesus. She had done all she could. But it struck her that Valdez wanted to discuss theology tonight. Perhaps his dad's passing had made him think more about eternity than he ever had before. Also, the fact that his dad had accepted the Lord on his deathbed must have had a profound effect on him.

Valdez was a dichotomy. On the one hand, he was

reaching out to her and admitting his need for the Lord. On the other hand, he seemed to be locking this same need inside him and isolating himself from facing his human frailty. He seemed lost and confused. She knew it frustrated him that her position with the Lord was unalterable.

He kissed her good night late that evening. Then he phoned a cab and went back to his hotel, leaving her spirit unsettled because of the unsolved issue in their relationship.

~~*~~

When Valdez phoned early the next morning, Ayita accepted a lunch date with him. In spite of knowing their relationship was a dead-end street she couldn't help the way she felt about him. Once she was finished doling out sympathy at the loss of his father, she would have to pull herself together and move on.

Tommy's, an industry hangout in Music Row, bustled with activity. Over Crab Louie and iced tea, Valdez shared a story with her. He'd met a lady realtor at an open house, and they'd clicked. She invited him to her sumptuous home and began telling him about various real-estate dealings. She also told him she was a believer and attended church regularly. He hadn't felt romantic toward her, but he thought she was amusing. A few days later, while scanning the local news, he was riveted to an article containing her photo. His new acquaintance had lost her real-estate license due to obscuring and altering facts pertinent to a real-estate contract.

According to the article, previous charges had been filed against her, as well. She had been grappling with lawsuits for many years. The judge brought down his gavel, saying "Young lady, you are not fit to sell real estate. I hereby revoke your license. This is the third and last time I expect to see you in my court. Your license was issued to you in good faith. You have seen fit to misuse your fiduciary trust, in addition to obscuring and altering facts relevant to the contracts at hand. As a menace to the public, I require you to contact your Real Estate Board and return your license at once."

Valdez paused. "She seemed like a nice lady. I had no idea she was a crook. By the looks of her residence and her lifestyle, I'd wager a guess that she never has to work another day in her life. She talked about relocating to the Bahamas. That's probably what she did."

He seemed to need to get this story off his chest, so she let him ramble on. "So this means all Christians are untrustworthy?" Ayita raised her eyebrows for effect.

"No, but it means I'm wary of people who call themselves Christians. I like to see proof. My point being that I think I'm a better person than some of them are, so why should I become a Christian?"

Ayita took a long sip of the iced tea. "For one thing, because the Bible clearly states that you will never enter the kingdom of God unless you are born-again. That, for starters, should jolt you into reality."

"But I believe in God, so I'll go to heaven."

"You still don't get it, do you?"

"So give me your version."

"We're born once of the flesh, but in order to enter the kingdom of heaven, we need to be born of the Spirit. You need to invite Jesus to come and live in your heart. When that happens, your priorities change, and you become a new creature in Christ. It's quite amazing, really."

"You make it sound so simple."

"Actually, it is."

"I'll have to think about it."

"Don't take too long. Remember, none of us ever really knows how long we have. We may not have tomorrow. Life is, after all, fragile. We could be killed in a car crash today. How do we know we won't?"

He frowned. "Oh, lighten up. Let's talk about something else."

"What would you like to talk about?"

"Us." He gestured to her and then back to him.

"We're at an impasse, Valdez. And you're the only one who can fix it."

"That's unfair. I would be good to you. I could give you a fabulous life."

She never would have believed that money could seriously tempt her, but it was wooing her, beckoning her, in spite of herself. Money would make her life easier. She lived beyond her means, but so did a lot of folks. She couldn't help it. Nashville's music industry was highly competitive, and to keep her edge, she had to stay ahead of the curve. New costumes had to be designed and created each time she performed on television. Scores sometimes needed to be rewritten. Musical directors, musicians and choreographers had to be paid on time, and so did back-up singers and dancers. Her expenses were astronomical. When her name got bigger, her manager would be able to negotiate astronomical fees for her live performances, but right now she was thrilled to be included in the Nashville clique of popular vocalists. She had outgrown her modest penthouse. Her mother was totally dependent on her. Although she hadn't mentioned it to anyone, she was slipping further into debt every month. Credit cards were fun, but she knew that the interest she paid was a waste of her hard-earned cash.

Ayita wanted to live in a house like other hot vocal artists. She needed a rehearsal studio and a gym. She yearned to get back to riding. All the people she hobnobbed with lived in spacious homes. She knew her mother would flourish in a house. She would probably get more into cooking and baking. Maybe even take up gardening. She'd always had a domestic bent, which had surfaced between drinking bouts.

Soon, Ayita would be working with costume designers for her tour. Then there was the bus rental and the cost of the back-up musicians. Her gross costs were enormous. She wouldn't be netting all that much on her first tour, but Lars Thalberg, her entertainment attorney, who handled all her business since leaving Tizzy, assured her it would solidify her as a household name.

Some days she didn't even want to think about how much she was spending. There were the bi-weekly massages, which helped to relax her body as well as her voice. There were the veneers she'd had done, her manicurist and her hairdresser. Yep, she needed more money.

Lately, she'd begun dreaming about buying a house, but she would need at least a couple hundred grand for a down payment, and she had nowhere close to that amount saved up. Valdez could fill that void. With his money, they could buy her dream home in Nashville and she would never want for anything, He could manage her career and she could focus on her career.

Reality struck. Why was she going through this exercise? Valdez continued to sit on the fence, spiritually speaking, and maybe he always would.

She reflected on her former relationship with Jerry.

Recently, she'd come to the conclusion that she needed a father figure, and Jerry had fit the bill. Maybe she could move forward to a healthy relationship with someone around her own age. *If only it could be Valdez!*

Deep in her heart, she knew she had to leave the problem with the Lord. She was only human, and leaning onto her own understanding was not working. She needed to tap into God's wisdom. She was done witnessing to Valdez. It was up to the Lord to work a miracle in his heart. She did have something in her favor, though. Over the last two years, since her attempted suicide, she had developed a deep, unshakeable belief in the power of prayer and God's sovereign timing in answering it.

Valdez phoned the next day, approaching his subject gingerly. "Don't read anything into my motives, but would you like to join me in viewing some properties today? I'd like to get a handle on what is available in Nashville, as well as an idea of prices. I thought we could start with some open houses. Maybe we could look at a couple of estates after that. I know your schedule. I'm thinking we could do opens Saturday and Sunday, maybe see a couple of estates by appointment."

"Actually, I would enjoy that, Valdez. I'll tag along."

"I'll pick you up around noon. I'll bring the real estate papers. We can get take-out when we get hungry. I took the liberty of making a couple of appointments. I hope you don't mind."

Valdez picked her up in his rented Mercedes, armed with maps. They drove to an upscale subdivision. Soon they were cruising down winding streets, following the *Open House* arrows. They were in and out of the spacious, lovely home quickly. "I want something more private, ideally with a couple of acres."

They cruised around ritzy areas featuring massive homes and walked through a couple of them. Just before 4:00, they drove up to an imposing, walled estate property. Debbie Shaw, a bright, attractive, bubbly gal, flashed a smile as she stepped out of her gold Mercedes. The pink designer suit she wore perfectly complimented her deep tan and well-maintained blond tresses. "Good-afternoon. Debbie Shaw." She handed them both her real estate card. "Shall we proceed?"

Valdez was slightly amused. "Absolutely," he said.

Debbie announced her arrival over the intercom in front of a private, gated estate. The tall, iron gates slowly parted. A pair of nasty-looking Dobermans sprinted toward their cars, barking ferociously.

A sleek, elegant woman clad in jodhpurs was just steps behind the dogs. She called them off, marching them to separate quarters at the side of the house and locking them inside. "The house is open. Go ahead in. I'll just go for a little ride while you're showing the house. Enjoy the tours," the owner said, smiling warmly at her prospective buyers. "Leave the doors unlocked when you're done. I won't be far away."

The Southern Plantation-style house stood stately and proud flanked by a backdrop of swaying palm and magnolia trees. Six towering white pillars graced the front of the house. Valdez and Ayita followed Debbie inside.

Debbie had done her homework. She spoke knowledgeably about the property, instantly gaining Ayita's respect and admiration. Glancing over at Valdez, she knew he felt the same way. She handed each of them a glossy brochure on the property and then toured them through the house.

According to the brochure, the house was seven

thousand square feet. "It makes it easy to recall the features of each room, at a later time," Debbie said, smiling at both of them.

"Could we see the pool and the gardens before we tour the second level?" Valdez asked.

"Of course."

Debbie guided them outside, through the main floor's French doors. They walked through a courtyard, beyond which loomed a colossal pool. The sparkling blue waters shimmered in the sunlight as swaying palm trees cast their shadows, bestowing shade over the pool. On scorching days, they would be welcome buffets.

Debbie led them back through the house, entering by another door, which accessed a separate wing of the house. She toured them through a state-of-the-art gym, beyond which was a large recreation room. The master bedroom was next. It was a stately room featuring tall, arched windows enhanced by peach floral balloon drapes, a white marble fireplace and a luxurious suite with a sunken Jacuzzi tub. Double French doors stood at the west end of the room.

Debbie opened one of the doors so she could show her prospects the sweeping vista below that encompassed the private gardens and pool.

"What a spectacular house," Ayita said, overwhelmed.

"I think I could live here," Valdez joked.

Debbie smiled. "I knew you would love this house. Wait 'til you see the closets!"

They trailed her into a deep walk-in closet brimming with designer clothing, shoes and handbags. Adjacent was a mirrored dressing room and wet bar, and next to that was a gentleman's closet. It, too, was well-stocked.

"And don't you just love that classical music playing?

It's piped into every room." Debbie smiled, confidently.

"It sure would be fun to live here!" Ayita blurted.

Once the tour was over, the three of them stood outside the house, gazing up at it. Debbie turned to her new clients. "What did you think? Can you envision yourselves living here?"

Valdez turned to Ayita. "It's yours for the asking."

The realtor did a double take.

Ayita gaped at him as though he had taken leave of his senses. "Why would you want a home this massive?"

"Well, it's my understanding that the more expensive the house, the fewer the buyers. I've heard you can sometimes get a better deal by offering on a pricey home."

"What *is* the asking price?" Ayita asked.

"Two point five. Actually, it's a bargain at that price," Debbie assured them. "But I still have two other estates lined up to show you. Maybe you'll like one of them better." She flashed Ayita a professional smile.

As they followed Debbie's convertible, Ayita studied the feature sheet on the house, fascinated. "You wouldn't really consider buying a house that costly, would you?" Ayita searched Valdez's face.

"Yes, I would. How do you think my father and grandfather made their fortune?"

"Through real estate?"

"Yes, through buying and selling high-end properties."

"I see," Ayita said. And she did. She was a fast learner.

"Dad owned a sixty-unit apartment building in Madrid. He held it for about fifty years and made a bundle when he sold it. He held on to the villas, as you know. Dad said he couldn't bear to be around Marbella after Mom died, because it triggered too many memories. So he liquidated everything in that area. But he couldn't bear to sell Mom's favorite villa, the one in Madrid. It was his grandfather's. I'll never sell it, either."

Ayita could hardly believe her luck. Valdez was not only gorgeous and crazy about her, but also wealthy and possessed business acumen. She admired him. *Maybe he'll become more spiritual in time...*

Ayita could hardly miss the way Debbie smiled flirtatiously at him when she probably thought Ayita wasn't looking. She was getting used to the way ladies reacted to Valdez. As they followed Debbie in their car, Ayita wondered how much Debbie knew about Valdez's finances. Had she qualified him carefully before showing him properties? Jerry had told her that the hot-shot realtors had a way of ferreting out financial information from prospects before ever showing them a single property.

She'd observed Debbie scrutinizing her, as though trying to figure out what she had going to attract a man of this calibre. For a moment, Ayita thought she had recognized the woman from a promotional campaign, when she was selling her CD's. But Debbie hadn't mentioned it, and Ayita was glad, because she preferred to be incognito during her downtime.

Debbie pulled up in front of another iron gate, punched in a code, waited until the gates magically parted, and then drove up to the estate. Valdez and Ayita trailed closely behind her in their car.

The French Chateau was a stark contrast to the colonial house they had just viewed. She had no idea what style of home she preferred and she hoped that by viewing various homes, she would get an inkling of what her personal taste was. She had a vague idea of what she liked from *Beautiful Homes* magazine, but it was far more exciting viewing the actual homes, as opposed to gazing dreamily at pictures in magazines.

The house was vacant. She caught a whiff of a musty smell the instant she entered the house. Debbie must have noticed it, too, because she immediately began opening windows. "This is my own listing. The owners have gone back to the South of France, and they want the house gone. They moved out a couple of months ago. We thought we had it sold, but the buyer backed out at the last minute. The owners' attorney has advised them to sue for Specific Performance, but they hope they don't have to incur that cost."

"What does that mean?" Ayita asked.

"It means that legally the buyers can be forced to complete-to make good on their contract of the purchase of the house."

"Why did they back out, anyway?"

"I'm not quite sure. The buyers got cold feet-buyer's remorse, they call it, in the business-and since then I've heard half a dozen stories as to why they backed out. Anyway, we're looking for a new buyer. We may accept damages, meaning a substantial amount of cash for the inconvenience of not completing, if we can resell it quickly. After all, the sellers made plans abroad based on the accepted offer. They've had to take interim financing while waiting for the sale and monies from this house. So the owners are very motivated."

"What is the asking price and square footage?" Valdez asked.

"It's only $950,000. A bargain, really. The house is over five thousand square feet. That's a full acre we're looking at." Debbie pointed outside. "Sorry I'm out of feature sheets. We've had a lot of showings in the last two weeks, since it came back on the market, because we've priced it well below market value."

"The house doesn't seem to have much light. When and where does the sun come in?" Ayita asked.

"It's west-facing, so you get the afternoon sun. I admit it's not that bright in the morning or early afternoon. The sun should be hitting the patio around this time," she said, glancing at her watch.

"Is the house being offered furnished?" Valdez asked.

"It's turnkey, yes. Mrs. Boujay didn't want the hassle and expense of shipping furniture abroad. They've already moved into their new residence. It's a villa in Cap Ferat. They just didn't like it here, much," Debbie explained.

"Why did they move here in the first place?" Ayita asked, curious.

"Jacque is a lyricist. He's sold hundreds of songs to artists in Nashville. I think he thought it would be fun living here and good for business. But Lilianna, his wife, hated it here. She couldn't seem to fit in. She's a bit of a snob, anyway," Debbie said, smiling.

They were passing a baby grand. A smattering of framed photos were perched on top of it. Ayita couldn't resist. She picked one up and studied it. "Is this them?" she asked Debbie.

Debbie glanced at the snapshot. "Yes, it's my clients. That's Lilianna with her husband, the Marquis, Jacque Boujay. He rather liked it here, but she's a socialite, and she tells me it's much more interesting socially in Cap Ferat."

By now Ayita was getting into the swing of things. She enjoyed seeing how other folks lived. She decided she would think of it as an education and not take it too seriously. What Valdez did was his business. He was over twenty-one and had a mind of his own.

She found their garden delightful. The central focal

point was a swimming pool. Surrounding it were a variety of statues and a couple of cherubs with waterfalls sprouting from their bellies. Rose bushes and dozens of flowers she couldn't name grew wildly throughout the yard. There was a white, wrought iron bench in the garden, and even a gazebo.

"Thank-you for showing us these houses. I'll think about them. But I would like you to line up a few more for tomorrow, if you would, Debbie."

"I would be happy to," Debbie said and waved good-bye, as they left and she started closing down the house.

"Would you like to come over for some iced tea, Valdez?" Ayita asked. "And maybe I can rustle up something for dinner."

His grin was his answer.

When they arrived at the penthouse, they discovered that Juanita had made Paella. "Of course you'll stay for dinner, Valdez. There's too much food for just the two of us," Juanita insisted.

Dinner was delicious, and Valdez managed to make Ayita and her mother laugh uproariously at his constant barrage of jokes. Ayita knew he was laughing on the outside and crying on the inside. People dealt with sorrow in many different ways.

"Good night, Ayita," he said, shortly after dinner. He looked over to Juanita. "Thanks for a great meal." She walked him to door, but he did not take her into his arms. He knew her mindset. It made her want him all the more. She longed for him to sweep her into his arms and smother her with his kisses. Yes, darn it, she loved him as exasperating as that was.

Valdez phoned Ayita early Saturday morning. "Debbie has lined up more houses for another tour today at 2:00. I hope that works for you, Ayita."

"I can't wait." Ayita was becoming enthralled with the house-hunting project.

18

Monday morning found Ayita resuming her hectic schedule of rehearsals and writing music. She took her mother out for dinner frequently, because she had great pride in showing Juanita around Nashville. In the three weeks since Valdez had left Nashville, he had called several times and even surprised her with more flowers. She couldn't stop thinking about the houses they had viewed. At night, she dreamed about them, and during the day, she studied the feature sheets and photos of the houses, as though *she* were the prospective buyer.

Normally, Ayita worked hard and didn't allow herself the indulgence of fantasies. In this instance, though, she couldn't shake the idea of sharing one of the grand homes with Valdez. Of course they need to be married, and that would take a miracle, given their differences. But she'd seen miracles before, and maybe another one was just around the corner.

She imagined what her life would be life, if she were to marry Valdez. Except for their unsolved issue, the idea appealed to her immensely. If she were to marry him, at least there would be plenty of room for her mother. All the houses they viewed had a games or recreation room. That space could easily be converted into a rehearsal studio. On the other hand, she would soon be able to afford to buy herself and her mother a nice home. Maybe not as lavish as the ones she'd viewed with Valdez, but a house anyway.

Producers had projected that given her rising popularity CD sales would skyrocket during and after the tour. She could make millions and be able to put in an offer on a house. As it was, she was getting substantial fees for her live appearances as well as her guest appearances on

Grand Ole Opry and other shows, coupled with brisk CD sales.

She was in the enviable position of being sought after by prospective managers. She would have to settle on one soon. Meanwhile, she adored having Lars attend to everything.

About a week later, Ayita got a cold and had to cancel rehearsal. Her voice sounded scratchy and awful, and she had to take a complete rest, like it or not. She phoned Debbie on a whim, asking to view the colonial house again. It was definitely her favorite. She wished she could buy it herself...that is, if Valdez didn't mind.

"Hi, this is Ayita High-Eagle. You showed Valdez Lopez and me through a colonial house, recently. I wonder if I could look at it again. I'd also like my mother to see it."

"Hey, Ayita, good to hear from you. I'd love to show you and your mom the house. When is a good time for you?" Debbie asked.

"Any chance of seeing it around 2:00 or 3:00 today?"

"That works. Shall we say 2:00?"

"Perfect. I'm not sure if I can find it, though. Any chance you could pick us up?"

"I'd be happy to-just give your address."

The house was even more enthralling than Ayita had remembered. She envisioned herself living in it. She and her mother would flourish here. A wave of sadness washed over her. Why was she torturing herself? She couldn't marry Valdez, and she couldn't afford to buy the house herself. Anyway, if she did decide to buy a house and managed to swing it, she wouldn't qualify for any of the houses she'd viewed with Valdez-not to mention it would be in bad taste, since he had selected the homes and *she* was just accompanying him. And Debbie was *his* realtor.

Ayita walked through the house, peering around, but when they got to the games room, she began asking questions about acoustics. It was then that Debbie twigged. "Oh my gosh, I just realized who you are! You're that incredible gospel singer I saw on *Grand Ole Opry!* Why didn't you say something?"

"Well, now you know. It's no big deal."

"It's a very big deal. I came out here to Nashville twenty years ago and had aspirations to be a recording artist myself. I didn't make it. I finally gave up and went into real estate. It's been lucrative for me."

"Good for you. I'd love to hear you sing sometime."

"You *would!* Wow. I'll take you up on that. Although...I *am* a little rusty."

"Don't worry about it. If you're good, I might be able to put you to work as a back-up singer in my new show. That is, if you're interested. No promises, though."

"Cool. Well, I'm going to call Valdez and see if I can get him to make an offer on this house. It would be so perfect for the two of you."

Ayita resisted responding to her comment. She knew everything started with a dream, and she really needed to dream about owning this house.

Debbie toured the mother and daughter team through the house, pointing out some features they could easily miss. Ayita was most interested in the games room. When she finally had spent enough time there, Debbie showed them the kitchen. "I love these granite counters. Aren't they beautiful, Mother?" she said, turning to her. Juanita was clearly thrilled to pieces at the prospect of one day living in a house like this.

"Tell me, Debbie. Do you think it would work to convert the games room into a rehearsal space so I would have the option of rehearsing here, instead of renting rehearsal rooms? My friend, Anne, did an acoustic makeover in her home."

"You and Valdez could make an offer, subject to an acoustics expert determining the viability of converting this space into a workable rehearsal space."

"Of course, I could. I mean...of course Valdez could."

"Okay, we can move on," Ayita said, embarrassed, because she didn't have the details fleshed out, and at the moment, she couldn't marry Valdez. *I shouldn't be wasting Debbie's time.*

The gym was next. Juanita enthusiastically started trying out the equipment by stepping on the treadmill and running for a couple of minutes. "I'd need a crash course on how to use this equipment," Ayita said, glancing around.

"Details, my dear. Just details." Debbie was soaring. She sensed herself getting closer to a deal.

Finally, they all plopped down on lounge chairs by the outdoor pool.

"For most people, the purchase of a home is the single most important investment they will ever make," Debbie said. "That's why I always encourage my clients to take their time. It's very important to make the right choice. You don't want buyer's remorse every time you make a mortgage payment."

Ayita chuckled to herself. Amused by the abrupt change in Debbie's attitude the moment she realized she was a recording artist. Suddenly, she was treated with great respect, even awe, as opposed to being treated as merely girlfriend of the wealthy, charming Valdez.

"Incidentally, Debbie, just so you know, Valdez might buy the house and live in it by himself," Ayita clarified. "We do not have plans to get married, and I don't believe in living common law. So, you see, this outing is a bit of an indulgence on my part. But I will probably be in the market myself soon, and I'll make sure I deal through you. You've been very kind and helpful, in taking Mother and me through the house."

Debbie dropped Ayita and her mother off at the penthouse. "I'm going to run right out and buy your CD's, Ayita. It's thrilling to...make your acquaintance." Debbie's mind whirred. *There's a deal here. I just have to be aggressive.* "Can you stand by for a few minutes, ladies? I'm going to try Valdez on his cell and see if I can get him to make an offer on that house, even if it's a low ball. At least that would start the negotiations." She punched in his numbers on her cell before Ayita could protest. "Hey, Valdez. It's Debbie, your favorite realtor. I just had the pleasure of touring Ayita and her mother through the colonial house. *They love it! You love it!* Why don't you put in an offer? It's not going to be around long at that price. I had another couple snooping around at that house the other day. So far, it's their favorite, too."

Ayita couldn't hear Valdez's remarks, so she had to fill in the spaces by listening to Debbie's responses.

"A three month close would be perfect. That's about the usual time...maybe a month longer. You tell me the numbers, and I can type up the contract and fax it to you for your signature. A fax is now a legal document. You probably know that." She paused and then said, "Sure...we could start with that. I know the owner is a motivated seller. He might even take it," Debbie said. Then she handed the phone to Ayita.

"Hi Valdez."

"I'm putting an offer on the colonial house. What do you think?"

"I think it's a great house, and I'm sure you would enjoy living there. There's lots of room for an art studio and lots of room to showcase your paintings," Ayita said, trying to be helpful.

"Am I to believe that you've finally come to your senses and you're going to marry me? Terrific!" Valdez said, not waiting for her response.

"I didn't say that!" She couldn't stop a smile she knew lit up her face. "Call me tonight, and we'll talk further. I'll give Debbie back to you," she said, handing the phone back to her.

They signed off. "So how did it go?" Debbie asked Ayita.

"We're going to discuss it further tonight. He wants to hold off on the offer and sleep on it. It's a lot of money and big decision."

"Yes it is. Sounds like a good plan," Debbie said.

Valdez phoned right after dinner. He launched into a discussion about the house. "Ayita, I'm seriously considering putting an offer on that house, but I don't relish the thought of rattling around in that sprawling mansion all by my lonesome. Don't hang up on me. I have an idea that might work."

"Which is?"

"Every year it becomes more expensive to maintain a home. There are taxes, pool upkeep, gardeners, household help, not to mention the mortgage..."

"At the risk of sounding like my attorney, make your point, Valdez."

"Of course. Well...we could buy the house together. It's a great investment. Both of our names would be on the title...and..."

She cut him off. "Nice try, Valdez. I don't have my

share of the down-payment for starters..."

"Money is not the issue. As soon as the estate is settled, I can close on it. You're jumping to conclusions. I was thinking that you and Juanita could have one wing of the house, and I could have another. You would have the option of buying into the investment, whenever you choose to. You could own half of it when you get the money for half of the down-payment. We can split the mortgage and taxes, etc. Meanwhile, you could both live there, rent free, so you could save the down payment faster."

"It sounds like a good financial move. But I couldn't possibly consider it."

"I think you *should* consider it. Lots of folks share the cost of running a house. Very few are comfortable living alone in a grandiose house like that."

Temptation soared through her, but as quickly as it reared its ugly head, she made a conscious decision to deny it any life. Not only would it be a poor witness, but it was against her moral principles as a believer.

"I won't even consider it, Valdez. Somewhere I've read that a believer must avoid the appearance of evil."

He sighed and then tried again. "I think you're throwing a couple grand a month out the window when you could be investing in a house and building equity. Plus, you have to shell out money for rehearsal space. You could have that in the house."

"I could. And I've thought about that. But the proposition is out of the question."

"So...were you just teasing me, then? Is that it?" He sounded frustrated and verging on anger. "Why did you go and see the house? What was that all about?"

She was silent for a long minute. "I don't know. I just couldn't seem to get the house out of my mind...so I finally decided to take another gander. I thought maybe then I *could* forget about it. Thinking about that house kept me awake a couple nights."

He chuckled. "I don't want anything or anyone to keep you awake at night, *except me.* You're pretty much a household name already. Imagine the explosion once you do the tour and another album. You're going to have more money than you can spend. But from a business perspective, house prices are escalating every month, so the sooner you invest in one, the better. Why pay more than you have to? I'll tell you how much I believe in your future, Ayita. I'd be willing to put you on title *now,* knowing that you're going to have the money to make good on it. I'm betting on you, babe."

"That's noble of you, Valdez. And it certainly is tempting." Her knees felt wobbly. She wanted him so much that she actually ached. She *was* in love with him. Whatever was she going to do about it? If only she had stuck to her guns and broken off with him ages ago. It was becoming exponentially more difficult to end their relationship as time progressed.

"Well, it *would* give us a chance to get to know each other better." Was that her own voice she just heard? "Who gets that amazing master bedroom?" She spoke as though in a trance.

"You do. I insist. You can make good use of the walk-in closet, I can't. And the sunken Jacuzzi. Leisurely bubble baths are a girl thing. As long as my room has a bed and the bathroom has a shower, I'm good."

"You sure know how to tempt a girl," Ayita murmured.

"Promise me you'll think about it," Valdez insisted.

She hesitated. He had her attention, there was no denying that.

"I'll think about it," Ayita said, knowing she would be thinking about nothing *but* that. She already knew she could not, in good conscience, go through with it. Yet somehow she needed to go through the exercise.

She tossed and turned all night. She had known from the moment he had asked her to move into the house that she could not proceed. Yet she couldn't get that house out of her mind, along with the dreamy thoughts of sharing it with Valdez-married, or otherwise. *Oh, Lord, forgive me for even thinking about it.*

~~*~~

Ayita phoned Valdez early the next morning, determined to close the door on any further speculation. She would simply have to tell him she couldn't see him anymore. It was the only way. She dialed his number. "Good morning, Valdez."

"Good morning, Ayita. Do you have good news for me?"

He sounded so optimistic, she hated to burst his bubble. "I'm afraid I don't. Sharing that house with you as a single gal is totally out of the question."

"Ah, you've finally seen the light. You're going to marry me!"

"Nooo, I'm not," she said, slowly. "I can't see you anymore. This relationship is officially over. That's not what I want in my heart, but it's the way it has to be."

He paused briefly. "I see. You don't even want to be friends?"

"No, because you want more than that, and so do I," she admitted.

Those last words had slipped out involuntarily, but it

was the truth. She wanted much more with him. In fact, if truth be known, she wanted everything with him-love, marriage, kids, a life together.

"Please," she begged, "don't ever call me again. It's the only way, Valdez. I have no choice in the matter, and it saddens me."

She heard him sort of gasp and thought she heard a sob as he murmured, "Good-bye," then hung up the phone.

Juanita sat on the sofa, listening to music. Ayita snuggled up next to her and then slumped, sobbing, into her arms.

"You are hopelessly in love with that man," her mother said, embracing her.

"I suppose I am, Mother." Tears trickled down Ayita's cheeks. "I had to end it. What else could I do?"

"Baby, we gotta pray about this." Her mother took both her daughter's hands in hers and then began to pray. "Lord, please make it right for my baby. She wants Valdez and he wants her, but he jest ain't a Christian." Juanita tightened her grasp on Ayita's hands. "And, Lord, do ya think we could have that house? It's the desire of Ayita's heart."

"Thank-you, Mother," Ayita said between sobs. She put her arms around her mother for comfort. Then she, too, poured her heart out to the Lord. *"Lord, give me the courage to forget about Valdez and that house. I want to pick up the cross and follow you. I want to love you with my whole heart. Your Word says that we must not be unequally yoked, so I trust you to do a miracle in Valdez's heart-or help me to expunge him from my mind.* She felt better after laying her desires and dreams at the foot of the cross. She would cast all her burdens on Him and leave them there. She refused to worry or think about it any longer. Scripture promised, "Thou wilt keep him in perfect peace whose mind is stayed on thee."

Ayita ordered their favorite pizza with five cheeses, black olives, green peppers and tomatoes. Tonight felt like girlfriend night. They put their pajamas on and channel-surfed until they found a good movie. Hanging out with her mother was just what Ayita needed tonight.

"Good-night." Ayita kissed her mother gently on the forehead. She settled into bed early, turning on her reading light and opening the Bible. As an afterthought, she went to the kitchen and poured a glass of milk for herself. It usually helped her sleep, though it wasn't good for her voice. But she wasn't singing right now because she was still recovering from her scratchy throat

In spite of the milk, Ayita awakened during the night after a dream. In the dream, she and Valdez shared ownership of the colonial house, and she was happily married to him. She lay awake thinking about him, wondering how she was going to live with the reality of cutting him out of her life. *Or was God giving her a glimpse into the future?* She'd heard of prophets in the Bible having prophetic dreams. She knew that God sometimes used dreams to communicate truths and wisdom to people. Was this a message from God to her?

She recalled a sermon, in which the minister said, "If God closes a door, no man can open it. If God opens a door, no man can close it." Yes, she had done the right thing by ending the relationship. If God wanted them together, *He* would make a way.

The next thing she knew it was morning. Her voice was fine, so she called a rehearsal for 10:00. "We need to wrap at 4:00 everyone," Ayita said. "I have a dental appointment," Ayita told the singers, dancers and musicians. Rehearsal is l:00 P.M. tomorrow."

The following day, Ayita had a meeting with The William Morris Agency regarding representation. It was long overdue for her to sign with a manger, but she had managed nicely with her attorney handling everything. It was becoming very costly.

Melvin accompanied her. The meeting was a preliminary meeting only. Armed with her two CD's and demo reels of various TV appearances, including her three guest spots on *Grand Ole Opry,* Ayita and Melvin waited in the reception area. They had an appointment with the famed Leonard Marx. He was responsible for some of the most brilliant music careers in Nashville. Melvin had briefed him about Ayita's lawsuit with Tizzy and her attorney handling her business.

The meeting with Leonard Marx couldn't have gone better. From the moment she laid eyes on him, she knew he would be her new manager. He couldn't wait to have her on his roster. But by now, Ayita was a seasoned artist. "I'll need to have my attorney look over the contract before I sign it, of course," she said,

"Of course." The manager stood them, shaking their hands. "Terrific to meet both of you." He looked over at Ayita. "I've got a lot of ideas to guide you to the next level. It will be my pleasure to work with you. I know your work. I don't need to see your show tape-but you can leave here if you like."

Melvin spoke up. After all, she was his find. "Ayita is also a song writer. She's hoping to publish her first songbook titled *Gospel Selections: Music and Lyrics by Ayita High-Eagle.*

"I can help you there. Once you sign with us, let's meet and go over the strategy I'll be developing for your career and we'll discuss publishers for your song book. I may even invite one to join us for lunch..."

Leonard was steeped in the music business. That much was apparent at that first meeting. Ayita was on cloud nine.

Going down the elevator, Melvin finally cleared things up. "He doesn't take brand new artists, Ayita. That's why I put you with Tizzy originally. I'm sorry how things worked out, though. But we're all better without him in the industry."

"It's been a great learning experience, Melvin. I think I'm ready for the new manager. Provided Lars doesn't see any glitches in the contract, we'll be good to go."

"You're on your own from here. Lars will take good care of you. I'll see you later. I have to get back to the studio." Melvin hugged her good-bye and they both drove off.

~~*~~

Ayita read the Bible every morning over breakfast and lots of coffee. This morning she was reading in Malachi. *"Bring ye all the tithes into the storehouse, that there may be meat in mine house, and prove me now herewith, saith the Lord of hosts, if I will not open you the windows of heaven, and pour you out a blessing, that there shall not be room enough to receive it."*

Ayita had followed this tithing principle ever since she became aware of it, and she had been blessed to overflowing. Somewhere deep in her heart, she believed that God would find a way for her to buy her dream house and connect with her dream man.

The jangle of the phone interrupted her thoughts. Valdez's name flashed on the screen. "Ayita, please have dinner with me tomorrow night."

She took a deep breath. He had chosen to ignore her decision to break off with him. That irked her, but she had a powerful yearning to see him again. His voice caught at her heart. She squelched it, because her desire to please God was greater than pleasing man. She had to stick to her guns or admit she had no backbone. "I told you it was over between us. Please do not call me again." There were tears in her eyes, her voice breaking toward the end of the conversation.

"I'll go to church with you Sunday, if that will make you happy."

"This is not about going to church; it's about you committing your life to the Lord. We've been over this so many times before." Ayita sighed.

"What can I say? If I'm dumped, I'm dumped! Fortunately, you're not the only woman on the face of the earth," he barked, slamming the phone down.

19

Valdez was fuming. Who did she think she was, anyway? He had had enough of Ayita High-Eagle, Miss Singing Sensation. She had an annoying habit of dictating her terms to him, and he was fed up with it.

He picked at his dinner of steak, salad and baked potato. He had lost his appetite. Room service was less lonely than eating alone in one of the hotel's restaurants. But now, as he picked at his food, he realized he had no appetite. Should he try coaxing Ayita into seeing him again tomorrow? Or maybe he would fly back to Fairhaven like he said he was going to.

He checked his image in the mirror. He was handsome, educated and wealthy. She wasn't financially solvent at the moment, so who was she to be calling the shots? *Irksome. That's what it is.* He knew if she was here with him and he brought it up, she would respond by saying gaily, "I'm a King's Kid." He grinned, in spite of himself.

Oh, who was he kidding? He loved her. He wanted desperately to see her, and he was willing to bet she felt the same way. She was in love with him; he could feel it, in spite of the fact she was keeping her feelings tightly under wraps.

He made a decision. He would fly back to Washington first thing in the morning. After all, he had the business of the estate to attend to. Then he had to decide whether to auction off his father's work at Christie's in London or Paris or offer the work to private galleries in Europe. He also had his own work, which would fill his next home, even if that home was the five-thousand-square-foot colonial.

He decided to make an offer on the house by fax once

he returned to the Fairhaven house. That would give him a little more time to mull it over. Maybe he would even ask that hot-shot realtor, Debbie Shaw, for a date. It wouldn't be all that lonely living in the new house. He could always hire a live-in housekeeper and cook. Maybe he would get a second dog. He's always wanted an Afghan hound.

Eventually, Ayita would come around. He had seen her eyes when she'd looked at that house, and if owning it made him more attractive to her, so be it. He had always been able to get any woman he wanted. It was ironic that he wanted Ayita more than any woman he'd ever known, yet she eluded him. He had to face the fact that he wasn't in with her as solid as he wanted to be. Somehow, he would have to find a way to win her hand without having to get overly pious. It was a good thing he thrived on challenges.

He'd given some thought to moving into the house in Madrid, but with both his parents gone, he had to make a new life for himself. He preferred America over Europe. Also, he wanted to be available in case Ayita changed her mind. It was a woman's prerogative to do so, after all.

It was time to refine his strategy for roping Ayita into marriage. He would resist the temptation of phoning her. If absence made the heart grow fonder, he would disappear again. Fly to Europe and line up some galleries to showcase and sell his dad's work for starters. Maybe some of his, as well. Since gallery owners in London, Paris, Rome and Madrid had been hounding his dad for years to allow them to sell his work, he knew it would be a cinch to arrange some art shows. He would keep a couple of his personal favorites, but it was pointless to put the work in storage and let it collect dust. No, his dad's work needed to be shared with the world. He would make it a point to attend all the galleries' gala openings in lieu of his father, as the "Artist-in-Residence." It was acceptable in the art world for the son of a great artist to represent the work. His dad's paintings would fetch much higher prices posthumously than they would when he was alive.

Not that Valdez needed the money. He'd been born with a natural business acumen, just like his father. But the unveiling of his dad's vast body of work would pave the way for his own work to follow later. It would also give him an opportunity to meet international collectors. He might as well increase the size of his estate, so the sooner he converted assets into hard cash, the sooner he could reinvest that cash into the money market and real-estate holdings.

The phone in his hotel room rang. He picked it up. "How about joining me and a couple of friends for some dancing at Utopia? It's the hottest club in town," Debbie Shaw cooed.

He'd had a feeling Debbie was interested in him when she'd shown him the houses, but with Ayita present, she had only thrown him subtle hints, when Ayita had been out of earshot and eyesight. He was weary of being rebuffed by Ayita. It was time to exercise his options. He was an eligible bachelor, after all.

"Sure, why not?" Valdez said.

"I'll pick you up at your hotel. Around 10:00 tonight?"

"Sounds good."

He was stuck here for a few days anyway, because of a bomb scare. Flights had been temporarily suspended. He might as well have some fun. He showered and dressed and went online to get an update on his flight. No change. He had two free nights in Nashville.

He checked out his image in the mirror, standing back to admire the pricey suit he had chosen for his night on the town. The cream color enhanced his swarthy good looks. The Ralph Lauren shirt would look great under it. It was crisp and new and had cherry-colored stripes. He flexed his muscles. Working out regularly kept him in great shape. Maybe no one would notice how crushed he was underneath it all. He knew it was rather in bad taste to be dating a realtor Ayita had met, but it was Debbie or no one. He didn't know anyone else in town, and he sure didn't relish the idea of spending another night alone.

He really wished Ayita would get off his case about God. After all, he believed in God in his own way, but he had no intention of poking his nose in the Bible constantly, the way some Christians did...Ayita, in particular. Yes, tonight he would forget about his dream girl and have some fun. It was just what he needed.

He filled in the extra time by watching FOX and CNN, catching up on news. The phone rang, and he picked it up.

"I'm downstairs." Debbie's voice sounded sexier than he remembered.

"On my way down," Valdez said, making an effort to sound more chipper than he felt.

Debbie was waiting in the lobby, gussied up for a night out. "Hey handsome," she called out as he strode toward her.

"Hi, Debbie," Valdez replied, trying to tone down the mood. He despised woman who came on strong. It was one sure way to turn him off.

"My car is parked out front," Debbie said a touch more demurely.

"I'll ask the valet to bring it around," Valdez offered.

Debbie was clearly at ease driving her red Mercedes to the club. She glanced and smiled occasionally at him. Her musky perfume wafted over to him, teasing his nostrils.

She was a little too obvious, but so what? Tonight, he threw caution to the wind. It was going to be a light-hearted evening, and it was just what he needed.

Utopia was a grand showpiece of Classical Greek architecture, flanked by imposing pillars at the entrance. A valet parked the Mercedes.

"The bar is fun. Should we start there?" Debbie smiled flirtatiously at Valdez.

"Why not?"

The disco was jammed with patrons. His quick impression was that of a yuppie crowd mingled with celebrity music folk. The club was dimly lit by candles at the tables, along with subtle recessed lighting in the ceiling. Most patrons sipped champagne in elegant, crystal flutes. Debbie ordered a bottle of Crystal.

"It's the 'in vogue' champagne," she said coyly to Valdez. "Nothing is too good for my favorite client." After the server had uncorked the champagne and poured their glasses, she lifted hers. "To you and your new home."

The rhythmic music blared. Lively tunes inspired dancers as they moved sensually in time to the music. With a little nudge from Debbie, Valdez took her hand and they weaved their way through the crowd and onto the dance floor.

Debbie was a graceful dancer and easily followed his smooth, skilled leadership with verve and fluidity. He had taught dancing many years ago in Madrid and knew a good dancer when he saw one. Tonight was an ideal deviation for him. As the evening progressed, he started to relax and enjoy himself. He even managed to push Ayita out of his mind for brief intervals. *I made the right choice coming here.*

They danced intermittently into the late hours of the

night. At one point, the band played some Latin American dances, including the Samba and Tango. They danced well together. Onlookers cheered them on, clapping in time to the music. Only a few couples remained on the floor, displaying their talents.

On the way back to the hotel, Valdez asked Debbie, "Could you work me into your schedule tomorrow? I'd really like to see the colonial house again. I want to go through it very slowly."

"I thought you'd never ask." She rewarded him with a big smile.

"Would first thing in the morning suit you? I'm busier in the afternoon."

"Perfect. Do you want me to pick you up?"

"Why not?"

Debbie picked up at 10:00, and they drove to her office. She poured him a cup of gourmet coffee and pulled out his file from a drawer in her filing cabinet. She handed him a folder she had printed out from the MLS listings.

"This is a list of the comparables-properties that have recently sold. They have similar square footage and are priced in the range of the subject property. All of them are on approximately one acre. This will give you an idea of what the homes are listed for, what they actually sold for, and how long it took to sell them in the present market."

"I'll peruse these comparables when I get back to the hotel. Thank-you. This will help me get an idea of what I should realistically offer."

"Exactly," Debbie said.

By the time the tour of the colonial was over, Valdez felt compelled to say, "I'll put in an offer after I've given it some thought and studied the comparables you've given me."

Valdez had lunch poolside at the hotel, took a leisurely swim, and then had a massage. Finally, he fell asleep in front of the TV. The lack of sleep last night was catching up with him. He felt vaguely guilty that he hadn't told Ayita about his date with Debbie, but really, it was no big deal. He enjoyed her company but had no interest in dating her. Yet she was a competent realtor, and he would use her services for real estate.

He had dinner alone in his room in front of the TV. Because he had taken a nap, he didn't feel tired. He had to fill in the evening. What would he do? He finally decided he would stop by the disco and kill the evening there. He selected a blue pinstriped shirt tonight and wore it with the cream-colored suit. He took a taxi so he would have the option of sipping champagne, if he chose to.

The doorman at Utopia greeted him effusively, doubtless recognizing him from the previous night and recalling his generous tip. He perched on a bar stool at one end of the long, art-deco bar. A long mirror ran the entire length of it, so that patrons occupying the bar stools could admire their images in it. He rather liked the dramatic black-and-white decor of the club, and the gold accents and gleaming white marble floors were nice touches.

Since he was nursing a mild hangover, he started the evening off with a bottle of Perrier, served with wedges of lemon. He would probably have a flute or two of champagne as the evening wore on.

A pert brunette with spiked hair and saucy brown eyes sidled up to the bar stool next to his. "Hey, handsome, how you doin'?"

Valdez couldn't help noticing how curvaceous she was in a slinky, white halter dress. It was so low cut that in spite of trying to avert his eyes from the cleavage, they kept darting back to it. She laughed merrily at almost every word out of his mouth. He had always fancied himself witty, but never before had he cracked up a woman every couple of minutes. It was heady stuff.

"Do you want to dance?" she cooed, oozing sensuality laced with sexuality.

"Why not?" Who was he to dispute how witty he was? Anyway, the babe was hot, and he would see where it went.

Valdez swung her around the floor, leaving her breathless and laughing merrily. The disco was even more jammed than the previous night. As he twirled his partner around the crowded dance floor, he remembered it was Friday night. That explained why the club was so jammed.

They were locked together in a waltz when he first smelled something. *Fire?* He took another whiff. *Fire!* No doubt about it. In one nimble, swift movement, he withdrew his arms from his partner, his eyes darting around the room frantically. To his horror, huge flames leapt ferociously across the entire front and rear walls of the club, masking both exit doors. His dance partner screamed and vanished into the crowd while he remained, shocked, rooted to the spot.

Most of the patrons seemed to have noticed the fire simultaneously. Pandemonium ensued as guests stampeded toward the two exits, only to discover the doors obscured by a towering wall of orangey-red flames. The club was devoid of windows.

He was trapped! They were all going to die here.

Panic seized him, and he gasped for air. A bottleneck of people clamored in the direction of both exits, shoving people to the floor in their frantic attempt to escape the inferno. It was a scene from hell.

It was no use. Dimly, Valdez was cognizant of the

horrific wailing and screaming as people were trampled to death on the floor. The screams grew louder. People gasped for air, unable to breathe. Clouds of ugly black smoke billowed throughout the room.

There was no air in his lungs. He crouched on the floor where the air was less smoky, holding his shirt over his mouth and nostrils to form a screen against the smoke. He searched in vain for a fireman. Every second counted as he crawled toward the exit doors, but the wall of flames impeded his ability to proceed.

It was a nightmare of epic proportions, taking on a surreal quality. He moved in slow motion. He could not breathe. He was suffocating. Terror griped him as smoke screamed through his lungs. His legs buckled beneath him.

I'm not going to make it. Waves of terror overtook him. He was dimly aware of the wail of fire engines.

It's too late. Scene of his life flashed before him in seconds. Soon it would be over.

The fumes were overtaking him. He had only seconds to live. A Scripture Ayita had loved flashed into his barely conscious mind. *Remember me when thou comest into thy kingdom."* The words had been spoken by one of two thieves, hanging on the cross with Jesus. "*This day you will be with me in Paradise."* Jesus had replied. "Oh God, forgive me for my rebellion. Help me," he gasped in a hoarse whisper.

Peace filled his heart in the midst of the hellish inferno. In that instant he knew he would live and not die.

Rescuers scrambled to employ digital holography on the Utopia. The 3D images produced through their infrared cameras enabled them to locate persons trapped in the dark, burning club.

Valdez was one of them.

~~*~~

A cacophony of sounds thudded in Valdez's ears-crackling noises of wood burning, walls crumbling, and debris flying wildly in all directions. He was vaguely conscious of two firemen rushing toward him. They strapped an oxygen mask on his face and dragged him up from the floor, rushing through the wall of fire. He screamed in agony as flames seared his body.

At last they were outside. They had made it. Emergency workers grabbed him, pouring cool water over him for several minutes and injecting morphine into him. He was on a gurney being transported to the back of an ambulance. Adjacent gurneys held victims moaning and screaming as attendants continued doling out morphine and other emergency medical treatment.

Barely conscious, he glimpsed a row of ambulances and emergency medical people working feverishly with burn victims. A cacophony filled the air as police sirens and fire trucks screamed onto the scene. Rescue workers worked frantically to save lives, while medical workers treated burned, hysterical patients.

He was dimly aware of the voice of a fireman nearby. "This guy is the last one we can save. If we go back in there now, we won't be comin' out."

The last thing Valdez heard before he lost consciousness was a deafening thud. He knew, without glancing back, that the roof of the Utopia was collapsing.

20

Ayita and her mother stared at the 11:00 P.M. news, horrified.

"Hundreds perish in crowded disco. Ironically named Utopia, it was a scene from hell tonight as the partying patrons were immersed in a hellish inferno. Most of the patrons died, unable to escape. Only twenty-two persons survived. Hospitalized survivors are undergoing emergency surgery or waiting for it. Helicopters are transporting additional surgeons and trauma specialists to assist emergency staff. Local off-duty surgeons and doctors have been dispatched. Police continue to search for families of survivors."

Ayita and her mother immediately prayed for the tragic situation and all those who were in pain and the families of those who had been lost. Then Ayita fell into a restless sleep, unable to identify what was disturbing her.

Ayita returned from rehearsal the following day, tired and hungry. She kicked off her shoes and was about to start dinner when the phone rang. She picked it up with one hand, holding an ice-cold coke in the other.

A nurse was on the line. She calmly explained that Valdez Lopez was in intensive care. He was a survivor of the Utopia inferno. "Emergency surgery was performed last night, and he is recovering."

"How did you get my number?" Ayita managed, despite feeling numb.

"A young woman by the name of Debbie Shaw came to the hospital to visit one of the survivors. When she learned Valdez Lopez was here, she insisted we call you immediately. She said she thought you were his fiancée. His face will have changed considerably, just so you're prepared when the time comes to remove the bandages. But he is thankful he's alive."

Ayita almost fainted. "I'm on my way. Will I be able to see him?"

"He's sleeping right now, and we won't wake him, but you're welcome to come in and wait until he awakens. He's been calling your name over and over. He must love you very much," the nurse said.

"I think he does," Ayita murmured.

"You will only be allowed to stay for a few minutes. If he hadn't been calling your name so persistently, you wouldn't be allowed to see him right now. He's not supposed to have any visitors."

~~*~~

Ayita drove to the hospital in a daze. Valdez was awake when the nurse showed her to his room Tears cascaded down her cheeks when she glimpsed him lying in bed, swathed in heavy bandages. "Valdez...oh, my darling..." She could see by his eyes that he was in pain. She tried to stay calm.

"Ayita," he rasped, in a faltering voice, "I cried out to God, and He heard me. I'm a real Christian now." The words were barely audible, but to her they sounded like the voices of a million angels, rejoicing for one lost soul redeemed.

The nurse signaled for Ayita to leave, but Valdez managed to rasp the words that had dominated his heart and mind for so long. "Will you marry me, Ayita?" His eyes shimmered with a deep, profound love.

"Only if you buy me a certain house." Overjoyed, Ayita winked at him.

In that instant, she knew the old adage was true: The eyes are the windows of the soul. For it was there, in Valdez's eyes that she saw reflected the love she had always dreamed of and the future she had prayed for.

Marlene Worrall is a professional actor and novelist. Theatre credits include a featured role in the original London West End cast of *Promises, Promises.* (AKA Angela Norviik) She has worked in TV, film and theatre in the USA, UK and Canada. She turned her hand to writing in 1994 after her professor challenged her to "Write an outline and first chapter of a novel." She went on to pen five more, as well as four screenplays. Her novella titled *Love Found in Manhattan* is available on Amazon through Lovely Christian Romance Press. She has published a number of short stories and was a contributing author on two Oak Tara anthologies.
MarleneBWorrall.blogspot.ca.
www.MarleneWorrall.com.

This book is a work of fiction. Names, characters, places and events either are products of the author's imagination or are used fictitiously. Any resemblance to actual events or persons living or dead is purely coincidental.

Angel in Shining Armor is © 2015 by Lovely Christian Romance Press. All rights reserved, including the right to reproduce in whole or in part in any form or medium.

All Scripture contained within is from the Authorized King James Version. Copyright©2000 by Zondervan. All rights reserved .Published by Zondervan, Grand Rapids, Michigan 49530, U.S.A. Library of Congress Catalogue Card Number 99-75836.

By payment of the required fees, you have been granted the non-exclusive, non-transferable right to access and read the text of this e-book on-screen. No part of this text may be reproduced, transmitted, downloaded, decompiled, reverse engineered, or stored in or introduced into any information storage and retrieval system, in any form or by any means, whether electronic or mechanical, now known or hereinafter invented, without the express written permission of the author.